"...me-noir at its finest."
— Edgar® Award-winning author

CITY FOR RANSOM

A NEW MYSTERY INTRODUCING
INSPECTOR ALASTAIR RANSOM

Terror stalks a metropolis in its finest hour...

ROBERT W. WALKER

BEA

FEB 1 6 2006

Advance Praise for
CITY FOR RANSOM

"Walker's masterful prose cuts like a garrote, transporting us with panache and style into an historical thriller with teeth. Ransom's the best new hero in period fiction."

JA Konrath, author of *Whiskey Sour & Bloody Mary*

"Walker's taken on Caleb Carr's territory, with a superb haunted protagonist with a graveyard on his back. Ransom your soul for this one; it's that mesmerizing."

Ken Bruen, Macavity Award Winner for *The Killing of the Tinkers*

"Gut-wrenchingly suspenseful, luridly atmospheric, and utterly plausible, Walker's creation is a brilliant mix of Conan Doyle, Erik Larson, and Wes Craven. You'll be shocked, stunned, beaten to hell, and riveted to the peerless quality of this page-turner."

Jay Bonansinga, author of *Frozen* and *The Sinking of Eastland*

"*City* is crime noir at its finest."

David Ellis, Edgar® Winner, author of *In the Company of Liars*

"*City* is ... deep, surprising ... vivid and passionate."

Barbara D'Amato, author of *Death of a Thousand Cats*

"Inspector Alastair Ransom's Chicago is brutal and violent, cloaking mysteries and intrigues in a facade of propriety as spectral and illusory as the grand and gleaming buildings of the vanished 'White City.'"

Richard Lindberg, author of *Chicago by Gaslight: A History of Chicago's Netherworld, 1880–1920*

CITY FOR RANSOM

ROBERT W. WALKER

AVON BOOKS
An Imprint of HarperCollins*Publishers*

This is a work of fiction. Names, characters, places, and incidents are products of the author's imagination or are used fictitiously and are not to be construed as real. Any resemblance to actual events, locales, organizations, or persons, living or dead, is entirely coincidental.

AVON BOOKS
An Imprint of HarperCollins*Publishers*
10 East 53rd Street
New York, New York 10022-5299

Copyright © 2006 by Robert W. Walker
ISBN-13: 978-0-06-073995-9
ISBN-10: 0-06-073995-9
www.avonmystery.com

First Avon Books paperback printing: January 2006

Avon Trademark Reg. U.S. Pat. Off. and in Other Countries, Marca Registrada, Hecho en U.S.A.
HarperCollins® is a registered trademark of HarperCollins Publishers Inc.

Printed in the U.S.A.

10 9 8 7 6 5 4 3 2 1

Growing up in Chicago in the fifties and sixties, I found a friend—a second mother, really—in Miss Evelyn Page, an extraordinary teacher of language and speech at Wells High, and when she made a gift of a small bookcase that I admired, she said, "You can thank me by filling it with books you've read."

I arrogantly replied, "How 'bout I fill it with books I write?"

She answered simply, "That'll do as well. Fill it with your characters."

"Deal."

"Deal."

Before she passed away, Evelyn Page knew I'd filled that bookcase twice over. She also knew that I was living my dreams—dreams she nurtured. A theater major and graduate of Northwestern University, she'd studied with Karl Malden, but she chose to become a teacher instead of Malden's co-star. My good fortune, for she championed me and gave me the opportunity to go to NU when it was my turn. But more importantly, she gave me a license to be myself and the courage, early on, to believe in myself; to believe myself a writer of purpose. For this reason, wherever her soul resides, I send out this dedication to find her . . . for she so loved Chicago and her house on Chase and Sheridan Road, and no doubt, she would've treasured a copy of City for Ransom.

ACKNOWLEDGMENTS

A novel like *City for Ransom* does not get written in a vacuum so much as a mineshaft. Thanks to an array of authors ahead of me, authors whose fascination with Chicago created a rich vein for a storyteller like myself to mine, *City for Ransom*, and its Dickensian ala Conan Doyle characterizations, came into being. My first novel, penned while I was a sophomore and junior in high school in Chicago, required research if I were to convey the inner workings of the famous Underground Railroad through the eyes of a fourteen-year-old Missouri boy (*Daniel & The Wrongway Railway*, 1982). Since then, all forty-two novels I've seen through to publication have conveyed research, whether police procedurals, suspense, young adult, even horror titles. To create *City for Ransom* and its sequels (*Vengeance for Ransom, Innocence for Ransom*, and hopefully more) the author was led to the "Mother Lode" by Mr. Kenan Heise, author, historian, *Tribune* reporter, and owner of the sadly closed bookstore, the Chicago Book Exchange. Mr. Heise, who gave assistance to my hero, John Jakes, when Jakes needed to dig into Chicago history, told me where to sink my pickaxe for the best titles on Chicago during the years I wished to write about—Detective Alastair Ransom's gaslight Chicago. The following $300 worth of books are by authors I must acknowledge, most of which were sold to me by Mr. Heise, as most—like all great books—are out of print:

Medicine in Chicago 1850–1950 by Thomas Neville Bonner; *Reminiscences of Chicago During the Civil War*, Citadel Books, *Chicago* by Finis Farr; *The Gangs of Chicago* by Herbert Asbury; *Gem of the Prairie* by Herbert Asbury; *Chicago* by Stephen Longstreet; *Wicked City* by Curt Johnson with R. Craig Sautter; *Chicago* by Lloyd Lewis and Henry Justin Smith; *Chicago Ragtime* by Richard Lindberg, *Crime in Chicago* by Richard Lindberg; *German Chicago* by Raymond Lohne; *The Chicagoization of America* by Kenan Heise; *The Journey of Silas P. Bigelow* by Kenan Heise; and *Perfect Cities—Chicago Utopias* by James Gilbert,

Other titles I stumbled on and devoured for my understanding of the city where I grew up include *The Pinkertons: The Detective Agency that Made History* by James Horan; *The Real World of Sherlock Holmes* by Peter Costello; *Chicago Then and Now* by Elizabeth McNulty; *Graveyards of Chicago* by Matt Hucke and Ursula Bielski; *Chicago's Famous Buildings* by Franz Schutze and Kevin Harrington; *Chicago—A Pictorial History by Herman Kogan and Lloyd Wendt; Elmer McCurdy—The Misadventures in Life and Afterlife of an American Outlaw* by Mark Svenold; *Forever Open, Clear and Free* by Lois Wille; *Central Michigan Avenue* by Ellen Christensen; *Man and the Beast Within* by Benjamin Walker, and *America* by Alastair Cooke.

However, the book that sparked the initial idea for *City for Ransom* goes way back to the 80s for me (it's been percolating for a long time). This title Dean R. Koontz insisted I read: Jurgen Thorwald's *Century of the Detective*. Even then Inspector Alastair Ransom was roaming about inside my head looking for a way out while I spent decades with Jessica Coran in my popular Instinct Series and Lucas Stonecoat in my Edge Series.

Thanks also to the wonderful team at Avon/HarperCollins, especially copyeditor and detail-conscious Patrice

Silverstein; May Chen, who handled me with grace; and brave young editor Lyssa Keusch, who proved the only person in all the publishing world to see the potential of the rough, early stages of *City*, and without whom Ransom would never have found his way out of this author's mineshaft (head), so that now this "gem of the prairie" named Alastair has finally come into the gaslight, proudly riding in a hansom cab, his scrimshaw wolf's-head cane tapping to the beat of hooves.

CITY FOR
RANSOM

CHAPTER 1

Illinois Central Train Station, Chicago, June 1, 1893

Yanked from a heated card game to investigate another murder, the third garroting in as many weeks, Inspector Alastair Ransom arrived angry. The rhythm his cane beat across the marble floor stopped when he hit a wall of odors—the winner: charred flesh. The smell dredged up memories of the Haymarket Riot and bombing, some seven years ago. The odors brought up another memory as well— one of a particularly grueling botched interrogation he'd conducted just before the infamous riot in Haymarket Square, a memory he'd hoped to have forgotten even more so than the labor riot itself.

But here it sat upon his mind, full-blown as if yesterday, thanks to this victim's fetid demise.

In an irritatingly gruff voice that made Inspector Alastair Ransom's hair stand on end, Dr. James Phineas Tewes shouted, "Inspector Ransom, finally, someone in charge."

"Can I help you?"

"I insist on a scientifically accurate, thorough phrenological diagnosis on the dead boy's cranium to determine his magnetic levels at the time of death."

"Phrenological what?"

"I'm conducting a study, you see and—"

"Magnetic levels? What nonsense! Read the dead boy's charred cranium? What possible good could your questionable art of reading skulls do either him or my investigation? He's dead, for God's—"

"But Chief Kohler approved and a—"

"His head's smoldering yet from being torched! G'damn you, Tewes! This is a murder investigation. You've no busi—"

"And your superiors, sir, sent me to examine—" Tewes stopped to catch another glimpse of the body, now half hidden by Ransom's considerable girth. Despite the black, smoldering lump of flesh leaning against the column, Dr. Tewes forged on. "I will make my observations and complete my mission here, Inspector! We're conducting an experiment."

Ransom tightened his teeth around an unlit pipe and tapped the floor with his cane. He scratched at his day-old stubble and stared long at the scrawny, parasitic scavenger everyone called a doctor, James Phineas Tewes—a little man of whom he thought little. He turned his back on Tewes to shout instead for his second in command. "Griff! Griffin."

"Yes, Inspector!" Griffin Drimmer called back.

"Get Keane in here to do the photographic work, so we can mop up this mess." Ransom indicated a blackened, charred faceless body propped against a pillar at the Baltimore and Ohio side of the building, second-floor balustrade. The marble floor around the body, also charred and blackened, told a tale in blood as it trailed from the men's room to the pillar.

The corpse's still smoldering head flopped forward, a quiet but echoing snap telegraphing a bone-cracking eruption at the terminus of the spine, incrementally giving way to the weight of the skull. The head had very nearly been cut off.

"You may ignore me, Inspector, but you can't ignore this!" Tewes, a dapper man in topcoat, suit ascot, his mustache twitching, claimed to psychically read people's heads as Gypsies read tea leaves or palms. But Tewes went to the extreme, claiming to diagnose illnesses and render cures to melancholia and other mental maladies with some sort of magnetic mumbo-jumbo in association with *laying-on-of-hands*. Little more than a snake-oil salesman.

Despite Ransom's attempts to stifle Tewes, the so-called phrenologist continued to wave a note. The note had the expensive watermark representing Kohler's office.

"Don't be a fool, Ransom," Tewes warned.

"Never, sir."

"Don't dare stand in my way. Not with this in my hand! An express order from your superior."

"You use the term *superior* too loosely, sir, and I don't react well to threats, *Doctor*." Ransom made the word *doctor* sound like *quack*.

"I know about you. Every law-abiding citizen in Chicago wants Kohler to give you the boot for your extravagant interpretations of the law," Tewes began in a more sour tone. "Your ill-treatment of prisoners, your questionable interrogation techniques."

"Really now?"

"The stuff of dark legend. Everyone fearing you!"

"Makes my job easier." Ransom gave a moment's thought to his ill-gotten, *half-deserved* reputation—the half that remained in people's minds. Tewes had kindly left out his addiction to gambling, tobacco, whiskey, quinine, and women.

"You can't stop the march of science or progress, Inspector!"

"Science? Progress?"

"Police science, yes."

"Really now?"

"I represent the hope that police operations improve evidence-gathering tech—"

"By paying out a handsome fee to the likes of you, Doctor?"

"You're as rough a fellow as I was warned!"

"Aye, I am that."

"And stubborn! Knowing that Kohler himself wishes my

participation on this case!" Tewes again waved the note in Alastair's face. "For God's sake, man. Read it!"

"Why? You've already revealed its content." Ransom punctuated his words with the unlit pipe, jabbing at Tewes. "Look here, my patience is in short supply, and you've no business here, mister!"

"This says otherwise!"

"You're not affiliated with the Chicago Police force or Dr. Christian Fenger's Coroner's Office. And if you dare get in my way again, I'll have you arrested for obstructing an ongoing investigation."

Tewes's curled handlebar mustache twitched anew like a tadpole under the muted train station gaslight.

Ransom saw a uniformed copper and shouted, "O'Malley! Take Dr. Tewes here out of my sight." Ransom turned his back on Tewes's raised hand, the note still flourishing birdlike over his head as O'Malley gently guided Tewes off. "You damned, daft fool!" Tewes shouted to no avail.

Inspector Ransom returned to the still-smoldering body that'd been doused with either petrol or kerosene, and then with water. In two previous such cases, the fire investigator had determined kerosene the accelerant.

Ransom immediately noticed a bloody handprint, left on the marble floor; the trail of blood led him to inspect the men's room. Drimmer pointed out the sliced off digits in the sink. Ransom went over to the body again, studying the handprint more closely. "The print has all its fingers. It isn't the boy's, unless the killer snipped off his fingers here and returned to the men's room to deposit each digit in the sink, but that feels counterintuitive."

Griffin Drimmer replied, "Then the print belongs to the killer!"

"If so, it needs to be photographically recorded, preserved. For should a suspect come about—distinguishable from the city's hundreds of likely vermin—then we can match said murderer to something tangible. How is that for scientific progress in police work?"

"Yeah, I overheard what Dr. Tewes said to you, Inspector."

Ransom continued to study the bloody handprint as if it recalled some secret memory.

A short, gaunt, angular- and grim-faced Griffin Drimmer, in a three-piece suit, fond of showing pictures of his children, looked more the part of Ransom's coachman than his partner. Their ages stood a generation apart as did their choice of clothing. His energy and diligence that of a river otter, while Alastair might more appropriately be called a pachyderm. Alastair believed his partner more enthusiastic than clever, more excitable than analytical, but he was young yet. There appeared much to recommend the new man, despite that Nathan Kohler had pushed Drimmer on Ransom.

"When we get the boy to the morgue," Alastair said to Griffin, "we'll stamp his palm and place it against Philo's photo."

"Easier than ripping up the floor tile and hauling it off."

"That'd upset people in high places."

"You mean along with Chief Kohler?"

Drimmer hadn't once had words with his partner about Kohler, but Ransom knew he was dying to do so—preferably after getting Ransom drunk enough to tell the whole sordid story as to why he and Kohler so intently hated one another from the inside out. Alastair considered Drimmer's position, its delicateness, working under him but ultimately for Kohler. "According to our good Dr. Tewes, Griff, we've already managed to piss Nathan." Alastair stared anew at the inexplicable mystery lying at his feet; three times the mystery now. It represented a third body that the coroner, Fenger, would have to separate from itself—like disentangling a melted sculpture created of limbs by the intense heat.

Both detectives staring at the bloody handprint felt a new aura surrounding it. "Could be the bastard's gone and got sloppy, Griff?"

"It must be his," Griff sounded hopeful. "You'll prove it so."

"Caution. It could as well belong to the night watchman who doused the body with water, or some careless copper got his hand bloody and kneeled here."

"But O'Malley's hands are too large to make a fit."

"Aye, it's a man no larger than the victim, from the look of it."

"Small hands for certain." Griffin placed his own small hands over the print, creating a shadow fit.

"Keep this between us, Griff. No one else is to know. Do you understand?"

"Absolutely, between us."

"When Philo gets here with that blasted photographic equipment of his, we'll have to stay on him, Griff."

"Stay on him?"

"He's coming off a drunk, and he can be a slacker when he's hung over."

"I'll stay on him." Griffin winked.

Ransom imagined Griff thought him on the same drinking binge as Philo, and he wasn't wrong. "Judging from the size of the handprint—if indeed it belongs to the monster we seek—our killer is hardly larger than the two women he's killed."

"About the size of that fella waving the note in O'Malley's face?"

"Tewes? Yes . . . yes . . . in that neighborhood. Doesn't take much to overpower a man from behind with a garrote." Ransom looked from the print to Dr. Tewes, who now waved Kohler's damnable note at Big Mike O'Malley. O'Malley's blue uniform looked purple under the haze of light from a lamppost that flooded in from an overhead window in the semidarkened stairwell—a stairwell down which Ransom would like to throw Tewes. He hoped O'Malley would escort Tewes to the door.

Tewes's silver tongue had gotten him Kohler's blessing and had gotten him past the police barricade, but Ransom's attention returned to the bloody handprint. He toyed with the cruel idea of getting a stonemason to lift it from the marble floor. To intentionally provoke Kohler.

Ransom's thoughts strayed to the so-called new and ingenious art of fingerprint and handprint evidence that was hardly new in other parts of the world. "Everything worth knowing comes out of the East," the taciturn medical examiner for Cook County, Dr. Fenger, once told Ransom. Then the spry old doctor added, "Of course, your chief of detectives thinks it's all mumbo-jumbo. Been trying for years to get the Chicago Police Department to invest in fingerprint-gathering techniques and devices."

Being the holdout of an old vanguard, Chief Nathan Kohler looked the part of Poe's most stolid raven: stocky, short, wrapped in a black coat the way a bird wrapped itself in its wings—indicative of how close he played his cards to his chest. A most secretive man, Kohler had been skeptical and resistant to the idea, as his custom dictated, distrusting anything new. Kohler finally put his opinions aside when the scientific evidence became too overwhelming to ignore—in large part due to Ransom's and Dr. Fenger's combined persistence and faith in the new science. In another part, due to the coroner's push for modern techniques and devices, and to wrangling a much larger budget out of the city. Dr. Fenger, one of the founding members of Cook County Hospital and the city's preeminent medical examiner, lent credence to Alastair's war. *And what is Kohler's answer? To hire on a mentalist?*

The newsmen, held in check at the stairwell, shouted for comments. Ransom counted on big O'Malley to keep the dogs of the press off his back, and while Alastair liked some reporters, and in fact knew a couple who proved better investigators than cops, today he'd immediately cordoned off the crime scene, and thanks to a Chicago miracle—greased with green—the sensational stories of two earlier garrote victims hadn't been reported in any major paper. All this, ostensibly to safeguard the "integrity of the ongoing world's fair." Ransom cared little for such concerns, but he did want to preserve what Dr. Fenger called the "amalgamate area wherein murderer and victim danced" or "the killer's parlor."

Fenger wrote poetry in moments of relaxation, good poetry in fact. And his poetical nature came through in his work. But Ransom took his meaning—keep undisturbed the space around the victim in order to do a thorough investigation. A common sense, scientific approach.

So today it was off limits even to his best friends in the press, those he drank with from the *Tribune, Herald,* and *Sun.* Reporters had gotten out of control in previous months. In fact, the sheer number of reporters in Chicago rivaled the vermin and rats. As many as forty-odd newspapers were vying for dominance within the city limits alone.

Naturally, the reporters clamored for a better view of the crime scene now—a closer look for photographs and drawings—but decorum in an investigation of a crime as heinous as this must, in Ransom's opinion, be maintained even at the risk of the public's so-called "right to know"— a card the Chicago press played like a two-dollar whore. When Ransom could, he gave the newsies far more access to the crime scene than Dr. Fenger thought prudent. He ingratiated himself with the press to gain access to their secrets—how they worked a source, how they got information. The lifeblood of an investigator. But he also nurtured a relationship with good newsmen who held doubts about official details of the city's investigation of the Haymarket Riot.

Ransom saw that some enterprising newsmen had found another way up to the third-floor promenade, and they now looked down over the kill scene. One or two photographs were taken from the odd angle, most likely useless.

O'Malley, in his nervous stutter, stood beside Ransom, sputtering, "In-in-insp-spec-tor . . . I think you've gotta deal with D-d-d-doc-doctor Tewes, sir."

Ransom rubbed his grizzled chin and fought the redness of eyes that'd seen too much horror and too little sleep, eyes now staring through O'Malley and Dr. Tewes, who'd joined them.

"You must take a moment to read this or—" began Tewes, the huge signature ascot bobbing with each speech.

"Dr. Tewes, we have standards that must be rigorously adhered to and scrupulously upheld to conduct a proper investigation, and they don't include the likes of—"

"Sir, I respect the vigor and integrity of your investigative procedure, and your long experience in police work. However . . ."

"Why must every review end in a *however*?"

"*However*, Inspector, every new idea to drag police science into keeping with modern knowledge of—"

Ransom dismissed Tewes—this time with the upraised bone-handled wolf's-head cane, a gift from his close friend, Philo Keane. He'd carried it since Haymarket, the riot that had ended in the deaths of seven of Ransom's fellow officers. The cane had become Ransom's trademark. Stories circulated all about Chicago of how Ransom put down any man who showed the least resistance by pummeling him with that cane. Tewes saw that the filigreed bone handle was cracked down one side.

Ignoring Tewes, Alastair called out to Griffin.

"Where's Philo?"

"I suspect he's on his way."

"Have him take pictures of the blood splatters in the men's room, the trail to here, and close-ups of that lone handprint. Using the modified identification-records kit, we can attempt to match the palm print to our records of known perverts and felons. How is that for modern, Dr. Tewes?"

The ID kit he referred to was a modified French police idea. The French believed a simple record of measurements of body parts kept on arrested felons proved as reliable as any eyewitness report. Many a man had been sent to the gallows via such matchmaking.

Ransom's examination of a crime scene took longer than any man on the force; he had a reputation for thoroughness but a kind of monkish quality of intense meditation as well.

"Zenlike isn't he?" Tewes, admiration in his voice, asked Drimmer.

"Not sure what that means," replied Griffin. "All I know is that Inspector Ransom is the man who modified the modern French Bertillon method of cross-identification cards to include fingerprints on known felons and repeat offenders."

Griffin Drimmer took the now infamous note from Dr. Tewes to examine it.

"The Chicago Police have put to use the Bertillon system?" asked Dr. Tewes. "I'm impressed."

"As I said, with modifications."

"Still, you won't find *this* killer in your card files."

"Now look, Dr. *Toes* is it? We know what we're doing here, and we need no additional help, I can assure you."

"Tewes," the small man corrected. "James, sir, James Phineas Murdoch Tewes."

Ransom erupted again, shouting for the missing photographer, startling everyone.

"His bark as bad as his bite?" asked Tewes, forcing a squint from Griffin.

Meanwhile, Ransom watched Chicago Police civilian photographer Philo Keane, and his new assistant, young Waldo Denton, struggle through the crowd of reporters on the stairwell, their hands full with the remarkable scientific tools of their trade. Ransom found the new art and science of photography—an invention catapulted to prominence during the Civil War—a godsend to police investigators. It'd become another new source of applied science in police detection. But the jaded crowd of reporters and curious onlookers rudely shouted at the inconvenience Philo and his assistant caused.

Keane and assistant together had hold of a long-legged specialized enormous tripod, which—once the carriage was assembled—stood twelve feet high on three giant legs. An entire ladder attached to it led to the top. This monster, once upright, allowed Keane special vantage point overtop the prone corpse, so as to photograph from above—the end result creating an effect like the eye of God looking in on death.

Ransom knew Keane's work and thought him an artist, and his equipment state-of-the-art, but the giant ladder-equipped tripod was the size and bulk of a giraffe. Still, the results—if Philo were not rushed and left to his own devises—often proved remarkable, if not uncanny. Ransom had known grown men on the force who did not care to be alone in a room with Philo's photos.

When Ransom reviewed such photographic evidence, he sometimes felt the hair on the back of his neck rise in response to the eerie appearance of a strange-looking halo effect around the depicted corpse—as if Philo had somehow caught a fleeting glimpse of the departing souls. Regardless of race, creed, religion, character or gender, Philo's glow— or *Philo's halo* as it had come to be known—was never seen on anyone else's film plates.

Of course, when called on this phenomena over a pint at Moose Muldoon's, Philo chalked it up to a reflection—flash of gunpowder in the pan—caught at the moment of squeezing off the shot, "Or just a dirty lens," he'd add.

Philo exchanged a grunt of salutation with Alastair, a glint of knowledge and bonding in each bloodshot eye. What these two men knew and shared of violent, unholy and unhappy endings culminated in a silent array of artistically rendered death photos. Sober, they seldom spoke beyond the necessary. So, Philo immediately began his normal routine of taking "cuts," confident that he knew precisely what Ransom must have.

Meanwhile, Ransom saw that Drimmer had gotten himself embroiled in a three-way conversation with O'Malley and Tewes; O'Malley quietly reading Kohler's letter aloud, his lips moving like a fish gaping for air.

"*JesusLordGodAlmighty* . . . if you want something done right . . ." Ransom muttered.

"Gotta do it yourself," replied the sloppily dressed police photographer. "I believe in old adages."

"Too bad you don't believe in lye soap."

"Unless I can afford Field's best perfume, I'll keep me stench." Philo's assistant stifled a laugh, while Philo laughed from the gut. "You're one to talk, old man."

"I want plenty of close-ups of the handprint to the side, Philo—see, right here?"

"Yah, yah, why're you badgering today . . . why? I'm way ahead of you."

"And, Philo, any blood splatters you see, and close-ups on the neck. Three hundred and eighty degrees. Do you understand?"

"You mean three hundred and sixty degrees, don't you?"

"Testing, Philo, to see how sharp you are this time of the equinox."

"Badgering is what it is, and I don't care for it."

Ransom whispered, "You ever think of getting off the sauce?"

"You're one to talk. What about that Chi-nee shit you smoke?"

"Keep it down, Philo."

Keane returned to work, placing a ruler beside the bloody handprint for scale. Escaping from him came an odd series of sound effects: "*Aha, ya-aha, mmm . . . uh-huh . . . ohhh . . . uhhh . . . bugger'at . . . gore-blimeyboy, whoa . . . ohhh-sheee-it . . .*"

CHAPTER 2

Ransom recalled how an army of stone masons had worked for over a year to build this massive Illinois Central Station, and how the marble had come out of the earth from a quarry near the Indiana state line. By contrast, the more recently completed World's Columbian Exposition train terminal had been constructed of wood and covered over with staff—a form of stucco. Where the solid graystone Illinois Central was built to last, the Expo terminal was intended only as a temporary structure—as with almost all the world's fair buildings.

Griff returned to stand alongside Ransom, now with Tewes's note in hand. "Tewes playing musical brains with you fellows? Stuff that damn letter. It's bloody three-forty A.M., Griff, don't-cha see?"

"See what?"

"It's a put-up job. Kohler's put this Tewes on to spy on us. He had to've called him in; how else would Tewes know to be here?"

"It's that dirty, is it?"

"Once Philo Keane's finished, Griff, call in the meat wagon. Get the corpse to Cook County morgue, 'way from all these vultures."

"Where is Dr. Fenger? Did he send word? An assistant?"

"Christian's facing several operations today."

Griff nodded. "And his classes are so full."

"Busiest man in the city," Alastair replied. "Sure, Kohler will forgive him. After all, he can do his job from his morgue as well as here, so long as we cover the territory."

"Autopsy, inquest—still, strange he didn't make an appearance. Not like him."

"Let's just say the good doctor is adept and not eager to enter a crossfire between the chief and me."

"You were warned about Dr. Tewes's coming onto the case?"

"You're catching on, Griff."

"Nothing gets by you, does it, Ransom?"

"This is my city."

"I've heard that. So, Dr. Fenger's playing it safe? Wouldn't have anything to do with that *Herald* cartoon?"

"Damn fools . . . calling him a 'Resurrection Man'!"

"Was kinda funny, putting a shovel in his hand beside a picture of a gold-filled coffin." Griffin's grin annoyed Alastair.

"The man received a raise! What's wrong with that? Christian Fenger deserves all he can get outta this city."

"Did you cook this up with Dr. Fenger? Just to get the body away from . . . *you know who* that much sooner?"

They both glanced at Tewes, standing with O'Malley. "How 'bout you, Griff? You think it's right, what Kohler's proposing?"

"Right?"

"A guy dies a brutal death, then along comes some bastard calls himself a wizard with magnetic hands. Just wants to turn a buck, pretending to read messages from the dead . . . from the contours of the skull. If it weren't so sad, it'd be laughable."

"Now that's an editorial cartoon."

"That Tewes guy just rubs me the wrong way. Makes my skin literally creep!"

"Me too. Same as you, Rance."

Ransom hesitated at this. Griff had never called him Rance. *Why the sudden chumminess?*

Griff pushed on while rocking on the balls of his feet. "All the same, it could be construed as an order, and if so, if you disobey—"

"Something's just not right about Tewes."

"All the same"—Griffin held up the note—"this note from Kohler is authentic, Rance."

"Leave it be, Griff."

"But Kohler's just hoping you'll foul up."

"It's all carefully orchestrated."

"Like I said, a setup. You make a stink over this, it's all he needs. So why not just let Dr. Tewes go through the motions?"

"Don't you get it, Griff? It's politics."

"Not everything in the department is about politics."

Ransom's laughter filled the train station. "Griff, this is the Chicago PD we're talking about. Everything in Chicago is about politics, especially the police force."

"You sure you're not being a little ahhh . . . overly ahhh suspicious?"

"Doc Fenger asked the same, except he called it 'unreasonably mistrustful.' Look, Drimmer . . . my friend and colleague . . . if I give in to Tewes, even if there is a note from my superior *suggesting* I do so, what happens to my investigation, one I am solely responsible for?"

"I don't follow you, Inspector."

"The bloody investigation turns into a circus."

"I see, a circus."

"A three-ring one as only Chicago papers can conjure, and as for me? I get the ax for my part in it."

"And if you should refuse that phrenologist?"

"Ahhh . . . a fine name for a charlatan, isn't it? So scientific and such a *magnetic* personality he has, too."

"Kohler's already declared you uncooperative. Seems he has it in for you. Like it's—"

"Personal, yes, but personal is political, Griff. Lotta water's flowed 'neath the bridge for me and Kohler."

"Goes back to Haymarket, doesn't it?"

He raised one eye to Griff. No secrets in a police department. "Your interrogative technique has improved markedly since working with me, Inspector. But hell, Griff, what in this city doesn't go back to Haymarket?"

"Where you got your leg busted up, isn't it? But they say a lotta good's come of it, too. Better labor relations, best labor laws in the country bar none."

"You've been reading old papers?"

"You and the chief see the Haymarket Square bombing quite differently."

"Aye, he wants it—"

"Buried, I know, while you . . . some might say you've obsessed over it since eighty-seven."

"Call me a student of history. And 'twas eighty-six, son, but enough down memory lane. We've plenty on our hands in the here-and-now."

The flash of explosive gunpowder from Philo's magic show now went off nearby, the acrid smell of the corpse's burnt flesh meshing with the sulfur cloud. All of it conjured up unwanted memories of that day at Haymarket.

"This boy's murder's connected to the other two, isn't it, Rance?" whispered Griffin, not wishing anyone else to hear.

Aside from the afflictions in his back and legs from that awful day in 1886, Alastair suffered from bad digestion, nosebleeds, headaches, and a low tolerance for administrative boobs who knew less than he did. And for the injustices abounding in Chicago from homelessness and joblessness to the inequities of political pork-barreling. He also had a low tolerance for the ignorance and tranquillity of youth. He secretly bemoaned his own lost youth, and he detested seeing youth wasted. And he worried about Griff's doing just that. "Of course, the killings are related."

Ransom saw Dr. Tewes disappear into the stationmaster's office, grateful to witness this obvious retreat until realizing that Tewes had gone in search of a telephone. Phones had been installed in many public places. No doubt the good doctor of phrenology meant to complain to Nathan Kohler about Ransom's rank insubordination, and this counterfeit doctor's inability to get past the inspector of record.

"Brace yourself, Griff, for a visit from the chief."

"Count on it, I should think. The uniforms are taking odds, and Rance—did I mention that the note is more than a suggestion, but a direct order?"

"No, you didn't, and let's keep it that way, shall we, Griff?"

Later Ransom found the wide corner concourse windows overlooking a black sky lit by thousands of lights creating a brilliance across *The White City*—the term everyone used for the temporary wood-and-stucco wonderland of Grecian and Roman edifices and architectural wonders of the astoundingly huge Chicago world's fair. This was the newly erected city within Ransom's city—Burnham's city, created almost single-handedly by the famous Chicago architect Daniel Hudson Burnham.

From the Illinois Central windows, Ransom saw a great deal more of the dark alleyways and shanties and the cutthroat Levee district than the extravagant fair. The two cities stood at odds—Burnham's idyllic dreamland lit like a many-tiered chandelier seemed to float over the lake. Chicago was a city of beauty and deeply cut cynical currents, its bedrock. Not even White City could hide the political expedience that formed her core darkness. Like a blinding chandelier, Ransom thought.

White City looked the dream, yes. Truth be told, however, it proved so much gilded illusion: a mirror of man's highest achievements, yes, that—so well presented—lulled one into Burnham's faith. One might for a brief moment, while walking the gas-lit stone paths garnished with flowers on either side and the lovely Lake Michigan as promenade, begin to believe in his fellow man, to believe naught a one of them capable of evil or murdering one another. That a man could never again do a harsh act against his fellows. Not even in the wee hours of the night when so much crime took place in the shadows as God slept.

"Not bloody likely in this or the next century, I warrant," he muttered to himself. "Lights or no lights, Mr. Edison."

In the distance stood the spinning lights of Mr. Ferris's giant wheel that dared take people soaring to a height of 176 feet—gaiety and light and a kind of euphoric madness all framed in a Romanesque window from which Ransom gawked and shook his head and chewed on a tooth-scarred pipe. If he tried hard, he could hear the unclear but separate German, Polish, Ukrainian, and Irish music welling up from the countless beer gardens. Something of a Babel indeed, he thought. In fact, the sound of lakefront revelers penetrated the vaulted waiting room ceiling here, bounced off and reverberated. By contrast, immediately behind Ransom, Keane's little photographic explosions created a too familiar, melancholic drama of its own: *click-whoosh, click-whoosh, click-whoosh.*

Ransom turned from the window to face Dr. Tewes, a smug look creasing the features below the little dapper's curled mustache. He stood rocking on his heels, flapping Kohler's letter. "I am a determined man, Inspector."

"Good for you, Dr. Tewes, but I have the dignity of the deceased to consider. Your questionable magic is unheard of. What do you think reporters'll make of it—your absurd play?" Ransom pushed past the smaller man.

CHAPTER 3

His work required Ransom's mind, but the old shrapnel wound to his leg, and ailments that'd plagued since the anarchist's bomb—the cause of his most grueling physical and mental pain—threatened always to break him. Today, seeing this horror perpetrated on a third victim threatened to break his resolve to remain aloof and in charge. More than once, his thoughts wandered to his opium pipe and his bed. It represented what little solace he knew— opium—any way he could get it. But here he stood in Illinois Central, all eyes on him with the damnable Dr. Tewes and his equally damnable "order" from Kohler. The best he might do here would be his rolled cigarette laced with hemp.

Ransom felt a headache coming on now. He'd begun to perspire despite the coolness of the station. "Look, Dr. Tewes, we've danced long enough here with the devil. Time to salvage what little dignity the boy has left, get him to our morgue, and you can examine him there to your heart's content. Deal?"

"You don't begin to understand, do you, *Inspector*?" Now Tewes sneered his title. "You've already wasted precious time."

"We need to return the train station to normal, fill out the paperwork, try to determine who the victim is, and get on the trail of his killer *before* the bastard strikes again, Tewes."

"Precisely why I'm here!"

Ransom turned from Tewes, but this time the smaller man caught his arm and confronted Alastair. "Just hold on there, man!"

"What in bloody hell do you hope to accomplish here, Tewes?"

"I have an order allowing me to examine the cranial structure." Tewes again held the letter up to Ransom's eyes, the signature unmistakable. "Look, Inspector, I'm not interested in taking over your case or your territory, or whatever it is you fear losing. Shit, all I want—"

"Fear? I don't fear anything from you, Tewes, believe me."

"If I can have a moment—just a moment—with the dead before all is lost—"

"Speak to the dead, is it? Through your gifted fingers, Doctor?" Alastair did not take the letter from Tewes but stared into the deep brown eyes of a man he'd been quietly investigating, a man he considered a consummate con artist.

Philo Keane stepped in when he saw Alastair reach both hands to his head, staving off a stabbing pain. "All right . . . *Doctor,* is it?" began Keane. "Time now for you to leave the area to us professionals. You find the morgue as Inspector Ransom says. Tug-o-war it out with Dr. Fenger."

Ransom put up a hand to Philo. "Allow me to introduce you, photographic wizard Mr. Philo Keane, Dr. James Phineas Tewes—"

"Dr. James Phineas Murdoch Tewes to be exact," corrected Tewes.

"A man who likely needs all his names to cover his tracks," added Ransom.

"Aliases?" asked Philo, taking Alastair's lead.

Tewes looked strange, a pale, thin, dismal face, hardly ever given to smile. He made slow movements, and his voice—always deep—somehow never rose above a whispering growl.

Ransom put a hand on Philo's shoulder, and spoke to him. "Dr. Tewes is well known in Chicago, mostly from fliers posted on every street lamp and shop window."

"Posters? Really?" asked Philo, squinting.

"The fliers propose that Tewes here can cure madness and depression. A new form of littering so far as I'm concerned." Ransom mentally flashed on the last such advertisement that he'd seen only that morning, tacked to a telegraph pole outside his police district house on Des Plaines.

Tewes gladly unfolded a bill now from his breast pocket and handed it to Mr. Keane. It read:

Phrenological & Magnetic Examiner
at his residence, 2nd house north
of the Episcopal Church.

DR. TEWES

May be consulted in all cases of Nervous or Mental difficulty. Application of the remedies will enable relief or cure any case of Monomania, Insanity or Recent Madness wherein there is no Inflammation or destruction of the Mental Organs. Dr. Tewes's attention to diseases of the nervous system, such as St. Vitus's Dance and Spinal Afflictions has resulted in some remarkable cures. Having been engaged for the past ten years in teaching Mental Philosophy, Phrenology, together with numerous Phreno Magnetic Experiments enable Dr. Tewes to give correct and true delineations of Mental Dispositions of different persons. A visit to Dr. Tewes can be profitable to any and all who wish to better understand their own natures, and how best to apply their talents in the world at large.

Ransom said, "I don't for a moment believe Dr. Tewes can cure a headache, much less a mental disorder, Mr. Keane, but as you see, he advertises himself a magician, capable of repairing mental disorders!" Ransom then said to Tewes, "What sort of game are you at here, Tewes? No one here has any need of your questionable services. Certainly, not this dead boy."

"I am a psychic medium, sir, as well as a phrenologist. I am informed that two similar cases of garroting murders have occurred here. The killer has not been apprehended in either instance, and I fear—"

"I fail to see how you can help out here."

"Kohler informs me this is the third garroted *and* fired corpse in as many weeks."

"My God," muttered Philo, "Kohler fights against finger-print identification, but he attaches a medium to the case."

"I assure you, none of these cases've been definitively linked by evidence," Alastair lied even as he wondered why Nathan would divulge such information to anyone not on the case.

"But there are *similarities* no one can deny—for instance, all three murders occurring at or near the White City fairgrounds."

Ransom silently agreed that the geography of these murders was correct. "As I said, no official link has been made."

"How can anyone of sense not see the glaring—"

"The other cases involved a young female—a clerk at Allen & Boynton's on State Street—and before that a park prostitute. Slash wounds were entirely different, and—"

"But the heads in either case . . . they were nearly severed."

"Look, both were women . . . both women sustained multiple stab wounds to upper chest and abdomen. There are none on the boy."

"So? It only means he is getting more adept at the garrote," countered Tewes. "And I'm given to understand that the store clerk was carrying child, making the death toll four."

"I see that Kohler has filled you in, but the two women had nothing whatsoever in common."

"Perhaps they do have commonalities to the killer. Perhaps their commonality is their mutual killer." Getting no response, Dr. Tewes, chin held high, added, "Yes, well then . . . Inspector, while you may be correct in your assumption that these murders are unrelated, if you do not mind, I would like to take a closer look at the boy's body on site. Your meticulous care, your photographs, your scientific approach not withstanding, you'll not have anyone in your Bertillon card files to match this killer."

Ransom lit his pipe and began smoking the Havana blend that he'd been thumbing in his coat pocket the entire time. Smoking calmed nerves, or so Dr. McKinnette said. He blew smoke into Tewes's eyes.

Dr. Tewes's soft features made determining his age difficult, but Ransom thought him born a conniving adult. The slight man proved unremarkable save how expensively he dressed— a broad Sampson Brothers overcoat layering a three-piece suit and a gold watch fob reflecting light off its surface. His title of medical doctor had been earned supposedly in France, but he had no such degree in America. A background check on the man only went back some seven years, and then nothing, as if he'd not existed before then. A similar check with authorities in France, and still nothing of a Dr. or a Mr. Tewes fitting his description could be found before he turned up at France's Royal Academy of Medicine. Ransom had made numerous police contacts in the Suréte, the oldest criminal investigation agency in Europe, and *Tewes* smelled like an alias even to them—as a Dr. François Tewes was reported as having died while imprisoned on charges of having killed a man in a brawl.

Likely enough, Chicago's Dr. Tewes was in his late twenties or early thirties; he with his full head of hair below the bowler, his small ears, dimpled chin, thin nose. This man was ambitiously working to build a reputation. What would solving a mystery do for his dubious practice?

"A garrote killer in New York left six victims in water— dumping their bodies in rivers, lakes," Tewes calmly maintained.

"Our Chicago fellow seems more interested in fire than in water," Ransom replied.

"He used a garrote?" asked Griffin, who'd rejoined them. "Like our madman here? Double-tiered?"

Ransom shot a wilting look at Griffin that telegraphed his disappointment in Drimmer's gullibility. "The good doctor here has something on Kohler, Griffin. That's obvious with his letter of recommendation. *Kohler* informed him. That's all there is to it."

"It's no letter of recommendation, Inspector," countered Tewes. "Read it. It's a direct order made to you."

Griffin tugged at Ransom's sleeve. "You can't afford any more trouble."

"Double wires," said Tewes mysteriously, "that crisscrossed in front to create a small diamond incision at or near the voice box in the females, and now the boy's Adam's apple. The deadly thing is likely a piano wire connected to two sturdy sticks, which he twists round the neck, making an immediate incision at once three hundred and sixty degrees. The tighter he winds it, the deeper the cut."

Ransom now knew for certain that Dr. Tewes had something on Kohler; only blackmail could've gotten the scoundrel this far. "I want the two-wire diamond aspect of this murder weapon kept under wraps, Tewes. Do you understand? We must not let the newshounds have it. We must hold some information in abeyance toward the day we pinch this maniac—to identify the killer with absolute—"

"I can be cooperative, Inspector."

"Don't think that you can blackmail me, Doctor."

"Why, Inspector, you give me far too much credit for guile!"

"If you mean skill in cunning and deceit and a cleverness in trickery, yes, perhaps I do."

"Look, I've seen the coroner's notes, true. But I first saw all this happening while laying on of hands to the cranium of a dying woman—"

"A dead woman now. Whooo . . . dying woman . . . how very mysterious," countered Ransom.

"A pauper buried in your Potter's Field a few months ago."

"It remains an incredible assertion."

"I read heads. It's what a phrenologist does."

"And you receive visions in the process."

"Perceptions . . . not visions, sir, and only sometimes, yes."

Griffin now stared at Tewes as if he were a magician. Ransom saw this and grew angry at his partner's wide-eyed response. "Nothing you've told us is new, Dr. Tewes. You may just as well have gotten your information from Kohler or some easily fooled police clerk."

"Yes, I suppose I might've. I certainly understand your skepticism. After all, you're paid to be cynical! But look here, I'm telling the truth about New York. And there's something else."

"What?" asked Griffin, eager to hear more.

"The instrument of death he wields."

"Yes?" asked Griff.

"The killer fashioned it himself. Made it with his own hands."

"However can you possibly know that?" asked Griffin, playing into Tewes's hand.

"The unique nature of the instrument. I've studied garroting devices. None that I have seen utilize two strands crossed into a diamond shape of this nature. X's yes—but using two strands, this is unique to our killer."

"And why the fire?" asked Griffin. "I mean if the victims are already dead . . . why then set the bodies aflame?"

"Usual purpose to set a dead man aflame is to obscure any chance at easy identification. Identification often leads to a killer, but this . . ." began Tewes.

Ransom cut Tewes short, saying, "Seems the fire was clumsily set, mainly to the torso. Features can still be made out, so whoever did this was not interested in throwing us off identification."

Tewes nodded. "I am surprised. He is brazen, this killer. As he was in New York."

"How can you be sure it's the same man?" asked Griffin, bursting to hear more.

"He follows the same patterns. In his patterns, his ritual, he leaves a distinctive mark of himself."

"Dr. Tewes has read some police manuals, I warrant," said Ransom.

"On that we can surely agree, Inspector Ransom."

"Perhaps we ought to be looking at anyone recently emigrated from New York to here, Alastair?" Griffin looked to Ransom, but Alastair held Tewes in his steely gray gaze.

"Only if you buy into this snake-oil salesman's ideas, Griff. Isn't that right, Dr. Tewes?"

Tewes frowned and said, "Please, just allow me a moment with the body, before it is too late."

Ransom did not like it when a man failed to answer a direct question. Something a man could not get away with in the U.S. Navy or aboard a whaler—two occupations Alastair had tried on as a young man.

"You may's well give in to me, Inspector," Tewes said, getting close enough to breathe on Ransom. "Nathan Kohler is on his way here this minute. He'll want an accounting if I am not allowed to read the victim's cranium."

Ransom ran his free hand through his bushy hair. A big man with powerful hands, Alastair went to the corpse. He then placed his cane under his arm to free up both hands. He next grabbed on to the corpse's blackened, singed hairless head at forehead and base of neck. He easily cranked the cranium from side to side, then front to back. With a sickening squish, the garroted neck released its tenuous hold, the head coming off in Ransom's now sooty, grimy hands to the chorus of gasping reporters who'd pushed the police line to the top of the stairs. Onlookers, cops, and medical personnel who'd rushed to the murder scene joined in a collective gasp, adding to the groans of seasoned crime reporters.

Photographer Keane flashed his pan and a fiery black

plume appeared with the odor of gunpowder all in a single *whoosh,* getting a shot of Inspector Ransom holding the dead man's head in his hands.

"Ransom!" shouted Griff in awe, expecting an oozing gruel to come rushing out of the huge cavity. However, the fire had dehydrated all bodily fluids; nothing but soot lifting and flying off the now completely severed head dirtied Tewes's white suit. Tewes's gritted teeth spoke volumes. Still, the doctor accepted and couched the severed head in the cradle of his arms.

Tewes's chin quivered like a girl about to burst into tears, his watch fob shivering, as Ransom said, "You wanna read the boy's skull, Dr. Tewes? Be my guest!"

Under Ransom's steady glare, the slight doctor refused to show another moment's emotion, holding his ground, earning more respect from Inspector Ransom than Griffin thought possible.

"I—I'll take it to the stationmaster's office," Tewes shakily said, "place it on a desk . . . for—for stability. You really . . . really should've left it intact, Inspector."

"Yes, find a square foot of privacy. . . . Good idea." Ransom's eyes scanned the reporters. "Or have you invited the press as well, Doctor?"

Dr. Tewes stiffly marched off with his dubious prize. Ransom tried to think of something clever to shout after him, but the absolute gall the man had displayed, in a bizarre way, held Ransom in check. "Hmmm, that Tewes fella, Griff, has more backbone than I'd've guessed."

CHAPTER 4

Griffin Drimmer had pushed back the police line to a chorus of questions from reporters, most of them wanting to know who Tewes might be. O'Malley had located a tarp, and crossing himself, the big Irish cop sent the canvas over the now headless, still smoldering corpse. The heavy cloth cascaded over the grim sight and made it disappear, save for the gnarled left hand and foot. Using his police issue boot, O'Malley nudged the errant telltale hand beneath.

"You can't cover it, O'Malley!" complained Philo. "I've still shots to get."

Ransom by contrast had returned to the body with his pipe lit, puffing calmly, and using his cane, he lifted the tarp for a final look at the dead boy.

"I thought, Rance, what with your having torn off the head . . . the tarp a good idea," said O'Malley. "Thought Tewes would wet his pants." O'Malley's laugh sounded hollow as it resonated off the vaulted ceiling.

"Not so much as a blink outta the little weasel," replied Ransom, "but his damn teeth chattered a bit."

Ransom kneeled, holding the tarp up with the scrimshaw tip of his wolf's-head cane. He stared anew at the once fair-skinned boy's bony body, imagining a child, hardly past a schoolboy, anxious for the bell to ring. "You did the right thing, O'Malley. Now keep those reporters at bay so Philo can take his cuts."

"I mean should Chief of Detectives show up . . . it being unseemly, sir, what with the head off. Not to mention, maybe Keane intends selling that shot of you and Tewes with that ghastly head between yous."

Ransom imagined staring at the scene in the *Trib* or the *Herald*. "I'll see to Philo Keane," Ransom shot back. "I think I know his game by now."

"Aye, sir."

"Still nothing of the young victim found in any nearby trash bin?"

" 'Fraid not, sir, but our boys're still on it."

Ransom knew that a certain amount of deference was paid him simply for being a detective on the force, but men like young, round-faced O'Malley foolishly respected him for his part—so-called—in the Haymarket Riot. "God writes plays for each of us, O'Malley," he'd drunkenly said to Mike at the bar the night before, "and in my script, he gave me Haymarket to suffer through." Then he'd shouted to the entire pub, "Who remembers the dead I served with?"

No one in the bar could name any of the fallen police at Haymarket.

"They erected a statue to them gallant fellows, do you know?" He lifted his glass. "A toast to 'em now! Erected their statue long 'fore your start of service, lads! Do you know where that statue to the common police officer is, O'Malley?"

"No, sir. 'Fraid not, sir."

"Relocated from its dedication pedestal. Buried amid the city's sprawling buildings and thriving commerce . . . outside the police station door at the intersection of Jackson and Taylor, where only cops and lowlifes hauled in and out might happen on it. Like a hydrant for dogs to piss on. Like they are ashamed of our boys. From the beginning, top brass, the mayor's office, didn't want it on Michigan Avenue, for sure, not in eighty-nine . . . and not now. "Ransom had heaved a sigh. "Dedicated May fourth in a downpour with a handful of us cripples like me on hand."

"No one wants reminding of Haymarket, old stick," said Philo at the end of the bar. "No heroes that day."

"Those men gave their lives," said Ransom. "And now they're stickin' it to old Birmingham."

"Birmingham, sir?" O'Malley had asked.

"Oh, Jesus, don't get 'em started on Birmingham!" Philo shouted.

Ransom gathered O'Malley and other young coppers to him. "I was aged thirty-two in eighty-six. Birmingham, he'd been a veteran forever."

Philo, ever the artist, added, "Birmingham posed for the statue commemorating those killed at Haymarket."

"A good man working toward a pension till they got something on him," continued Ransom. "Some nonsense 'bout dereliction of duty. You know what he does today?"

"No sir, what?"

"He guides folks from the White City fair yonder to Haymarket Square; shows 'em sites of the running battle and riot. Gives 'em a firsthand account."

"Makes most of it up as he goes in that sotted mind of his and—"

"Philo!"

Philo raised a glass. Laughter erupted, but Ransom didn't join in. "And study the man well, Ransom," Philo kiddingly warned, again toasting, "because you'll be guiding the tour one day if you keep at things so stubborn!"

Ransom ignored these remarks. Too much truth therein. Instead, he'd continued talking to Mike and Griff and the younger men. "Old Willard Birmingham's come a long journey from Liverpool to Chicago. A bloody good man, but he's sure on his way to pennilessness in his old age. We're getting up a fund for him, boys, so pony up—come along, every one of yous."

Griffin Drimmer gave up a silver dollar to begin the pool

and curry favor. As Griff then worked the crowd for Willard's pitiful pension, he asked Ransom, "How well did you know the men killed at Haymarket, Inspector?"

"We were all of us two-year men. Of the seven killed, only Thomas Redden was more than two year on. None of the killed held supervisory positions, that's sure. Degan had hold of me, helped me from the blast when he collapsed and died, poor bugger—a severed artery killed 'im. A good patrolman of the Lake Street district, he was, a fixture . . . and the first to go."

Philo, as old as Ransom, piped in. "Got some great shots, but all were confiscated during the drawn out inquest. Never got them back."

"Part of the cover-up, I warrant," said Ransom, beginning to slur his words.

"Cover-up indeed?" asked Griff.

"I tell you, boys! Maybe those pictures show something they don't want no one to see. After the bomb hit . . . over the next twelve days in hospital I was. Cook County, where George Miller succumbed to his wounds, then John Barrett with his family looking on, and next Timothy Flavian, Nels Hansen, and Nicholas Sheehan. Degan and another of our men died on the street."

"Must've been hell losing so many comrades," said O'Malley, Griffin agreeing to a chorus of other cops.

"And a helluva big Irish wake," added Philo.

"Boys, I don't want to talk about it, not without sufficient drink." And then they all became sufficiently drunk.

Now a sober Inspector Alastair Ransom, leaning on his cane, contemplated a baffling murder spree. Three dead. All since the opening of the fair on May first. The fingers found lying about the men's room in a pool of blood, two in the porcelain basin, Philo had photographed. Griff held them up in a glass vial to Ransom's eyes.

"You know, Griff . . . O'Malley," he quietly said. "I once knew a fellow who'd auction off items like these."

"What kind of a ghoul was this guy?" Griff erupted.

"A cop. . . . Unfortunately, all too human. We called him The Reaper."

"Jesus God."

Griffin shook his head, hardly believing.

"You know, famous case and all, souvenirs, relics."

"You'd never do anything like that, sir," said young O'Malley, his boyish eyes filled with anxious curiosity about the infamous Inspector Ransom, anxious anew to tell his friends on the force what he'd witnessed here—how Ransom had literally handed Tewes a handful of what he'd deserved! And to brag that for a few pints the other night that he could now call himself Alastair Ransom's drinking comrade—*the* Alastair Ransom, a man famous for tracking down all manner of muggers, burglars, rapists, maniacs, killers, and anarchists.

"You really ought to keep a safe distance from the likes of me, Mike," Ransom whispered in his ear. "I go down, they'll likely go head-hunting for what few friends I have."

"I'll not be a fair-weather friend, sir."

"But you will likely be fearful one day at having to explain our connection to your superiors."

"Not at all, sir."

"You're a good cop, Michael Shaun O'Malley, but you ought to be more careful. And why aren't you using your head instead of that nightstick?"

"Yes, sir. I'm going to put in to take the detective's exam like you said."

"Good . . . good for you, O'Malley," said Griff, slapping his back. "How did this fella you spoke of who took the valuables, sir," continued Griff, "just how'd he ever get away with it?"

"Promoted."

"What?"

The department got 'im off the street and behind a desk, and today . . . well, today there he stands." Ransom's segue pointed to the chief of police, who rushed for the station-master's office.

"No! Kohler himself, is it?"

"That's me story, and I'd not lie about a thing like that."

"You two go way back then," said O'Malley.

"For a time, he was my training officer. Till I could stomach him no more."

"How could the department let a thing like that go on and then promote someone so lacking in morals?" asked Griff.

Ransom smiled at his young partner. "You've still a lot to learn about the department, Griff."

"Did things differently in those days, hey?"

"It still goes on, Griff. For Kohler at a higher level. Things don't reform in Chicago so much as they permutate."

"They didn't have evidence manifests in those early days?" asked O'Malley.

"Oh, sure, but they could be doctored, you see, palms greased. Didn't have photography on every case either, not like they do now. The eyes of the brass are upon you, son."

"If it's in Keane's photos," added Griff, "it'd better be in a lab or in lockup."

Alastair laughed. "But if it ain't in the frame . . . well, then it don't exist, boys."

"The fingers . . ." began O'Malley. "None can be mislaid or lost or else, sure, but tell me, what good are they?"

"If our boy here," he punctuated with his cane, "if he dug his nails in during the struggle, even got hold of the killer's wrist or pinky finger and laid a bite on him . . . well, I've solved cases by matching a scratch line to the size of a victim's nails or his dental impression. Fenger claims there're no two alike."

Griffin objected. "That's not very scientific. Sounds impossible to prove."

"Not if the killer *thinks* it can be proved. Call it voodoo detection."

"Voodoo?"

"Hell, I tell 'em we're in the new scientific age . . . I show 'em a vial of animal blood and a vial of human blood . . . I declare which is which by running 'em through a series of tubes and *whamo!* The guilty fellow confesses, because he is *found out*."

"But there's no such science separates animal from human blood, sir."

"No . . . not anywhere but in my head, but when I shove the evidence down their throats, they confess, I tell you."

"You think the scientists will ever learn to determine animal from human blood?"

"Perhaps . . . some day."

"In the next century perhaps?"

"Time will tell, but I know there are men in the universities working on it. Just imagine it, lads, a case in which we can get a blood-type match to prove it is indeed human blood on the man's shoe or apron and not some slaughtered animal."

Griff shook his head. "I still have no clue how they intend ever to do blood typing."

"Trust me, nobody knows," replied Ransom. He took a long drag on his pipe. "Now, Michael Shaun, how'd you like to do some detective work under Inspector Drimmer's guidance?"

" 'Twould be an honor, sir."

"Have O'Malley here help you go through the Bertillon cards for a match on that handprint, and boys, go at it with a vengeance."

O'Malley's eyes rolled as he realized that Ransom and Griffin had snookered him into doing the most tedious time-consuming, brain-numbing police detection work on the force, going through the Bertillon cards. He silently mouthed a string of curses.

"If he's never been arrested in our city, Ransom, he won't be in our card files," cautioned Griff.

"If not, we try New York's—with O'Malley's help."

"Then you think Tewes was telling the truth about New York?"

"Who knows?"

O'Malley mildly protested. "Sir, I—I've me own duties, and with the I-ID cards, we're talking hours, possibly days, and—and me duty sergeant, he—he ain't likely to OK—"

"And your duty sergeant's name?"

"P. J. O'Hurley, sir."

"I'll smooth it over with the man, Mike. We all want you to make junior grade, and I'm sure O'Hurley, too, has your best interest at heart."

Griff took Ransom aside. "Do you give any credence to Dr. Tewes's claims?"

"Sure and why not, Griff? Tewes is as psychic as that Jack terrier of yours."

"Now you're getting personal."

"Our guy, whoever he is, certainly likes playing with fire."

"So we gotta check for all firebugs in the system first."

Ransom nodded. "I suspect it's just his way of adding one more element of the *spectacular* to his crime."

"After headlines?"

"That or he plain bloody likes to watch 'em burn. Maybe something symbolic in it for the bastard. Shakespeare used fire as a symbol, and Plutarch before him, so why not our killer?"

"Whataya thinking? He's a gentleman of refinery, knows Shakespeare?"

"Did I say that now?" Ransom scowled across.

"I was just—"

"—thinkin' aloud? Some sort of evil genius? Evil yes, genius no. Find it odd, though, that the faces in every instance have been spared."

Ransom thought the victim himself far too young and innocent to have a criminal record. In fact, he looked, beneath all the smut, like a child in a Rembrandt depiction of a Dutch peasant family. A fingerprint from the severed fingers would in all likelihood prove valueless. Still, that tedious chore of doing something useful in a scientific method with the fingers would be left to the coroner, the now famous, indefatigable Dr. Christian Fenger.

Just after Haymarket, Chief Nathan Kohler's intelligent predecessor had made a deal for space at Cook County Hospital for police morgue work. What Dr. Fenger got in return was an endless and steady supply of John and Jane Does—cadavers. Christian's operating theater, where he taught surgery to a generation of doctors, never lacked for cadavers, not like the University of Chicago, Northwestern University, and many other surgeries and medical schools. Before this arrangement between Cook County and the CPD, the earlier police coroner had been a former barber turned pathologist named Louie Fountenay who knew little to nothing about police science and investigation. A man without imagination as well.

"Be sure to point out the situation with the head and fingers to Doc Fenger when you accompany the body to the morgue, O'Malley."

"Yes, of course, Inspector." O'Malley jotted a note and mouthed, "Fingers . . . give fingers to Fenger."

CHAPTER 5

Chicago had almost as many train terminals as police districts, but the Illinois Central Station had just opened this year as the busiest terminus for Columbian Exposition fairgoers. Designed as a through station—as many of the suburban trains used tracks that went through the terminal and on to Randolph and Lake streets—New York architect Bradford L. Gilbert patterned it on a Monet painting of the Paris train station. Opened to serve the tourist traffic to and from the great fair, Illinois Central stood a sight to behold with its towering, gangly turreted clock tower, gaudy Romanesque exterior, and its ponderous Richardsonian office wing extending outward from one side of the tower. Spindly iron columns that appeared ready to collapse at any moment under the weight of the massive masonry supported this penitent-looking wing. The whole an ugly symbol of the city's progress, felt awkward, a hodge-podge of random, hastily got-up gore, so far as Ransom could see.

Still, trains of every size and stripe bellowed and roared and whistled in and out, some suburban lines only slowing, going on to their next destination, while the huge engines of the Illinois Central and the Baltimore and Ohio sat at opposite ends like two bulls sizing one another up.

The interior of the building featured an enormous elliptically vaulted waiting room straddling the tracks, and a grand staircase leading up to where Ransom stood. The marble steps opened wide, butterfly-fashion on two sides, going up to the second concourse. It was from up here one found stairs going to the top of the clock tower.

Two uniformed officers who Ransom had sent up to the clock tower and roof to investigate returned now with a brown paper bag in which they'd gathered six cigar butts, all the same brand, their bands proclaiming them Cuban Valenzas. Could the killer be so foolish? Had he staked out his victims over a period of days from the clock tower? Looking down over the panorama of the world's fair from that vaulted position?

"None of the workmen here claim the habit or the brand, sir," said the officer in charge of the tower hunt.

Ransom's partner added, "A costly brand—Valenzas— not sold everywhere in the city. I smoke them myself on occasion."

Ransom nodded, taking this all in, mentally picturing the killer dousing the young man with kerosene and lighting the corpse with his cigar. "Should I put you on my suspect list, Griff?" joked Alastair. He also made a mental note to call Stratemeyer, Chicago's foremost fire investigator. Get him down to Fenger's morgue to help determine the exact nature of the accelerant, and if it might've been touched off by a cigar. If any man could find residue of cigar in the ashes of the boy's clothing, it was Harry Stratemeyer. Ransom had already drawn on Harry in connection with the previously torched garrote victims, and Stratemeyer assured him that neither had been torched *while* alive. Alastair imagined it so in this case as well, as the fire had remained stationary, the grime and creosote trail going nowhere. People afire who are alive tended to spread it around.

Ransom had taken no notice that Drimmer had stiffened, rankling at the suggestion he could be a killer.

Instead Alastair was watching the trains come and go below, like herding elephants in India, recalling his time there a few years ago while on holiday. Just outside the huge, marble-columned, marble-floored concourse, just outside the west and south windows, lay the infamous red-light Levee district and beyond, a slum wasteland. Closer to hand, directly below the window where he stood, Ransom studied the warm but limited glow of the gaslights that lined the little "cow paths"—so-called by students coming and going from the University of Chicago campus. The same lanes once led cattle to the slaughter at the Chicago Stock Yards— a standing joke with the students, but now rail lines hauled the cattle to slaughter, and the slaughter paths had been left for the students going to exams.

The paths also led people from the locomotive engines of the Illinois Central to the Alley L—the first elevated train line in the city. The Alley L journeyed folks on toward the South Side and the Hyde Park campus, but not without the stench of the infamous Chicago Stock Yards filling the cars. The odor of slaughter wafted for six city blocks in every direction. On a bad day with the wind blowing in from the lake, this foul odor blanketed the entire city.

From the second-floor balustrade, Ransom looked out over the solemn main concourse where uniformed officers, with little enthusiasm and smaller hope, questioned people, asking if anyone had seen anything out of the ordinary. The sound of steam-powered trains wafting up to him, Ransom returned to stare out the window at a growing and often troubled metropolis, reflected here in the terminal district where so many different rail lines crisscrossed as to boggle the mind.

He'd been on the scene for an hour and a half now, and his bad leg and back were conspiring with stomach pains from having not eaten. Having had to deal with Tewes atop the gruesome remains had left his nerves in disarray. The sheer cowardice of the killer infuriated him, so evilly Machiavellian down to the instrument of murder: its street name the *Devil's bow tie*. In a sense, a garrote was a hand-held guillotine, also created and perfected by the French—purveyors of culture and horror at once, as with all mankind, Ransom thought.

His skin-crawling need for an opium hit kicking up, his maimed left leg aching, and dry heaves threatening, Ransom—perspiring heavily now—excused himself and walked away from Griff and the others. He bypassed the men's room when he looked inside at the floor still polished in blood. Swallowing hard, he pushed through the doorway to the stairs leading to the clock tower. He wanted no one to see his fevered restlessness as the opium addiction withdrawal of mere hours now grapple-hooked his insides and crept along the epidermal layers of his skin.

Alone in the clock tower stairwell, Alastair struggled to regain control. He pulled forth a flask and emptied its contents—Bourbon whiskey—swallowing in rhinoceros fashion. Light filtered down from the top of the tower, which looked a thousand steps away. Ransom took the stairs, struggling against his own heft and body to wind his way up the spiraling steps like those in a lighthouse.

At the top, he stood and stared down from the window the killer may've gazed from; may even have watched his young victim's approach from. What kind of internal slings and arrows and horrors beset the madman? How much did the killer hate God, mankind, society, people, Ransom's city, and in the end himself—his own horrid soul? And how bloody similar were they, this phantom and Ransom's own shadow self? The one that crawled up out of him during his most private moments?

From below, young Griffin Drimmer banged clumsily up the first few steps, his voice spiraling up to Alastair. "Rance? You all right?"

"Just catching the view!" he shouted back. "Preparing for the Ferris wheel!" he joked.

"Ahhh, not a bad idea. It'd take an act of God to get me that high off the ground!" Griff's voice grew louder with each footstep. "If God meant for us to fly, he'd've given us the equipment."

"Give me time for a smoke, Griff. Wanted to see where they found the cigar butts."

"Yeah, sure, Rance . . . sure."

With Griff sufficiently persuaded to leave him in peace, Inspector Ransom stared from this six-story-high vantage point at the grand new buildings of the Columbian Exposition lining the coast of the largest lake in the Midwest. Most prominent was the Ferris wheel. Everyone asked these days, 'Have you dared ride the wheel?' and few people had for fear of its dizzying heights. Ransom had as yet to brave it. A marvel to behold, a symbol of what mankind had accomplished, along with all the other wonders of the fair, which had given law enforcement officials special headaches, as every day people were mugged by hoodlums and pickpocketed by street children. The complaints had kept the CPD understaffed for over a month now, and for Alastair the fair could not come to a close soon enough, but not before he rode the wheel—perhaps while under the influence of his opiate.

But he had time, as the fair was slated to run through summer's end. Everyone in Chicago—including off-duty police—had flocked to the exposition, the crowds enormous, just as they were this morning. Food vendors, merchants, and manufacturers showing their wares could not be more content. But rumors, reports, and leaks about a "Chicago Ripper" had begun to filter through, and people at the top like the governor, the mayor, his people, the architects of the fair feared the worst. No doubt, this new killing would alarm the entire city, and everyone would hear the fanciful epithet cops'd begun to whisper: The Phantom of the Fair—who wielded a garrote like a butcher with a de-boning knife.

Alastair pulled on the tobacco blend he'd mixed with marijuana. He'd given some thought to marketing it as a healing smoke known to the ancients and rediscovered—make a buck or so on the side like that Tewes fellow. Food no longer tasted as good, but winters in Chicago seemed shorter. Fact of the matter, Alastair liked Chicago cold—more human hibernation and less crime in the cold.

Griffin had quietly come up the stairs after all, and he

called out from the landing below. "Thought . . . you gave up ta-ta"—he fought for breath, panting—"ta-bacco . . . for lent."

"Lent? No . . . *rent*. I gave it up so I could pay my rent."

"Oh, yeah." Griffin made the final landing. He fell silent at the sunrise coming over the fair. "Weird paradox. They build this station so more people might come in for the fair, and now this."

"We're going to catch this son of Hades, but until we do, the bosses want us to somehow keep it out of the papers. So it won't affect their precious fair."

"But the reporters're all over this."

"The dyke will hold a bit longer, Griffin. Mayor Carter Harrison has his thumb on every publisher in the city."

"All the English language papers're going to go wild for sure."

"No, they won't. Any city editor stupid enough to print a word of it, and he'll be handed his hat—unless they all wise up and decide to simultaneously print it in every paper at once."

"What about Thomas Carmichael at the *Herald*? He was downstairs in the crowd, Rance."

"Carmichael, I'll deal with Thom personally." Ransom was beginning to like Griff's calling him Rance.

"Whataya going to do? How can you stop his mouth?"

"The old-fashion way—"

"Politics!" They said it in unison. Then they laughed, the sound of it spiraling down the stairwell. Ransom took a long pull on the pipe.

Sniffing, Drimmer said, "Unusual odor that blend you're smoking."

The smoke created a halo over his head. He pointed to the fair. "At the moment, the party is all that matters. It's the largest, most expensive blowout in history, Griff, rivaling Rome, twice the size of the Paris World's Fair, and it will be protected at all costs."

"Three killings, the work of the same lunatic . . . can't be hushed up for long."

"You're smart, but you're new to Chicago politics. If the mayor and commissioner want it kept out of the papers, it'll be kept out of the papers."

"But the papers're so critical of Commissioner Mc-Donoughue."

"All for show. Keep the population believing they have a voice."

"God, Rance, you're cynical."

"I've earned my cynicism, every poisonous drop of it." He tapped his cane against his injured leg. "Not like I can escape it."

"When is your injury not with you?"

"Rarely . . . rarely . . ."

"When you're using opium or hemp, or both?"

"Ahhh, so you do know my secrets."

"It's no secret, my friend. Kohler has wind of it. Asked me to report on duty use."

"He did indeed?"

"Yes, he did."

"And will you? Report me, that is?" He indicated his pipe.

Griffin hesitated a moment. "I've only seen you smoke tobacco."

"Good man."

"A lot of people want to see you go the way of this Willard Birmingham fellow. You must take care."

"I'm always careful, Griff, and not to worry unduly. You'll only get warts worrying o'er the likes of me."

They watched the sunrise stream through the thousands of taut wires and metal slats making up Mr. Ferris's giant wheel. Griff finally said, "You ever going to tell me exactly what happened at Haymarket Square that day in eighty-six?"

"Maybe . . . one day."

"This year?"

"Perhaps when all the evidence is in. . . ."

"But Kohler says there was a thorough investigation, inquests into the deaths, everything that could be done . . ."

"Let's just say it was an official investigation—and all that entails."

"Inquests are supposed to finish a thing."

"Yes, inquests were done, but I would not use the word *thorough*. Thorough might include the truth."

Griffin studied the older man's features while Ransom stared off into the distance, his eyes again drawn to the big wheel, its splendid synchronicity, its scientific perfection.

Of a sudden, Alastair had enough of the ornate clock tower window, feeling calmed. He and Griffin made their way back down the spiraling stairwell. "I want to thank you, Griff," he said.

"For what?"

"For your kindness in not judging me too harshly. Gracious of you, actually."

"Oh, not at all. I understand your addiction to the opiates, Rance, I do. We've all some bloody crutch or other."

"What're you talking about? Alastair Ransom? A crutch? To hell with you, Griffin Drimmer." He grabbed the other man by the scruff of the neck and kiddingly shook him.

Griff laughed and pulled away. "Part of the human condition, I'd say, like decaying teeth. God giveth teeth and he taketh 'em away."

"From perfect alabaster skin to boils and bunions."

"From paper cuts to falling debris."

"Unraveled ties and crashing platforms!"

"And safety vaults."

"From six stories up."

Griffin kept it going. "Locusts and all manner of insect pestilence."

"Melancholia and stillbirths, amoebic dysentery and the slats."

"Gallstones and tumors!"

"Failing hearing."

"Loss of sight, taste, smell, and touch."

"Tapeworms and tomato mites."

"Ships lost at sea."

"Coal mines collapsing."

"The sky doth fall."

"And G'damn satanic bastard bedbugs!" finished Alastair.

Together they laughed at the competition. "All part of God's grand design, and certainly not to be challenged," finished Ransom. "I think Mr. Darwin may be right. It is a world belonging to parasites."

"Allowing evils large and minute, no doubt to so bedevil and confuse our souls as to send us leaping into His open arms?"

"No doubt—but, Griff, I wasn't referring to any addiction of mine when you began all this."

"Then what were you referring to?"

"To my, *ahhh* . . . my rough handling of Tewes and that little matter of the head. I shouldn't have lost my temper."

"Lord, Rance, you held your patience longer than anyone ahhh . . . *expected*. That is among the lads."

Ransom's laughter filled the clock tower entryway and spilled out the door and into the death corridor as he pushed through. Reinvigorated, he returned to take charge of his investigation. The photographer, Philo Keane, had continued to work from atop his ladder-step tripod, getting himself and his camera into position. He next fitted his bulky camera into a glovelike vise that framed and held it steady. Below lay the uncovered body, the tarp held now by Philo's young assistant, who stared in stark horror at the sight.

"What in the name of St. Elmo's Fire is taking Philo so long?"

"Keane can't finish his work without the head, as Dr. Tewes—"

Ransom marched for the stationmaster's office, shouting, "Then what in St. Elmo's is taking Tewes so damn long?"

Griffin muttered, "Oh, shit."

Keane, atop the ladder, shouted at Griffin. "Out . . . out of the frame, please, Inspector! I've got to get a few *headless* depictions."

Ghoul, Griffin thought an instant before slipping on a ruler alongside the body. He then righted things and scurried out of the viewfinder's range just as, ahead of him, Ransom disappeared into the stationmaster's office to the sound of the *click-whoosh, click-whoosh* of Philo's master camera.

Meanwhile, timing each shot, Philo's assistant on the ground, having discarded the tarp, now shakily held on to the flashpan and ignited it with each click of the shutter. The two of them soon created enough additional acrid smoke that everyone began to cough.

CHAPTER 6

Stationmaster's Office, Illinois Central, 6:09 A.M.

The seared, blistered, fire-blackened head told Dr. James Phineas Tewes how horrid the suffering had been for the young man. The blackened eye sockets now painted in human creosote told Inspector Ransom how the soft tissues of the eye had been boiled and mottled by the flames. Still if one worked at it and stared long enough, the boy's anguished features came forth from this fired negative. The dead young man's rictus smile appeared as an ironic grin, but Ransom knew it for what it was—muscle contraction as with the pulled-tight withered arms—a detail learned attending autopsies conducted by Dr. Fenger.

Still, the grotesque grin, seeming so inappropriate, proved difficult to look at, even for a seasoned veteran with the CPD. For Dr. Tewes—a relatively young fellow—Ransom imagined it a far worse sight than any cadaver he'd worked on in a sanitary medical school in France. For Tewes it must be an excruciating sight, regardless of Tewes's having *asked* for it.

Running gloved hands over the severed head, reading the skull from bumps and indentions, Tewes looked as if in trance. The con man's white gloves came away with grimy soot. "He was thinking of home, family, his loved ones somewhere beyond Chicago . . . homesick, he was for . . ."

Ransom shook his head at the mock reverence in the room, and he audibly groaned on seeing Tewes's eyes roll back in his head, while his hands continued to hover over the scorched hairless cranium. Surprised to see Thom Carmichael of the *Herald* beside Chief Kohler, Ransom tapped Thom and said, "Phrenology—as bogus a science as ever concocted."

"Yet the chief of detectives of the second largest city in America"—whispered Carmichael in response—"a city on the verge of modernism, wishing to join the ranks of Paris, London, Berlin, St. Petersburg, and New York, approves of this *black art*? dressed in the laurels of science?"

"How the bloody hell did you get in here, Carmichael?"

"Kohler . . . he insisted. Special invite."

Carmichael, a cagey, crusty fifty-year-old, hard-drinking, hard-working reporter of Irish and English descent allowed nothing past him. "I loved your handing Tewes the head of John-the-Doe out there—only the platter was missing."

"Tewes had it coming, so to speak."

"You do make my life interesting, Rance."

"Trust me, it wasn't for your benefit or the *Herald*'s, and before you print a word of what you've seen, I wanna sit down with you, understood?"

"I am a little short on my rent this month."

The phrenologist gasped twice in quick succession as if an electric shock had gone through him. The hefty and misshapen, bearded stationmaster, a man named Manfred Parthipans, stood wide-eyed, lashes atwitter in an oversized face, his mouth agape. Ransom imagined him soon at the nearest pub relating all he'd witnessed today. "At least the boy was thinking pleasant thoughts at the end," Manfred opined.

"Hence the smile," said Kohler, faking a watery eye.

Ransom could not let it pass. "The constricted smile results from torched muscle—as a good autopsiest will tell you, Nathan."

"You can as well wait outside, Alastair," replied Kohler.

Tewes quickly added, "The boy let go of this earthly coil believing himself reunited with loved ones on the other side."

"I'm glad you think so, Dr. Tewes," piped in the cynical and equally skeptical Carmichael. "Reunited now in the celestial realms."

"That is correct."

"And precisely what part of his skull told you this, Doctor?" asked Ransom.

"I see through touch, Mr. Carmichael, Inspector Ransom." Tewes addressed the skeptics without looking away from the black orbs that'd once been two distinct human eyes. "I saw what was in his heart moments before death."

Carmichael vigorously pursued. "And just what sort of *arrangement* do you have with Chief Kohler's CPD?"

"I hired Dr. Tewes for his special talents, Mr. Carmichael!" announced Kohler. "As Ransom has brought me no results!"

Tewes had gone back to *reading* the severed head.

Ransom frowned and thought Tewes a wily con artist indeed—smart. Smart enough to know not to lock verbal horns with Carmichael. Ransom too thought of the corruption in the department, and the sleaze at all levels of city government—politics these days, synonymous with corruption—inviting in every sort of hoax and con game and pork barrel, and hair-brained scheme imaginable, and some not so imaginable like this. He thought of the payoffs he'd himself made over the years to people like Carmichael to keep them in line, and he thought of the bribes he'd himself pocketed over the years—the way of this place called Chicago by the indigenous Indian tribes like the Sauk, the Pottawatomie, and the Blackhawk, all of whom referred to the immense wild onion fields surrounding Fort Dearborn as *Chicago*—"land of mighty stench." The stench of wild onion had been replaced by the stench of slaughterhouses and politics, so that *Chicago* remained apropos.

Certainly, the story of any city's development was, after all, a story of crime and corruption, but somehow Chicago had been born in a greater cesspool of greed and on a grander scale of graft than any other before or since. Perhaps it was due to having been reborn in fire in seventy-two in the thick of the Guilded Age.

Still, in all his years in the mud hole, Ransom hadn't a dime to show for it. He had always meant to rectify this with some large-scale land scheme or venture of his own, but nothing of this nature had ever come about.

Ransom's thoughts drifted back now to the victim, and how many other ways the foolishly naive and innocent were routinely plucked in Chicago.

Stationmaster Parthipans said, "Train schedules might indicate when the young man got off an inbound train, or if he were boarding an outgoing train, *if* we had a name."

"His name is . . . was Cliffton . . . Cliffton Purvis of Davenport, Iowa . . ." said Tewes.

Griffin had stepped into the office at this moment, blinking dumbly, astonished at this assertion. In fact, the room erupted with a collective groan of wonder.

Ransom immediately challenged with, "And just how would you know that?" His mind raced with possible explanations: Tewes must have previous knowledge—as the features were recognizable through the soot and burned portions of flesh, along with portions of clothing, or perhaps some item on the body? Certainly, the dead boy's head hadn't imparted a name!

Tewes lifted his smut-covered white gloves and spread-eagled his fingers. "Phrenology told me so."

"Yeah, and I believe in the tooth fairy."

Meanwhile, Parthipans had rushed to his records and had begun flipping through ticket stubs. "Sorry, Dr. Tewes. There's no Purvis purchasing a ticket either inbound or outbound according to records."

"He must've purchased a roundtrip far in advance. Try earlier dates."

"I'll give you this much, Dr. Tewes," began Ransom. "In life, the victim might've looked like a farm boy from Davenport . . ."

Carmichael erupted in laughter. This was followed by an epidemic of laughter all round the room, Parthipans and Griffin joining in.

Tewes managed to hold his head high, but his face flushed red. Parthipans then came around from behind his cage. No longer laughing, the burly round man quietly extended a file card to Kohler. "Hold on, sirs, l-l-look at this."

Kohler's eyes lit up as he read the card:

```
Cliffton Purvis, depart Homerville,
    Iowa,
May 6th, destination Chicago.
    Return date open.
```

"Is it . . . is it him?" asked Parthipans. "Homerville is neighbors to Davenport."

"Coincidence, no doubt," Kohler said, amazed at the information. "Get on your telegraph and contact Homerville. Find out if this fellow Purvis ever arrived."

Carmichael and Griffin surveyed the card after Ransom. All three men looked at Tewes as if he were the killer.

"What?" asked Tewes.

Ransom bit his pipe hard and squinted.

The other men continued to stare at Tewes.

Tewes dismissed them all, going back to holding gloved hands within a hair's breadth of the fried cranium. But in a moment, he tore the gloves off and used his bare hands in a show of gaining more information.

For the first time, Ransom noticed how soft and feminine Tewes's hands were. *That's what it is about this man who is so . . . different. He's bloody effeminate.*

"Registered student . . . university . . ." began Tewes, ostensibly reading the head. "No, no! *Visiting*. Signed on . . . late summer term . . . Northwestern University . . . months ago. Returned for President's tea."

"This is getting us somewhere!" exclaimed Kohler.

Tewes continued. "Stopped to take in the fair . . . lost money . . . barkers and flimflam men . . . gaming . . . left him with only his ticket home. Cashed it in, but too late to get a cab back to the dorm. Fell asleep here. Woke up . . . stepped into the men's room . . ."

"I think it's time we reunited head and body and get all to Dr. Fenger," Ransom said, making a play for the head.

"He wants us to know that no one—no one!—can fight off an attack from this fiendish garroter!" Tewes dramatically added. "No one is safe." Something in the message or perhaps Tewes's resonant voice dredged from the diaphragm, or a combination of the two held Parthipans, Griff, and even the cynical Carmichael suddenly enthralled along with Kohler. Only Ransom remained skeptical.

"To hell in a sailor's dream," muttered Ransom. "Griff, see to it the head is returned to travel with the rest of young 'Purvis' or whoever he is. I gotta get out of here."

Ransom, his cane tapping a kind of personal anthem on the hardwood office floor, left Tewes to mesmerize the others.

CHAPTER 7

Still in the train station, going mad inside his head, Ransom paced wildly along the corridor outside the stationmaster's office, his crime scene now a circus so far as he was concerned. He toyed with the notion of just immediately shutting the crime scene down, when O'Malley rushed up, panting, holding out a wallet and papers. "It's the boy's student identity card. A freshman at Northwestern, sir."

Another coincidence? An educated guess? Or a sixth sense?

O'Malley extended the wallet to Ransom, who opened it on the ID, which read: Purvis, Cliffton O., address 194 Blount St., Homerville, Iowa.

"Where? Where was this found, Mike?"

"One of the lads spotted a ragged fellow with burns to his hands."

"Where?"

"In the food commissary slurping coffee, stuffing ham and eggs, sitting at table pretty as you please."

"What tipped your men off to him, O'Malley?"

"His clothes were sooty . . . the hair on his forearms singed. We think it's our man, but—"

"No garrote?"

"Sorry, no sir. That'd cinch it, I know."

Ransom asked, "Where's he being held?"

"Downstairs in Dr. Fenger's meat wagon, under lock and key to be sure."

"I don't suppose you found any Cuban cigars on him, O'Malley?" Ransom didn't wait for an answer, going for the "suspect" instead.

Ransom followed O'Malley to where the horse-drawn medical wagon awaited the release of the murder victim. A faded whitewash showed an earlier sign on its side in faint letters: OSCAR MEYER. It'd indeed seen an earlier life as a bona fide meat wagon.

"Get the suspect outta there, O'Malley."

Mike did so, his fingers twitching over his nightstick. Soon Ransom was shaking the dead man's wallet in the homeless drifter's face. The poorly dressed, elderly fellow immediately told his tale.

Alastair felt convinced of the man's version of events, which metamorphosed from having simply found the wallet lying on the floor, to having been awakened in a stall in the men's room where he routinely slept since arriving in Chicago. He'd emigrated along with tens of thousands of others from the prairies and surrounding states. Once in the city, he could find no work. He'd been in town for two days and two nights when he was awakened to the sound of two men conversing.

"Then what?" asked Alastair. "What in blue blazes did they speak of, man?"

"Not too many words passed before it happened. Awful . . . murder most foul, sir, most foul!"

"Can you recall the tenor of the conversation? Angry, argument, foul words, what?"

"Oh, no, sir, as friendly as you please and the boy spoke of his girlfriend and the fair and how he was so happy, and suddenly the killer lit on him with a horrible attack."

"Friendly—draws the boy into talking, relaxing, washing his hands in the sink—was he, when the attack came?"

"Yes . . . but how'd you know?"

Ransom imagined that his own recreation of events must represent as much magic to this homeless vagabond as Tewes's sideshow disclosures had made on brighter fellows like Griff and Carmichael. After all, he had himself imagined the boy a student at a nearby college. Still, Tewes had known the boy's name and where Purvis hailed from. Tewes knew too much—more than enough to incriminate himself but not enough for an arrest! "Did you have a talk with anyone about this at any time before O'Malley and me?"

"No one, I swear."

"Then you showed the wallet to no one? Spoke to no one named Tewes?"

"I swear . . . the madman talked to the boy as if he knew him, and then suddenly he is cutting his throat, and next setting his body out on the column and setting him aflame."

"You saw all this?"

"Yes, God forgive me! All happened so fast . . . no intervening, sir."

"Did he say a word over the body? Anything at all, man?"

"He laughed and he sang."

"Sang?"

"Badly, he sang."

"What tune?"

"I don't recall. Something familiar."

So much for Homerville Cliff going out of this world in a pleasant, smiling reunion with his ancestors, Ransom thought.

"I—I—I wah-wah own-ly—" the drifter stuttered and stank.

"Spit it out, man!" shouted O'Malley, his nightstick raised overhead as if it'd come down of its own volition.

Ransom placed a soft palm against O'Malley's chest. "Easy on the man, Mike. He ain't used to our ways, are you, mister *ahhh* . . . what'd you say your name was?"

"O-rion . . . Saville, Orion Saville."

"All right, Orion. Tell us what you saw. Every detail. You want to help the authorities, don't you?"

"Y-y-yes-sir . . . only . . . only got a fleetin' glimpse of the killer's legs and shoes—"

"Through the slit in the stall?"

"Yes. Thought he'd see me, turn on me, and—and kill me."

"Tell me what was noticeable about the shoes?"

"Shined up nice, fine leather. I know leather. Was a tanner before coming here."

"Expensive wear."

"The best quality it was."

"Go on."

"And when I escaped the bloody men's room . . . and—and saw the body aflame, I shouted for help but nobody 'round that time o'morn. I tried to put out the fire. And the whole time this madman was whistling a tune as he rushed off."

"What sort of tune?"

"Why . . . I believe it was 'Listen to the Shepherd' . . . no, no! Twas 'Coming Through the Rye.' "

"Hmmm . . . OK, tell me just how you put out the blasted flames. Exactly how did you accomplish that?"

"Yeah, how'd you do that?" mimicked O'Malley.

"By—by . . . by dousing it with my own mother's coat— only thing left me in this world." If true, this made a liar of the watchman, who'd claimed that he'd hosed down the body while yet aflame.

Ransom noted the moth-eaten coat, parts of it showing obvious signs of fire damage. The homeless man's gesture had been successful, and he'd salvaged his coat, along with the boy's wallet. In the process, he'd burned his hands.

"And the name you gave is no alias, sir? What is your given name and where indeed are you from?"

"Orville then . . . Orville McEachern is my true name. Feels good to say it aloud again."

"An outstanding warrant out on you from where?" Ransom had seen scores of homeless and hobos, and most had had at least one run-in with the law.

"Boston."

"So you came here to rid yourself of problems in Boston?"

"I did. You have found me out."

"And how did you arrive here? By mule, pack train, afoot?"

"I come by the rails."

"Indeed . . . in style."

"A—a stowaway from the Ohio Reserve on the Baltimore and Ohio."

"You fled Baltimore after leaving Boston then, Mr. Saville?" Ransom was careful to use his alias, and a half wink told McEachern that he'd come to the right city to start over with a new name. "The truth now I'm asking from you."

Saville-McEachern cleared his throat and scratched himself all over, clearly uncomfortable under Ransom's and O'Malley's combined gaze and in need of a bath. "I *ahhh . . . ahhh*, hell . . . I fled . . . fled Baltimore after robbing a bartender of twenty-four dollars and some change."

"There's no work in Baltimore, I've heard, no more than in Chicago."

"Then you have some idea how it is with me. No work for an honest man," he lamented.

"So desperation creates liars and thieves of us all?"

"I was without choice."

"You speak like an educated man beneath all that grime, sir."

"I was schooled in Boston." He said this as if it were a badge of honor.

"You say you're a tanner?"

"Aye, it's my father's gift passed on."

"Then it is your gift. We must help Saville here, O'Malley! Get 'im fixed up with the right people all properlike. What do you say, O'Malley?"

"Oh indeed, Inspector Ransom."

"So's the man can use those hands for honest work and rob no one in my city, what? O'Malley'll see you to a hot meal at the shelter. Get round then to see me, and I'll introduce you to some friends who can get you solid on your feet."

Ransom told the wagon driver, "Now Shanks, take Orion here to Cook County! Ask Dr. Fenger to set him right!"

"But, sir, Gwinn and me're only here to transport the dead."

"So now you do something for the living!"

Shanks began to protest. "But . . . but . . . this is an official ambulance."

"Make it one trip, soon as I can get Purvis all put back together again and out the door."

O'Malley's nightstick had disappeared into its sheath. "Doctors at County'll patch up your hands, old-timer," O'Malley agreeably added. "And not to worry. Inspector Ransom's a man of his word."

Ransom's mind still could not wrap around exactly how Dr. Tewes had gotten the information on the victim. He stared at the boy's ID. Tewes had made some striking hits. It smacked of collusion. To know the name, and so close on the boy's hometown—too odd. Just too odd. And Ransom was supposed to believe all this factual data had been somehow mysteriously "pulled" from the dead cranial matter— "raised" from the silent brain through touch? Nonsense.

Tewes had to've known certain facts beforehand, Ransom reasoned. Prior knowledge of the victim, just as in those bogus spiritualism tents and séances. But how? With whom had he consulted? Had he run into the killer at a local pub? How close was he to the killer? Or had he run into the victim sometime earlier, perhaps casually.

He felt a heart flutter. Instantly interested to learn what else Cliffton carried in his wallet, Ransom searched the billfold. Nothing but stubs from the fair, an old photo, presumably his parents posed before an ivy-covered building, perhaps visiting the campus. It looked like the black stones of Scott Hall. No paper bills—as these the drifter had spent. Only a cache of nickels and dimes in the zippered pouch.

Robbery was no more a motive here than in the previous two deaths. Cliffton had been killed out of some twisted purpose Ransom hoped to determine before the killer might strike again. But just how did Tewes figure in all this?

If the killing motive were personal, he must find answers among Cliffton's acquaintances. The *answer* would lie in a handful of small details, perhaps a falling out, perhaps a lover's quarrel, perhaps a debt, or a building jealousy or misguided revenge, but how could it be personal since the previous victims appeared, on the surface, to have had no contact with Cliffton whatsoever unless young Cliff had partaken of the services of one or both of the previous victims—one a known prostitute, the other perhaps destitute and desperate as she was with child. They were from entirely different worlds, one a Polish girl living alone, and another a seasoned prostitute known by police to ply her trade near the gambling dens of the Harrison Street Levee. Was Cliffton a lost soul who wandered Chicago's Levee as well, addicted to gambling or whoring or something worse?

Somehow he doubted this.

The three victims must have something or someone in common. Their paths must have crossed at some juncture somewhere. In this he agreed with Tewes, who had likely picked up this tidbit of police science from having hung about enough police houses to know how detectives talk and operate. He likely also read Pinkerton accounts, Conan Doyle, and dime novels.

Certainly, many traditional investigative tools and measures *did not* apply here. Still, what other choice had he but to look for a tenuous pattern?

These thoughts filtered through his mind as Ransom returned to the station interior. *And if no pattern existed?* he silently asked himself. *Then the bastard remains faceless and free to roam my city.*

Three bodies . . . mutilated throats *fed* to a garrote, each set aflame . . . each left in high-profile areas—one, the prostitute, left on a well-worn path in Jackson Park, used by the fairgoers and police patrolling the area; the Polish girl, barely twenty-three, left on the steps of the world's fair Natural History Pavilion—her unborn child found during autopsy by Dr. Christian Fenger. The killer may have honed his garroting skills on the other two, so that stabbing to subdue his latest victim was unnecessary—three times the charm.

From the evidence in the bathroom here, the struggle was quick and the attack overwhelming; over within seconds— certainly no more than fifteen to twenty seconds before Purvis succumbed to blood loss and a deathly euphoria. Ransom had seen the results of the garrote from time to time—a weapon of choice by the weak and cowardly and usually those without recourse to a direct attack. A cheap weapon, cheaply made, it proved deadly in its simplicity, and frankly speaking, Alastair wondered why it was not used more often. After all, it was an easily concealed weapon, not so noisy as a derringer nor so messy as a blade. Tidy it was. Despite the blood, little could spill onto the killer, as the victim's own body shielded him from the pumping major artery—the one Dr. Fenger called the carotid.

In Cliffton Purvis's case, his death was delayed only long enough for him to see his killer in that mirror at the public basin—such a modern convenience!—when the attack took place. Dying away in a matter of seconds . . . dying away like a pulse.

The sweltering summer heat and humidity had earlier plagued Alastair beside the stuffy odorous horse-drawn coroner's wagon sitting idle on 12th Street where he'd held the impromptu interrogation, but this same heat could not penetrate the cool stones of the train station. With the perspiration on his brow chilling, Ransom guessed that room temperature here would keep a bottle of ale a perfect seventy-two degrees. He renegotiated the marble stairwell, his cane tapping out a rhythm. He hoped against hope that the body and head had by now been reunited, that Philo had finished, and that the resurrection man, Gwinn, was wrapping the body, preparing it for Christian Fenger's morgue—

characterized once by Carmichael as an "eerie cadaver dump for every unclaimed body in the city."

O'Malley, a master at delegating responsibilities, shadowed Ransom. Realizing that Mike was over his shoulder, Alastair asked, "Wonder why the boy was here in the wee hours . . . on the little-used second floor?"

"Men's room?"

"But there are rooms below. Look, if he were broke from his day at the fair and was sleeping here on and off, he may well've found this area safer for his purposes."

"Apparently, so did his killer."

"It's what I like about you, Mike. You cut to the chase."

O'Malley had informed Alastair earlier that the aged night watchman who'd lied about his having doused the body with a hose while it was still on fire—a retired train conductor— had gone into a babbling state of shock. He'd been taken to nearby Cook County early on and was of no use.

Ransom realized that the bloody handprint could belong to the watchman or even to the drifter, another reason to keep him near.

Chief Kohler and Ransom now passed at the top of the stairwell. All eyes were on the two. Kohler said, "Work with Tewes! He's a remarkable man!"

"Look, Chief, due in part to a drifter, in part to the actions of the watchman, the damage to the facial features was minimized."

"Well, yes."

Alastair showed him the find of the wallet and its contents, giving Kohler a moment to digest this development, allowing Kohler to say it: "So you think Tewes had some prior knowledge of the boy?"

"And is withholding information and—"

"Not so loud. Keep this between us, see . . ."

"—and ought himself to be detained and interrogated." Ransom brought it down a few octaves. "How else to explain his knowledge of Purvis down to his studies? That's not even in the billfold."

"Perhaps the man is psychic after all."

"Phrenologically gifted I suppose," Ransom mocked.

"Look, Tewes makes a good point. Predicted we'd find papers on the boy. Said our killer cares not a wit that authorities identify his chosen victims."

"What has that to do with—"

Kohler held a finger in Ransom's face. "Other than torching his earlier victims, he took nothing away save a few items of jewelry. Tewes asked a sound question. What does this portend? What does it say about this phantom?"

"I suppose your leaving means the séance is over? And I can have my crime scene back?"

"Yes, the doctor is finished."

"Thank God."

"Once again this madman threatens the peace of the fair and our city," said Kohler, his eyes scanning the enormous station. "Sad place to die, don't you think?" Kohler's question surprised Alastair.

"We've both seen far worse."

"That flop house on Monroe?"

"Try that warehouse on Kingsbury a hundred years ago."

Kohler shot him a look of utter disdain. "Let it go, Ransom. The dead bury the dead." Nathan then stormed off.

Ransom guessed that Kohler, for a moment, was touched by a feeling of disconnection he himself felt here in the train station. "Place does make a big man feel small," he muttered to Griffin, who now stood alongside him, watching Kohler disappear, a trail of newsmen on his tail.

"Small, you mean? Insignificant?" Griffin's eye had fixed on the vaulted ceiling above the main concourse.

"The place is designed to do just that, to architecturally turn working stiffs like you and me into ants. Nathan's reacted predictably—exactly as the city fathers and the railroad tycoons want us to."

Griff smiled and fired back, "But not you, right, Alastair? How could anything make you feel small?"

Ransom scratched at his mustache, turned to his partner

and wondered at this question. "We don't need towering columns, vaulted ceilings, and massive Ferris wheels to make us feel small. Police work alone'll do that for us, Griff. Seeing what we see on the job—enough this day alone to make a man feel helpless and disposable." They'd been here now for three hours, from three to six A.M.—through morning's darkness, dawn, and sunrise.

"Disposable? That raises the question: How're we going to explain to Dr. Fenger how the head came off the body, Rance?"

"He's the medical genius. Let him tell us. And as for that matter, I have a few choice questions for Dr. Tewes. Where is the man?"

"Oh, he left in rather a huff down the opposite stairwell, avoiding you, I think, with a stop, that is, in the men's room where the boy was garroted. Seemed quite shaken afterward. Hey, Rance, do you ever think this new contraption, the phone, will ever replace the telegraph?"

But Ransom was looking down on Randolph Street, watching the strange Dr. Tewes where he awaited a carriage this busy morning. "I suspect that man of more collusion in all this than I can prove, but I will."

"What sort of collusion, Rance?"

He shared the wallet with Griffin, watching his eyes for a response. With the shock still on Griff, Ransom said, "I suspect skullduggery. Tewes recognized Purvis *before* I handed the kid's head to him."

CHAPTER 8

Philo Keane had packed up what he could carry,
leaving his young assistant, Waldo Denton, to arrange trans-
portation for the bulk of the photographic equipment from
the crime scene. Philo had one single desire for now—hide
away in his darkroom. To bid the annoying world and his
assistant good-bye. To be alone with his creations and his
music.

He dearly loved sleeping to the sound of a symphony
playing on his newly purchased phonograph—his only expensive indulgence, this awe-inspiring invention that placed
the decision of a musical score into his hands. He loved live
theater, opera, almost as much as a good beer garden. And
now he could afford the next best thing! He'd placed on a favorite, Wagner's "Rides of the Valkyries." The sound of the
orchestra wafted throughout the cramped apartment, and the
beauty of it mesmerized and relaxed Keane. Accompani-
ment to his art and passion that he now wished to immerse
himself in. The sooner he was done with the crime-scene
cuts for Ransom, the sooner he could sit down to contemplate the photographic art he'd created from his most recent
model, Miss Mandor. God, she was gorgeous, and as she
was a mute, so perfectly manageable.

For now, he must concern himself with commerce. Aside

from what Ransom needed, which he did purely for the money, he did shoots for area merchants. Another passion, his camera, was the specially designed 1893 Hetherington magazine camera. Sealed in leather with no projecting points, it had a continuous rotary shutter requiring no attention and could be set on slow, medium, or rapid speed. The lens was a beautiful Darlot #1 hemispherical with a lovely revolving diaphragm working between the lenses. Aside from a focusing dial, the camera was outfitted with a tally that kept a record of the number of exposures made. Finally, it had a rack-and-pinion focusing movement, and a back-and-forth double swing back, as well as a side-to-side swivel. Everything in one camera! And it had set him back sixty dollars—a fortune. Purchased through Montgomery Ward & Company, along with his oversized tripod that'd cost another $9.98, his outlay for equipment had put him in the hole. However, he'd talked Ward & Company into barter for partial payment through a commission to create a photo array accompanying a line of veterinary instruments.

Philo was in the process of fulfilling this agreement on the side, but the angst involved, the frustration, the sheer hatred of the project had grown like a cancer inside. A ruddy little account executive named Trelaine kept turning down his concepts for selling, with some attempt at flourish, such items as stricture cutters for cow teats, French poultry killing knives, Whisson's improved pig forceps, de-horning saws, Farmer Miles's castrating *ecraseur*, and, worst of all, the disgusting Gape Worm Extractor for worm disease in fowl. This terrible looking instrument, essentially a brass probe with barbed fishing hooks, Trelaine billed as the only sure way to pluck out the offending worm and dead matter from the windpipe to save a chick from a gasping death.

Men like Trelaine infuriated Philo. So did all the prudes at Ward & Co., as they'd turned away his best, most imaginative solution to selling such god-awful products—a lovely bonneted model playing the part of farm maiden, holding a precious chick in one hand, the chicken-torturing device in another, while smiling at the camera. Their alternative? A boring full-page add made up of words. Words that spilled over the edge of the page; words without let-up, no visual counterpoint, like looking at a page in the *Encyclopaedia Britannica*.

Still he had to pay the piper, to defer to his patron, to swallow his artistic integrity. To abolish his perfectly rendered ad for the *milksop* they proposed—a simple picture of each probe, each extractor, each bailing iron and plier.

But first to CPD business, make some money by developing 8-by-10 cuts of dead people. Another side business, an underground market catering to the bizarre and gruesome, would pay handsomely for a shot of Ransom shoving that severed head into Tewes's hands—not to mention headless, crispy-fried torso shots.

He slipped a small silver-coated flask from his coat pocket and swallowed its contents. With Denton still not back, he'd had to mix the chemicals and float the cuts himself. By now, he hoped the death shots from the train station—submerged in a brackish solution that told him he needed to clean his tray—ought to be taking form.

In his darkroom, he found it so. The results made his rent, and a sumptuous meal and bottle besides. "Where in hell is Denton?" he wondered aloud. His new apprentice was a glutton for punishment. In fact, Waldo brought it on himself. "But like God, I never put more on the boy than he can bear." Helplessly, Philo always took the tone of a British lord engaging his lowliest subject with Denton—lord to peasant; he did so only because Denton invited it, seemed actually to expect it. "It's as if comforting to the boy," he'd once told Alastair when Ransom had pointed it out.

Philo stared into the watery solution as the prints below the surface began a hazy, formless chemical dance. The term *solution* seemed apropos. Unfortunate that his friend Ransom had no easy solution to this bizarre series of garroting murders.

Waldo Denton noisily pushed open the door to Philo's

residence, his clatter at odds with the stirring sound of Wagner's valkyries down in the deep interior of the lower level apartment. Over the musical rendering of the twelve handmaidens of Odin riding their horses over the field of battle to escort the souls of the slain heroes to Valhalla came Denton's complaints as he placed the monster tripod in its corner. Too large to stand straight up, the tripod—used only in photographing murder and suspected murder victims—reached out to trip even the cat, Kronos, a tom that came and went of his own accord.

Philo slipped from the darkroom, his hands waving, mimicking a maestro. Waldo stared at his mentor's antics. Philo's orchestrating left hand continued, while his right swooped rhythmically down, dipping into his pocket, and returning with a bank note dangling before Waldo.

"The equivalent of U.S. currency, my boy!" he assured his apprentice, handing him the note instead of the promised dollar bill. Denton stared at the bank note from the Prussian Bank of Chicago as if it were a hundred dollar bill, his eyes wide with wonder. "I've never seen a bank note with this kind of pale pink color, and my . . . the Roman Caesar's got such a strange scepter, and usually his nose is a whole lot bigger, isn't it, Mr. Keane? I mean don't get me wrong. It's quite lovely in its detail."

"It's a new bank just opened off Lake Park Avenue . . . you know, Adams Street. So you know it's legitimate."

Philo himself made little in the way of payment from the CPD, but he'd wisely catered to not one but all seven district station houses, and the work was beginning to pick up.

Philo's darkroom amounted to a section of the apartment he'd covered in black material purchased from a mortuary. In what little space remained of his apartment, one corner was filled by a bed shoved against the wall, while another wall held up his bookshelf and desk, cluttered with all manner of photographic paraphernalia and books. Philo had studied the new and amazing science of photography since its inception and even before: the various stages of man's desire to reproduce reality in his own hands—through his own eyes—from cave art to present . . . *the Matthew Brady deluxe camera and tripod now available in any Sears Roebuck store and catalog across the country.* Photography had taken off like a brushfire in a tornado, and sadly he knew the only ones getting rich from it were the manufacturer and the merchant. At times, he'd cursed himself for having turned down that job to sell cameras at Fields Department Store, turning his back on a normal life, a regular paycheck, and perhaps some friends he'd have encountered among those who loved the new science. But sales was sales and he was no salesman, and he had always shunned what others called normal.

Perhaps for the same reason the science of photography had captivated Philo as a child. The history of reproducing and depicting the world around mankind, all of it fascinated him. Even as a child, he watched in awe as a Civil War photographer named Clemmens displayed battlefield shots and spoke of his adventures in the war. This man inspired him, giving Philo a wartime print that he'd signed.

Philo now ushered Denton out of his front door, chastising him for being late getting back. "Come round when I send a messenger for you, Waldo, and not before."

"Right, sir, but are you sure, sir?"

"Out Waldo, now!"

The sound of Waldos closing the door came as a gift just as Wagner ended. "Sometimes silence and aloneness is all that will do," he said and raised his empty gin flask. "But this will not do."

Inspector Alastair Ransom had left the Illinois Central train station and waved down a city hansom cab, one of a fleet of horse-drawn carriages that collectively beat a rhythm against the brick and cobblestone streets. Once seated inside, Ransom called out to the cabbie through a small portal that slid open and closed as needed, shouting, "One forty-one Clark Street."

Clark Street was the center of a great deal of activity, shops and taverns lined its way along with bawdy houses and gambling dens. In order to remain open and operating, Ransom knew that every pub, inn, tavern, bar, brothel and flophouse paid a tribute to the beat cops patrolling the area. Rent in the area had remained low.

The quiet interior of the cab and its plush cushions had an instant effect on Ransom, whose recurring headaches, stiff right leg, and frayed nerves did battle with him. He hated having to deal with people he thought belligerent—like Tewes and Kohler. This placed him in a foul mood that only Merielle might render neutral.

Not even Merielle's lithe body and experienced hands could end his suffering altogether. In her arms, beneath her warmth and her strong massaging hands, with her lips on him, with her giving herself entirely over to his needs without judgment, without harangue, allowing him to indulge his most secret desires, Ransom at least had the illusion that someone loved him unconditionally and without reservation. Merielle did not recoil at his burned flesh where the bomb had mauled him; she didn't recoil at the size of him, as did many a woman. She did not recoil at his often lurid, often horrific stories of things he'd seen on the street as a cop, tales more terrifying than anything penned by her favorite author from *Harper's Illustrated*, Edgar Allan Poe. Once, during an all-night session after they'd made love, he'd shared tales he thought would send her running from him. He'd confided the truth behind his reputation. Instead of leaving him, she leapt into his arms. He learned her real name that night. Before this he'd known her only as Polly Pete. Ever after, he'd called her Mere. Still, she'd withheld the details of what had led her into prostitution.

Alastair believed himself in love with Merielle, and he nowadays paid her a salary to be on call exclusively, setting her up in an apartment. She no longer needed to sell herself to men, he'd told her, and she'd tearfully accepted the arrangement. With his generosity and what she made modeling for Philo Keane, she needn't make a whore of herself ever again.

She had come to love him, and to love him unreservedly, despite the disparity in their ages. He was old enough to be her father. In fact, of late, she'd begun to treat him like a father, and this made him uncomfortable, but not so uncomfortable that he did not go to her for comfort.

She was a balm to his mind—*body and soul*. His working day was spent amid a dismal, depressing landscape; amid the poor and homeless, the wretched and out of work, the abandoned and orphaned—all ignored and given not the least human tolerance by city fathers whose god was money. The city he loved, the city he had always called his, had disappointed Ransom in cascading fashion.

An English reporter who'd recently pleaded persuasively to gain entry into the Harrison and Des Plaines streets' lockups was a close friend of Alastair Ransom's. The man wanted to publish a sensational exposé of conditions in Chicago, along its South Levee district and in its corrupt political scene, and in its treatment of the poor and indigent; to get at this, he wanted to see firsthand how people in the jails were treated, and he wanted Ransom's input. While it had yet to be published, author William T. Stead had confided in Ransom, over ale one night, the title: *If Christ Came to Chicago*. Ransom had laughed, finding it both fitting and hilarious at once.

"You can't be serious," he'd cautioned Stead.

"I am deadly serious, my friend."

"But you will scandalize the gentry, the wigs on Michigan Avenue, the merchants on State Street."

"As it should be!" Stead raised his glass and loudly exclaimed, "If Christ himself came in on a box car, he'd be pummeled and dragged off to a cell the likes of which I've not seen the world over, gentlemen. I tell you, I have seen more Christian charity in China, nay even Russia. Ransom

here has shown me that Chicago's got the deepest holes
other than Calcutta."

He'd gone on that night, adding that Chicago had no equal
for squalor on the planet, thanks to the cruelty of the guards
and the city fathers who'd created the dungeons here. "Your
city, Ransom, allows it," he'd said.

Ransom felt the stinging truth in Stead's words. Any visit
to the Harrison Street jail, which Stead characterized as
worse than the prisons of St. Petersburg, proved this truth.
Gaslight and shoulder-to-shoulder prisoners and makeshift
areas for the homeless, so many sleeping in one place. All
conspired to create a thick warmth and an atmosphere that
strangled the man who dared inhale. The floor a carpet of
humanity, the fetid atmosphere choking, the bars sweating
with condensation, the lockup proved the picture of
Hades—straight out of a Hieronymus Bosch painting of
Paradise and Hell. While actual prisoners slept behind the
barred gates, homeless tramps slept in the corridors between
barred cage and wall, there on the stone floor. "Pigged together like herrings in a barrel," Stead had written. "A pavement of human bodies." As the reporter finished each
chapter of his proposed book, he'd asked Ransom to read it
for authenticity and detail. All this on the promise he'd help
Ransom research Haymarket for his next exposé. The man
missed nothing.

But unlike Stead, Ransom had to work under these conditions and to live with them. Stead could write his book and
feel good about himself, feel he'd served man and reportage
gods, and could be on his way . . . onto the next social problem or issue in another city in another part of the world.
Stead had left his manuscript with Laird and Lee, a small
Chicago publishing concern likely to go bankrupt, while
he'd returned to England. Ransom held out little hope his
friend would ever work on Haymarket, and he imagined that
Stead's book on political corruption would likely never see
light of day. But even were it published, Alastair predicted
the sum total would be a mere ripple effect; certainly not

enough to embarrass Chicago's elitists. Nothing substantive came of Reform with a capital *R*, of new laws, new resolutions, of cleaning house, and all the clichés of politicians caught hands down. That only happened when someone died, as in the Haymarket reforms.

Chicago's wheels turned on the greased axle of corruption, and with graft came all manner of crime. Nothing against Stead or his naiveté, but the chances of his brave and devastating tirade against Chicago's politicians, money changers, officials, city councilmen, aldermen, her underworld and upper-world bosses would likely get fifteen minutes of anyone's attention. Chicago's corrupt nature somehow endeared it to those who lived here, even as it alienated and disenfranchised its own.

Amid this growing mad dragon of a city, with booming skyscraper construction reaching these days to twenty and thirty stories, people tried to make a living in an economy that favored those with resources, but circumstances only favored a widening gap between takers and the taken. And those who were *without* came flooding into the city from every conceivable direction on a daily basis. Every business in the city was exploding. Every school growing. Every trade erupting. Including the black markets along Maxwell Street, but hardly at the clip of the increasing population. As a result, every human vice had its own district, and professions like gambling and prostitution were as rampant as the opium trade.

The cab Ransom rode in bumped about the brick streets. The rhythmic *clop-clop-clop* put him near asleep, but then another pothole would wake him. The work at the train station had been grueling on a body he warred with daily.

Ransom had lived with pain since '86—seven years now. He experienced no relief save the dance with the occasional opium pipe, or the bedroom dance with Merielle, and sometimes he combined the two, and she joined him fully in the ballet.

The cabbie snatched open the latch and called out, "Clark Street, sir. You'll be departin' soon, sir."

Ransom contemplated a good stiff drink as he fished out payment for the cabbie. He dropped two bits into a paybox with a jingly bell attached. He needed to lie down with Merielle . . . get everything off his mind.

The carriage passed through the noise and bustle of new construction. While there was a great deal to recommend Chicago to newcomers with ready capital to invest in real estate or some new undertaking, the explosion of construction, land speculation, and development only made Ransom uneasy in his own home and in his own skin. He'd always imagined that Chicago would never become another New York, that it would always maintain a kind of small Midwestern flavor and friendliness, but such romantic notions had burst just after the Great Fire and multiplied after the Civil War.

Neither the Civil War nor the Great Chicago Fire could be set straight, but Ransom had been secretly investigating the cause of the *murders* at Haymarket since the day he'd walked out of Cook County Hospital on wooden crutches. Five friends who'd also been taken to County that day never walked out, victims of the bomb supposedly set off by agitators—union rabble, heads full with communistic ideals and radical notions of fair work practices. Two other cops dead on the street. No one ever learned the truth of it. No one ever claimed responsibility, and no one ever pinned that responsibility on anyone either, despite their hanging one man for each killed police officer. All Ransom knew was the single fact that seven good cops died that day. A devil's bargain that left him wounded and wondering who to lay it on. Official reports left as many questions as physical injuries. He gave little thought to emotional injury. But he gave a great deal of thought to what'd become a crusade to get the CPD to pay restitution to the families of the slain officers, but in his zeal to do so, he'd raised the ire of the mayor, his lieutenants, city fathers, and Chief Kohler.

Oddly, the more he poked and prodded, the greater the protests against him, which only led Ransom to dig in his heels to uncover the truth surrounding Haymarket.

As he dug deeper into a past that wouldn't let go, Alastair began to suspect the unimaginable . . . that the highest authorities in Chicago may have wantonly conspired against the labor movement in an effort to make them all out to be anarchists, and thus hatched the idea for the anarchist bomb in Haymarket Square. Could it have been conceived and implemented by labor bosses and by men in his own department?

A horrid notion when Alastair first came to it; it'd hit him like a stone wall. He refused to believe it, and for a long time it'd sat—while he pursued other leads, talked to other sources, went down other paths . . .

Each only led back to a single persistent and ugly conclusion. As actual eyewitnesses disappeared, moved on, died, became mentally unfit, or had graduated from incarceration to death itself, memories and details and so-called facts had become scarce, drying up.

But he remembered the doctor who'd patched him up and tended his burns, Dr. Christian Fenger. What Fenger knew, however, he had no intention of telling Alastair Ransom. He felt the matter rightly belonged in the grave of time, better left with those dead on both sides of the labor wars. On this score, Dr. Fenger had all these years remained adamant.

The cab stopped abruptly. The end of movement and the sudden silence against the cobblestones raised Ransom from his reverie. He climbed from the cab, tipped the faceless, silent cabbie and walked from the tavern address fronting the street to the back alleyway. Here he climbed stairs to the second floor atop the tavern, and knocked on Polly Pete's door in the sure belief that Polly no longer lived here, replaced by his beloved Merielle instead.

No answer came at the door.

This surprised him.

He checked his watch.

He'd given her everything she needed to pursue her fascination and interest in painting oils, and she was an amazing artist, after all. He'd seen the result of his patronage; his benevolence such as it was on a detective's pay. She simply needed to be discovered by Crocea or Barhid or any of the major galleries now legion here. Along with commerce and industrialization, the interest in opera, theater, ballet, and the arts had blossomed. In fact, Chicago's new art institute was this year completed in Lake Park, standing alone and set apart on the lakeside of Michigan Avenue facing the buildings of commerce and banking. The arts building at Congress and Michigan Avenue also stood out in his thoughts now as he again knocked at Merielle's door.

Where might she be?

Then he heard someone on the inside.

He banged louder.

Louder still.

Finally, the door crept open, wide enough he could see her eye in shadow. It was swollen red and cut so badly as to be closed. Opening her injured eye sent a shock of pain through Merielle that she could not mask, contorting her soft features. Someone had beaten her, and he knew exactly the man—if the term could be applied to Elias Jervis.

"Don't say anything, Alastair," she said. "Just listen. I'm no good for you. I let you down."

"Jervis did this to you! The bastard. I'll kill the *sonofa*—"

"No, it wasn't Elias!"

"Who then?" Jervis had been the last man who'd tried to keep her, but he only knew her as Polly Pete. It was rumored he'd once put her up as partial payment on a bad debt. Ransom goaded Elias to toss her in as a prize during a heated poker game when both men were drunk. Ransom had had his eye on her since seeing a photograph that Philo had sold him. But at that poker game, he saw something pained and solitary and quivering and in need when he gazed into her eyes. He cajoled Elias into the bet, upping the ante, saying it must be a permanent arrangement, and Polly's eyes lit up with the possibility. And so he'd won her fairly, and once they were alone, he offered her enough money to leave Chicago, to go home. But she continually claimed there was no home—that it no longer existed.

That had been the night they'd first made love, but also the night they'd watched dawn arrive together. The night Alastair learned her real name.

"I slipped back, Alastair," she now tearfully said. "I don't know why . . . don't know what's wrong with me, but he got ugly, the bastard, but I swear it never came to nothing but a beating. It's all my own fault. I shouldn't've let him through the door, but . . . but he was going to go forty bloody dollars. Damn me! Damn my—"

He pulled open the door and took her in his arms. When he'd first met her, his friend Stead had warned him off, characterizing her as a woman "shut up in sin," one destined to tread the "cinder path of sin," as he'd called it. But Ransom refused to give her up.

She stood shivering, surprised, expecting him to hit her.

"It was Elias, wasn't it? I want a piece of the bastard."

"Forget him, Ransom. My own stupidity and foolishness got me this way."

"No, Merielle! No man has a right to do this to you!" He shoved the door closed. "No one!"

"You don't know my final secret, Alastair . . . sweet, dear Alastair."

"Christ . . . I thought we'd gotten through all your secrets."

"We got through all of Merielle's secrets, yes. But not . . ."

"—not Polly's?"

" 'Fraid so."

"Whatever will make you happy?"

"Something's wrong in my blood . . . in my head even, Alastair. I need someone to tell me why . . ."

"Why?"

"W-why I like to be hurt . . . why I like pain. Why I want to be treated like dirt. Ground beneath your boots, Alastair."

"Baby, it's—"

"Shut up and listen! I'm telling you the truth, finally, so listen!"

"All right . . . go ahead, sweetheart."

"Can you, old man, tell me why I want to be Polly and not . . . not this princess you want me to be, Alastair, the one I've been trying to be! Like your bloody dream of some child I once was?"

"We can talk to Dr. Fenger."

"No! Not him!"

"Then another doctor. Chicago's full of doctors."

"A doctor for the soul? How many treat your soul, Alastair?"

"What're you talking about, baby?"

She went to her bureau drawer and snatched out a piece of soiled, torn paper. She held up the advertisement to his stunned eyes. A frayed flier for the services of Dr. J. Phineas Tewes.

"Tewes . . . why'd it have to be Tewes?"

"I've been seeing him."

"How long? For how bloody long?"

"Two weeks, a little more. He's helped tremendously!"

"I can see that," he replied sarcastically. He snatched the flier, ripped it up, and paced the floor boards above the London Royale Arms Tavern like a bull caged in a stall.

Given what he'd gone through today with the quack at the train station, it felt like a blow, this desire of Merielle's to visit Dr. Tewes for a phrenological exam to determine why she felt mentally scattered. It was as if two people occupied her cranium: Merielle a cultured, educated, and sweet young woman Ransom might take to any cotillion in the city, and Polly, the brash, dirty-talking, crude, uncultured, unread, uneducated poisonous wench who *enjoyed* dirty money for dirty sex.

"He says you're just using me, Alastair."

"Tewes said that?"

"He says a lot of things about you, yes."

"Bastard. What else?"

"Says you beat people to within an inch of their lives when you interrogate them."

"It's only what everyone on the street says. He knows no more 'bout me than what I want people to think. If they think that way, I get 'em talking, believe me, without laying a hand on 'em."

"Dr. Tewes says you're only after one thing from me, Alastair."

"Really? And what might that be?"

"What lies between my—"

"Why the *squirmy little runt quack*! What business is it of his to get involved in our affairs? Last time you held me, you called me a comfort, said you loved me, Mere! And I believed you, and I've never lied to you, ever, and—"

"Dr. Tewes says your attention and help is only trading one kind of bondage for another—"

"Just tell me, who in hell beat your eye to a pulp!"

"Dr. Tewes thought it was you."

"Who?"

"I ain't tellin'. I don't want you going raging off like my—my father to slay the dragon. Merielle might, but I don't!"

"I'll just find out another way, Mere." He refused any longer to call her Polly. "It's what I do, after all."

"You won't get it from me."

"Stubborn little . . ."

"Bitch? Now that's the kind of talk I like, Ransom. Call me dirty names and be as rough as you can be, and you'll please Polly, and with Polly in your bed, you'll have the buckin'est best time of your—"

He grabbed her up in a bear hug and stole her breath away with a passionate kiss. He hurled her onto her back and ripped away the robe she wore, revealing her red lace lingerie. He tore away at his own clothes even as he kissed and touched and held her down all at once. "As rough as you want it," he hoarsely whispered in her ear. "Maybe after this, Dr. Tewes can go to hell, Polly!"

"Oh, god, Ransom! Yes, yes! Being Polly for you"—she caught her breath—"that could work . . ."

And to hell with that creepy little bastard Tewes, he thought, his hatred of the man rising with his passion. He said aloud as she came in multiple orgasms, "Promise you'll never see that quack again, Polly baby. And give me the name of the blackheart who hurt you! Now or else I will never stop this!" He taunted her with each thrust. "Tell me . . . tell me now . . . now . . . now . . . now!"

"Damn fine . . . *in-ter-ro-ga-ti*on tech-technique! Ran . . . som . . . style, damn! Said you'd . . . get it outta . . . out of me . . . one way . . . or another . . ."

CHAPTER 9

In a darkened Chicago flophouse, same time

In the waking vision, the killer sees the dead unborn eyes alight with a strange preternatural recognition of who has killed him. The unborn one stares into his soul from somewhere the other side of Styx.

The killer sits up, sweating in the dark, a storm of hatred raging inside. He stares at the black eyes in the mirror. "Have a tumbler of that elixer that Dr. Tewes sold you," the voice in his brain tells him. He'd purchased the concoction a week ago from the little doctor of phrenology and magnetic healing. He'd wondered now for hours about Dr. Tewes's having shown up at the train station, wondered at his taking the victim's head off to the stationmaster's office and doing a mystical *reading* of it. Ransom amused him, while Tewes frightened him.

How much did Tewes know of him and his private business?

"God blind me! 'Twas a regular cockfight between the big inspector and the little dandy!"

But what of this strange new science—phrenology? What had Tewes learned from the dead cranium? Did he cross a line into the spectral world, or was he a consummate con artist? But suppose . . . just suppose the dead man had revealed something to Dr. James Phineas Tewes? What then?

Dr. *James Phineas* Tewes knew that one day the mask must go to reveal *Dr. Jane Francis-Tewes* beneath, so that she could come forward, if for no other than for herself and for Gabby. The balancing act, always difficult for her, was, she believed, even harder for her daughter, Gabrielle, conceived with her French lover and dead common law husband, the real Dr. Tewes. The real Tewes had been her first major heartbreak; finding herself pregnant and alone in a foreign country had been her second. Returning to America as a surgeon unable to work due to her gender, proved Jane's third major disappointment.

All the same, she refused to cling to remorse or regrets. Jane Francis-Tewes instinctively knew that an out-of-wedlock pregnancy could end her professional career faster than any preconceived notions of the American public about women practicing medicine. So James Tewes had become Jane Francis-Tewes's cover, and the phrenological exam and diagnosis his/her unorthodox answer to creating a clientele in her medical practice—a practice that failed when she'd attempted to set up shop in New York, then Philadelphia, then Indianapolis as herself.

Unable to feed Gabby and finally tiring of the world's idiocy, she traded for a world she would mold instead. Thus, she began dressing as a male doctor of magnetic medicine and phrenology. As a result, her practice here flourished.

On arriving here, as Gabby turned eleven, the widower physician, now "James Phineas Tewes" had gotten himself a bank loan! Something Dr. Jane had never accomplished.

And so it went.

The longer she was Dr. James Phineas Tewes, the better their lives, and the more independent she and Gabby were. Clients here in Chicago, having come with *his* fliers in hand,

flocked to Tewes's promises of relief from all manner of
mental and nervous disorder.

And in fact, Dr. Tewes—Jane and James working in
tandem—did indeed do good and not harm as people like Inspector Ransom believed. So what if the patient believed J.
Phineas's hands those of a man touched by God, that his fingertips conveyed some sort of magic that could actually read
mental states from mere touch alone?

The plight of women in general and female doctors in particular hadn't much changed even now in 1893—seven years
before century's end. They still hadn't the vote, nor the confidence of the medical community men that they were worthy of professional training. The man's world within the
man's world was the male bastion of medicine and surgery.

Her father had been the exception to the rule, encouraging
her curious spirit, despite the medical establishment's barri-
ers. To make a living as a female surgeon in 1893 proved
difficult to impossible. The few women Jane knew who actually got work only did so as doctor's assistants or midwives,
and even these only in the loneliest outposts of the West
where anyone knowing *anything* about medicine was prized.

Now Jane, acting as Dr. James Tewes, had enrolled her
child at Northwestern University Medical, and in the meantime, Gabby was an indispensable secretary and accountant.
For long years now Gabby had gone through stages: not understanding to enjoying the charade to, at age eighteen,
questioning her mother's actions on grounds of ethics.

They'd arrived in Chicago at the outbreak of Haymarket,
when the papers were filled with those arrested and on trial
for killing seven policemen. Jane paid little heed to the papers then, set on her new stratagem and determined on success. A lot of fliers had been printed and circulated since
1886, but her patience had paid off.

She'd had a patient today under her touch who'd reminded her how fragile was her ruse. A strange young fellow
she'd seen at the train station, assisting the photographer.
Denton was his name and he'd commented how lithe and

sweet the doctor's fingers had felt over his scalp. He'd almost fallen asleep in the chair as Jane probed the calming centers just behind each ear where a bit of pressure and rhythmic action could put a grown man to sleep. She'd curtailed the diagnosis and provided him with some particulars of his condition—after gleaning some anecdotal information about what precisely had been troubling him, where his aches and pains lie, and how long he'd been suffering. Denton happily allowed Tewes to place "his" hand on the area of his abdomen where the real complaint might be diagnosed.

Before it was over, Dr. Tewes told Denton, "Sir, your mental malaise has a quite physical and banal cause—"

"Really?"

"A hernia from lifting that huge tripod."

"What do you propose?"

"Find other work."

"But I wish to learn photography from the best."

"I can give you an elixir for the pulled muscle, but you really must see a surgeon like Dr. Fenger."

"A surgeon! But I fear going under the knife."

"It is a simple procedure." She could perform the surgery herself, but to do so would end her ruse as a man. Any new surgeon coming to Chicago was instantly spotlighted by the medical establishment, his credentials gruelingly questioned. And not without good reason. Many a cruel hoax was perpetrated in the name of surgery these days.

She now sat at her elaborate makeup mirror. The bright lights were the same as those any actress required for makeup. In a sense, she'd become the consummate actress. She began wiping away the makeup. Gabby would soon be home, and office hours were over. She gave a moment's feeling of pride in Gabby. The promise of children, to see one's love come radiant, full-bloom, and for her to become Jane's closest, dearest friend . . . all a blessing. *My greatest accomplishment*, she thought. Gabby, along with her professional success, pleased her greatly.

This new direction Jane'd taken—getting work in police

circles as some sort of mentalist—this her father would condemn completely, wholly, royally as far too risky and nervy, a fool's show of bravado. *How ultimate was this,* she silently asked herself of the subject . . . *to step into the world of police detection in this guise and walk out with not a one of them recognizing a ruse?* How wicked to pull it off before the disturbed eyes of Inspector Ransom, and he once a childhood sweetheart? They had gone to the same schools together in those far ago early years of their lives in the Prairie City.

As a child, she'd loved him unreservedly. But what'd he become? Jane knew well that reputation, however blown out of proportion, was based on a core reality. Perhaps he didn't beat people he arrested with quite the gusto or vigor depicted in the lurid street tales, but he did engender fear in all who thought Ransom interested in talking to them. He seemed also desperately lonely—hence Polly-Merielle, who'd confided far more in Dr. Tewes than Jane'd wished. Polly, addicted to a need deeply imbedded, had in fact begun a heavy petting session with Dr. Tewes, who blocked her overtures and had insisted on a purely professional relationship. Taken aback, Polly actually showed signs of rehabilitation after all sexual advances had been refused.

Jane now stepped to her bed and pulled forth a black valise, one that'd been her father's. She spread out the tools of her buried trade—most of her father's surgical instruments. She ritualistically handled each surgical instrument in turn. She did so swearing to her image in the mirror, "One day . . . one day I'll again hang out a shingle as Dr. Jane Francis—Surgeon." Some day when Chicago—*and the rest of the world*—might accept a female surgeon without reservation. In the meantime, poor Gabby'd had to memorize a pack of lies associated with being the daughter of Dr. Tewes as Dr. Tewes's "wife" had died giving birth to Gabrielle. It proved increasingly maddening for the child.

Perhaps we should've stayed in Paris was a phrase that'd become a mantra. So often did she say this to Gabby as a child that Gabby had made up a lyrical song around the phrase. *Perhaps . . . oh, perhaps . . . we Pariii . . . we Pariii.* Perhaps.

For now, she remained the mysterious Doctor Tewes. "What would Father say about all this waste of talent?" she asked the empty room.

She heard his resonant bass voice now saying, "Take heart, Jane."

Her father'd had to deal with his own generation and problems endemic to it . . . or rather *epidemic* to it. Ailments like malaria, typhoid fever, and digestive malaise when Chicago had been Fort Dearborn. The military base, finally unnecessary, evacuated in 1836, four years after the Black Hawk War but not the threat of disease. And so Dr. William Francis stayed on and started a private practice. How crude medicine and surgery were then. The diseases that laid men low in those days—all across the continent—such as pneumonia and "graveyard" malarial fevers, sometimes called miasmatic fevers wiped out 80 percent of one Illinois county in the 1820s. Attacks from these fever diseases continued almost unabated for decades after. Her father had once told her that in each case where a doctor could not determine the cause of the disease, he invoked the word *malaise*.

In Chicago, cholera and small pox inspired the greatest dread. Even rumor of such pestilence roused officials to pay heed to her father and other medical men to make sanitary reforms, appropriate money for the neglected Board of Health, and to enact laws designed to reduce the incidence of fever diseases. No one else in the country believed Chicago a safe place for his wallet, but worse yet, no one on the continent believed it a place for one's good health. No sewage system worthy of the name existed before 1851. Garbage and refuse continued to be tossed willy-nilly into the Chicago River or allowed to accumulate in filthy alleyways. Drinking water came either from shallow wells or from the lakeshore. Her father had himself succumbed to pneumonia during a ravaging epidemic.

Jane had grown up self-reliant, as her mother had died of a brain tumor when Jane was only six, and her father, William Francis, left Chicago for Europe in a fit of self-doubt, wishing to learn far more. Death and pestilence in Chicago had frustrated all his efforts. When he returned, Jane, living with her aunt, was four years older. By now she'd been estranged from her father, which suited his needs, as he was a workaholic and as she was a painful reminder of Charlotte, her mother.

William had returned with plans for a serviceable system of sewers to rid Chicago of pestilence. He'd studied with Dr. Xavier Bichat, the man who'd demonstrated that tissues and not organs were the seat of disease. A decisive step in the localized pathology movement. The concept of disease invading the solid parts of the body implied a revolution in medical theory and practice. But even now, 1893, many a medical professor clung to the mad notion that blood was the carrier as well as the starting point of disease—thus a lot of old fools calling themselves doctors still insisted on leeches and bleeding a patient to "remove bad blood."

When Jane had gone through medical school, she'd been taught that to combat disease, she must "treat the blood" either withdrawing it through venesection, or by purifying the "life's blood" with medicine.

Thanks to the new pathology, what men like Bichat and her father insisted upon challenged this classical, centuries-upon-centuries held notion. The French medical community also began the meaningful application of statistical techniques to clinical data. The value of postmortem records, vital statistical studies, and using clinical tests in the diagnosis of illness had been embraced by forward-thinking men and women. Her father's return to Chicago to reacquaint himself with Jane was also to *acquaint* the established medical community with Bichat's methods. With the acceptance of the localized concept of disease, and with modern surgery just coming into being in the second half of the century, surgeons began doing far more than setting fractures, treating flesh wounds, abscesses, bladder stones, and hernias, as the idea of surgery as a last resort faded.

As far as Jane Francis-Tewes was concerned, this new belief in Bichat's localized pathology of disease had, even more than the discovery of anesthesia, marked the turning point of modern surgery. It initiated the kind of surgery the now famous Dr. Christian Fenger performed daily at Cook County Hospital, where he also took charge of the dissection of the murdered and the victims of questionable deaths for the CPD as chief coroner. Working through Kohler, Jane as Tewes, had made it her business to get something on Dr. Fenger, to blackmail him, so as to get a close look at the reports on the first two victims and a firsthand look at the next victim—who happened to be the Purvis boy.

She felt badly at having gotten Fenger's cooperation in the manner she had. He'd come to see Dr. Tewes on Nathan Kohler's urging, but even more out of desperation. He'd come with a brain full of racing circuitry and stress and recurrent headache and depression, and Dr. Tewes being who *he* is, could not be expected to disregard an opportunity to leverage a small favor from the infamous Dr. Fenger. One word of Fenger's level of intense mental stress, and Cook County Hospital would put him out to pasture, as might the CPD.

It was not a thing she'd relished doing, as she respected and admired her one-time instructor in surgery, a brilliant man and a wonderful mentor, and her father's friend. He'd been one of the few instructors she'd had this side of the Atlantic who had trained her as he might a man. Few men were as ahead of their time as Dr. Christian Fenger, and he so reminded her of her father, and Jane believed that his fine reputation brought more thousands to the operating table than did the use of ether and chloroform. She hated using him, but there seemed no other choice.

A noise came from without. Gabby had come home, and she was talking to someone. Jane Francis cursed under her breath. How often must she tell Gabby she simply must tell her friends that her doctor father can't abide anyone in his clinic or his house as he had a morbid fear of the microbial world?

She peeked out to the next room, her forceps still in hand, to see Inspector Ransom standing in her parlor. "Jesus!" she gasped. The man stood nervously rocking on his heels, looking about, as Gabrielle explained, "But Father is not here."

Jane looked for some out. The bedroom window, but that was a drop into the bushes and neighbors already kept a prying eye on Tewes. Then she saw an apron hanging on the back of the door. She snatched it down and tied it on, and in an instant, stepped into the parlor and asked, "Can I be of any service? I'm the doctor's caretaker, maid, fix-it person, and sister, Jane. Can I help you, sir?"

"I'm looking for your . . . ahhh brother." The bull shoved his weight from side to side. "I have a bone to pick with him."

"I see. I'm sorry, sir, but he is not at home."

"Then I'll wait."

"Aren't you Inspector Ransom, sir?"

"Oh, oh, yes . . . Ransom. Sorry . . . thought I'd said so." He held up his inspector's badge—a gold-plated shield.

"And I am Miss Ayers."

"Really? Jane Erye like in the book?"

"No . . . no . . . A-Y-E-R-S . . . quite different. Jane Francis ahhh . . . Ayres."

"So is there a convenient place for me to wait?"

"Outside perhaps . . ."

"Outside?"

Merielle-Polly is right about him, she thought. *He is a bit thick-headed.* "Yes, please, outside. We are two women in the house, and doctor would not be pleased if he returned to find us alone with you, sir. Only polite to wait outside."

"Not in the study?"

"Sorry."

"Not in the doctor's office?"

"No, sir, now please . . . outside. There's an ample porch, a swing."

Gabrielle erupted in a laugh she stifled.

Ransom frowned, placed on his bowler hat, gave a fleeting glance at the spinster sister, turned, and stepped through the door. From the door, Miss Jane Francis 'Ayres' shouted behind him, "I do hope it is not too important. If so, you might find doctor at Cook County. And if not there, Hanrahan's on Archer near—"

"I know the place." Ransom tipped his hat at the woman. Odd, he thought, how her eyes and those of young Gabby—who'd introduced herself as Dr. Tewes's daughter—had looked so much alike, aunt and niece, but then rumor had it the child was adopted for usury by Tewes. Perhaps Jane was the actual mother?

The afternoon shadows were lengthening, and in the distance, a thick roiling cascade of clouds threatened to invade from the lake to Chicago's downtown, the army of storm clouds forming like a regiment over skyscrapers in the distance, no doubt worrisome for the fairgoers and merchants. *Nature had no business cutting into profits,* Ransom imagined on the lips of every Chicago merchant.

He stepped off the porch and into a thin, surprisingly chilly silver downpour, having decided to go in search of Dr. Tewes at Hanrahan's. Not likely he was at Cook County. Most likely he told people that he was on staff at Cook County along with most all the luminaries of the medical profession in Chicago, and the thought made him laugh. Imagine Tewes alongside a man like Christian Fenger.

"Hanrahan's . . . far more likely." The South Levee was the den of lowlife in the city. As a cop, he knew every section of town and its character, and the Levee maintained the deadliest reputation, even above Hair Trigger block. Called by many the Old Tenderloin district, the South Levee had become firmly entrenched twenty-odd years before any thought of a Columbian Exposition. Now there existed *two* South Levee districts—a new extension of the old reaching like icy fingers toward the world's fair, close enough to the Loop office buildings as to be within view from the Union League Club windows. A horror and an abomination to the gentry.

Ransom climbed into a waiting cab he found a few blocks from Tewes's place and shouted up through the window at the driver to take him to Hanrahan's in the South Levee. The cabbie hesitated and stared down at his fare as if seeing him for the first time.

"Official business," said Ransom, displaying his inspector's badge.

The man's face sank like stone turning to dough. He knew to get his fare he'd have an hour's headache just filling out the paperwork, and the wait for the reimbursement would take months. *Police business*, it was termed.

Ransom heard the driver's guarded curses as the cab lurched forward without grace. As the carriage made its journey through busy, crowded streets for the south Loop area, Ransom thought of this turn of events with Merielle. She'd made him promise to not harm Dr. Tewes or his hands.

"The man's hands're unbelievable!" she'd exclaimed.

"Drink your absinthe," he'd shouted back.

"But Alastair, he possesses some sort of *Rasputin-like* ability, totally relaxing you while reading you like a book."

But his foul mood against Tewes and against the bastard who'd beaten Mere, fueled by each rhythmic *clop-clop-clop* of the carriage horse, was further fueled by having to go near the area not far from where he'd been born and raised, now an area of indecent trades. God, he felt like thrashing Polly from out of his Merielle, or in some way combining the two, and somehow making both sides of her love him unreservedly.

Perhaps she was incapable of such a love. She did indeed seem "shut up" in sin. She had let him down. Disappointed him. Falling back into old habits, and going to this snake-oil salesman when he should suffice. And then the nerve of the little creep. Giving bad advice to Merielle, warning her off him! All this had come about *before* Ransom had shoved the dead boy's head into Tewes's hands! How galling.

Just when he'd begun to feel that all was well. That he had control of his life. That he had the woman he loved. That she loved him. Now this.

Plus Merielle had taken to lying to him, something he expected and saw every day on the job. But not from her. It infuriated him. She swore that it'd not been Elias Jervis who'd blackened her eye. Swore on her mother's memory that Jervis had left for Milwaukee as certain friends of Ransom's—toughs on the force, she'd called them—had made life in Chicago too "hot" for Jervis, the worst sort of pimp, to continue in "Ransomland," as she'd put it. Merielle added, "I don't know the man's name, only that he wore a black cape, a top hat, boots all shined. A real gent," she'd finished.

"Some bloody gent! Strikes you 'cross the face?" he replied.

Where Hanrahan's sat, square between these two levee districts, was the southern tip of the Loop, bounded on the east by Dearborn, Clark on the west, and Harrison on the north. This had more recently come to be called the wicked Custom House Place Levee. The "Gem" of the prairie continued its reputation as America's wickedest city, its reputation that of a bacchanal the likes of which must make Rome blush.

High-minded temperance leaders and aldermen who didn't care about getting reelected blathered on about one day burning out the cancer of the entire South Levee—both new and old—in the name of the Lord, as done with other areas in the early days. Some nights a parade of angry citizens marched through the South Levee with torches held at the ready, but unlike The Sands and Hair Trigger Block, an actual burn-out hadn't come to pass. Still an uneasy tension between the so-called socially conscious and the vice merchants always hung over Chicago like a pall. Thirty-seven to forty houses of prostitution squatted within the confines of the new levee alone. Forty-six saloons and growing. Eleven or twelve pawnbroker houses. A shooting gallery or two, and an obscene bookstore. Many a dipping house operated here, in which a closet-sized room was opened on a waiting prostitute, the John mugged and robbed, girl and pimp splitting the proceeds.

It'd taken him a long time, but finally Ransom had gotten some useful information out of Merielle. She came across with what the "gent" called himself—"Mr. Sleepeck Stumpf" which sounded ridiculous to Ransom's ear, but she insisted on it.

He'd passed the name along to Dot 'n' Carry and other of his streetwise friends to hunt him down—he wanted a word with Mr. Stumpf. The result so far pointed to a fictitious name.

Alastair placed his cane with the wolf's-head bone handle at ease alongside him as he leaned back into the cushioned seat of the hansom cab. This particular cab was indeed plush and the burgundy seats rich and warm. The interior, no doubt, had been done by the Pullman Company or Fischer. The Studebaker carriage company had lost out repeatedly to the other two for large contracts; Ransom had read as much in the papers. He tried to recall a time when he'd had a moment to read a paper, fatigue washing over him.

Alastair closed his eyes as the cab made for the destination suggested by the handsome petite woman whose features were surprisingly memorable, although he'd given her scarcely a nod. He wondered if she had any idea of the Levee district's reputation. Surely no, or she wouldn't've pointed out that her brother, the good doctor, frequented the area.

Or had she wantonly wished for an officer of the law to know of her brother's questionable proclivities? How much did this woman know of Dr. Tewes, or of his comings and goings? Perhaps, in the future, she could prove useful?

CHAPTER 10

Philo Keane had fallen asleep to the sound of a Strauss waltz on his phonograph while thinking of Miss Chesley Mandor. Philo had one other vice than drink, and this was his prurient interest in the curvaceous body of a woman—as he'd all his life engaged in the search for the perfectly formed female, a dream that possessed him. He purely loved and respected the feminine form, from the tender half flush along the nape of the neck to the luscious ripe oval of the breasts, the deep valley of the cleavage, the enrapturing triangle of the crotch—a magnet to his eye and camera lens.

He loved the species, fussing with her lips, her eyebrows, her lashes, her ears and adornments, and her neck and necklaces and chokers and lacy things from items on a bonnet to items on her privates. The way she tossed back her hair; the way she tossed back a pint of ale; the way she stood hands on hips when angry. Yes, he loved this vivacious creature called woman. He loved this ideal in his mind's eye, but he also loved the flawed ones, the fallen ones, the sad and swollen ones, but most of all, he loved any woman—prude or prostitute—who'd had the decency to retain the beauty given her early in life.

Philo wanted more than anything to combine his interest and love of the female form with his art. To make money with these two interests simultaneously had become his driving obsession. He had to be careful, however, as the Victorian prudishness of many if not most of his prospective clients in such a venture reared its ugly head and suddenly some fool is calling a cop, shouting "pornography" when in fact, Philo created art.

All round him, Philo saw the most god-awful advertising. Fliers created by fools. No use of negative space. No visual component. As an artist with a camera, he found the advertising people settled for appalling and garish and foolish and redundant and boring and pedestrian and on and on . . . Not a *whit* of thought in it and no *wit* besides! But he had plans for Chicago advertisers. He had now a library of photos of beautiful women in various poses in Grecian and Roman dress, some quite suggestive, and should he find a backer, someone with gumption and capital—why then, look out. And should he superimpose the lady with a farm implement or a tin of snuff, a soft drink or hard liquor, or that new contraption invented by Thomas Crapper called indoor plumbing? What limits remained? If only he could squeeze money out of some of these old duffers like Sears, Roebuck or Field, there was a fortune to be made in advertising.

It all seemed God's plan for him.

Born in Canada, Philo Keane had immigrated to Chicago in search of work like so many before him, except that he was a skilled lithographer. But he gave up this career for what appeared a far more lucrative one—photography—which he'd grown to love, and which he suspected would supplant all lithography someday, making his older profession obsolete.

Philo had studied with a fellow Canadian, the famous Napoleon Sarony, himself apprenticed to the celebrated lithographers Currier & Ives. Napoleon, now near death in a New York hospital, had made history when he sued a clothier who expropriated a photograph of none other than Oscar Wilde posed by Sarony in an artistic rendering—as Sarony had pioneered the celebrity portraiture business.

The case was the *Burrows-Giles Lithographic Co. v. Sarony*, and its roots went back to an advertisement for hats that'd used 85,000 reproductions of Sarony's print, while ignoring Sarony's copyright!

Sarony, on learning of the outrage, took his case to court and won, but his opponents appealed to the Supreme Court where they argued that since the technology of photographs hadn't existed in 1790, then photographs could not be covered under the copyright laws framed in a 1790 Act of Congress.

The Supreme Court disagreed, citing that the founding fathers had anticipated all manner of futuristic discoveries in both patent and copyright law. Justice Samuel Miller, who wrote the ruling, added that an author is simply the one "to whom anything owes its origin." As Sarony's #18 Oscar Wilde was ruled a work of art and the "product of plaintiff's intellectual invention, and as a class of invention for which the Constitution intended to secure to the author for exclusive right to use, publish, and sell . . ." and so it went.

The ruling made Sarony and his company a household name.

And while men with vision like Sarony had gone full tilt into the photographic portraiture business with a passion, and their reward was great, Philo disliked portraiture as ironically "lacking in art." At least he could not make art of it, but he could make art of a beautiful body.

He'd gone broke filming naked women—prostitutes on the whole, but women to whom he'd paid homage and greenbacks. His collection of feminine beauty was, in discreet gentlemen's circles, legend, and Philo'd begun to turn a profit on some of this trade, as clients—quite specific in their demands—had grown.

"—a redhead fully nude, a redhead partially nude bent over a barrel, a nude blonde doing a pirouette, nude brunette in a tutu doing a pirouette, a nude from the waist up, a nude from the waist down with a cigar in one hand, a brandy snifter in another . . ."

He gulped down another drink. Surprisingly, he did his best work, when either angry or tipsy. Regardless of client and demand, Philo always carefully posed his models in an artistic manner with attention to detail and decorum, using his extensive collection of luxurious sheer nightwear in a pose reminiscent of sculptured goddesses, sometimes . . . never always and never for certain . . . but on some rare occasions, he did reach a pinnacle of stellar art, like the piece that Ransom had purchased for three bottles of rye and two of whiskey for a likeness of Polly Pete. Polly was spectacular, as close to Philo's ideal as he ever hoped to come, but Polly was Ransom's woman now. Now there was a beautifully rendered piece of art if ever there was—Polly . . . real name Merielle Spears. She'd gone rough-hewn and hard-edged early in life, and yet under the right conditions and upbringing, she may well have been a lady of high society. But even Polly was eclipsed by Chesley.

Philo returned to the darkroom to examine cuts taken at the train station. Gruesome. But the impromptu one of Ransom handing that charlatan Tewes the head proved priceless. Philo laughed anew at the incident. How like Ransom to lose it like a rattler without a rattle, so suddenly and without warning.

Keane ogled the developed photographs, hanging each now to dry and talked to himself. "Must make more prints. Limfkins, Haldermott, and Janklow pay well for photos of the dead, and this series of 'head' and 'headless' shots'll go dearly. As for the photo of Alastair in all his raging glory—*what a bull of a man he is*—well that one any newsman in the city'll pay a premium for."

But he pulled up short in his enthusiasm, remembering that Alastair was the only friend he had.

"Damn bloody dilemma, what old man?" he asked himself. "Bloody friendship." The Canadian accent he'd worked years to conceal filtered in whenever he was alone.

The phonograph record in the other room had continued a rhythmic irking as it had come to the end of the music and repeatedly ran in the final groove.

He stumbled toward the phonograph, anxious to put on

another Strauss and dance with himself. As he did so, he gulped down another drink.

Along State Street the same day

The killer lifted what had been Purvis's handkerchief—or more likely his girlfriend's, as it smelled of perfume. The smell quickened his pulse as he relived the bloodletting. Stumpf could do that, imagine it all as if happening over again, even here, standing below an awning to avoid the late-afternoon shower. Nearby carriage horses slick with rain stood silent vigil amid the bustle of Chicago commerce. He stared at his reflection in a Field's window and saw the four mirrored eyes—his and Purvis's. Saw the right hand fingers popping off like so many escaping tadpoles. Then blood spurting from his victim's neck, painted both mirror and basin. Young Cliffton had instinctively covered the leaking dyke of his carotid artery with his left hand, but by now every vein and artery in the neck had been severed. No holding back the flood.

Even here in broad daylight on Chicago's hard-packed streets, the killer felt a sexual release beneath his clothes, so clearly had Sleepeck Stumpf recreated the killing, reimagining the event by simply sniffing repeatedly at the purloined handkerchief—a souvenir of achievement. His first male. It'd been interesting the way the boy's legs had buckled; how like a marionette he'd become, giving way to the gravity of death . . . like a stone sinking. The feel of it . . . his power over life at that moment of death's weight taking the boy down to his knees—it all held such absolute charm for the assassin.

How the victim slid so easily over the marble floor as I dragged him along in his own blood. A wondrous emotion welling up. Something never imagined. How like the slaughter animal, the way his carcass gave itself up to my control.

Firing of the bodies held no excitement for him. It was merely for show . . . something extra for Inspector Ransom.

Cliffton had died of massive blood loss. Traumatic, hemorrhagic shock due to the neck wound. He hadn't felt a thing after that, certainly not the fire. In fact, he was so suddenly dead that he hadn't time to think of anything but the enveloping arms of death. No time for questions of why or of eternity, heaven or hell; nothing normal or natural in the way he went.

Young Cliffton—at the point of attack—in Illinois Central Station, second-floor concourse men's room no longer gave a rat's ass about examining the architecture, or studying under the finest architects, or recalling how sweet his girl's kiss was beneath the Ferris wheel. He had been jabbering and washing his hands—just as his mother, no doubt, had taught him—when the garrote leapt round his neck.

Quick efficient silent death slipped from a coat pocket.

Again he covered his nostrils with the aroma of the stolen handkerchief—Cliffton's possession. It conjured up another aroma, the last odor Cliffton smelled—his own blood. He sucked it in, and his brain filled with the images of holding life in his hands.

Not only had Cliffton been the first male he'd ever killed, but the only victim he hadn't assiduously stalked. Opportunity had simply presented itself there in the train station. His third killing since arriving in Chicago. He'd only killed small animals until now, practicing on them with the garrote. But he'd never been found out or arrested. So he wasn't in their various card files.

Another of his victims had been a tender, lovely, young milk-skinned little family girl, a Polish princess named Milka Kaimeski—Cliffton's female counterpart. He liked killing the innocent and unblemished.

Friends of Milka's had left her in the company of a gentleman the night she lost her life. Descriptions of the phantom gentleman were as varied as those of Christ himself and so rendered useless, but all were in agreement that he carried a cane, wore a top hat, expensive leather shoes, coat and tails, and that he was smitten by the beautiful young Milka. Most accounts put the man at thirty or thirty-five, the age he effected when prowling for prey. In point of fact, he carried no cane. Canes were for crippled old men like that fanciful copper, Inspector Ransom. He didn't himself need a stinking cane to take down that fat screw, as he was young and strong, having just turned twenty. Sure, the old hero of Haymarket had a hundred pounds on him, but the great equalizer lay silent in his pocket, the mini-guillotine.

As for his first Chicago victim, she too, had gone to the fair. But she'd been a tough, gaunt, hard-edged, leather-skinned cigar-smoking working girl named Hannah O'Doul, a red-light district prostitute. She'd gone to the fair on a lark with friends, but having run short of funds, Hannah separated, intending to acquire more funds by picking up a John at the fair. She'd found him. Or rather, he'd been stalking her.

She wanted most of all to ride the Ferris wheel, and while frightened of its enormity, she remained fascinated at the idea of reaching out to touch a bird in flight. He'd dumped her body along the forested lane where police routinely patrolled, mimicking the playful taunts of old Jack the Ripper himself. Hannah's death only made a few sentences, buried on the obit pages.

Killing prostitutes got no play in the press, and little had been made of the Polish girl in the Chicago press either. It disturbed both him and Sleepeck Stumpf that these heinous murders had been given so little attention. They'd both expected outrage. They'd expected a flood of ink devoted to the killer. But surely now they'd see results in the dailies; they must give it front-page mention now, thanks to his having upgraded to the murders of an unborn along with the Polish girl and now a fresh off-the-farm school lad—all in a matter of weeks. The response must now be outrage.

He imagined the morning newspaper accounts in the *Chicago Tribune* and the *Daily Herald*: POLICE STYMIED BY PHANTOM GARROTER, AT A LOSS FOR CLUES.

News of the killings on the street ran ahead of the reporters, outstripping their efforts and accounts. News had also spread wide about the Polish girl's pregnancy. He hadn't known it at the time; not that it'd've mattered a whit to Stumpf. Apparently, no one else had known she was a spoiled dove, left to fend for herself. That is until the autopsiest, a Dr. Christian Fenger, declared it so. This news spurred belated outrage. Authorities had arrested the boy Milka had been seeing—father of the child being their prime suspect.

Afterwards, Sleepeck Stumpf called her another Hannah O'Doul in the making, a street tramp—no better. Getting herself knocked up in such fashion. A sign of the times, end of century coming on—the *end time*! And as for the unborn child, what bloody chance might it've had at a future anyway?

"When the Twentieth Century does arrive, God means to destroy all the Earth and Sky overhead, and to begin all over again anyway," Stumpf assured him just as Mother had on her death bed. "This according to Revelation and Stumpf— spirit of the spirit. So what matters? Naught . . . naught matters." All the same, if the unborn counted as a life, he'd *taken in* four souls, each saved from the horrors of the end time.

Four souls . . . three of which he'd felt enter him as he drained each life. But not knowing of the child, he hadn't felt the child's spirit enter, and this led to a doubt of Stumpf and his purpose in all this killing. Stumpf promised power and knowledge of the universe, familiarity with the Creator beyond that of normal men—and a sense of well-being to override the chaos of this world. All the same . . . whether Stumpf was just talking or not, the taking of lives did have a profound effect. He felt it religiously—a deep, abiding, and contented feeling—especially when twisting the garrote to hear death and to breathe it into his nostrils.

He imagined an orderly or nurse standing beside an autopsy slab at the Cook County morgue, arms extended with the linen winding sheet, the wrapping held wide and open to receive the dead fetus from Milka's womb. Imagined Dr.

Fenger's cold forceps lifting out the four-month-old child from the burned girl's charred abdomen, and handing the lump of flesh over to the tearful nurse. And as the child is being transferred from the doctor's hands to the linen hammock, the child's eyes open and fill with an awe that speaks of life and death entwined.

"When are we not with death?" he asked aloud. Passersby below umbrellas stared dumbly, but a nearby horse whinnied as if agreeing.

CHAPTER 11

Dr. Tewes had rejoined the world, and as quickly as Jane could become James again, she got her other self over to Cook County Hospital. She'd been weary, but with that bull detective on Tewes's tail, she'd suddenly become energized, taking a carriage for Dr. Fenger's. Should Inspector Ransom now seek out and find Dr. Tewes, he'd be in one of the two places spoken of. In fact, sending him to the South Levee district was a stroke of genius. He'd likely want to catch the good doctor there in a questionable or compromising position, she reasoned, so he'd go there first. Unable to find him there, he'd come looking at Cook County Hospital. *Perfectly played,* she reasoned.

On arriving, she—as Tewes—learned that Dr. Fenger was still in the autopsy and inquest phase. Having a number of living patients to see to, Dr. Fenger had only now gotten round to a full autopsy of the Purvis corpse.

She stepped into his operating theater. Rows of male students filled each aisle in the area built for this man. He'd become a legend in Chicago, indeed in Illinois, and in Europe. Fenger belonged to all the medical associations in the city and the state, and some abroad. As a surgeon and a pathologist, as well as a medical school professor, Christian was the first to join the latest specialized medical groups. In fact, he'd spearheaded the Chicago Pathological Society that'd come into being immediately after the Great Chicago Fire of 1871.

For most of Fenger's professional life, he was called a "curator of the deadhouse" but this medical genius was far more. He'd come on at Cook County in 1873 when the famous pioneer bacteriologists Drs. Isaac Danforth and Robert Koch paved the way for Christian Fenger's inspiring and educational medical demonstrations—demonstrations that Jane's father had insisted she see at age fourteen and fifteen. Fenger's fascination in the evolving neurological sciences and neuropsychiatry, an infant science only hinted at in individual case reports, came out of an interest in neurosurgery. It was this area that a young Jane found fascinating—what explained the mind of humankind? To encourage her, Fenger insisted she take home copies of *Northwestern Medical and Surgical Journal*, the *Journal of Nervous and Mental Diseases*, and the *Chicago Medical Journal and Examiner*.

Her father had seen to it that she study German and French so that she could read journals and reports coming out of Europe. But when it came time for her to complete her studies under Dr. Fenger at the Rush Medical College of Chicago, she found all medical reference libraries in the city inadequate to the task. In Chicago, no more than two sets of the great German yearbook, Schmidt's *Jahrbücher* or the Virchow-Hirsch *Jahresbericht* could be found. In fact, these volumes could only be had at the abeyance of the founders of Rush Medical's chief rival for students and publicity—Northwestern—and only by personal favor of the chiefs of medicine there. A long-standing feud between the leaders of the two institutions kept this from becoming a reality for Jane.

This and a general lack of concern for developments in Europe, especially with regard to neurosciences, sent her off to Washington, D.C., to complete her dissertation for her Ph.D., but even in Washington, the competition to gain ac-

cess to such journals proved impossible. This led her abroad
to finish her studies toward her medical degree.

However, she failed to heed her own internal advice
against getting emotionally involved with a silver-tongued
Frenchman with a probing eye and a soft caress. François
Tewes derailed her up-till-now obsessive love affair with
medicine. She found herself alone in France and pregnant.
Still, determined to finish what little remained to accomplish
her medical degree while hiding her pregnancy, she forged
on to Germany, where she gained acceptance as a doctor.

Her having had to leave Chicago due to a lack of books
had outraged Dr. Fenger, who had, since her father's death,
become like a father to her, certainly a benefactor. She believed him secretly in love with her, but their age difference
prevented him ever to broach the subject, and the sad creases
about his eyes had only increased and deepened with each
day. Seeing her off for D.C., he looked stricken there at the
train station. She could only imagine how he felt when she'd
wired him that being unsuccessful in Washington, she'd
booked passage for France and eventually Germany. Using
his recommendation, which she still cherished, she felt certain that a major medical facility in Paris or Berlin would accept and attach her, a woman, to a medical program in which
she could attain her final goal—to practice surgery and
eventually neurosurgery. However, such a position never
materialized.

These memories flooded in alongside the moment here in
the surgical theater. Jane had learned only recently that after
she'd left Dr. Fenger's care and Chicago, that Christian had
spearheaded a campaign to create a ten-thousand-volume
surgical-medical library to be housed in the Newberry Library in the heart of the city. Later, in 1890, the John Crerar
Library was founded by the wealthy railroad magnate, willing two million dollars to launch *his* medical library. By this
time, when all the medical books at the Newberry had multiplied to well beyond thirty thousand, Dr. Fenger swore that

no more promising medical students would have to leave America for Europe.

Christian had loved her, had taken her under his wing, but he'd lost her to the same intolerance she faced daily as a woman in medicine. She'd stopped corresponding on learning of the pregnancy. And when she saw him nowadays, she saw the depth of his hurt smoldering as coals in a hearth. As much as it pained them both, Jane still could not tell him of her return, or her deception, not now . . . perhaps never.

Fenger absolutely hated Dr. J. Phineas Tewes almost as much as he'd loved Jane Francis. And since Gabrielle looked so much like her in her youth, Jane had sent her to the rival school instead, out to Northwestern where Gabrielle had known the murdered boy—Cliffton—only too briefly. It'd been Gabrielle who'd been with Cliffton the night he died, and Gabby had pleaded with her mother that they go to the train station and offer him a place to sleep so that he'd not be in that cold and lonely place by himself without a dime. They'd argued, and then came the middle-of-the-night call from Nathan Kohler saying, "Our opportunity for your experiment has come."

She learned that a garroted body had been discovered at the train station. She'd prayed it would not be Purvis—and she feared that if it were and Gabby learned of it, she would never forgive her mother.

Chief Nathan Kohler was the only one in authority who knew that she and Tewes were one and the same. She'd confessed it to him when he'd detected her utter discomfort in having to follow him into the stationhouse men's room during their discussion over allowing Tewes access to the crime scene and victim. She'd lost composure as Kohler and others used the wall-length trough urinal.

Nathan Kohler had read her well and had cruelly turned her scam on herself, threatening exposure if she failed him. At least Dr. Tewes had gotten into the crime scene even if it was as Nathan's spy. So much drama in the horrid wake of the garroter. She sadly imagined the night of magic the victim and her Gabrielle had had at the world's fair, and how the boy had depleted his last dime on Gabby to please her with ice cream and carved animals.

And now the boy was a specimen for a room full of medical students to see what fire did to flesh and how an autopsy *around* the charred flesh was done.

Dr. Fenger proved his usual able genius, making the autopsy look easy. He somehow remained above it all while his hands worked busily over the body as an artist's hands might paint in oils.

Fenger's appointment to Cook County had indeed marked the coming of age of pathological specialization in Chicago in 1878, and now it was fifteen years later, and he showed no sign of slowing down, not superficially anyway. But Jane— as Tewes—knew better.

Christian Fenger had come to Tewes out of a sense of desperation, having tried Spiritualism atop his Catholic upbringing, had even attempted the new fad of graveyard séances in a failing hope of reaching out to his dead parents, and he'd sunk to the level of looking for solace in the bottle, in various drugs such as opium and heroine, and finally searching for that elusive answer to all he sought in the arms of a series of philosophizing prostitutes. Something to do with having struck his father during an argument, and the elder Fenger dying of a heart attack hours later, and Christian, late in life, had become obsessed with making amends. Fenger had seen the guru of phrenology several times before breaking down and detailing the depth and longevity of his search for this personal Holy Grail, and the salvation of a tortured soul he showed to no one.

As she watched his deft hands now from the gallery, she wondered what kind of surgery he'd seen during the Civil War as a field surgeon. He'd never spoken of it, not to her or her father. He'd come for dinner in those days, the only time she'd ever seen him relaxed, smiling, laughing. Most of the time, he complained of a morgue sorely lacking in rudimentary supplies and elementary equipment—from microscopes and alcohol to specimen jars and burners. He was ever searching for benefactors to improve the circumstances for all medicine in Chicago, and today there was seldom a medical professional who'd not learned from this man who read and spoke some twelve languages so that he could keep abreast of all medical breakthroughs the world over.

The autopsy and teaching session came to an abrupt end. Fenger, exhausted but daring not show it, looked his age when he turned to find Dr. Tewes watching over his shoulder from the gallery.

Their eyes met. *If silence could kill,* she thought. *God . . . how he hates what I've done.* His initial fear had been that someone might discover he'd come to a phrenologist for help, but he'd left Tewes's apothecary and consulting room with a great more dread than when he'd entered, having divulged all to Tewes in a flood of confession sorely needed, a confession he could not make to his priest.

She knew how easily he could strangle her to death, he was that angry and filled with venom for Tewes. At the same time that Tewes had made this proud man a victim, Jane's heart bled for Christian.

"Dr. Tewes . . ." Fenger found his voice. "My office, please."

All of their dealings behind closed doors.

Others no doubt wondered what a man of Fenger's caliber had to do with the likes of a Dr. Tewes.

She followed him down an institutional gray corridor to his office.

Alone with Tewes, fresh from the Purvis autopsy, Dr. Christian Fenger liberally washed his hands even though he'd been wearing rubber gloves during the autopsy. He splashed about at the sink in his office, taking his time, in no hurry to learn what Tewes wanted next. He toweled off and tossed the towel over his left shoulder, went to his desk and yanked a drawer open.

For a moment, she feared he'd pull out a pistol and shoot her. Instead, Fenger pulled out a large bottle of whiskey and two glasses. She couldn't blame him, as Tewes held sway over him even here in his own office; a continuing threat, seated vulturelike, wanting *more* of him. He must think the demands on him would never end.

"Will you join me in a drink, a toast to a successful difficult autopsy that told us nothing we didn't already know?"

She took the drink proffered only because Tewes would. She must constantly do what Tewes would not hesitate doing, such as blackmailing the most respected medical man in Chicago.

"I am only here to thank you, Dr. Fenger."

"Indeed, and why thank me?"

"As a result of your gaining me entry to the crime scene, I was able to meet my . . . my objectives."

"I am supposed to be comforted that you met your goals then, Dr. Tewes?"

"If there'd been any other way, I can assure you—"

"Assure me? Assure me, you? The rest of my life you can say that word, and I would not be assured, sir. You are the worst sort of vermin crawling about this anthill we call a city."

"But you love Chicago and always have."

"What would you know of love?"

"Perhaps more than you realize."

They stared across at one another. "Did you face someone's rope once, Tewes, the way you protect that neck of yours? Where was it they wanted to hang you?"

She reached instinctively to the ascot worn to hide her lack of a protruding Adam's apple. She played the hand he dealt. "Let's just say that in Europe, the locals can get nasty."

"Trust me, Chicagoans can get nasty, even those in high places."

"Shall I take that as a threat, sir?"

"Take it any way you wish." He downed a second whiskey.

"Aside from your womanizing, you've taken to drink, yet you continue to practice as a surgeon, Dr. Fenger. If I had any morals, I should report you to the American Medical Association and let the authorities deal with your—"

"Just what in flaming Gomorrah'd you come here for, Tewes?"

"Your findings, of course, on the boy from the train station."

"You miserable . . ." he muttered then checked himself. "So, it's a private report you're wanting?" His grip on the whiskey glass threatened to shatter it. "You have my early report."

"I need to know one way or another all you can tell me about the killing. I'm doing my part in . . . in creating a kind of explanation as to the killer's motive and method and . . . and what this might say about *him*—for Chief Kohler, to help in apprehending this madman before he should kill again. It's that simple."

Fenger looked stunned at this. "Really . . . a kind of sizing up of the killer. It hadn't occurred to me."

"I believe if we could understand the makeup . . . that is the mental makeup of this madman . . . perhaps through the very clues he's left us . . . then perhaps we might know better where to find him or how to lay a kind of pigeon—"

"—trap for him, indeed. Tewes, have you sufficient knowledge of human nature and the *homo sapien's* mind to . . . to begin to affect such . . . such magic?"

"I welcome your help, Dr. Fenger, sir."

"And this has been your goal . . . all along?"

"It has been, yes, as the boy . . . sadly . . . has had some history with my daughter, you see, being in university together—he studying architecture and she, *ahhh* . . ." Jane hesitated a moment.

"And she is studying?"

"Medicine."

"Really? Doing her work at NU . . ."

"Same as young Purvis in there," she eluded to the morgue. "Enrolled at Northwestern."

"Ahhh, yes . . . fine school, but she'll face harassment at the hands of backward, stupid instructors and ignorant fellow students who've difficulty with the notion of women practicing medicine. I . . . I once thought that way myself until . . . well, that's a long story."

She swallowed hard. "Then you will consult with me on this matter of creating a kind of mental map of the killer?"

"If you can do this, and if it proves a useful investigatory tool, Dr. Tewes, you'll've made medical news, a new use for neuropsychiatry—forensic in nature. The idea of it . . . intriguing."

"It is an idea born, sir, of many years of observing human nature . . . the mind."

"Then all of this phrenological business, what you advertise? All for show?"

"Not entirely, sir. Magnetic healing has its place alongside other methods of relaxing and helping the patient."

"The medical community here has you down as a cold and calculating, money-grubbing fraud, Tewes. Nothing I can add to that will condemn you further."

"I guess I've honed my reputation well."

"Part of your cover to get the ailing and sick and *malaise ridden* into your clinic."

"Most of the population are superstitious, and abhor going under the knife, your new anesthetics notwithstanding, sir. They come to me for relief of their mental stresses so often associated with—"

"—their physical deformities and diseases, yes—like my own. So am I to congratulate you for taking my patients?"

"I only offer succor and advice. Dispense known medicinals from my private apothecary. And while we are so openly speaking, when I was a mere child, I saw you operate, and I heard what you said about mind and body—"

"What're you saying?"

"—having to be treated as one. I never forgot that."

"*You* were in my lectures?"

"Years ago . . . in the company of an adult."

"Your father?"

"Yes."

"I see. I'd've never guessed it. You are full of surprises, Tewes."

Today Christian Fenger had people flocking to see him work; so many in fact, the crowds had to be regulated. He now put bottle and glasses away. "Did I know your father?"

"No, sir. We were passing through on our way to the Northwest territories." *Damn it, why don't I end this ruse and tell this dear man the truth,* she asked herself, and her hand went to the ascot to pull it away, and she leaned over to reveal her cleavage when a gunshot-pounding knock came at the door.

Jane straightened and turned away from Fenger, tightening the ascot all in one fluid motion as Fenger cried out, "Enter! Come on in, Inspector." To Tewes, he added, "I know his signature knock."

Ransom stood in the doorway.

"Well now," said Fenger, "I see we are all here."

"Kohler informs me, Christian, that it was your idea all along to have Tewes here sticking his nose in on my case."

"He's right."

"What're we coming to when a street charlatan can just waltz in on an official police investigation?" Alastair's voice rose with each syllable, "Claiming divining powers by reading bumps on a dead man's head!"

"Now, Alastair—"

"What's bloody next? Tewes here telling us what steps we need take, and who we interrogate, and who we let slide, and who we shadow? Christ! Tell me that!"

"Just calm down, Alastair. Don't get your feathers up."

"And a fine hello to you, too, Inspector," said Tewes.

"Tewes, if some night I see you coming along a dark alleyway—"

"Just so politic is this man, such a wit with words."

"Calm down! Both of you!" shouted Fenger as Tewes and Ransom glared into one another's eyes.

Ransom thought the man's eyes familiar, and he put them together with the sister. They were damn near identical; definitely related.

"Alastair, James here is—"

"James?"

"Yes, James has a useful plan to help discover who your killer is. Now this fiend has struck three times we know of, and any fresh perspective as unique and as thoughtful as James's bears a hearing."

"I don't believe you're buying this nonsense, Christian."

"Dr. Tewes has a *plan* you can only benefit from."

"What's he got on you and the chief, Christian? Is it your lifestyle, your—"

"He's got a plan to psychologically examine the killer's methodology, his steps, his choice of murder weapon, his very thinking, Ransom."

"That's my bloody job!"

"You need bloody science on this one, Alastair. Get used to the idea."

"I don't take orders from you, Dr. Fenger."

"Stubborn, hardheaded Irish Mick-cop!"

"This is not the way I solve cases, *kowtowing* to a so-called psychic."

"I claim only healing powers," corrected Tewes.

"Reading the bumps on a dead man's head—that is not my idea of solid police work, Dr. Tewes. And as for you, Christian, *you* ought to know better."

"Every new science has its critics so why should phrenology be any—"

"I've seen Tewes's clinic, Christian. Like a carnival wagon full of bottles and potions and colored water so far as I can tell."

"You've gotta be the tightest wound man I've ever met," countered Tewes. "Do you have a single friend?"

"I want to talk to you about your bad-mouthing me to the few friends I do have, like Polly Pete."

"*Ahhh,* the young thing you've taken under your wing. You do her no favor. Substituted one—"

"I do not hold her in bondage."

"You won her in a card game! How wonderful is that for her esteem? Do you know she's slipped your firearm into her throat on occasion as you slept nearby, contemplating blowing her head off with you in the room?"

"What? Never. You lying—"

Tewes did not quake or shirk or back off, but rather leaned into the coming blow. "Go ahead, strike me like you did her! I saw her blackened eye! Go on! You don't frighten me, Ransom. And I tell you this in strict confidence, what she's revealed. Whether true or not only Polly or Merielle knows."

Ransom held the shaking fist at bay. Tewes knew both her names; how could he know this unless Merielle had confided it? What if sad Merielle *had* contemplated suicide with his .38 Smith & Wesson five-shot? He imagined her caressing the blue steel, center-fire hammerless automatic while he slept inches from her. *Could it be?*

Fenger met Ransom's eye. They had had long, deep conversations about Polly, and Ransom had not even told him about her dual nature or the depth of Polly's sexual needs and masochism. Fenger had only told him that he understood what a pull love—any brand of love—could have on a man. Christian didn't judge him on this; he only feared for Ransom's own soul in this twisted relationship, that he could lose it as surely as Polly could slit his throat one night— actually or metaphorically. Fenger'd had a similar experience with a lady-of-the-night to whom he'd given his heart.

"To hell with you! To hell with you both!" Ransom dropped his bull stance and rushed out, his face flushed.

"Well . . . that went well," Fenger said sarcastically.

"I've come to expect very little of the man."

"He is an excellent investigator."

"He must be for Chief Kohler to put up with him. I think he is a crude barbarian."

"You have to get to know him to appreciate just how polished he is, given what he's been through."

"You mean the limp, the burn marks at his neck? Haymarket bomb incident?"

"He survived it . . . physically. Mentally, he is still warring with it . . . here." He pointed to his head.

"Does everyone who knows this man excuse his behavior?"

"Tell me exactly what did the man do to you at the train station?"

"It's an involved story."

"Will it harden me against Ransom? I've long wanted a condemnation of the man so's to excuse myself from his company."

Jane described that moment when Inspector Ransom lost his temper, wrenched the boy's head from its loose moorings and shoved it into Tewes's white suit and hands.

Dr. Fenger laughed uproariously. When he settled, he choked out, "That is so like Alastair . . . so like the man. Had you known him better, you might've seen it coming."

CHAPTER 12

Christian Fenger went in search of Alastair Ransom . . . knowing one, that he could not possibly understand his relationship with this lowlife Tewes, and two, knowing that Ransom's respect was something he needed. He had also seen the look of hurt and betrayal on Ransom's face, and he somehow sensed that Alastair had an animosity toward Tewes all out of proportion, and he wanted to get to the bottom of it. What did Alastair know of the strange little man's background, and what, if anything, might Ransom be willing to do for Christian to end this sordid fellow's stay in Chicago?

He knew Alastair like a brother, a younger brother to be sure, but a brother; Ransom was one of the few genuine and sincere people Christian knew. With Alastair you knew where you stood. A man of action, he let you know what he thought by what he did. In his every action resided his inner self, and he made no excuses for living as he did, whereas Dr. Christian Fenger lived in a world of duplicity at every turn.

Being a physician, Christian could seldom say or do anything without fear of repercussions, so staid and stodgy was the Chicago medical community. Although he got away with what other medical professionals in the city called "murder," there was no way around the politics that'd embedded itself in every aspect of Cook County Hospital and every medical school in the city. Graft and greed proved rampant even here, in the field of healing, and when he'd told his story to Ransom's British journalist friend—Stead—about how things were in Chicago with regard to the growing indigent problem and its effect on medicine in the city, the reporter listened transfixed at the callous disregard for human life and limb shown the homeless by city fathers and merchants. Stead had promised an exposé, which hadn't come. No doubt finding a gutsy enough publisher for the work had proven impossible.

Conditions the Spanish would call *que horrible* had continued to plague the city for as long as Christian had lived here. These thoughts filled Fenger's mind even as he pushed through Hinky Dink's tavern door where he felt relatively certain he'd find Alastair sipping red ale.

He spied him in his favorite corner, the dark one at the back. Hinky waved to Christian and shouted, "Good to see you, Doctor. Your usual?"

"Yes, thank you." He headed straight for Ransom, and as he neared, he saw the familiar scowl.

"What was that little fruitcake doing in your office, Christian?"

"We were engaged in private conversation till you trampled over the man."

"Private is it? And you're hoping to keep it private? What's the creep got on you, Christian? I'll wring his scrawny neck, and if it snaps like the twig I think it is, then he'll bother you no more."

"And how much is your fee?"

"Fee? For doing that skunk? You've no idea how he's turned Mere against me."

Hinky hefted a huge beer glass before Dr. Fenger. "Your usual, Doctor, and how're we tonight? You know me ailing *murther*-in-law's still abed? She ain't no help on her back, and me wife's 'coming scruffy-looking 'n' mean-tempered as a 'ell."

"I'd call Dr. Hale on Adams, Hinky," replied Fenger. "He's a good GP. I'm a surgeon."

It was a dance he and Hinky did each time Fenger entered this swamp, and for this reason, he'd stopped coming. He imagined Ransom had specifically chosen this place, believing that Christian wouldn't follow him in.

"Well . . . all the same, for a medical man such as yourself, the draft is on the house, sir." Hinky moved off, waving a hand at the bill Dr. Fenger held out.

"Please, take payment for the beer, my good man."

Hinky ignored this, returning to his work behind the bar.

"So what *would* you do to this miscreant, Ransom, *if* I asked you to make him go away . . . maybe leave the city?"

"It's a big lake out there."

"I see."

"No, you don't see. I'd do nothing of the kind without sound reason, and you've give' me none. Why didn't you tell me that this was going on?"

"It's a recent problem. I've wrestled with it. I've never had such evil thoughts as this man's created in me . . ."

"Ahhh . . . thoughts of the darkest order are due every man."

"Not me . . . never before now."

"So you've fantasized the man's death?"

"Appears we both have."

"Some would call this a conspiracy to commit murder, Doctor."

"Goddamn you, Alastair, I know that, and it turns my stomach what my mind is juggling."

"The little man maddens people."

"And how has he got your ire up with Merielle?"

"Has to do with Polly, actually."

"Polly, Merielle . . . I can't keep her straight. But tell me more."

"She fell for his flier . . . went to see him. Sat under his hands, and soon she's telling her life's story, and he tells her she needs to save herself—"

"From you, of course."

"He advised her to leave me!"

"Hey, friend, I've advised the two of you do exactly that for how long?"

"That's different. You . . . you're a friend."

They drank more.

"It's worse than his having insinuated himself on my investigation."

They ordered more drink.

"What about you, Christian? What does this . . . this *information pimp* have on you?"

"He had some creep with a camera get photos of me in . . . well, let us say that if these photos come to light, my enemies would have a field day, and my time at the university and Cook County'll come to an abrupt end." Christian believed Ransom would more easily believe this lie than he would the truth—that the mere accusation that he'd compromised the safety of his patients by performing surgery while under the influence was enough to end his career.

"Blackmailing little weasel." Ransom downed the remainder of his ale. "Certainly enough reason to plot a man's demise."

"You could, I suppose, arrest me for all I've said."

"Yes, I could, but I won't." Stepping up his drinks, Ransom signaled Hinky for another red Irish.

"You're a good friend, Alastair."

"I need you precisely where you are, close to the Haymarket records."

"Damn it, Alastair, are you now blackmailing me for those damnable records?"

"Hey, a favor for a favor."

"The Chicago way, yes."

"Hardly blackmail."

"*Ahhh* . . . a euphemism for it? How deep or shallow runs our friendship, Alastair, and how many men can you call your equal in this city? Do you wish to die a man apart as you've lived since Haymarket?"

Ransom tapped the wall with his cane. "I still have physical problems from that day, and I'll likely have problems with the official cover-up till the day I die."

"Your friends're dead. You can't bring 'em back, Alastair, and pursuing Haymarket can only end in your becoming an even bigger target than you already are. There are vested interests in keeping Haymarket in its grave."

"Like it never happened."

"Like it never happened."

They sat in gloomy silence.

"Besides, your hands're a bit full with this mad garroter."

"Damn press is calling the bastard the Phantom of the Fair."

"Do you have any idea how many people are attracted to the fair on the off chance of seeing some shred of this maniac's handiwork? And then you, juggling that boy's head at the train station? My God, man. You must do something about your public persona and that bloody temper."

"Not to worry about me, Doc."

"Who then worries for you, Ransom? Polly Pete?"

"Leave Polly outta this."

Fenger threw hands up in defeat. "All right, all right . . ."

A silence engulfed them, and they listened to some traveling minstrel switching from a whaling tune to a ballad of a lover who'd lost all sense of the world, lost in the arms of a woman.

"Are you still getting the headaches?"

"Stop with it, Doc."

"Then the answer is yes. You try the elixir I concocted for you? You using the brace on your neck each night?"

"Don't always sleep at home, and I don't carry the damn brace with me, Christian."

"Of course . . . I see . . ." Fenger laughed and finished his beer. "Maybe you should go to Tewes for a phrenological examination. Find out all you can about him. I've checked through my contacts in Washington, New York, even Europe, and no one knows anything about him; it's as if he simply hung his shingle out one day."

"Should I fall off my chair with the revelation he's a fraud?" Ransom's hearty laugh interfered with the balladeer's music. Several grunts and catcalls escaped from patrons listening intently and crying in their foam.

Christian whispered, "*Hold* on the matter of Tewes."

"What? I thought—"

"If we can learn more, then perhaps we can trump him with his own bloody past. That way, we don't leave this world as assassins."

"At least you don't."

"I only believe half your boast and none of your bark, Alastair."

"I could tell you stories, Doctor."

Fenger matched Ransom's stare, and in the man's eye, Christian indeed saw a pair of burning coals from the hearth of Hades when a bent shadow crept across their table. A fast-moving, athletic, well-dressed man in black cape, carrying a gentleman's cane, obviously just for show, and the cane had a glistening, metallic head—a wolf's head like Ransom's own but not scrimshaw. Ransom instinctively felt as if evil had passed by, and he followed the shadowy figure, leaning to glance at what sort of footwear he had. High boots. Ransom could only make out a pair of shining black heels as the door closed on the man. His mind flooded with what the homeless witness had described of the killer's clothing and boots; this drove him to his feet, wanting to tail the man . . . *senseless, futile act*. For how many men in Chicago carried a cane and wore boots and cape? But even as he started up, he realized a new shadow split the table. Dr. Tewes now stood before them.

"So this is where the three of us talk?" Tewes challenged.

"How did you know we were here?"

"I tailed Dr. Fenger."

"You've a helluva nerve, Tewes, and you disgust me," began Ransom. "D-I-G-U-S—"

"I know how to spell it, Inspector."

"What more do you want from me, Tewes?" asked Christian, his forehead creased in pain, eyes drooping. "What more could you possibly need tonight?"

"I appreciate all your help, Doctor, but I also'd hoped that you and I, and perhaps Ransom here, could put our differences aside for the good of this case."

"You ask too much."

"You think you are such a cunning bastard, Tewes," added Alastair, sitting again.

"I know that you two'd as soon plot my death, gentlemen . . . than share a drink, and yet . . ." Jane for a moment came to the forefront, a tear threatening to expose her. She worked to regain her composure.

"Take a seat, by all means, as I'll be going," said Alastair. "Seems I've got some patchwork to do with my woman, thanks to your muckraking in my personal affairs."

"Polly's my patient now, one with serious mental problems, which I've discussed with no one but you, Inspector, as I suspect your misguided feelings for her are genuine if not—"

"What the deuce would you know of what goes on between a man and a woman!" The place silenced at this.

Tewes spoke through grinding teeth. "Look, Inspector, just because you're nice to her . . . well, this doesn't mean you or this city's *good* for her."

"She's been wanting me to take her to the fair, to ride that damned wheel in the sky and—"

"By all means, indulge her, but in the end, her best hope is a young man her own age who'll take her far away from here."

"Who gives you the authority to make her decisions?"

"I cannot make decisions for her; I can only advise, and I advise you to come back to my office some day by appointment and allow me to help you with those headaches and what is troubling your mind, Inspector."

Ransom shot to his feet, towering over Tewes, wondering how long he'd been in the tavern and eavesdropping. "God, but you have balls for such a puny fellow."

"It's not balls, sir . . . but the wisdom of knowing what

makes a man strong and what makes a woman brave. Polly knows now what is at the root of her troubled mind—her father . . . a man about your age when he raped her. She ever tell you that, sir?"

Ransom, like an elephant shot through the eyes, dropped back into his seat.

"That she is the victim of incest by not a stranger, not a stepfather, but by her own blood father? You, sir, are a sick stand-in for a father she is still trying to please, though he's in the grave . . . to make sense of and to—"

"Enough! Shut your mouth. Polly loves me, and I'll be the one takes her outta the cesspool she's made of her life! Not some fool who tells people's fortunes by the knots on their flaming heads."

"—and to understand herself, independent of you and your nightmares." Tewes settled back as if resting his case.

Ransom gritted his teeth, shot Fenger a glaring look, exchanged a dark thought with Christian, then rushed from Hinky's, pushing out the door so hard it creaked on its hinges, threatening to come off.

Hinky shouted at the big cop, "Hey! Keep such brutishness outta my place, copper!"

"I could help that man to calm down to a much needed catlike mental state of serenity if he'd let me." She once again sat before Fenger as James Tewes. She so wanted to reveal herself to him at this point, to end the dark ties that bound them in this pretense, and the awful way that things had developed. She feared his reaction, and yet, she wanted his warmth, his renowned caring, his respect, but how?

"I thought I'd seen the last of you tonight. What else've you come to milk me of?"

"I would like to tell you something important . . . and it is difficult to broach, Dr. Fenger."

"What is it? You want my blessings? Want to address me as *Christian*? Want chumminess from me?" Fenger's scowl could not be masked.

"Damn . . . this is so hard. You only led me to believe you

thought my idea of creating a mental picture of the killer a good one. I took you at your word when—"

"I am a master of facetiousness. Even Ransom knows this. But now what on earth are you driving at, man?"

She pulled away her neckerchief, revealing her throat. She needn't say a word. Her fingers trailed a faint red glow that died along her milky white neck. No protrusion of Adam's apple, and a makeup line gave Tewes's face and neck a darker hue. "You're not a man! My God, woman, who are you and why? Why this elaborate ruse?"

"It is me, Christian, Dr. Jane Francis."

He squinted and blinked all at once.

"You once loved me, respected my father . . . and you . . . and . . ."

". . . and you left me."

"Not you. I left Washington for Europe to further my studies, to gain access to—"

"Your future."

"—a true medical library, recall?"

"Yes but you stopped writing, and all these years I had no idea. I thought some awful fate'd befallen, that you were . . . dead. Now look at you."

"I can explain."

"What have you done to yourself?"

CHAPTER 13

They had brought their voices down and spoke under the minstrel's songs, and the muffled conversations of Hinky Dink's.

"I've a daughter in medical school. Can't do that on what a woman makes—not in any womanly profession or in my *chosen* profession."

"But you're a gifted physician with surgical skills touting phrenology and nonsense and selling snake oils! And doing it as a man. A waste on more levels than I can say."

Hinky interrupted, asking if the young Dr. Tewes would care to partake of a drink. She ordered Amaretto liquor.

"My God . . ." Christian moaned, "Ransom—"

"What of 'im?"

"—has the wrong idea about . . . and—"

"No one else is to know, Dr. Fenger. No one! You must promise. You must reveal my secret to no one, and especially not to Alastair Ransom."

"But the blackmail and the—"

"I'd never've gone through with it, sir, never."

"But Tewes may've?"

"A means to an end."

"To gain access to Alastair's case?"

Jane nodded. "I can explain why."

"You don't understand. As angry as I am at Tewes, you must know—"

"I can sense Ransom wants to hurt me . . . ahhh, Dr. Tewes, that is."

"Hurt you? He wants to drown you in Lake Michigan, and I just handed him all the justification."

"That's his knee-jerk reaction? Kill Tewes?"

"He could be lurking in the shadows of the alleyway just outside right now."

"Then the two of you . . . you really were plotting—"

"Dr. Tewes's demise, yes."

"My God . . . perhaps I play my part too well."

"I'd say . . . yes."

"How can we stop him without telling him the truth?"

"There mayn't be any stopping him short of his discovering you wear knickers!"

"Shhh! Please." She looked around but no one heard above the lament being sung of unrequited love. "But Ransom's a law enforcement official, a police officer, an inspector in the—"

"All the more reason to fear him."

She gulped and Hinky handed her the Amaretto at the same instant. She threw it back and swallowed. "I needed that."

"We have to tell him something."

"No!"

"I . . . we left it with his calling on you at your office . . . asking for a miracle cure for those recurring headaches he's suffered since the bomb."

They sat in silence. The balladeer song changed to a mother's child lost to war. Finally, Jane said, "All right . . . when he comes to see me . . . do you think him foolish enough to . . . in my own home . . . that he'd—"

"No, actually, I think he'll gather information on you— Dr. Tewes—for now."

"Clumsy . . . comes 'round ostensibly for an examination? For the headaches?"

"A phrenological exam, during which he'll interrogate you—Tewes that is. We agreed at the last only to get some dirt to counteract Tewes, but . . ."

"But what?"

"For one, he's bloody unpredictable, and I didn't like that look in his eyes when—"

"Far from pleasant, agreed. Funny . . . as children, I admired him so, but he's so changed . . . and I rather doubt he has any memory of—"

"As children?"

"I have the dubious honor of having gone to the same school when I was four, before Father moved us to the far north side."

"Can't imagine Ransom ever having been a child."

"But in so many ways . . . he still is."

"Aren't we all?"

"This new science of the mind and neurosurgery fascinates the child in me, I suppose."

"I insist on walking you home, Dr. Tewes. In the event you should encounter any unpleasantness."

"A big unpleasantness named Ransom, you mean? That won't be necessary, Doctor."

Christian released a twenty-year-old sigh. "My God, so it's now Dr. Jane Francis. Had you not gone off—"

"Believe me, sir. I learned more from watching you work than anything in all my studies, both here and abroad."

"And now you're back. Declare yourself, Jane, and I'll do all in my power to get you an appointment at Cook County."

"As what? I would be put to work doing nursing and scut work, and we both know that, dear, sweet Christian."

He stared into her knowing eyes.

"Don't look that way at me. You know it's true. You, sir . . . you live in a world of your own making, but the rest of us . . . we live in *this* world."

"In the end, we all of us create our own reality. You're foolish to've created yours as Tewes!"

"You say that . . . that it is up to me, yet you know why I had to leave Chicago, and why I had to return as Tewes."

"A woman asking for a look at a private collection of medical books to fulfill her dissertation so she might graduate on to medical school, yes."

"And I was turned down."

"You ought to've fought them!"

"With what?"

"With the strength your father instilled in you!"

"You sound like my Gabrielle."

"Your girl . . . now in medical school?"

"Yes, and she is such a dreamer."

"Dreamers are needed in this life."

"Perhaps . . . but my dreams were done in by reality."

"But reality is what *you* create of it, my dear."

"You and Gabby will love one another."

"You . . . daughter."

"Sadly, the young man murdered at the train station was seeing Gabrielle, and God forgive me, I'd forbidden their seeing one another, and now this."

"Poor child."

"She can't be distracted from her studies—not by anyone or anything, not if she's to succeed."

"Succeed like her mother or like Dr. Tewes?"

She bridled at this. "We've had disagreements . . . over not allowing anything to distract her from her goals."

"Her goals?"

"Yes, her goals."

"Well, Jane . . . I am an outsider here, but—"

"The young man who was killed, he'd walked her home from the fair. It was to be the last time she'd see him! That's what I told her . . . and prophetically and sadly . . ."

"And how is she taking it?"

"Too calmly . . . too well. Going about . . . my God, as if nothing of the sort could possibly've happened."

"A holding pattern; in order to deal with it. Grief must

manifest itself in some form or other. Keep her close; keep a watch on your daughter, Jane."

"I have."

"To lose someone close is difficult enough, but to lose someone to this madman afoot in Chicago?" Dr. Fenger looked profoundly sad for Gabrielle.

"Yes, so here again is reality. Like a hurdle everywhere."

"Still . . . inside here," he said, pointing to his head, "you can and will one day turn a corner, and when you do, you'll be living your dream, as Dr. Jane Francis."

"Discouraged, disillusioned, hurt. How do I ever dream again?"

"You find a way."

"Hell, Christian, you've heard the views held by Dr. McKinnette and the great Dr. Banefield Jones and Dr. Stille. That women haven't the disposition or the stomach for medicine, and especially surgery."

"They harp the belief of the general population."

"Fools all!"

"Unfortunately, yes, but Jane, that was years ago, my dear."

"Not for me, sir. For any woman in medicine, that is today."

They sat silent, each thinking of the vile words of McKinnette, Jones, and Dr. Alfred Stille, that day at the symposium; words leveled at the few women in the room, including Emily Blackwell, sister to Dr. Elizabeth Blackwell.

"Rush Medical College refused Emily Blackwell permission to allow her to finish her medical studies. Rush—your medical school—in 1852, and why? The Illinois State Medical Society censured the school for admitting a woman!"

"That was 1852. This is 1893, Jane."

"And the problem of training women in medicine continues unabated. My Gabrielle faces it every day at Northwestern, the same narrow-minded pig-swallop that constitutes the average doctor's attitude toward us, that we are as mentally unfit as we are physically unfit for—"

"You needn't recount—"

"—for even a business profession."

"I know. I know all this."

"But you left the room when Dr. Stille finished his remarks during his presidential address to the American Medical Association."

"You've read the minutes, and I suppose you're right to condemn me, but I was only eighteen. Have you carried Stille's words with you since?"

"I have, yes. Shall I recite?"

"Please don't."

She did. " 'All experience teaches that woman is characterized by a striking uncertainty of rational judgment, capriciousness of sentiment, fickleness of purpose, and indecision of action—which makes her totally unfit for professional pursuits.' "

Fenger knew the truth of it. What women in medicine faced. Prejudice, backward beliefs, amazingly parochial attitudes. Not only were women, in the eyes of most medical professionals, mentally unsuited for professional study, but in the case of medicine, there were additional "reasons" to bar them. These had to do with modesty and morality that caused awkwardness during physiological discussions and in dissections—both of which felt like venues no *lady* ought attend. *Quite unladylike* is how Dr. Byford had phrased it. "But Jane, more recently . . . was it sixty-nine? Bill Byford at Chicago Medical solicited and accepted young women to—"

"Yes and again the male students petitioned at close of term that women be removed!"

"Making idiotic charges against Byford and other faculty as I recall."

"Claimed they'd prudishly omitted a number of observations and clinical techniques due to the presence of women." Jane paused. "Damn, some of the leading physicians of Chicago are *still* the biggest blowhards and the loudest opponents of women in medical education."

"I remember when Nathan Smith Davis advocated separate female colleges for medicine, and for halting women from gaining a foothold in the American Medical Association," said Fenger. He laughed.

"What?"

"Sarah Hackett Stevenson took him and the status quo on."

"Now there was a hell of a woman."

"Your greatest advocate, Jane."

"Aside from you, but true enough, she kept me on my game."

"The first seat in the AMA ever occupied by a woman. Courageous lady."

"A student of Darwin and Huxley at the famous South Kensington Science School in London."

With gnashing teeth, he shook his head. "Has she returned to Europe?"

"Not quite. She's removed to Springfield. Point is for all the eyes women've opened, the problems persist."

"I'm not blind, but this is a societal problem, dear, and it persists in all areas of commerce and business—not just medicine." Fenger lifted his drink for a sip.

She drank a second Amaretto.

He shook his head, gathering his thoughts. "I recall once we got a cadaver in, and the man, kind enough to leave his body for scientific study, had one stipulation else his body goes to the earth."

"Let me guess. Rush Medical must preserve the body from any and all indignities. Meaning no female medical student could work over him."

"Even in death, a man remains modest." He held up a finger. "Look, Jane, Sarah Stevenson graduated from the Woman's Hospital Medical College, an outgrowth of a hospital established in 1865 by—"

"Mary H. Thompson, a hospital for indigent women and children—"

"—which only last year became a department of—"

"I know, Gabby is studying at the Thompson School at Northwestern University now, but as I said, she's having similar problems as any woman in medicine has for the past sixty years! Mary Thompson herself finished for her degree during that one-year experiment for the Chicago Medical College, the same year three other women were stranded in their studies. Now it's 1893 and soon it'll be 1900, Christian, and you want me to believe things have improved?"

"By degrees, yes."

"Degrees?"

"Women are now admitted into competition for internships at Cook County Hospital and Asylum."

"And how many of those internships've gone to women at your precious medical facility?"

"The numbers improve each year, I assure you. Hopefully, by the turn of the century coeducation in medicine will be an accepted reality."

"Do you know what happened to my reality, sir, when I was no longer at ease at Rush, made to feel that way by the male students?"

"You disappeared."

"Not entirely, no. I first wound up at the Hahnemann Medical College."

"No."

"Yes."

"That place occupying several rooms over a drugstore? On South Clark?"

"The one that prospered last during the Civil War, yes."

He bit back a show of anger.

"Not long there, I moved on to the Bennett College of Eclectic Medicine and Surgery, where the systematic teaching of pathology and bacteriology has only now begun. I got some smattering of laboratory work in chemistry, a bland education in surgery, histology and nothing of physiology."

"Little wonder you ran to Europe, but you might've come to me first. Why didn't you?"

"Pride perhaps . . . anger . . . the anger of youth." She failed to say she feared he'd fallen in love with her.

"Ahhh . . . fire of stubborn youth," he replied.

"I've no regrets of going abroad. I returned with a medical degree and my Gabrielle."

"A good thing, I'm sure."

"Look, Doctor, you ask that I deal with reality now. *Deal with it* was your most oft repeated admonition to all your med students." She indicated her disguise. "I dress in drag to fit the reality that makes it a man's world."

"It's ethically wrong, Jane."

"And you? How do you deal with reality? You torture yourself for countless years?"

A brief stunned look as if struck by a sudden pain and Fenger calmly replied, "Me . . . me and reality . . . how do I deal with it?"

"Your hands're in it each day."

"While I find beauty in the human body, I also find suffering. Yes, I suppose I do recreate this thing we call reality in my work every day . . ."

"Yes, in order to do what you do."

". . . in order to remain standing and doing surgery for eighteen, twenty, thirty hours at a stretch at times."

"Like when Haymarket happened, the Great Fire?"

"Haymarket, yes, and as a much younger man, the fire. Actually the Great Fire benefited my reputation. Soon after, I was teaching at Rush and practicing at Cook County at age thirty-seven."

"You patched up Ransom when he was hurt in the bombing at Haymarket, didn't you?"

"Everyone was called to help."

"And you saved Alastair Ransom's life."

"Any doctor would've done what I—"

"No, sir. I looked at the hospital record."

"Really now?"

"Another doctor had written him off, and even then, you understood how ninety percent of wound infection occurred, so you took sanitary steps to see to it that he did not lose his leg or his life for that matter. You were so far advanced over the other men practicing medicine then."

"He proved a strong patient."

She half smiled at the characterization. "Being bull-headed may've saved him in some situations, but you saved him that day. It's what you do, Dr. Fenger, what sets you apart."

"Please . . . being set apart is a lonely proposition."

"Regardless, you . . . you save lives amid all this circus— this passing parade of angels and demons in this . . . this—"

"This floating opera we call Chicago?"

"Precisely." Jane stood and bid him good night, taking her leave.

CHAPTER 14

Later the same night

Jane gasped, startled to find Alastair Ransom on Dr. Tewes's doorstep, wearily smoking. In a cornice window, she saw Gabby staring from behind curtains, that damnable pistol—an ancient old breach-loading Sharp's longer than Gabby's forearm—poised. Jane had removed the firing cap, rendering the thing useless whether loaded or not. Apparently, Gabby found Alastair not only an exotic fellow, but at least as frightening as if a bear had wandered up onto the porch.

She wondered momentarily at the strangeness of life in its permutation through the aging process; how such a handsome, bright-eyed, intelligent, soft-spoken, pleasant, sweethearted, concerned, giving creature as Alastair'd been as a child could be so different now. How had he become such a clod, a sot, a womanizer, and a fool?

"What are you doing here, Inspector?" she asked as Tewes. "Surely, you've not come to beat me senseless or to shoot me?" She said it loudly enough for neighbors to hear, but primarily, she wanted Gabrielle to calm down.

"Here to offer my apologies."

"Really? This comes as a surprise," she lied.

"I know you mean well."

"And what has brought you round to this startling conclusion?"

"I'm trying to apologize for what occurred at the train station."

"You're here about Polly . . . Merielle."

He glared. "Yes, was 'round earlier on that errand. Look, you had no right browbeating my Merielle and—"

"Browbeating?"

"—and running me down, using dubious methods to demoralize her and—"

"Dubious? Demoralize?"

"—to set her against the only man who's been good for her, and who has her best interest at heart. If you'd bothered learning the nature of our relationship, you'd know—despite my shortcomings—I bring a certain stabilizing force into her life, a certain, *ahhh* . . ."

"Normalcy?"

Tension palpitated between them.

"Yes, damn you, normalcy."

"I doubt, sir, you've any acquaintance with normality."

"And you do, I suppose, you the magician of Belmont Street, espousing magnetism and this . . . this bogus science of phrenology, no better than reading the stars or tea leaves."

"If the tea leaves fit."

"Look, I did not come here to argue—"

"But that is all you've done!"

"I want you to advise Merielle of my strengths, the list of reasons why she should remain mine."

"You men—" she stopped herself. "Fellows like you, I mean—police and others in authority . . . you really do believe you can *own* someone, don't you? Body and soul."

Their voices had risen and there came a tapping on the windowpane. Both men stared at Gabrielle. Finally, Ransom asked, "She any good with that hog leg?"

"She's quite good with it," Jane again lied.

"I suppose you taught her at an early age to point guns?"

"In this environment, is that so wrong? Seems the norm, in fact. Hair Trigger Block is a short stroll."

"Then you value your daughter well."

"That I do . . . yes."

"Perhaps then we should continue elsewhere, say Muldoon's end of the block?"

Jane feared going off with this man anywhere, but as Tewes, she must show no flinching—just as she'd not failed the test of manliness at the railway station. "Give me a moment to settle Gabby then," she calmly replied.

"Agreed."

"Then we'll reconnoiter how to civilly work together."

"Work together?"

"On how best to help Polly."

"Ahhh . . . yes."

"And on how best to pursue a killer?"

"Hold on. My being here's in no way a conciliatory gesture in that direction."

"Fair enough. Only a moment then." Tewes disappeared into the house. Alastair could hear the daughter giving Tewes hell about going off into the night with Inspector Ransom. The young thing was wise. Tewes must've told her what had transpired at the train station. Ransom relit his pipe beneath the gaslight and paced the sidewalk, his cop's eye reading the night street. A ragged little Italian family searched through discarded items in an alleyway. Two desperate-looking men stepped from a darkened doorway, perhaps engaged in a shady deal. Along the packed Clark Street, a hansom cab rolled by, pulled by a weary horse favoring its right front hoof. "Likely your mare's thrown a shoe!" he called after the driver, but the warning went unheeded.

Merielle let him in again. He seemed harmless, and he'd been so complimentary when she really needed complimenting, and he'd apologized for striking her, after all. So she let him back inside, or perhaps she did so, just so she'd have something to tell Dr. Tewes. She'd tell Tewes, "Yes, I opened the door *because* he struck me." She knew that Ransom wouldn't return tonight. How devilish to conduct an affair behind Alastair's back. How devilish indeed to have two men in one night handle her as roughly as Polly preferred.

The gentleman calling himself Mr. Stumpf had asked if she'd seen any of the fair. He spoke of the Ferris wheel, how glorious the lake and the land and the town looked from the sky. "Like a blanket of stars fallen to earth," he'd said, adding, "what with the lights below instead of above!"

How marvelous it'd sounded, and so she'd gone out with the man in cape and top hat to feel for once like a lady, to allow Merielle an opportunity to play herself. Merielle did not disappoint either Polly or the gentleman. She held on his arm like a proper lady, just like her *mum* had done for her *dah*.

So they had gone out and taken a carriage ride, something Alastair had never done for her. The gentleman spoke of the great art treasures from around the world housed in the various pavilions of the fair. He spoke of sculpture and artifacts from Asia and beyond. He spoke of it as another world she must see before she died.

"Silly," she twittered, "I won't be doing that for some time."

"Of course not," he'd replied.

Twice more he apologized about the moment of anger in which he'd blackened her eye. He'd brought a cosmetic just for her to cover it.

To further make up, he'd paid her admission to the fair. He'd showed her a magnificent night of extraordinary sights, sounds, odors, tastes, and touch. She'd had a popcorn-peanuts-molasses confection called Cracker Jack, and she'd seen how they made saltwater taffy, and she'd seen farm animals and amazing new inventions, all amid a Grecian world of fake white marble.

Polly'd felt stirrings that she'd never felt with any man. Here was a man who'd not just talked about showing her the world but showed her the world! Sure, he was younger than she, and sure his manhood was small—the reason he'd hit her when she'd laughed—but here was a fellow who didn't just talk of improving her lot, of keeping her from boredom, but a man who actually followed through on promises, unlike the too busy Ransom.

This little man was Alistair's opposite in so many ways, except for his roaming hands. Even on the Ferris wheel, so high above the fair, she remained the focus of his attention. He'd placed his fist up her skirt and dug his fingers into her, making her laugh. He claimed never to've touched a woman there before. Claimed himself a virgin.

She'd assured him, "I'll be gentle."

She said so again now that they'd returned from the fair, as she teasingly dropped her dress about her feet.

While she tied hair from her eyes, he seductively sidled up, one thing on his mind, Polly'd surmised and giggled. She leaned back into him, as Stumpf slid something thin and fragile about her throat, a fine wire-width bauble, she thought, when she gasped at her mirrored image on seeing the blood necklace.

Stumpf took his time cutting into her soft flesh. An eighth of an inch at a time, whispering, "In truth, dear Polly, this bow tie's a gift from Alastair."

She sputtered, her words choked by blood.

"His vile blessings on it, Polly girl."

She coughed up the sumptuous meal he'd bought her at the exquisite Palmer House downtown. It came up with blood as she succumbed to death. Blood and bile her last earthly memories. She neither felt nor smelled the kerosene doused over her, nor the fire that lit up her body.

Her dress still about her ankles had soaked up the kerosene too, and it quickly caught flame, and the fire took on a wild life of its own, jumping to the curtains as if alive. A killing acrid smoke filled Ransom's love nest.

In a panic, the garroter swept from the place, rushing just ahead of the fingers of fire chasing him out the door of this tinderbox. A final glance back as he slammed the door was like looking into the fiery maw of Hades. In minutes, the entire second story was feeding flames; a handful of minutes more, and the growing fire began consuming the ground floor from above.

From a safe distance outside, where Clark met Halsted, the killer stood watching the flames devour Ransom's home away from home. A giddy laugh wanted escape, but now he realized his vulnerability as an oddly curious odor of burnt hair rose to his nostrils. He lifted the cuffs of his overcoat to find hair on his arms curled into miniature bits of brittle bush—entirely singed.

They strolled the gas-lit street toward Muldoon's.

"I'll admit, I didn't know that Polly was a Merielle until late in our sessions," began Tewes, who'd pulled forth his own pipe and had accepted a light from Ransom. "Nor . . . nor that it was you she was—had an arrangement with. Odd coincidence that."

"I'm not a big one for coincidence, Tewes."

"Does it so kill you to call me Doctor?"

Ransom only grunted.

Tewes struggled to keep pace with his gait. "Things in Polly's case . . . they just came to a head recently, and only recently did you come up, sir."

"What do you mean things came to a head?"

"What *doctors* who deal with emotional and psychological matters call an *epiphany*, Inspector."

"An epiphany?"

"The unexamined life is not worth living, Inspector."

"Is that an epiphany?"

"Epiphany comes of self-awareness, a realization of one's own needs or weaknesses, or source of power, or . . . well, you get the idea—Greeks knew of it."

"I see."

"Good."

"I'm sure that you're . . . beneath it all, Tewes, a relatively . . . *ahhh* . . . *ahhh*, normal fellow yourself."

"As my title is so hard to get over your tongue, Inspector, it's James. Or if you prefer Phineas, Inspector ahhh . . . Alastair . . . may I call you Alastair?"

"I suppose it can do no harm."

"God, man, you can be infuriating. May I or mayn't I? Or shall we carry on with Inspector and your mix of snipe-and-grumble-and-mutter for doctor?"

"You're likely the most difficult man to accept an apology that I've ever met, *James*."

"Ahhh . . . so your answer comes out, *Alastair*."

They continued in silence. The heartthrob of the city buzzed, all the drays, the cabs, the clopping of horse shoes against earth here, cobblestone there, the more distant sounds of the train yards, the stockyards, ships in the great harbor that was the lakeshore, down to the sound of the gas lamps that lit their way.

"There's talk of getting electric lampposts, or so I hear," said Tewes, looking at a lamp that sputtered on and off. "To replace these old things."

"We're rushing into a new century with all our fine inventions, aren't we?" he calmly replied.

"So much progress . . . and so much loss."

"Ahhh . . . something we agree on."

"I suspect you a bit old-fashioned, Alastair."

"Aye . . . I'll admit to a touch of it."

They arrived at Muldoon's door, and Ransom held it wide. His newfound manners made her suspicious. "Your talk with Dr. Fenger has improved our relations, I'd say."

"Some, yes."

"Some . . ." She wondered what *some* meant. Wondered if Fenger had somehow contacted him, perhaps by phone, and if so, how much Christian had confided.

"Gave me a general dressing-down, he did. He has a far higher opinion of you than I'd imagined possible. Says your techniques may be somewhat experimental, ahead of times, even extraordinary—"

"Said that did he?"

"OK, he said you were eccentric."

"I see."

They found a seat in the dimly lit, wild saloon, replete with gunmen at the bar, spittoons lining the dirty floor littered with the leavings of the day—mostly bones thrown to prowling dogs, Muldoon's more obvious friends. Muldoon stood an enormous man behind the bar, slack-jawed giant that he was, and according to a whispered remark into Tewes's ear, "Muldoon'll truck no undo criminal activity on the premises unless he gets a cut, so don't go plying your trade here, James."

Jane decided her disguise as Tewes remained intact, as Ransom's body language, speech, and swagger, all but the added politeness, remained the same toward Tewes.

They ordered two pints of ale and a pitcher besides, Tewes putting up a hand at the suggestion they could drink so much.

"I need steady hands for my practice when the door opens tomorrow."

"Oh, come, by then you'll be steady again."

Tewes nodded, accepting Ransom's generosity. "All right, but I don't intend to stagger home."

"Ahhh . . . then you are a better man than I." Ransom laughed at his own remark.

Tewes raised his ale to Ransom's toast, accepting her plight for the moment. While Dr. Tewes liked ale, Jane did not.

"To a new beginning between us, Doctor Tewes."

"Why, thank you, Alastair. Coming from you, I'm most pleased."

"As you should be. Drink up!"

After a moment of awkward silence, Ransom said with open palms, "Oh, I shouldn't've been so hard on you to begin with, really . . . I mean, when you look around . . . there're so many ahhh . . . unusual new methods and techniques, just as Christian says, and your magnetic healing is really mild by . . . say compared to—"

"Mysticism, séances, hypnotism, spiritualism—raising the dead at a cotillion party?"

"Balancing sieves on a fork, or divining by Quija board?" She raised Tewes's glass in a gesture that said touché.

"I'm trying to say that you're almost within the realm of . . ." began Ransom. "That is to say at least close to . . . I mean at least scientific sounding . . . and something *natural* about magnetic fields. So, I'm just saying—"

"That you accept me as *somewhat* less than eccentric? Perhaps normal?" She laughed at this.

"What's so—"

"Funny? You might care to know I've never been called *normal* by anyone's standard."

"Are you saying you've never been normal?"

"Normal . . . what is the norm, Inspector? If normal means staid, stodgy, keeping in one's place . . . I am afraid not."

"Seldom does an officer of the law see normal, as I saw it today at your home."

"At my home?"

"That sister of yours you use as maid, Jane, and your daughter, one who works your books. Both I'd characterize as normal as normal gets."

"Normal is as normal does? I'm glad you approve, and that you found my . . . my Jane and Gabby so . . . presentable."

He lifted his glass as if to the memory. "A pleasant, comely woman she is, your sister."

"Not when in her ill-temper, I assure you."

"She seems a woman of . . . of—"

"Yes, spit it out, man."

"Of obvious good character. A woman apart."

"Struck you as a woman of substance, did she?"

"Aye."

"After all, she is my sister." *Some detective*, she thought.

"And you, Doctor . . . so . . . so . . ."

"Different, say it, man! Different as night from day, indeed . . . I am quite *different*."

Lifting the pitcher of room temperature rich red ale, Ransom poured Tewes's glass full again. This done, he asked, "How so? I mean . . . how do you mean, different?"

"Damn *different*, man! Friendly, fascinating, strange, odd, weird, gifted, bright, charming, delightful, intellectual, insightful, all of it."

"Curt, abrupt, intense, too direct," added Alastair.

She answered between sips, the taste of ale growing on her, "Don't leave out funny, hedonistic, artistic, expressive!"

"Expressive, yes, agreed!"

She pushed on. "Creative, self-absorbed, spirited, sincere, straightforward, lively, both patient and impatient, loyal, sad, depressed in turns . . . at times lonely, *waaay* too sensitive, sarcastic, can't keep my mouth shut when angry or irritated, or around stupidity—especially stupidity that costs me in time, energy, or money, and—"

"Like now?" he finally interrupted the flood of words.

She ignored this, continuing with "—and inhibited at times, fearful at times, as I know too damn much for my own good, but I don't trust anyone, which makes me distant."

"And I suspect you are a challenge for any woman."

"Do you see that too? It's me . . . in my own mind, I'm larger than life, despite my height."

"Really? I could introduce you 'round to some women."

"So that I can be like you—loud, obnoxious, a skirt-chaser?"

"You really have me wrong, sir."

"I've misread you? You are actually curious, thoughtful, meditative—at least Christian says so."

"Fenger says that?"

"Especially about medicine, the human body and the mind."

He snickered. "Whatever helps me solve a crime. Strange that Christian's never said as much to me!"

She looked at him as if for the first time. "What started this conversation off?" She was beginning to feel the effects of the amaretto and ale mix in her system. "Ahhh, yes, well, I know no one who'd use 'normal' in describing me, no. Would you?" Tewes stood, a bit tipsy, even as Alastair poured the phrenologist another glass of ale. Tewes declined another sip. "It is home for me. Have to look in on my little girl. Had liquor with Dr. Fenger, you see atop this."

"Your Gabrielle is a beautiful young woman, Dr. Tewes, and we should have a toast to her at the very least." Ransom held up another full ale to Tewes.

Determined, Jane gulped down the tribute to, as Ransom put it, "the fairest lass in all the city," and she did so in manly fashion.

Unable to hold his liquor, Tewes had played into Alastair's plan too well, as he could not find the door out of Muldoon's. Muldoon and Ransom exchanged a look of knowing, and so Ransom must help Tewes home. The entire way—having to hold Tewes up. What at first he found disturbing soon became curiosity. *How is this fellow so slight?* He imagined lifting Tewes over his shoulder. It'd certainly make getting him home a simpler proposition as Ransom himself had a buzz on. But the sight of her father slung over Ransom's shoulder might set off Gabby with the gun. *And soft. The man's shoulders and arms soft and hardly a tincture of sweat.*

A strange fellow indeed, he concluded as he rang the bell.

Gabrielle rushed out, gun in hand. "What've you done to him?"

"Afraid, young miss, he's sotted."

"Drunk?"

"On ale. Do apologize. Hadn't the slightest inkling he was gone until . . . well, he was gone."

"Bring the doctor inside, please."

He threw Tewes over his shoulder, the doctor's pants leg revealing as small an ankle as he'd ever seen on a man. It made him think of the Bertillon method, the fact no two men had the same measurements, and he wondered if he were to "take the measure" of this man, and send it to contacts at the Suréte in France, if he might not get a match to a wanted fugitive or fraud under another name.

Ransom always carried a tailor's measuring strip in his pocket. Normally, his subject was awake and frightened or beaten into complying with having his measurements taken. But he'd also performed it on a few with whom he'd struggled and knocked senseless, and he found measuring the unconscious a great deal faster and easier. Thirty seconds alone with Tewes now was all he required.

"Get him some water, and I'll get him into bed," Ransom now barked orders at Gabby.

"I won't leave you alone with him under any circumstances."

"I mean your father no harm, child! Now go! Get water or better yet, black coffee!"

Gabrielle waved the gun before his eyes. "All right, but you just lay him out on the bed, and don't touch him in any other way!"

"I've no desire to touch him in any way, child. Now, please as I say!"

She acquiesced, backing out the door, gun weighing down her hand like a pipe.

As soon as she disappeared, Ransom whipped out his measuring tape and gave Tewes the Bertillon once over, memorizing each figure in his head as he measured forehead, distance between eyes, nose to chin, eyes to chin. Circumference of neck; shoulder to shoulder. Chest. Again the sponginess of Tewes's body struck him. He then measured the waistline. The man had none! He noticed how the man's belt looped one and a half times around the waist. He hadn't time to contemplate this more, as he now measured length of leg from crotch to knee, then knee to ankle, finally tearing off his shoes to measuring foot size.

But he failed to finish as Gabrielle was returning; he pocketed the unraveled tailor's tape. What'd alerted him to her quick return, he realized only when seeing her enter, was her gun clinking against the glass on the crowded tray she carried. She had a pot of coffee on the tray alongside the water.

"I'd made coffee earlier," she explained. "Father never stays out so late, ever."

"And you were worried."

"And rightly so, it appears."

"He tells me that you knew the victim at the train station." Fenger had told him this.

"I had only known him for a few days at Northwestern when we met quite by accident at the fair, you see. I was playing hooky from my studies. Gabby's eyes had filled with tears. "We were to meet at the fair again next eve . . ."

"He was quite taken with you, then?"

"He was sweet . . . smitten, I'm afraid." She teared up and he offered her a handkerchief that she accepted.

"I had no idea your father couldn't, you know, hold his liquor. I do apologize."

"I've never seen him this way, ever."

"You take good care of your father. Admirable."

"I do my best."

"He is not always making wise decisions, I would hazard a guess."

"Certainly not tonight! Going off with you! No . . . I mean, yes. He is not always showing the best judgment, but he is my father, and I . . . I love him dearly."

"That much is obvious." Ransom poured himself a cup of coffee and sipped at it before asking, "What about your aunt, his sister?"

"His sister?"

"Your aunt . . . who I met earlier?"

"Ahhh . . . Mrs. Ayers . . . Jane Francis."

"You do not call her Auntie?"

"I've not known her long."

"Ahhh . . . I see."

"She's only recently joined us."

"From France?"

"Ahhh . . . I believe by way of New York."

All facts he could check later, he told himself. The young one seemed absolutely befuddled. She'd not gone near the gun in all this time. Perhaps she was getting used to Alastair. He could only hope. "It's a fine gun you carry about."

"It is mother's," she blurted out. "I mean . . . was my mother's. The . . . the only thing she bequeathed me."

"Interesting heirloom then. But I was given to understand she died in labor, giving birth to you, so how was it she bequeathed you a gun? Or is that mere street talk, rumor I'm repeating?"

"She set it out in a letter in the event anything should happen to her during her pregnancy."

"Ahhh . . . foresight she had, perhaps a premonition?"

"I am told she was sickly . . . always."

"Difficult pregnancy?"

"Hard labor came as no surprise."

"I see. Your father here, being a doctor . . . he must've known the risks . . ."

"Aye . . . I mean, I should think so, as he's a medical man."

"But they had not consummated their wedding? He then had to legally adopt you, his own child is how I heard it."

"No . . . common street talk is that, sir!"

Was Gabby embarrassed by this? Her clenched hands spoke of discomfort, perhaps a lie. He lifted the gun, and her allowing this felt like a new, fresh start between them. They smiled across at one another, the gun held up between them while Tewes mildly snored.

Ransom examined the gun for the missing cap that Tewes had mentioned. The firing pin was in place, and the cap in the caplock. Either Tewes failed to tell the truth about the gun, in an attempt to ease Ransom's fears at having it pointed at the back of his head, or Gabby knew as much about guns as her father'd intimated. Likely the latter.

"Whataya think of my gun?"

"It belongs in a museum."

She looked indignant. "That gun is in fine working order. I keep it clean."

"It's a cannon, not a gun. Blow a hole the size of a medicine ball in a man."

She threw her hands up to cover her laughter. "Now you exaggerate."

"Not by much."

"My . . . my family wants me to pursue a medical degree, but I'm so fascinated with what men like you do, Inspector Ransom."

"Really?"

"I've read Alan Pinkerton's accounts of heroic deeds during the late war, about his army of spies—*We never sleep!*— what a motto and that evil eye they use to signify themselves, it's all so . . . so adventurous and . . . and . . ."

"Romantic it is *not*, I can assure you."

"Oh, but it is . . . what you and other Chicago detectives must see daily! I bet no two of your days are alike! Can I tell you that medical school is a bore down to my . . . well, to my core!"

"But isn't medicine in your makeup?"

"I hate it. Hate that it's in my blood, too!"

"It should come easily to you, following in your father's—"

"The last thing in the world I want to become is . . . is my father."

He stared grimly across at her as if taking this blow for Tewes. "Does your father know your feelings?"

"He's rather wrapped up . . . busy with patients. Hasn't seen me . . . not the real me in . . . in . . . well, in forever."

"But all that tuition going to Northwestern . . ."

"If I could figure out a way to use it . . . my studies . . . in tracking down and catching killers . . . what you do . . . then it might be worthwhile, but just dealing with sick and depressed and grim people all day as Father does. I know I'd rather be a copper like you, working with the dead!"

"Hmmm . . . perhaps you should talk to Dr. Christian Fenger then."

"Dr. Fenger? The famous surgeon?"

"And pathologist. Does work for the police . . . helps us identify victims of foul play, and determines just who is and who is not a homicide victim, and how precisely their lives ended."

"I . . . I've not given this area of medicine a thought, not a single thought."

"It's not entirely new. Been with us since King William ordered a medical man to investigate suspicious deaths."

"The first coroner? I wonder who he was."

"Physicians working for the crown, only now you work for a municipality like Cook County."

"Coroner . . . I rather like the sound of it."

"Call on Dr. Fenger sometime, and tell him of your interest."

"It'd be behind Father's back."

A way to get back at Tewes, Ransom thought. "Ahhh . . . once you've established yourself with Dr. Fenger, how can your father balk? No one has a greater reputation as a surgeon." *Complicate Tewes's blackmailing effort.*

"I'll visit him at his office tomorrow!"

"You'll never catch him in an office. Does everything afoot. Go by County Hospital at exactly ten A.M. He'll be there. Tell him two things."

"Yes?"

"That Inspector Ransom sent you, and that your father is Dr. Tewes."

"But with my father's reputation as a mentalist, Dr. Fenger'll toss me out."

"Not so. Your father enjoys a good relationship with Dr. Fenger," he lied, "and I am sure that if Christian finds you as determined a pupil as you seem, why then he'll side with you."

"Imagine it . . . Dr. Christian Fenger in my corner."

"Stranger things've happened."

She looked at the prone figure of Tewes, who was out and had no need of water or coffee.

"Will you have more coffee and stay longer, to tell me harrowing tales of cases you've worked on, Inspector?"

"It grows late, and I fear we'll wake your aunt."

"Oh, *poooh* on her! She sleeps like a stone a way off in the other part of the house. You must tell me of your cases!"

"Really, it is late."

"But the coffee, and I made cookies earlier."

"Hmmm . . . you can be persuasive, young lady."

"Then you'll stay awhile?"

"One cup of coffee, two cookies—"

"And three lurid tales?"

"Let's make it my *most* lurid case."

CHAPTER 15

Fire alarms from several directions sounded a distress that would wake the entire city. Still, Ransom ignored the Chicago Fire Department at work in the black of night, instead launching into the story of how he'd almost single-handedly caught Morgan Nels and his equally deadly wife, Nellie "the Hawk" Nels, a twosome who'd begun as flamboyant con artists, but had graduated to murder when a con went bad. "Found contract killing far more to their liking—faster results—so they embarked on a career as a tag team."

He was in midsentence when the phone rattled to life in the other room.

"You have a telephone?" he asked.

"We do. It's needed in a medical practice."

"A most helpful new tool for the police as well."

"So I've read."

"Read?"

"I know a young policeman who sneaks the police news to me whenever he can."

"I see . . . the *Police Gazette*."

"I love it."

"You really do have the blue bug then, don't you?"

"Is that what they call it?"

The phone continued to ring. "I'd best get going," he said.

"But you didn't finish. How precisely did the Nels do their murdering?"

"I suspect you've already read of the case."

"I have, but to have you, the man who brought them to justice to tell it . . . this is such an . . . an honor."

Am I blushing, he wondered.

"I did some checking up on you; learned a lot about you, Inspector, and I'm not ashamed to say it, but"—she had begun a blush now—"I so admire you, sir."

"Why thank you."

"So few people . . . so few men could possibly be as brave as you."

He swallowed hard at this. "I cannot remember a time when anyone has said as much to me. I don't know what to say, except . . . well . . . thank you, Miss Tewes."

"Gabrielle or Gabby . . . you must call me Gabby, yes."

"All right, Gabby. I take it as an honor."

"But for now . . . we must keep our alliance between us. Should Father learn, he'd scalp me, and most certainly send me to convent."

"Really?"

"He says you're not to be trusted, that you're a scoundrel, and that he suspects you have, on occasion, crippled or killed men to make them talk."

"I had no idea he held so high an opinion of—"

"Is it true?"

"True enough."

"I'm not sure I believe either of you." She threw one of her cookies at him, making him laugh.

The sound of sirens continued closer now. The phone had stopped rending apart Ransom's head, but it'd left a throbbing. His contorted features telegraphed the depth of pain he entertained.

"Are you all right, Inspector?" she asked.

"Have this headache, you see. Should be off to bed."

"You ought to've had Father diagnose your problem 'stead of spending the evening drinking, the two of you."

"So right." He stood to leave.

"I suspect the headache is the tip of the iceberg," she hazarded a guess.

"You're going to make a fine doctor."

She escorted him to the front door. A red glow against the sky in the distance made them both stare in wonderment.

"Whataya suppose?" she began. "Fireworks at the fair?"

"Another fire. They break out routinely. So many of the original homes built substandard before the new laws were enacted, and when they go up in flame, well the way they are atop one another over there on Broadway, Clark, the Lincoln Park area . . ." he paused, giving a thought to Merielle. She lived in the area in question.

"Can you imagine someone calling here at this hour?" she asked.

He banged the floor with his cane. "By my word, perhaps the doctor is being called to assist at the fire?"

"I think not, but who knows."

"If it should ring again, answer it. If they need him, get that coffee into him and get him there."

"Are you going to see the fire? Would you take me with you?"

"No," he lied and grimaced. He did indeed mean to determine its origin and extent, but he certainly did not want her on his arm at the scene of a fire.

"You really should take care of your health, sir, that headache."

"I've tried all cures."

She nodded. "All but my father's. Come by for it. He does good work, despite what people think."

"If it'll afford me the pleasure of your company, Gabrielle, then I may just do that."

Ransom said good night, his body silhouetted against the red sky. She called out as he grabbed a passing cab, "Do take better care of yourself, Inspector. Chicago needs men like you! Many more I'm afraid."

"Make for the fire, my good man!" he shouted to the cabbie as he boarded. Out one cab window, he saw Gabby waving him off; out the other, he saw an oddly shaped black plume of choking smoke rising over Chicago. He cursed the fool who'd fallen asleep over his stogie, or the overturned lamp, or the careless fellow with one of those newfangled gas stoves kicked over at the foot of a bed.

The devastating fire reached beyond the London Royale Arms Tavern, threatening to destroy other tenement houses around it. Most builders at this time, having learned the lessons of the Great Fire of '71, used brick and mortar and the new concrete, especially in high-rent districts and for the high-rise structures of Michigan Avenue and other downtown locations. In such places, the city upheld new fire standards, but here on Clark new construction followed old paths: payoffs and graft to aldermen and building inspectors allowed substandard housing to again flourish.

After the debacle of flame that leveled Chicago, headlines had read:

**FIRE DEVASTATES CHICAGO . . .
CITY TO NEVER RECOVER . . .
GREAT LOSS OF LIFE AND PROPERTY . . .
END OF GREAT RAIL HUB!
GONE THE WAY OF ASH . . .**

Such headlines abounded in the few newspapers whose presses the Great Fire hadn't silenced. People who'd lived through the fire in '71 now stood in shock and fear at the sight of *any* conflagration that even appeared to have the possibility of becoming the next Great Fire. Tonight's inferno looked far too familiar; older citizens standing and watching the rain of ash and cinder trembled at the prospects while blood orange, red, and blue flames licked at all surrounding structures. Nearby trees and fences ignited. Was

1893 to be the next year of the failure of the Chicago Fire Department?

As Ransom's cab neared, all about the street, people ran shouting and pointing and trying to steer clear of the hooves of racing horses pulling the latest in fire fighting equipment— which remained inadequate to the task. Antiquated equipment, too little, too late. The images and sights and sounds of the fire numbered so many, no one could see or hear them all: multiple fire wagons descending on the scene from three directions. Firemen appeared in chaos, hauling out axes, picks, hoses, buckets. Some worked the hoses, others the ladders. It took some to quell the terrified horses that'd supposedly been trained for fire emergencies.

Ransom felt a stomach gnawing sense of a losing battle. No lessons whatsoever learned since '71 save those of graft and fraud and phony land speculation. When it'd come time for the displaced families of the Great Chicago Fire to collect on all those many "church" and benevolent society funds, there were no funds. They'd all been systematically disposed of by the shrewd promoters who'd thought up these fine-sounding benevolent "societies." The funds had gone into the purchase of ash-strewn downtown lots on streets of loss, where nothing but a lone charred and blackened water tower and firehouse made of native limestone sat forlornly at the end of Michigan Avenue. A boon and a lure as it happened for those with deep pockets. Men with both vision and selfishness in mind, greed and glory all balled up in one idea of a phoenix rising from the ashes, making the Gem of the Prairie shine again. But tonight only one thing mattered to the firemen whose very skin was seared and scorched and blackened by the fire at hand. *Save the block* . . . lose the whole tavern and entire building, the outbuildings, possibly the building to the immediate right and left, but stop it here and with no more loss of life than might already have occurred. An entire heavy oak bureau drawer with mirror, and a four-poster bed, mattress and springs had fallen through with fire-blackened flooring. The cross beams held longer, but as more and more became compromised these heavy beams—forming the crisscross support that made up the second floor—tore away in groaning complaint; the insatiable flames had licked at this area for too long now.

To the untrained eye, it might appear the flames had begun on the bottom floor, but not so with Chief Harold Stratemeyer, whose experience told him just the opposite, and this belief was given more credence when all the upper stairways caved in from the center. And now after this small explosion of debris amid the flames, Stratemeyer could see the result after the smoke cleared a bit.

Ransom stood alongside Stratemeyer unbelieving. Sitting atop the charred bar . . . like a mockery of Alastair's former love nest, the bedsprings and still burning mattress precariously balanced. This was art of the devil.

Harry Stratemeyer was acting as the new fire marshal—old Warrick having been found floating in the Chicago River's north branch. Death by what was being called an accidental drowning helped along by alcohol, but there remained the curious part—no wallet or money in his pockets. At any rate, Stratemeyer, who'd been Warrick's second in command, ordered men to water down surrounding buildings, having long since given up on the clapboard two-story and its surrounding outhouses. Chicago firefighters had in fact evolved greatly since the devastating fire in 1871. While still in need of more and better equipment, they did have far better access to water, as sewers now carried needed supplies to hydrants throughout the network of streets. And their tanks were larger and their horses faster and generally—but not always—better trained on chaos. His men were also better trained and outfitted.

Strateymeyer grabbed Ransom the moment he saw the big inspector wandering in a daze toward the flames, pointing and shouting about someone he called Merielle. But it was no easy grab; Stratemeyer had had to subdue Ransom with the help of several of his men. Otherwise, Alastair would've surely rushed into the flames—flames in their acme, rabid, licking, unstoppable.

Stratemeyer, a large man himself, had thrown a massive bear-hug onto Ransom, and with the two others, had wrestled his friend Alastair into a sitting position below the cinders that rained down around them all like searing fireflies discovering freedom.

Finally, two large firemen now sat on Ransom where he beat the earth with both fists.

Alastair Ransom had sat all night on the street corner, feeling his life going off into the night sky with the smoke that discolored the moon. Head in hands, eyes arched and watching, Alastair said a prayer for Merielle as the final boards caught flame, only to fall into the center of the gutted two-story. The place had housed the old London Royale Arms Tavern, a pretentious title for a pub, and his Merielle's rooms above, now no longer above.

Stratemeyer would not let him set foot onto the scene until one hundred percent certain that first the fire was under control, and until he could determine if it were arson or an unfortunate accidental occurrence. Two burly firemen stood guard over Ransom where he sat while Harry kicked through the rubble in a methodical going over.

As it'd been a large, sprawling thing that went far back of the yards, a number of other apartments rented by the owner of the Arms had also burned. But everyone living in the building was accounted for, all but Polly Pete.

Now at daybreak, the fire under control, Ransom stood to shake off the weary firemen guarding him. He began a strange tiptoe amid the squalor and fumes and blackness of the gutted house, working to remain in Harry's footsteps so as to disturb as little as possible of Stratemeyer's possible arson investigation, and he thought of the last time he'd spoken to Merielle.

The second floor had caved in on the bar below, and all of

Polly Pete's frilly adornments had gone up in smoke, along with her trunk, her bureau drawer, the mirror blackened with smutty, grimy smoke now atop chairs and tables in one corner—somehow miraculously intact, a still-life painted in fire meant to mock Ransom, to rend his heart. Peering into her eerily intact mirror was a look into a bottomless abyss of smut. Nothing reflected from it save a single eye—his eye, reflecting where a single dewy quarter-sized square remained somehow unblemished. Satan winking at him. Then he saw the bed again—*their bed*—straddled atop what was left of the bar, the mattress gone save for the seared, hoary black tufts of it. Black spider webs clung to rails, to exposed conduits for the gas burners, pipes, leftover standing boards, leftover standing glasses half melted, to an array of exploded bottles of rye, rum, whiskey, gin, vodka and other spirits. Only the bedsprings remained of their bed, and the coiled springs, like the mirror, painted in satanic abandon.

"Where is she? If not here . . . where?" he asked. A glimmer, like a fleeting bird from his deepest recesses of—hope for Merielle—rose in him.

A completely ash-covered Stratemeyer looked him in the eye. "Alastair, you should go home . . . go home, now."

"Where the bloody hell is she?"

Stratemeyer gritted his teeth. "You're a hard man to stay liking, Alastair. You should take a friend's advice!"

He pushed past Harry, searching, tearing at boards, cutting hands on debris in his mad hunt for Merielle, but he found nothing when he came around a wall on his right side that'd somehow grotesquely remained standing, as a magician's trick . . . like the trick of the intact mirror. Still, no body.

"Damn you, Harry! What's become of her?"

Stratemeyer merely lifted his chin, and Ransom followed his eyes upward. Above, caught on an exposed daggerlike protrusion of steel pipe—part of the upstairs plumbing—her body dangled: a charred disfigured doll, and ghastliest of all, she was headless.

Ransom went to his knees, bellowing like a wounded

beast. All of the hurt, all of the pain she must have felt, he screamed out in her name.

Stratemeyer called for some of his men to escort Alastair out of the devastation.

When Stratemeyer felt confident that Ransom had been put in a cab and sent home, he went around the bar and stooped below the bedsprings to reach in for the other part of the woman he'd only known as Polly Pete, the woman Ransom had made a reputation on with his winnings as a gambler. Harry'd never heard her called anything else. He wondered about the name Merielle. Guessed it Polly's nickname, else the one given her at birth by parents, whoever they were . . . wherever they might be . . . if even alive.

One thing he knew was to treat Polly's body with all the respect of a queen, Alastair Ransom's queen. He knew not to assume anything, knew to pass this along to the medical chaps who'd ultimately take her in their care, knew not to willy-nilly bury the remains in Potter's Field, not without consulting Ransom.

An assistant rushed to Stratemeyer's opened arms with a large paper sack to receive the head. This done, Harry pointed to the dangling corpse overhead. "Somebody get a ladder against that wall! Determine if it'll hold! And confound it all . . . if God willing, snatch that poor woman down."

"Sir, if I may volunteer for that duty," replied Rodney McKeon. "Alastair Ransom's been a good friend, sir."

Harry concurred, nodding firmly, thinking Ransom had done so much for so many. He dropped his gaze and jerked his head to hide a creeping tear. "That man doesn't deserve this."

"Some bastard's taken her head off," muttered another fireman.

McKeon added, "Yaaa . . . looks the same bastard as did the others, but this time . . ." He paused to bring home his point. "This time, he's gone too far."

Harry said, "And he's not goin' to get away with it, not after Ransom finds his wits."

* * *

Alastair Ransom hadn't gone home in the cab they put him into; instead, he wound up at Muldoon's, unsure how he'd arrived here. He pounded on the door, demanding he be served, until Muldoon pulled it wide. Muldoon argued the law that shut taverns down on any given Saturday midnight not to reopen until Monday noon. Ransom pushed past the giant Muldoon, who snatched out a blackjack and slammed it into Alastair's head, knowing he had the law on his side. This just as Mike O'Malley'd arrived.

O'Malley arrested Muldoon for assaulting an officer, and Ransom was taken into custody for a drunk and disorderly, orders of Chief Kohler himself, and ignobly thrown into the drunk tank. With no beds left, they laid him out on the floor, unconscious.

Muldoon was booked for battery on a police official and told his court date would come round when it came around, despite his continual plea: "I was trying to uphold the drinking laws put forth by authorities!"

It fell on deaf ears. Muldoon's use of the sap to the back of Ransom's head had caused a concussion, and saps were as illegal as drinking on Sunday—which actually changed from one week to the next, depending upon the level of graft. In fact, the drinking laws proved as mercurial as the tides.

"He knows the rules but chose to break 'em! I pay good money to run a business, and this is how you treat me?" complained Muldoon, his gigantean features terrifying even through the bars.

"You daft fool, Muldoon! Have ya no sense? That's Alastair Ransom you knocked cold, and he has friends all over Chicago."

"I know who he is, but he pushed into my establishment shouting orders!"

"Have you not heard the news, man?"

"What news?"

"Christ man, why news of a black-hearted bastard who's going about the city cutting off heads!"

"Every day it's all I hear!"

"About this morning's victim! Found in the fire on Clark Street?"

"What's it to me?"

"It was Ransom's Polly who was *murrr-durrr-ed*, man!"

It finally hit Muldoon, sinking into the thick walls of his head. "So he decides he'll take it out on me, does he?"

"He needed a drink, and he needed it badly, and you ought've given it up."

"It's me license I worry about."

"Aye . . . like every merchant in this city."

"You coppers don't make it easy on a man, the way you scratch honest earnings!"

"Honest is it? Your place is a bloody front for every vice known to—"

"—and now they got fees for this, and fees for that, and soon it'll come to having to pay a fee to keep a rooster in your own bloody yard!"

"Dare you now swear at your jailor?"

"Look . . . is Ransom going to be OK?"

"I dunno. Moans a bit now and again; still outta his head. Didja have to hit him so hard?"

"I didn't want that man getting up after I hit 'im, for sure."

"Well . . . you succeeded . . . least till he comes to. Best think of selling your place and getting out."

"Ne'er saw a copper so liked by other coppers."

"He's a good man, a noble man to be sure."

"And I suppose, O'Malley, you're one of his henchmen?"

Mike O'Malley grimaced at Muldoon. "I shoulda beaned you!"

"All right . . . I should've thought before I swung on 'im."

"Inspector Ransom's done more for police and the personal safety of every cop in this city than all the captains, and all the chiefs, and all the commissioners, and all the mayors combined."

"And I grounded him."

"And you won't hear the last of it with me or many another copper, I can guarantee you, Muldoon."

"What're you saying? Huh?"

"I'll say no more."

"That if he's to die, God forbid, that . . . that my time's truly up here?"

Michael Shaun O'Malley only turned the key and walked from the lockup, saying not another word.

CHAPTER 16

Griffin Drimmer stumbled amid still smoldering ashes of the fire that'd killed Alastair Ransom's only dream. Alastair had confided in a word here and there that he had found someone special, someone he'd spoken about in connection with the word *future,* someone who, as he put it, might help him put away all his ghosts. Someone he thought he might devote all the rest of his life to, and in doing so, he could let go of the past, let go of the horror of Haymarket and the lingering questions and suspicions, to end his years-long quest after the phantoms of another time.

Now this.

And it was worse than first he'd heard—that Ransom's woman had died in a terrible fire. Worse by far, as she'd been garroted—beheaded—and set aflame. He could hardly imagine Alastair's grief and suffering. Surely the work of the fiend they'd been tracking. Had the madman turned on the hunters? And if so, how safe was Griffin's own family? He must think of his own loved ones now.

He made his way from the sight of Polly Pete's severed head and the blackness of the fire-charred building and went in search of a messenger to send a hastily scratched note reading: "Pack children—go to mother's in Portage. Stay till you hear from me!"

Everyone in Chicago, it seemed, had come out to see the fire, a mob held back by uniformed coppers. People in mass who needn't be here. People who could contribute nothing. Still, the CPD and CFD had learned something since the days of Haymarket, to circulate plainclothes undercover cops and snitches in among the crowds to feel out the word on the street.

Nathan Kohler had come down to the site to oversee the investigation, barking orders for Griffin to get to the bottom of things. Philo Keane, hearing of the matter, had rushed down to gather what photos he might, not knowing of Polly's murder by garrote and by blaze. He'd arrived just in time to get shots of the body being courageously eased down by a fireman Philo knew only as McKeon.

Despite a hangover, Philo rushed into the midst of the rubble for shot after shot, made to pause only by the surreal sights—the mirror, the bedposts and bedsprings atop the charred bar, and then he saw the head being lifted from a bag to display to Drimmer and Kohler, and Philo's camera caught this, too.

Some of the firemen thought Philo a complete ghoul, but he knew that Alastair Ransom, had he been here and of sound mind, would be barking at him to get all these cuts. He told himself he was doing it for Ransom, although a whispered voice from the deepest reaches of his psyche said otherwise, said he liked it, the stark beauty that fire and charred remains carried into the frame. An artistic-minded man must understand the stark painful reality inherent in the scene—like storm devastation.

"How I would've loved to've been on hand during the Great Fire . . . to've photographed its majesty, its finality, the uncompromising wasteland," he said to arson investigator Stratemeyer.

"Yes . . . I suppose a fine artistic soul such as yourself, Mr. Keane, can find beauty e'en in death. But trust me, you would've wept to see Chicago so crippled as she was then."

"You must have been—"

"I was a bloody eighteen-year-old at the time. This"—he pointed to the devastation lying before them—"this is something like it only if you multiply the loss of life by hundreds and the property damage by millions."

"Still, the stark beauty of it. I've seen early photos, but a frame always limits the perspective of reality."

"Not sure, sir, but would you move just to your left a foot or two, Mr. Keane?"

Philo did so, and the wall and fixture pipe that'd snatched Polly's body while her head had fallen, now came crashing down, sending up a plume of smoke and ash to choke Philo and paint him ashen. He stepped out of the billowing cloud caused when the firemen had intentionally brought down the unsafe wall.

Small fires still flared up around Philo as he moved off. Stratemeyer and his men stayed inside the mushroom cloud of debris, while Philo caught glimpses of these ghostly figures and snapped pictures. Under his breath, between choking bouts, he cursed his young assistant, Waldo Denton, for having not shown up for this. *How was the boy to learn a damn thing?*

Then from out of the dust cloud stepped the man with the brown bag stuffed with Polly's head, and following him, two men carrying a reed stretcher on which lay Polly's charred legs, torso, arms, and half her neck. The cooked cadaver did not look real; it looked for all the world, he thought, like a fake rubber blob, something a rubber factory might cast off as damaged molding.

Philo bumped into Griffin, and their eyes spoke, both feeling the torment of grief for their friend and colleague, both knowing they could not possibly feel the depth of pain that Ransom, this moment, must be feeling for his loss.

"Shocking . . . awful," Griffin mustered two words.

"Horrible, satanic is what it is," managed Philo.

Enough said. The body parts were whisked off to Cook County morgue by Shanks and Gwinn, who'd taken direction from Christian Fenger, also on hand. Fenger had re-

mained on the periphery, watching from afar. How long he'd
been on scene, no one hazarded a guess. Kohler asked it of
Drimmer, and when Griffin had no answer, Kohler muttered,
"Everyone thinks him a Renaissance man, a Leonardo of the
prairie, but I think him rather a ghoul who likes his work too
much."

"Unlike some people," muttered Philo.

Kohler gave Keane a withering look. "Look here, photographer, just do your job and mind your business. I was speaking to Inspector Drimmer."

"Sorry, sir."

"Just get those cuts to us as soon as possible, and if you've
not already delivered the others from the train station to Inspector Ransom, then get them to my office as well. And for
that matter, where the deuce is Ransom?" he said loudly for
all to hear. But he fooled no one. News of Alastair's one-
sided run-in with Muldoon, and his lying in a cell at the Harrison Street Lockup on Kohler's orders had spilled onto the
street like beer from a busted vat. Chicago's premiere detective, Inspector Ransom, lay unconscious in one of his own
cells, locked up with derelicts, drunks, and scavengers of
every stripe—some of whom might care to take a daggar to
his throat.

Philo just stared at the well-dressed politician cop, and
was quickly losing his temper when Waldo Denton stumbled
up, the boy's face painted with fire grease and smoke, damp
with tears. "I can't do this no more, sir. No 'mount a scratch
is worth this . . . every time somebody is killed like this . . ."
An audible moan rose from Denton's gut. "Damn it, this . . .
this is too hard, Mr. Keane."

"I ask a lot of a man, agreed."

"Perhaps too much."

"Whataya know of hard?" Philo sharply asked. "You ever
go hungry, boy? I mean falling down hallucinating hungry?"

"No, sir."

"Hell, asking too much! Why, you didn't even know Polly,
not like I did."

"I saw her at your studio once, and—and in your photo collection."

"God, boy . . . go get yourself straightened out." He handed Denton fifty cents. "Come by when you're feeling better. You may still have a job! Now get!" Philo threw rocks as Denton ambled off, dejected, apparently in shock, but over his shoulder, he called out, "I stole a picture of her once."

"From me?"

"She was beautiful."

Kohler glared at Philo. "How'd you know the victim, Keane? And what sort of *pictures* is this young man referring to?"

"Art." Philo quickly returned to his work. "Artist and model, and that was the extent of it." Philo had seen the glint in Kohler's eye as if he'd discovered some gold nugget fallen from the sky. He'd never told anyone of his practice of taking a woman's body for his payment on occasion, and Polly had found it a thrilling proposition.

"Yes, Mr. Keane—I see." Kohler sometimes hissed.

As Philo worked, he saw Dr. Tewes join Kohler. Likely here was the only man standing who had no idea what'd become of Alastair Ransom this day.

Jane could not concentrate on what lay before her as either the man she pretended or the woman she was, as both personae had taken this hard. Polly had been Jane's or rather James's patient, and Ransom's lover, and now this. How angry Ransom had appeared the other night did not connect or make logical sense. Yet, it would be the perfect murder indeed if, in a fit of rage, Ransom had killed Polly and made it look like the work of the killer the press now called the Phantom. How simple to cover her murder. And Ransom, being Ransom, knew how to cover up any mistake that might be made or badly juggled. But, in fact, this hadn't been her notion but rather Kohler had floated the idea past her.

Was it possible? Did it go with what she knew of the man, despite all the dark tales of Alastair's temper and questionable morals? Could his police life have spilled over into his private life, and had he used Dr. Tewes as both his excuse and his alibi?

She then decided it too preposterous and not in Ransom's makeup as she stood here, staring at the ruination of Ransom's life, his goals, his plans. It led to her own epiphany. "Nathan," she said to Kohler, "I can go no further with our charade."

"The hell you say!"

"Suppose I were called to testify in a court of law over events? To swear on a Bible as Dr. Tewes? It's preposterous, untenable."

"Look here! We had a deal. This"—he indicated the fire—"changes nothing."

"It changes everything. You don't need me to bring Ransom down. He is on his back now; you need but crush him, but I'll be no party to the kill, and no longer part of your web of deceit."

It'd been Nathan Kohler who'd led Polly directly to Dr. Tewes's for the care she sought, as he had led Fenger to Tewes. "Information gathering," he'd called it.

"You cross me, *James*, and you'll be exposed for what you are, *Jane*." Kohler had investigated Dr. Tewes the year before and had learned Jane's every secret.

"Perhaps for the better."

"Really? You think so?" His half grin curled snakelike on itself.

"I've accomplished so little, nothing meritorious about my time spent here."

"You can do well here."

"I am not speaking of Chicago."

"What then?"

"I shouldn't expect you to understand."

"Try me, Jane."

"Accommodate the bloody world so as to fit comfortably

into it is what I've done, when in fact, I should make the world accommodate *me*. It's what good people have been trying to tell me." She thought of Gabby, Dr. Fenger, her father, and for some odd reason, Alastair.

"Whatever are you trying to say?" Kohler replied. "If you're in control of your senses, then the world makes perfectly good sense."

"You mean, the sense of the world is what you make of your senses?"

He looked into her eyes, confused.

"Nathan, it is so damnably easy for you with your syllogisms to live by, but it makes no more sense now to me than ever it did as a child, this place."

"Live with it."

"I've never understood the people with whom I share this world, why they do what they do—*usually self-sabotage*," she thought of Polly and Ransom—"it's all a mystery . . ."

"We're not here to understand every mystery of life."

"Blindness is no mystery."

"Blindness?"

"Blindness to the results of our own confounding decisions."

"So you retreat into your considerable intellect, Doctor? This is your answer?"

"When I can no longer take another single second of the insanity of the world, why not?" She indicated the fire devastation spread before them. "I have this nice dark, under-the-rock place where things are black and white, and where *what has been* rules *what is* right now, where insane behavior is explainable."

"You're speaking of understanding this madman again? But no one can penetrate the mind of a maniac."

"Science must someday do so."

"And in the process of your scientific inquiry, you cut yourself off from your own feelings," he countered. "How adventurous it'd be to open that Pandora's box you pretend into nonexistence along with your real self, your real gender."

"We set things in motion, Nathan. You set me a-spying on Alastair Ransom, and I've been dutiful, and now this? This is an unacceptable result. I'm done with it."

"Done indeed?"

"Think of it, my prying into this woman's life not to help her as a physician, but to learn of Ransom's comings and goings? I did harm. Had I not poisoned her against Ransom as you instructed, then perhaps—"

"She'd be just as dead; Polly asked for this."

"That's a horrible thing to say; no one asks for this."

"She lived the life; every day she chanced some awful thing happening."

Some awful thing like you, she thought but said, "It's not something I want to be a part of any longer, not for any amount of money."

"Not even to keep Gabrielle safe from attention?"

Her clenched jaw quivered. She stared into the rubble and curling smoke.

"Not so easy to walk away from me, Dr. Tewes."

"Damn you, sir."

"I can make your life hell in Chicago."

"You said you admired my savvy and determination, and yet you can do this?"

"Think you've too few patients now? Imagine should I put out a single word against you. Besides, that little matter of Gabby's having been born a bastard, all that about her father . . . all quite nicely locked away for now, sealed in my office."

There was the rub. Gabby's father, all the terrible reports of how he'd died so ignobly in a prison in Saint-Tropez, France, where he'd been caught cheating at cards in a casino brothel. He'd been beaten to within inches of life and then arrested. Dead of his wounds in that cold cell, uncared for, alone, disgraced. Kohler had dredged it all up from French authorities.

"We both want what's best for your child."

She'd worked to shield Gabby from the truth.

All the volcanic negative raging storms self-created within us that make us do and say stupid hurtful dumb self-destructive things, she thought. And a parent will do anything for a child. Gabby, so much like her, had always and still lived inside her feelings, inside her instincts. Gabby knew. She knew something in addition to Cliffton's murder troubled her mother's soul. It had a name—Nathan Kohler.

"I'm glad to see you're thinking it over," said Kohler. "That you won't act impulsively."

Kohler had no idea how impulsively she might act. Staring at the charred remains of this day, she realized all her rampant thoughts ended with setting Kohler afire—images of his suffering flitting by like a series of daguerreotypes on a spindle. They were replaced by Gabby dancing riotously in her head, dancing with the phantoms of what was and is and what might be.

"Our bargain stands then." He kept calm, smiling, his well-groomed mustache gluey with pomade.

She stared forward, wondering where she might purchase a garrote. "I don't think until this moment that I've ever fully realized just how profoundly different Gabby and I are."

"Really?"

"My intellect is just a tool, Nathan."

"Of course, to make sense of experience."

She agreed, "All things large and small, corporeal and spectral."

"Intellect helps us communicate."

"But my intellect, much as it is my 'cover,' isn't me. So don't put too much faith in its always being there for you to manipulate."

He was the picture of perplexity now.

"I don't live in my intellect. I live *elsewhere*."

"Elsewhere?"

"Where the heart lives." Her gaze remained on the ashes.

"And where is that?" He brushed her hand with his, making another of his crude, awkward passes.

"A place few get to be part of or see, a place that some—like you, Nathan—don't even know exist."

"*Annnd* . . . you're saying this is a bad thing?"

"I've been induced to live outside my feelings in this matter, induced by people like you and circumstances."

"Get control of yourself, Jane! There're reporters all around here. At least pretend interest in the current problem we face, and in what I'm saying."

"Feelings—source of my strength, why people listen to me, trust my deepest felt senses. My father, God rest him, he used to tell people—"

"Perhaps you should be having this conversation with your daughter, Dr. Tewes?"

"Yes, for once Nathan, you're correct. While I'm at it, I'll tell her everything. That way no one the likes of you can harm her with your dirty reports."

"Look here," he began, snatching at her arm.

"Tewes" pulled away from him, making curious reporters even more curious. She stormed off, wondering where Ransom was at this moment, knowing how hurt he must be, wondering if there wasn't some way to help him.

CHAPTER 17

The following day at the cold site of the fire . . .

Some anonymous benefactor had paid his bail, but for now Ransom's concern rested on an enormous egg protruding from the back of his head where that damn fool Muldoon had struck him, sending him into a blinding black light. He gave a fleeting thought to having to face Judge Grimes for misbehaving on a Sunday. Jacob Grimes brooked no chicanery but his own.

As for now, Ransom made a beeline for Cook County morgue and Dr. Christian Fenger. When Fenger heard he was outside his autopsy room, he sent assistants to keep him out. They did so and forcefully, but Ransom hadn't the heart to put up much of a fight. Aside from his head killing him, and the back pain from lying so long on a stone cell floor, he felt like one of those bulls in the arena, stabbed full with swords, knives, and lances, bleeding from multiple wounds. Whoever this madman running about the city was, he'd brought police to a standstill, and Alastair Ransom to his knees.

When Fenger came out, his lab coat discolored not with the hues of a blood rainbow but rather soot of Polly's remains, he asked, "What can I do for you, Alastair? Why're you here?"

"Her ring."

"What ring?"

"One I gave her. I want it."

"Ring? There was no ring . . . no jewelry whatsoever."

"Thanks to your men, no doubt."

"I hate to think—"

"Give those ghouls a clear message: If I don't have her ring, they're going to lose something of far more—"

"Look here, Alastair, this is not the wild prairie town of your youth! And you're not a law unto yourself. If I find Shanks or Gwinn've engaged in theft of a body then, by God, they'll be arrested!"

"I want to hear *punished, fired.*"

"Any inquiry will follow a civilized course."

"Civilized course?" Ransom laughed.

"You don't know that they did this. The killer may've taken the ring. Canvass the pawn shops."

"Why . . . why her, Christian? Just a sweet kid beneath it all . . . for what purpose?"

"Perhaps Tewes can profess to understand the mind of a killer," said Christian, "but I'll not attempt it."

"You talk to Shanks and Gwinn."

"I personally trained those two, and they know better, Ransom."

"Human nature being what it is . . . sometimes no amount of training's going to overcome a theft of opportunity."

"You're upset, favoring your head. Let's have a look."

Ransom submitted to his impromptu examination. "You've a considerable lump back here."

"Astute of you, Doctor."

"God, you can be a surly bastard."

"I've gotta run. Give you the day to locate that ring. I know your men have it."

"Go home. Rest, and Alastair, I'm truly sorry about your Merielle, and given the circumstances, I'm going to overlook it today, but don't ever come back to my hospital making threats, or again stretch our friendship to its bounds."

"What, no balm for my head?"

"Ground aspirin in water three times a day for the pain. Nothing else I can do. If you want any further help with it, go to Tewes."

"Tewes really?"

"Submit to Tewes."

"Submit?"

"Under his hands, you just might get some relief for that lump, and more importantly, you may get some long-term help with your temper and your suspicious nature and those recurrent headaches."

"I am gone. Good-bye."

Fenger called after his retreating figure, "Home, rest, Alastair!" Under his breath, he cursed Shanks and Gwinn, the two who'd transported Merielle's remains. "Wouldn't put it past the two of 'em to pawn items from a cadaver. Scavengers . . . first come, first served." Fenger went in search of Shanks and Gwinn.

Ransom had no intention of going home, despite the pain in his head, shoulders, and back. He'd caught a cab for the scene of the crime. The ride across the city on a crisp, clear morning, a hint of promise in the air, a hint of the goodness of life just out of reach, and Alastair cursed the illusion—this intangible called happiness. How many years now had he cajoled himself with jokes about it, comforted himself with rationalizations about it. Happiness for him remained a kind of cloud toward which he aspired, but once inside, the thing dissipated. Some old Gypsy woman at the fair would likely tell him he caused his own bad luck, his own suffering, and maybe she'd be right.

Ransom now paid the driver through the slot and painfully climbed from the carriage. He stood before the stark remains of the old tavern and apartment house, made starker by the sunlight beating down on smoldering blackened beams still crackling with heat.

He went into it, like walking into a grim Rembrandt, filled with odd light and an enormous sadness. Wandering about the ashes, kicking about the debris field for the ring that Fenger said wasn't on the body, he lamented the loss. It'd been a special gift, an heirloom, once his mother's. He knew Shanks and Gwinn's police records. A couple in more ways than he cared to give thought to; their in-tandem, small-time larceny had landed them in jail on frequent occasions. Dr. Fenger had come to the jail, bailed them out, insisted on their good behavior, and gave the miscreants employment. They took to the work of coroner's men like rats to cheese, and on the side, they remained larcenous. Only now, their victims couldn't report them. And the two deemed *anything* left on the body, once they got hold of it, fair game, a tip from the dead. Until now, Ransom had cared little about such petty theft. But this was personal.

His relationship to the killer had also become personal in the deepest way—hunter and hunted now joined by victim on an entirely new level.

From a distance, on the street corner, Jane watched Ransom, looking a ghost of himself, going amid the rubble. She'd guessed that he'd return to where Polly'd died once Dr. Tewes bailed him out. He hadn't disappointed her.

She sensed the truth of one conviction: the murders had come home to Ransom. It'd suddenly, dramatically become personal for Alastair, having seen Polly's blackened, headless torso . . . having seen her hideous death. Torn from his life. She wondered if in some strange, twisted way if he'd somehow brought it on himself.

Body and head—according to Stratemeyer and confirmed by Dr. Fenger—had come apart in the fall due to the severity of a wound sustained to the neck—by a garroting device.

*   *   *

Angry, hurt, in pain, hardly able to blink out the sun, Alastair watched as Dr. Tewes came toward him. Tewes abruptly stopped when the big man lashed out. "Get the G'damn hell outta here, Tewes. I'm in no mood."

But Tewes kept coming on, entering the ashes, the little bow-tied, mustached fellow unmindful of smudging his newly pressed white suit.

"Whataya want here, Tewes? To gloat over your success with Polly? To see the results of your therapy? How good of you to follow up!" He grabbed his throbbing head, shouting only increasing the painful stabbing.

"I want to offer my sincere—"

"Keep 'em!"

"But I am so truly sorry, Ransom . . . really, I am. I couldn't've foreseen this. No one could. Not even Alastair Ransom."

"I should've been with her. Should've hunted down that bastard she called Stumpf. And you, Mr. Psychic. Why *couldn't* you've seen this coming?"

Neither Tewes nor Jane Francis had an answer.

"Your crystal ball out for repairs?"

"Get it back tomorrow."

"Day late . . . dollar short . . ." Alastair muttered and leaned on a table that collapsed, sending him into the ash, throwing up a cloud. The image of the broken man completed.

As he fought to his feet, he said, "'Spose you come to read Mere's head like you did Purvis's? G'luck. It's with your friend, Fenger."

"I came to help you, Inspector." Tewes helped Ransom find his cane, taking charge, telling him, "We'll get a search party down here to scour through the rubble for Polly's ring. I promise."

"Merielle's ring . . . her name was Merielle."

"Yes, of course . . . Merielle's ring."

"Fenger told you?"

"He did." Tewes led the dejected inspector down the street and to a table in the Bull Terrier Pub on Clark near Lincoln where early patrons drank dark ale and talked of nothing but the fire and the rumor that Polly'd been beheaded and set aflame.

Ransom sat now, head bowed, sipping at hot coffee in one hand, a tall Pabst beer in another. Tewes was soon on his second glass of heady Krueger dark ale, Jane having acquired a taste for it. Ransom wondered if it were for show, to demonstrate his masculinity to the detective. Tewes also appeared absorbed in the busy pub's clientele, fascinated in fact. He examined people nonstop, telling Ransom a bit of history on each that he merely surmised from the size of their foreheads, ears, noses, arched brows.

"You can't really believe you can read people from the shapes of their heads and features. That this phrenology con of yours actually has any merit."

"You're ignorant of the science of phrenology."

"And you're gonna educate me?"

"The magnetic energy of our bodies flows strongest at the head, and it gives me, a licensed medical practitioner, Inspector, a picture of the mental state. Besides having a calming effect."

"To what end?"

"Talk. In the best tradition of the family doctor, even the homeopaths with whom I do not always agree, believe in talk."

Ransom remained skeptical, sipping his coffee. Tewes read skepticism in his frown, but merely pointed out another guest in the pub, saying, "See the fellow with the bowler hat at the bar?"

Ransom saw a man with narrow eyes staring into his food, occasionally sniffing at what dripped from his fork. "What about him?" Ransom knew the street tough and petty criminal from repeated arrests.

"He's plotting some mischief as we speak."

"That does not surprise me, Dr. Tewes. He's an habitual criminal, one you likely know as well from careful reading of the *Police Gazette* your daughter has subscribed to."

"*Police Gazette?* Gabby?"

"I saw it in her possession at your home the other night when I put you to bed."

"So that explains my nightmare regarding you."

"Just as you knew something of Purvis, and just as you knew something of Merielle, you know something of Darby over there."

"I can't say that I knew Purvis or even Merielle in any true sense of—"

"Your daughter was seeing the boy, and you counseled Merielle."

"You don't seriously think I had anything to do with either death, do you?"

"I'm saying you know how to milk information. It is, for all its sprawling largeness, a small city made up of a series of ethnically divided communities, and you know a smattering of several languages, yes?"

"Rummaging in search of suckers in seven languages," Jane said. "I resent the implication, and as for Merielle, you still remain blind to her inner turmoil."

"Yes, I admit to blindness, but . . . convinced myself she was . . . that she, she . . ."

"That she could find salvation in making you the center of her universe? That she loved you more than she loved her addictions . . . the life?"

"Something like that, yes, confound you, Tewes!"

A silence settled over their table. Jane realized that each in turn had come to suspect the other of evil. A man with a violin began to play a soft melody imported from some far corner of the world, perhaps Prague or St. Petersburg. The sounds he manipulated from the strings reached into Ransom's deepest sorrow and spoke of his own wrongdoing in all this: his part in Merielle's death. It felt to him as if the violinist had been paid and sent here just to torment him.

"Nothing you might've done or said, no amount of money you may've thrown at her would've saved her from this madman," Tewes counseled. "She wanted to break away from

Chicago and you, Ransom, making her an easy target for—"

He flinched even as he shouted, "Lie!"

"She saw you as a problem, Ransom, a major problem."

"You give a man no quarter, Tewes. Careful over thin ice."

"She liked you better'n others who'd kept her, yes, but she resented the economic bondage you repre—"

His fist slamming onto the table silenced Tewes. Ransom sat seething, unhappy, silent. Jane feared he might explode and strike out with both fists, or with that cane he carried.

But he did neither. He sat brooding instead. *A bear whose meat's withheld,* she thought, but then Dr. Tewes abruptly returned with, "Look, to prove a point—I've seen this fellow at the bar many times but do not know him. Not even so much as to say hello."

"Name is Charles Darby, alias Anthony Guardi, known as Tug."

"Why Tug?"

"Short for Tugboat."

"OK, why Tugboat then?"

"For his size and ability, he can push around men twice his size, and if they disobey, he runs them aground . . . beats 'em to a pulp."

"Tugboat? Quite handy with his Irish fists?"

"But he can pass as Italian. He's done some prizefighting. The man is a poster boy for Lombroso's method of detecting the criminal mind among us, I think, don't you?" Ransom referred to the now famous Dr. Cesare Lombroso, the Italian psychiatrist and criminalist who'd studied hundreds of thousands of convicted felons, taking measurements of their heads and facial features in an attempt to prove all criminals were evolutionary throwbacks—Cro-Magnons among civilized society.

"He does have a sizable pair of ears and that brow is as deep as a canyon, hiding menacing eyes," Tewes said.

"Not exactly the most reliable method of identifying a criminal, Doctor."

"No, I am sure of that. Still, I've read Dr. Lombroso's

work, his *L'uomo delinquente*." The book created a•stir among scientists the world over. "Even if he is wrong, Lombroso has created more interest in criminal science than anyone living."

"Well, give it time. Science in detection will mature, but I remain skeptical of body measurement identification techniques."

"Really? Then that tape measure my daughter saw hanging from your coat pocket the other night was what, for show?" Tewes put up a hand to curtail rebuttal. "Look, we can agree, Lombroso's evidence is riddled with suppositions, as is Bertillon's method."

"You mean, what else do we have to work with? Shall we arrest Darby there for the Phantom, here and now, on his looks?"

"Lombroso is a first mewling step, and others with even less to go on have only cataloged known offenders, stating no two men can possibly exist with the same physical measurements outside the phenomena of twins."

Ransom began listening more intently. Apparently, Tewes was a serious student of Dr. Lombroso and the first criminal identification system in history, and why not? It lent credence to the study of phrenology. "To be sure," Tewes continued, "his studies remain extremely controversial, as—"

"As well his theories should!" he countered.

"—as his theories are based on measurements and statistics derived from insane asylums across Europe, but Lombroso used the science of phrenology—skull reading—to determine whether or not a true criminal was *under* his thumb or not."

"That's funny." Ransom downed the final half of his second Pabst.

"Lombroso measured the forehead and skull, and his findings said that a certain percentage of the population remain nihilistic cave men in heredity—where it counts! Here." Tewes pointed to his brain. "That evolution is not so tidy a business as it is haphazard, random even. De-evolution may play a major part."

"And others say we're all descended from a meat-eating killer ape. Ever e't raw meat, Doctor?"

"Regardless of mad notions that we're all descended from murderous apes, Lombroso's theories and statistics say that criminals are *born*—often with telltale knots on their cranial bones."

"My God, that would not include me." Ransom gingerly touched the knot left by Muldoon. "So we put away anyone with a knot on his head? Please, Dr. Tewes, I was just beginning to take you seriously, and now this. You can't honestly subscribe to the theory that killers are born and not nurtured?"

"I do and I don't. I think it a bit of both."

"Then you can't seriously go by Lombroso!"

"Only one technique of many I use. I combine a number of approaches to reach my conclusions."

"But deciding a man is guilty by the size of his brow, how deep set the eyes? How many bumps on the head? Isn't that extreme . . . like stepping back in time, say to . . . to the Salem witchcraft trials and spectral evidence?"

"It's only a starting point to jump off. We're all of us working in the dark, and thank God for the microscope, so that one day in the not too distant future—in the early 1900s I predict—we'll be capable of distinguishing animal from human blood."

"To separate the murderer from the neighborhood butcher, yes. That would be a boon. You've no idea how many guilty blokes've got off claiming chicken blood!"

Tewes stopped short, realizing Ransom was engaged with the man at the bar, their eyes locked. Jane watched the small drama unfold: Ransom raises a glass to Tug, and Tug offers his up and drains it. Each sizing up the other, each knowing their paths will cross again in a less amiable setting. Tug tosses down a coin and stalks out. Ransom's eyes never leave him until he is completely gone, but he continues to speak. "If a man is apelike in appearance, perhaps he is a gentle giant. But not your man Tug."

"But suppose others who react to your gentle giant have treated him like an ape all of his life due to his very appearance? Doesn't it make sense for him to commit a crime to get back at a society that condemns him for his deformities?"

"He who is treated like an animal becomes one?"

"Yes."

"Like that elephant man in London?"

"All right, there is an example. When treated with respect and dignity, he became a gentleman, but treated as a sideshow freak, he lived life as a carnival animal."

"Hmmm . . . point taken." Ransom finished his coffee and then downed another beer that'd appeared. "Sounds as if we agree more than we disagree on Lombroso, Doctor. But tell me, why'd you get involved in this case?"

"I thought it a quick way to build a reputation, to use my phrenology in a manner . . . well as a way to—"

"Bombast the public? Scam, hoax?"

"All right. I was getting desperate, and it does not speak well of me, but I saw or rather felt I must do it, not for myself but for Gabby. Tuition and clothes and all her medical books."

"And the whole show with the head, a freak show?"

"Not entirely. I've had more people coming to me for help, and I've helped more than I've harmed."

"Yes . . . well, your dubious services did not take with my Merielle, now in her grave."

"She's not the first patient who's come to me in a state of deep emotional distress and depression that has lingered for years without relief. Sometimes I don't get them soon enough. Sometimes they come as last resort, when only if they'd come sooner, then perhaps . . . well . . . it's all supposition."

"I've some notion of this killer myself. I've feelings that are like his, feelings of wanting to kill someone or some thing. And I feel him near."

"That's . . . well frankly . . . frightening."

"As well it should be, Doctor. I glimpse only small snatches of Merielle's attacker. The fellow who once pimped her out, Jervis, I hear from my snitch, that he's left the city fearful I'm coming for 'im."

"Do you think this fellow Jervis killed her?"

"He'd never have the guts. So afraid now, according to O'Malley, that he ran on the assumption I'd be coming for him."

"What sense then do you have of this multiple killer, Ransom?"

"What sense do you have of this killer?"

"Vague . . . a dark presence at her back, a fleeting glimpse of a cape. Expensive, well-polished boots, something out of a State Street window."

"You talked to the homeless fellow who grabbed the wallet, didn't you, Tewes?"

Jane confessed she had. "It may not've been a coincidence that mirror coming down with her head."

"Meaning?"

"Her place was no larger than the men's room at the train station."

Ransom considered this. "She spent a lot of time before that mirror."

"She'd've been held against the mirror in the same manner as the boy."

"Blind me . . . looking into her eyes as she died."

"In top hat and cape, he'd pass for a real gent in Polly's eyes."

"And he whistles tunes." Ransom held out a small coin but it was no coin. It was a silvery metal button with the letters CPS stamped on it.

"What is it?"

"Found in the rubble."

"But what does it mean?"

"It may mean our killer shops at Carson, Pirie, Scott, the department store."

"He shops at Carson's?" She sounded incredulous.

"Speak of State Street windows. He may perhaps work there."

"What's next? How do you proceed to interrogate everyone who walks in and out of a department store on the busiest street in the city?"

"Maybe . . . just maybe she ripped this from his coat in the hope I'd find it."

Jane gave him this fantasy. "Yes . . . most likely."

"You think so?"

"In one fashion or another we're all interconnected. Her last thoughts were likely of you crashing the door down, saving her."

"Connected. Sounds right."

Tewes leaned in toward Ransom, sensing he needed to hear more. "Call me a fraud if you like, a spiritualist, a necromancer, but I believe images we retain in our minds that become our personal ghosts are electromagnetic in nature. And I believe that we're all intertwined with magnetic rays that live in and around us."

"Magnetic rays that live inside us?" He sounded both skeptical and curious.

"In our minds, yes, and our bodies. We're made up of millions of atoms. This much science tells us, and how are these atoms held together but by a magical magnetism of soul and miniature telepathy between these atoms? They hold our very cells in harmonious bondage."

"I suppose you're writing a book on all this"—he stopped short of calling it nonsense—"I mean how it all relates to your phrenology, your visions."

"Do not tempt me. In this magnetic field I refer to, we all touch upon one another's thoughts, feelings, aspirations in an empathic field that God wants us one and all to acknowledge but most . . . well most of us are blind to it, blind in sight and touch."

"And I suppose you're more attuned and open to this field than anyone else?"

"Than the average, yes. It's a biochemical connection that holds our thoughts in place and creates the miracle of thought leaping across time and space just as there are necessary *interstices* between cells in the body."

"*Inter*-what?"

"Damn it, Detective, have you never seen living human tissue below the microscope?"

"I have . . . at the morgue . . . on occasion, yes."

"Tissue in a dead man living on, yes."

"I never thought of it quite like that."

"And that life can be sustained in a Petri dish indefinitely."

"It can? I had no idea."

"The magnetism inherent in all life, sir. You've seen it with your own eyes. And the human brain, that marvel of nature . . . it's the single most complex organism in the universe. An electrochemical device not unlike Philo Keane's camera in that regard, powered by electrochemical energy."

"You're losing me, Doctor."

"I believe the brain somehow stores messages, even after death, in some strange way only the future or God might reveal."

"Stores images like a camera, as in memories—even *after* death? Philo Keane know about this?"

"Memory lives on . . . at least at the cellular level, the level too miniature for the human eye. Cells living on, functioning for a time even after all activity ceases in the body."

"Cells living on after . . . continuing to store messages? Do you know what this sounds like, Dr. Tewes?"

"I know what it sounds like, Jules Verne, H. G. Wells, the fantastic ravings of some lunatic storyteller, but science has always lagged behind the prophets. Look, if you pluck a leaf from a tree and place it below the microscope, the cells are still alive and active."

"And you think the same is true of the brain?"

"Yes, on a cellular level, absolutely. Look, I know you could have me committed, but I'm trusting you with my innermost beliefs here. Do you see this table before you, Alastair?"

"Of course, I do. Why?"

"At the microscopic level, the atoms in this tabletop're spinning about, bombarding one another, electrically charged both positively and negatively, in a constant state of flux—movement, but not to the naked eye! We only see—"

"A solid, a cold dead block of wood."

"Cut from a long dead tree."

"So in a sense . . . it remains alive although in appearance dead."

"Take comfort that your Merielle's soul is at least as active now as this tabletop."

He'd meant to entrap this phrenological medium by encouraging him to "read" his sore head, but he hadn't counted on such talk.

"Your killer is a man no one suspects; like the table, superficially apparent yet not so apparent."

"Taken for granted, you mean. . . . I could go to Carson, Pirie, Scott, stake out the store all day, see him more than once come and go and still not see him?"

"Precisely. Dead perhaps on the surface, comes alive only when he kills. A man with well-polished boots and his clothing tailored, a cloak, a cane, a top hat."

"A description fitting thousands going about our streets. It's not a great help, Doctor."

"But it tells you *not* to focus on the usual suspects like Tug."

"Agreed, it'd only be a waste of time."

"Comparatively speaking, the Tugs of Chicago're mere muggers to this monster deviant."

"This creep is no known entity."

"No anarchist, second-story man, or habitual wife beater, no. This madman is unique, clever, educated, possibly upper crust."

"Or plays it well?"

"He's interested in shocking us all, Inspector, from the police to the citizen at the fair. It's a bloody game to 'im."

"A game? Of course it's a game. But what is the goal? Why does he kill? Just to shock us? There must be more."

"As mundane a motive as it may seem, you must accept it.

There's a strong possibility he's only interested in the hide-and-seek, the hunt, his mind in some manner captivated . . . in rapt awe with the idea of controlling when and where death occurs."

"A twisted angel of death."

Dr. Tewes finished another lager.

"Is there any more? Are you withholding anything?"

"If Fenger's not told you, you should know that Polly passed out after the carotid artery was compromised. The same moment that the garrote sliced a three hundred and sixty-degree cut around the neck, she was gone. Mercifully, she'd've felt no lingering pain from the garrote or the fire."

"Thank you, Doctor."

"Trauma of the attack itself would've been like an attack of chills to the system, but I suspect her last thoughts were of you."

Ransom held back a tear.

"All guesswork, but I believe we must try to understand both the victim and him—our killer—in order to prevent future killings."

They sat in silence, imagining the horror this monster had brought to Chicago. A pair of warriors fighting a ghostly plague they didn't understand. And they felt alone against the enemy. "What next indeed," Ransom muttered.

"The killer is mobile. Moves 'bout the city effortlessly. Likely means money, well-to-do family, I fear and so—"

"Yes, has his own carriage and driver." Ransom brightened. "They theorized old Jack the Ripper did it that way."

"Blends."

"And is well versed on our city terrain."

"He's cunning and quite possibly enjoys working with his hands. Perhaps likes to make things . . . as with his garrote. It is unique to him. He loves his weapon. It grants him power."

"Ahhh . . . but it's not so unique after all." Ransom held up the same garrote—crisscrossed with a diamond center.

"There is then something unique about this man's relationship with the weapon, I tell you. It's that twisted."

"All right, perhaps he talks to it. I won't argue the point."

"And one more thing."

"Yes?"

"While he may be as well off as Mr. Field himself, he is small in stature."

"How can you possibly know his stature, Doctor?"

"The angle of the garrote—the force—pulling downward. Polly was as tall as you, yet—"

"Yes, he'd pulled downward even on Purvis. It appears the killer is rather short. Clever of you to've noticed, and right."

"I find the so-called investigation full of holes."

"Ahhh . . . you would. Look, we'll soon have a break in the case. I get reports daily from Dot'n'Carry."

"Dot and who?"

"My street snitch. My most reliable spy. If ever I write my memoir, my homeless friend will have to be acknowledged. The poor wretched gimp."

"Gimp?"

"He has been with you for days, Doctor, so unobtrusive you've not noticed. Blends as you put it."

Jane did a 360-degree turn, taking in everyone here and on the street through the window where Chicago's teeming life passed by. Commerce continued unabated. Vendors rolled portable carts, selling anything imaginable. A number of people with canes limped by, along with black hansom cabs rolling in and out of the window frame.

The fiddler in the corner had stopped to swill his ale, halving the glass before starting up a lively rendition of "Comin' Through the Rye." The tune livened up the patrons all round, and even Ransom's toe began to tap, although he seemed unaware of this, as his thoughts remained on the killings, how the only witness they had said the killer was whistling this same popular tune.

Dr. Tewes was not unaware of Ransom's toe-tapping, as he was tapping on Tewes's shoe—a man's size seven, stuffed at the toes. A man with a harmonica joined in with the fiddler. Patrons began to clap as if clawing their way from a dull hell.

Young Waldo Denton entered and ordered up a bucket of beer. "Fetchin' for Philo, no doubt," said Ransom to Tewes.

Waldo gave a glance in Ransom's direction and nodded at him and Tewes, grinned before rushing out again, the bucket of beer slopping along his pants leg. "Boy acts as if Philo might beat him if he dallies." Ransom then looked with a mix of disdain and admiration at those having fun.

"Garroting's a cowardly method of dispatching someone, catching 'im from behind, not facing your victim, eye to eye," he began. "And yet twice now he's killed victims before a mirror."

"If you're right . . . he likes to watch 'em die—"

"And to see himself in the act."

"Behavior says something about who he is," Jane explained.

"I believe a lot of what you say about the makeup of this monster is well . . . useful information."

"Almost sounded like a compliment in there somewhere. Now . . . with whom do I speak about recompense?"

"Recompense?"

"Yes, I'm sure you've heard the word before. I expect pay as an independent consultant to you, Inspector."

"Aha . . . like any other leech on the Chicago payroll."

"Have you seen the cost of bread lately? Been to the fair?"

"I've no time for such trivialities."

"Perhaps had you taken time . . ."

"Go on."

". . . you'd've been on that wheel in the sky with Merielle last night instead of pumping me for information."

"Damn your hide, Doctor! What about your daughter, Gabrielle? Have you given a moment's thought to the possibility that she, rather than Purvis, could've been killed that night they were at the fair?"

"It has indeed kept me awake nights."

"Perhaps had you bothered taking Gabby to the fair, she'd not've been with Purvis that night! And what about your sister, the one you treat like a housemaid?"

"Leave Jane out of this, and Gabby as well. They're none of your affair." Jane sensed her ruse was finally up with him, but she could not be certain. She held her silence. She wanted so much to reveal her true self to Alastair, as she had Dr. Fenger, *before* he read about it in one of Chicago's twenty-six newspapers, or heard it from Fenger, or got it between the eyes from Kohler, or his snitch!

As if taking up a challenge, Ransom boldly replied, "I just may call on your sister, Dr. Tewes."

"What?" Tewes was clearly stunned by this.

"She's new to the city. She must be curious about the fair."

"Is this some sort of threat, Alastair?"

"Threat?"

"Worm information out of my sister to get—"

"I'm merely wondering if she's curious about the wheel, the fair, the pavilions?"

"Of course she is but—"

"But you've had no time to show Jane the city or the fair?"

"Yes . . . I mean, no, but—"

"Someone should."

"She is seeing a fellow who intends just that," Jane lied.

"*Ahhh* . . . that's good."

"I will take my leave of you now, sir," said a more composed Dr. Tewes.

Ransom watched the funny little doctor saunter from the tavern as if a sudden fear had overtaken him.

CHAPTER 18

His father's name was Campaneua, his mother Jarno, and together they straddled the earth, wreaking havoc in both Europe and America as anarchists. Mother had kept a scrapbook, clippings on train derailments, bombings, bank robberies, and even assassinations they'd carried out. They'd been lovers in a war against established government, communists of a sort, and they had a son born of their union, but wedlock in their estimation amounted to just another social contract meant to make sheep of people, right alongside religion and centralized government. Just another fabrication, a contract with myth—another tool of the enemy. They purposefully abstained from marriage as just another form of mind-slavery, a ritualized cultural iconoclastic opiate. As such, marriage looked, felt, tasted, sounded, and smelled like just another part of the cultural bag of tricks undermining true opinion and intellect. A conspiracy to keep the common man in place, from the Bible to the U.S. Constitution—all designed to keep a harmonious peace among the sheep.

His anarchist parents had named him Roberre Jarno-Campaneua the Second, and his mother had brought him up to believe in himself entirely and in the causes of anarchy. But anarchy appeared on the wane, and he could find no compatriots this side of the ocean—someone not brainwashed in the mores and values of capitalism, someone who might appreciate him—men willing to die for the cause, as his father had seven years ago at the hands of one small-minded, now crippled police detective here in Chicago. Another killer like himself—one he hated with all the venom inside him—Alastair Ransom.

Sleepeck Stumpf—a secret name given him by the ghost of his father—had met few men today to rival his father. He'd like to set a bomb in a busy thoroughfare or train station himself. Do the old man proud. But it'd have to wait until after his vendetta against Ransom was settled for good and all.

Times had gone sour for anarchy in America. While the movement of the anarchists thrived in Europe, dotting the continent, here in America, it'd quelled to a murmur—thanks in large measure to the enactment of labor laws resulting from Chicago's Haymarket Riot. The enemy had won that day.

Ransom had almost been killed by a bomb that his father may well have set, the same bomb that killed seven coppers at Haymarket. He'd no way to substantiate this. Nonetheless, no one among the anarchist communities had ever claimed responsibility for the Haymarket bomb, and as his father'd been murdered before the bomb went off, it could well have been his work. Several prominent labor leaders and a handful of anarchists had been arrested, given blanket injustice, tried quickly, and hung—seven all told. There ought to've been a world outcry at the injustice of it all, the quick *prairie justice* as some called it, but none came. Blood was required. One imprisoned anarchist managed to kill himself in his cell, cheating the citizenry of Chicago of their justice.

One anarchist, a woman, had slipped away; she'd gone all these years undetected, living a quiet retirement after learning of her common law husband's death. Roberre's mother.

He had memories of his father holding him, playing with him, caring for him, but it'd been too long and his features had faded. All he had was a worn, aged daguerreotype, what little Mother'd told him, the news clippings of his father's doings, and a rough police sketch done as a wanted poster by some long-ago police artist created from faulty accounts. According to his mother, they had his nose too large, too flat, his ears exaggerated, along with his lips, and they displayed his eyes as wide and maniacal, along with an overhanging brow—all wrong. In fact, his father had mild features and could pass for a bank teller or accountant. "Put 'em in a suit and tie, and the man could step through any door," Mother would say, a twinkle in her eye.

"You should've known your father, such passion," she'd drummed into him. "Such a blazing fire in his soul. So inspiring, and all he wanted was a better life, not for himself alone, not even for just you and me, his family, but for the masses."

Roberre heard this every day of his young life, from his mother, whose maiden name had been Stumpf.

And so he'd come to Chicago, where he'd dug up his mother from Potter's Field and buried her anew on the farmstead outside Chicago she'd called home until the bank had taken it from her. But he'd also come to avenge his father, and he meant to do it his way, and not by bomb—as it left too much to chance. He meant to serve up this vengeance against the man who'd executed his father by fire in the manner of cold vengeance, a vengeance that would bring that giant of a man to his knees before killing him outright.

He'd do it quietly, carefully. He'd made himself invisible to go about Ransom's damnable city freely, and he would strike viperlike with the garrote he'd made with his own hands when just a boy, when Roberre Jarno-Campaneua the Second, a.k.a. Stumpf began contemplating killing the man who'd turned his father into a human torch.

Across the city at Ransom's home and in his nightmare

It felt as if it were happening all over again; even the sounds in his ears on the day they'd cornered that Frenchy bastard, who planned to set off a bomb. Ransom had tracked down the son-of-a-sow, and during a Chicago storm, deep inside a large warehouse, several coppers had worked the man over. He sat beaten and strapped to a chair. They tried to pry from him where he'd planted the bomb and the names of accomplices.

"I tell you nothing! I am French citizen. Have rights. You can't detain me like this," he kept saying. "You are law in Chy-cago! So must obey rules. Is not so?"

Angry at his smugness, Ransom kicked out the chair, sending him toppling. Another uniformed cop named Nathan Kohler then doused him in the kerosene that Ransom had threatened to use, the fumes so powerful they made both Campaneua and Ransom choke.

Now Campaneua and Ransom stared wide-eyed from each side of the huge wooden match. Unlit for the moment. Neither man saw anything else—not the other men in the room, not one another, not their surroundings. Neither man saw the vegetable crates or the huge warehouse door that stood so near. Neither saw one another any longer as Ransom contemplated striking the match, the storm outside replaced by hollow silence in his ears.

Ransom didn't see Kohler, just back of him, strike a match either, and when Nathan tossed his lit cigar onto the man lying tied in the sawdust, all he heard was a *whoosh*. The flaming, flailing sight backed him off as the dying man cried out his name: "Roberre Jarno-Campaneua!" The last words he uttered as his body burned before the amazed eyes of the four Chicago policemen who'd been ordered to get information from him at any cost.

And Ransom sat bolt upright, awake, a feeling of Campaneua's ghost in the room, alongside all the garrote victims, including the unborn child and Cliffton and Merielle. They'd stalked him to his bed, each whispering some unintelligible gibberish understood only by the dead as Ransom broke into a blistering sweat.

The following day at the home of Dr. Tewes

The phone rang several times before Gabby picked up. She still felt tentative using the new invention, but the moment she heard it was Inspector Ransom, she calmed and brightened. They made small talk of the weather until finally Gabby broke down in tears, telling him how sorry she was over the news that he'd lost a friend as she had—"possibly to the same maniac roaming the city. And all while I pushed pastries on you the other night."

He asked her not to cry, telling her all would be put right. Then he added, "I actually called to speak to your aunt."

"My aunt?"

"Have it in mind to perhaps take her to the fair, if . . . if that is, you do not forbid her seeing me, Gabrielle."

"The fair? Really? You and . . . Jane?" Gulping, she added, "I guess that'd be up to my aunt, although my father might have something to say."

Suddenly, Tewes came on the line. "Jane is a grown woman. She can make her own decisions in such matters."

"Good of you to say so, James."

"I see no dependency issue that was the foundation of your and Merielle's relationship, Inspector. I suppose, if Jane Francis is of a mind, then by all means—"

"Then how early may I visit?"

Is he baiting me? Had his squirrelly, wooden-legged snitch, called Dot'n'Carry, seen me change from Tewes to Jane through a window sash? Does the detective know about Kohler and me? Play it out, she finally decided, wherever it goes. "Ahhh . . . I should think seven, sevenish . . . after dinner."

"Very good."

"Then I shall *warn* Jane of your calling." Jane fought off a feeling of confoundedness. Here was a man in mourning one day, brokering a courtship the next? It must be to unmask Tewes, part of the hunt.

"Then I shall soon come 'round."

"G'day, Inspector." Jane placed phone to wall cradle to find herself held prisoner by Gabrielle's disbelief. "You preach that I not play with fire! A man like—"

"This doesn't concern you, young lady. Get to your studies."

"But only the other day . . . what was it you called him? *A thug with a badge!*"

"Keep thy enemies close."

"You hypocrite."

"Gabby!"

"Go then! Dance with the devil! Draw attention! Yet you shout at me with poor dead Cliff? What of your *precious* practice? What if Inspector Ransom sees through it all?"

"He won't."

"He came damn close getting you drunk! He's notorious!"

"He's . . . that is, his asking me—*Jane*—out . . . it's—"

"A surprise?"

"He is unpredictability personified."

Gabby looked at her mother anew. "Hold on . . . you're flattered, aren't you?"

"Why nonsense. I must take care is all. He's seen me. I must be . . . natural."

"Ahhh . . ." Gabby paced off and returned. "All right, but if you're to do this right, we've got to do up your hair, and Mother, a little rouge and lipstick, please."

"I'll not waste a moment primping for that man."

"Really? Mother! You must lay a foundation, make some preparations. I'll help you. I've got new cosmetics from Carson's, so be here at six."

"An hour before his arrival?"

"Right . . . more time's needed. Make it five."

Gabby hugged her mother and whispered in her ear, "Still, I worry."

"Stop it."

"He's so darkly . . ."

"Mysterious?"

"Notorious."

"Ten percent true, ninety percent bull-swallop."

"Mother! Bull-swallop? Is that the same as bullshit?"

"Gabby!"

Gabby followed her mother into her bedroom. "Well . . . Inspector Ransom uses the term pig-swallop for—"

"*Gabby!* Watch your tongue! Is this what you're learning at Northwestern Medical? How to swear like a sailor?"

"I'm a liberated woman, a suffragette now. I think I can say *bullshit* when the need arises, and this is a time for—"

"You've been sneaking to meetings with that fanatical friend of yours, Lucy Wistera, haven't you?"

"Lucy talks sense! It's time we had a say-so in politics. Look at how G'damn awful the world is with men running things since Roman times!"

Jane sat at her makeup counter, carefully applying her mustache. "You, young woman, are going to get your mouth washed out with lye soap if you—"

"Oh, please, Mother!"

"I raised you a lady! Not a tramp of the streets!"

"You ought to be in the rally, Mother. You'd be a beacon to all women everywhere as Dr. Jane Francis, but no! You've gotta go about dressed as a man!"

"That is enough! Taking such a tone, young lady! What is happening with you?"

"You taught me to stand up for my rights! It's time you did! As for taking God's name in vain, if he's a man like *men* insist, then Lucy says it's time He got us the vote!"

Turning from her mirror, Jane stared Gabby in the eye. "Look here, I'm trying to make a life for us, to—to keep you in school, and you need to put all effort and con—"

"Concentration, I know, into my studies! But damn it what confounded good're studies when the end result is . . . well, look at you, Mother! Having to masquerade as a man in order to get equal pay and equal treatment? Do you plan to vote in the upcoming elections as Dr. Tewes as well, Mother?"

Jane's voice cracked when she replied, "I raised you a lady, groomed you a professional, not some pseudo-

ntellectual, Bible-thumping, horn-blowing brat with a cause
nd a flag made of bloomers! Do you have a notion what's to
ecome of Lucy Wistera and her pack once they've been
toned and arrested and jailed?"

"Stoned and jailed by ignorance. People who haven't a
clue as to what a suffragette is!"

"Well, you're right there. Most of the city can't read English! In fact, most can't read in any language!"

A huge silence came down around them, and as Dr. Tewes
stared back at Jane in the mirror, the doorbell rang. "See to
the door; if it's for Dr. Tewes, show them into the clinic."

"Oh, it's just Waldo Denton. He's becoming a nuisance."

"Where did you say you met him? At the university?"

"Not exactly, but yes."

"What?" Jane's confusion was clear even through her
makeup."

"I catch his cab most days out to the school, and . . . he's
made it his business to flirt."

"I hope you have enough sense to not encourage it. A
cabby!"

"He's apprenticing as a photographer and is trying to get
me to sit for him."

"Don't fall for it!" Jane bristled. "Get rid of him. Get your
mind off the vote, photographic modeling, boys, and onto
your studies!"

"You're so romantic, Mother."

Evening at the Tewes residence

"It's him! Inspector Ransom," Gabby called out to Jane.
Just the other side of their sheer drapes paced the pipe-
chewing Ransom.

"Now behave, young woman. Use civility but stall him."

"You talk of civility," Gabby replied, stealing a glance at
the infamous Inspector she secretly admired, "while lying to
a police official?"

He looked the size of a Montana grizzly she'd seen depicted in *Harper's Illustrated Weekly*. Ominous and threatening and alluring at once, always striking just the right pose—in tune with his reputation. Her friend Lucy had once, in passing, said of the notorious detective that he doled out his own unique brand of justice before any judge or jury got the case. Said Ransom gained full confessions more than any other inspector in the city, the county, and perhaps the country by employing horrible instruments of torture like the widow-maker, the thumb screw, the rack, the spiked cage, the firebrand, and jagged broken bottles fused to chains, while ordinary coppers used only nightsticks and saps. According to rumors repeated by Lucy— "Occurs in a secret place 'long the river, close 'nough when a prisoner expires, his body's tossed out a window into the dirty waters to float far from any *interrogation*, and no one the wiser."

Such talk had begun with Millie Thebold saying, "No one speaks of it, but this is Ransom's city . . ."

"Meaning?" Gabby had asked, taking the bait.

"Meaning," replied Lucy, "nothing happens without getting back to him in one fashion or another."

Millie chimed in again. "Police talk! Means Chicago is Ransom's city, like Paris, France, is Vjdoc's city or was 'fore he died." She then held up a dime novel, the title reading *The Adventures of Inspector Vjdoc.*

Gabby opened the door, smiling wide. "Welcome once again to our humble home, Inspector. You look quite dashing tonight."

The sounds of the World's Columbian Exposition competed with horse hooves over the cobblestones as cabs came and went, bringing people to and from the gay lights and activity of the fair this warm summer's eve. Ransom had been feeling awkward, unsure what they might talk about, he and the lovely Miss Jane, until he finally blurted out a comment. "I am often too serious, too involved in my work, with not enough time to relax much less visit a place like this."

"I'd've never guessed," she teased.

He felt comforted that she could so easily joke with him. "What about yourself?"

"What of me?" she countered.

"I never see you about. Is it *workworkwork* with you as well? When do you smile . . . I mean have fun . . . have a laugh, an afternoon in the park?"

"Me? Smile? I can smile even when screaming inside!"

"Then perhaps you ought to have been in the theater?"

"I meant only that I can sing when I wanna cry, and cry when happy."

"Anything else I should know about you, Miss Jane?"

How much did he know? Had Dr. Fenger given her up? What else but cloddish, male curiosity prompted these questions?

"If I may ask," he added.

"I fight for my every belief . . . stand against injustice when I see it."

"You sound a *resolute* woman, Miss Jane."

They'd arrived at the Ferris wheel, and he purchased a ticket for each of them. Climbing into the enclosed gondola, designed like a train car berth, she replied, "Resolute? Hmmm. Well, when I see a perfectly good solution going unused, yes, I can be resolute."

"And I sense in you a caring, giving person just in seeing how you treat Dr. Tewes's daughter—almost as your own."

"I'd go without shoes if it'd help Gabby get through medical school. I love her unconditionally, and I cry when that child excels, and I cheer when she succeeds."

This seemed at odds to him with what Gabby had imparted of her relationship with her aunt. "Then you have no children of your own?"

"I do not, but I'm happiest on hearing of a new birth or a new marriage in the family."

"But you are not married?"

"No . . . I am not, sir."

The gondola swept upward with them in it, creating an exhilarating, whirring breeze all about. It was a feeling of flight that neither had ever experienced.

"And what else can I learn of you tonight?"

She looked deeply into his eyes. "Well, I'm just a normal woman. My heart breaks when a family member or friend dies, yet I feel strong in the face of death—as I know certainly that death is no end."

"Must be comforting, your certainty." Ransom thought of Merielle's awful end, still like a festering wound in his chest.

"I know of a certainty that a hug and a kiss can heal a wound," she countered, "or a broken heart."

"Is that so?" *She reads minds, too,* he thought.

"And I believe the heart of a woman can change this world, and is in fact what makes this world work."

"Bully then for you, madam."

"I know a woman can do *more* than give birth."

"And what *more* is that, if I may play devil's advocate—the vote?"

The wheel had brought them full circle and was up and away again. Her hair lifted in the wind.

"It is long, long overdue for women to have the right to vote in this country, sir, and the suffrage movement will one day triumph. Imagine it, men systematically withholding the rights of women because of their misunderstanding us, assuming tears a weakness of the heart, assuming emotion a faintness of character, making it a crime to have feelings, and to label emotion as somehow *damaging*."

"Please, I didn't mean to start us on the wrong foot. I'm on your side."

"Really? A rare fellow indeed."

"I think it a just and fair cause."

She nodded, a smile softening her features. "All true. Did you feel the same way about the labor movement when you had to stand against the protestors and agitators and anarchists?"

"Haymarket got completely out of control. A lot of unanswered questions still."

"The explosion, you mean?"

"That and what led up to it. What happened at command, the orders we got, the bad timing of it all. We marched down there to our fate as if . . . as if it had been—"

"Scripted?"

"Exactly."

"But isn't all history from hindsight going to appear to us as having been fated or as you say, scripted? Do you really think anyone meant to set you up, I mean anyone within the ranks of the department—your own leadership?"

"How do you know my thinking on this? Who've you gotten all this from? Dr. Tewes?"

"I keep my ear to the ground. Met your snitch the other day on Dr. Tewes's back stair, sneaking around like a rat. I see why they call him Dot'n'Carry. That rattle he makes with his crooked little cane—"

"He lost good use of the leg and an entire foot in the war. Inside the man's head there is more of Chicago than anyone I know. He is fascinating to listen to if someone takes the time."

"Or puts him on the payroll? Perhaps you're a softy, Mr. *Ahhh* Inspector Ransom."

"Please, call me Alastair."

There was a silence between them, the sound of barkers and the fair music rising up to where they rocked in the gondola. She then broke into his thoughts. "Black men have had the vote since just after the Civil War. Women are only asking for the same rights as any man, and in the U.S. Constitution and the Bill of Rights, the term men in 'all men are created equal' is genderless and refers to all mankind!"

"You'll get no argument from me."

"Well what fun is that?"

"You're really quite the woman."

"Really now?"

"Perhaps just the woman to bring the vote to Chicago."

"As I said, I can do a lot more than be a . . . a . . . an incubator for some man's seed. I have it within me to bring joy and hope and compassion and ideals into the world. Every man and woman does."

He straightened at her words, quietly weighing each.

She continued, nonstop. "I can bring moral support to family, friends, and colleagues."

"Then you have a lot to say and do in this life."

"And too little time to do it in."

"Sounds to me like you've a lot to . . . to give a man . . . any man."

"Nooo, no, no sir, not just any man will do for me, Inspector. Most men fail to appreciate a woman of intellect, opinions, and—"

"Again no argument from me."

"You can be such a good listener, Alastair, when you sit long enough. This inventor, Mr. Ferris, perhaps the true purpose of his wheel is to make people stop and sit and talk."

"To speak of things that otherwise would not get said?"

"Perhaps . . . to get things said and done."

"Things like . . . like well . . . this!" Alastair surprised her with a kiss, and she surprised him by returning it, as hers was a long, hard, soft, changing kiss that meant to steal his breath away, and it did—just as the ride came to an end.

They disembarked the wheel, she laughing and stepping off ahead of him, leaving the big detective feeling awkward and unsure and a little self-conscious and guilty. All the things he'd wanted for Merielle . . . all the promises to ply her with attention. All of it he was doing now, so soon after Merielle's death, with another woman—a woman he hardly knew. *It's police business is all*, he kept telling himself.

He had as yet to make arrangements for Merielle's burial, but he instinctively knew that Fenger was taking good care. He worked to banish thoughts of Merielle for the time being, following after Jane instead.

She abruptly turned on him and breathlessly asked, "Can we go up again? It's the most amazing feeling . . . like flying. So liberating."

Ransom only partially frowned as he patted himself down for the change to purchase additional tickets.

They sat atop the Ferris wheel once more, staring down at the dizzying lights of Chicagoland from the spiraling buildings of downtown along the waterfront and Michigan Avenue to the rustic old homes and the worst, lowliest hovels of the South Levee district. The multitude of lights and burning fires blinked like stars aground. It was made the more magnificent by the gas-lit street lamps.

He began pointing out the tallest downtown structures, giving each a name. "There is the Studebaker Building. Four hundred ten South Michigan. Built by Mr. Beman in eighteen eighty-five."

"Where they make all the fine carriages?" she asked.

"That'd be it, yes, and there, see the Auditorium?"

"Yes, but what is going up beside it?"

"Across Congress Street, an annex hotel to the Auditorium."

"Yes, yes . . . so amazing from up here."

"Bit farther south is the Richelieu Hotel, also built in 'eighty-five."

"And the trim building beyond?"

"Chicago Athletic Association—just gone up this year. Beyond that the Smith, Gaylord & Cross Building—old at 'eighty-two."

"I suppose every inch of Michigan Avenue will have been cleared and sold and a building put up to reach to the stars."

"So-called progress. Land speculation and real estate development."

"You disapprove?"

"Ahhh . . . it's not all to the good, no."

"Larger isn't necessarily better, you mean?"

"I know I'm in the wrong business, but the sorta money worship that's swept the city . . . it's just not for me."

"Still, way up here it all looks beautiful. The lights at the Art Institute and along the boulevard."

"I warrant it's the best way to see the city—day or night."

"And the pavilions of our magnificent White City."

"The city spared no expense on the fair."

"Mind-boggling, how huge it is," she agreed.

"A nightmare for a small police force to cover."

Despite the wheel's having filled with people as it made its 270-foot arch above the city and lake, the couple felt alone, unable to see any other passengers from their gondola cocoon. Below, the fair crowds moved like schools of fish: coming and going, darting here, chasing there, the fairways teeming.

Alone yet every gondola occupied, and in one of them sat a killer, a killer who with eyes closed relived his murders, particularly his last two life-taking adventures. In his mind's eye he again killed Polly Pete, tightening his fists around the garrote that now dangled between his knees.

As if happening this moment, he brings the garrote to its full cutting power through *his* hands, the daydream so vivid, so real, so fulfilling—made the more so by holding tight to Polly's ring while riding the Ferris wheel he'd shared with her so recently. He smiled, eyes closed, as he calmly reminisced about *this night* . . . a 270-foot above-ground dream.

Just as he feels Polly's life in his hands, under his complete dominion, slipping away, just as he becomes the god who decides she dies, on that eclipse of time during which he might've allowed her sorry life continuance, or not . . .

Stumpf too had had a good time with Polly—he and Stumpf—as when Polly had taken her last gasp, tasted her blood spewing from both sides of her mouth, deepening that faint provocative tincture painted in her cleavage. It'd all made Stumpf and him giddy and wet.

From high atop the Ferris wheel, the killer stared down at the gathering crowd around the lagoon boat rides. Uniformed police'd converged on the Lover's Lane Canal.

Appears Stumpf's been a bad boy again, he thought, knowing that he and Stumpf were one and the same—like two men inside one brain.

Other passengers on Mr. Ferris's wheel noticed all the to-do at the lagoon, seeing a strange fire on the water. While Stumpf appeared a gentleman alone on the wheel, he'd in fact begun the evening with two lovely companions. They'd taken two boats out on the lagoon—double the pleasure.

His friends remained in the lagoon far below. One in the water, at least in part, the other in a now flaming rowboat; both dispatched by the Phantom.

Through the trees, flames winked, and Stumpf watched authorities hook and drag the fiery craft ashore. Desperately, men doused his latest victim.

The killer saw from this moving position, every second another perspective. Interesting altogether, each separate moment of the ride as if sitting inside one of those hand-held daguerreotype machines people paid to watch at the 3 Penny Opera on Lincoln and Fullerton.

Around him, he heard others speculating from the safety of their perch on the excitement below. A series of gasps, whispers, cooing like pigeons, and the sound of giggling and kissing.

A slight scent of kerosene adhered to him, and his nails had become ragged at having scaled the bridge abutment from the lagoon. But he had soaked a handkerchief before then to swipe at the larger, noticeable blood splotches on his boots, pants leg, and cape.

He gave more thought to the girl in the flaming boat. Most assuredly as lurid an image as anything created by Edgar Allan Poe. It must garner front-page attention and eclipse the Columbian Exposition. As the giant wheel lifted up and up again, he braced himself and watched the activity he'd set in motion below. When the wheel stopped with him atop it, he stood to open a small window. He shouted into the wind as he had that night with Polly Pete, perhaps in this very gondola, crying against the wind, "I'm King of the Fair!"

*   *   *

The Ferris wheel continued its rise and fall. Above the killer in black, Ransom and Jane Francis peered out over their gondola to get a look at the noisy fellow some six or seven cars below. Ransom stood, giving the gondola a start backward in reaction to his weight. Jane gasped, but in a moment she, too, was standing to see the man who'd been shouting from below, now coming round, lifting as they descended. "He looks like Dr. Jeykll, I think," she commented.

"You mean Hyde, don't you?" They faintly heard the wheel operator at the bottom shouting up. "In your seats! Sit the bloody hell down!" They did so and rocked the gondola more as a result. Then Alastair again craned to see all he might, and she thought him so childlike in his enthusiasm, and so she began rocking and rocking the gondola in a madcap fashion she believed he'd enjoy, when suddenly the suspended car holding them began to sway too dangerously for comfort.

He threw his arms round her, pulled her into his chest, and she felt safe there, no matter what, while below them in rotation, the single man's rantings had only increased with maniacal laughter.

"You bitch, you've just laughed your last," the killer shouted and backhanded the spectral image of Polly Pete whose eyes opened on him despite her head wobbling near off. His erection came with her pain even if she wasn't really present.

Still she sat here bleeding and whimpering, and the more she bled out, the tighter the garrote and the more sexually excited he became. *Who on this planet could possibly understand this,* he wondered. *Sherlock Holmes perhaps, but the man was himself a fiction. Perhaps Stumpf and I oughta submit to Tewes's magnetic therapy—witchcraft he calls phrenology.* But a part of Stumpf feared the idea that Tewes might see right through him, to know his innermost thoughts.

"We should make love right here!" Polly's ghost whispered in his ear.

"There isn't time . . . or space!" As beautiful and wild as

Polly'd been, he knew he could not keep her. He could not keep any of them.

She persisted, grabbing his crotch. "What? Are you afraid? You're not one of those who can't get hard in a woman?"

"Shut up! You don't know what you're bleedin' talking about! Shut up!"

"What are you in real life, heh? A lawyer, a professor, a doctor, perhaps?"

"I'm none. Now, Polly, be a good girl, least till we're at your place."

She pouted. "You're as boorish as Ransom, wantin' me to be a cultured lady till we're in bed!"

In the end, the gondola and Polly both settled down, and they sat safe and secure in their seats, and he stared at her, thinking she had a death wish. She needed Stumpf to kill her. She wanted it; begged it. *Right, right?*

"Yes and I want it again," her spirit said in his ear.

He regained himself—in the here and now place—and watched the building excitement he'd created below. Stumpf had given him a quota, and he always demanded more blood; always from the back of his head came Stumpf's voice. Not even lively Polly had been able to drown out that voice.

With their ride over, he and Stumpf and the ghost of Polly stepped from the gondola to an angry operator who failed to appreciate his antics. A tip shut him up, and as the killer joined the maddening crowd on the fairway, he heard the operator also shake down Ransom for a tip.

He soon sat on a bench deep in shadow, nerves raw and exhilarated at once. Polly had been right. He'd never enjoyed normal relations with a woman. Born incapable. Withered testicles and deformed penis. Nothing whatever doctors could do. Despite the efforts of his mother to take him to the best surgeons on two continents, including Christian Fenger. They opened his urinary tract, but they couldn't produce a miracle any more than God himself might. No one could induce *feeling* in the lump of flesh he carried between his legs. That came only with the kill, only in *taking* life. What defense would he and Sleepeck Stumpf have if ever they were apprehended and tried?

He'd spent countless years in and out of hospitals, as Mother refused to accept his condition as irreversible. How many silent nights he'd spent with Stumpf—as his mother insisted on calling it, a name from his nursery, from his sleep murmurings. Mother was the only one on the planet who'd unconditionally loved him. When she'd died, penniless, he'd had to bury her in that damned Potter's Field. Although starving, he'd refused to sell her body to the medical men. After that something snapped inside him. He ran. Only months after this, he killed that first prostitute at the fair.

Polly made three, Chesley four. *Four* Chicago women, and now *two* young men, as well as *one* unborn child made the total seven. Chesley had proven a quite humorless thing compared to the vivacious Polly. And as for Purvis and now Trelaine . . . each beautiful in his way and so filled with life and love and happiness as it spilled from them with their blood. "Have all to live for," Trelaine had once confided to the very man who had, this night, taken his life.

He'd shut Trelaine's joy down with a delight of his own. As he'd felt with Polly and the others . . . and again with young Chesley Mandor, who'd so wanted to ride in that boat with Trelaine on her arm here at the fair . . . and 'twas a flaming good time she had. . . .

CHAPTER 19

Guiding Jane Francis by the hand, Ransom rushed from the Ferris wheel the moment the gondola stopped. His cane beating an anthem, Alastair shouted over the noise of the fairway. "We need to find a cab stand, get you home! Something's amiss at the lagoon, and I fear the worst."

"God, not another murder!"

"I pray I'm wrong. But to be safe, you must be off."

"But Alastair—"

"I don't want you seeing anything upsetting."

"I'm no shrinking violet! I'm a midwife; perhaps I can help."

They failed to notice a man in shadow across from them watching their every move, reading their lips as best he could.

"I will not allow it, Jane."

"Did you not hear a word I said?"

He relented. "OK, if you're quite sure. I must get there as quickly as possible."

"Then why are we wasting time?"

The boat lay half in, half out of the lagoon, the charred remains of the corpse partially covered in the waterlogged bottom. As Jane began to see the truth of it, the eerily fired body like a discarded heap of trash along the keel of the rowboat, seared clothing did a *danse macabre* along the surface. She only half heard Ransom's order: "Jane, stay back . . . do not move from this spot. Promise me."

She held herself in check, saying nothing, her body trembling at the sight that he tried to shield using his frame. *Stop trying to spare me, damn you!*

Someone foolishly shouted, "Is're a doctor here?"

Jane wondered at the emotional cost of being Ransom. And what of being *with* Ransom as Polly'd been? Still, she instinctively remained close to Alastair, seeing him take charge, ordering reluctant men into the water to grab the gunwales on each side and guide what remained of the boat onto firmer ground. "Easy! Easy! Don't lose her!" came Ransom's encouragement to the younger men.

One last thrust grounded the boat, and the waterlogged, burnt bottom split apart.

"Get her outta the muck! Lift below the arms and at the ankles. Use your gloves if you must, but do it." The uniformed police obeyed, but they seemed Ransom's children in need of chastising and scolding. "I'll take a stick to every last one of ya! Do it, do it now."

Together, the younger men lifted her out.

Jane wondered how many killings he'd seen and overseen, and who this latest victim might be.

"Outta the tunnel aflame all on its own, I tell yous," the shaken attendant kept shouting.

Alastair grabbed the ride attendant by each shoulder, holding him like a plow. "But going out on the water, man! Who'd she get in the boat with?"

"Fine-looking gent, but he didn't come back."

"What'd he look like?"

His description fit the Phantom, but the attendant ended with, "But they looked so in love."

"Allow me to help the man with his memory," came a feminine voice from behind Ransom. He turned to find Jane beside him.

"I told you to stay put."

"But I'm trained in hypnosis, and we ... I mean you ... you could greatly enhance someone's memory if—"

"I hardly believe a parlor trick is going to be of any—"

"Give it a chance. No one's come forward with any useful information. No witnesses beyond this rum-soaked attendant." She near whispered, "The killer has declared war on us all, Alastair. That could as well be Gabby or me in that flambéed condition!"

Even on quinine and opium gotten from Dr. McKinnette, Alastair feels Jane's sincerity, her genuine desire to help. Here stands a woman who understands the complexities and vagaries of a cop's life and work and is accepting of them. Not only accepting but supporting.

It was a new and odd thing for Ransom.

He felt unsure what to do with it. With her.

What to do with the feelings she imbued in him.

Just how to behave.

Just what to say.

Should I kiss her?

Thank her?

Hold her?

All three?

Say nothing, do nothing, oaf, Jane thought but said, "I'll get that cab now." To herself, she muttered, "Had you shown one sign, I'd've told you—confessed everything. Men!"

"Y-yes ... get home. Tomorrow, I'll call 'round."

"Whether you know it or not, you've just lost the best thing you never had," she shouted back.

"Griffin!" he shouted over her on seeing his young partner push through the crowd. "See that my lady gets home by cab." He forced a silver dollar into Griffin Drimmer's palm. Griffin stared from coin to Alastair to the woman he didn't know.

"I came as quickly as—"

"Get the lady to a cab and safely off." Ransom remained adamant.

"Sure . . . sure . . ."

"I'll come 'round tomorrow," Ransom repeated to her. "Now please, go along with Griff—my right-hand—"

"Dismissed like a pet!" her anger surfaced further.

She went out of view on Griff's arm, swallowed by the crowds, as Ransom watched, rapt in thoughts of her, a vague idea of life with a woman of substance, but this notion lost out to the moment. Over his shoulder the murder victim stared at him, an obvious connection to the ones before. *Maniac's stepped up his timetable.*

Like a man shackled, he studied the victim's features— not so mangled as to be unrecognizable. He called out to the crowd, "Anyone know her?"

"Here sir, a purse," offered one uniformed officer dripping from the waist down.

Ransom pulled out papers, letters. Love letters addressed to a Chesley Mandor, from a suitor named Joseph Trelaine. "Chicago address. Where is he now?" *Is he our Phantom? And if not and she got into a boat with a man . . .* " Then it occurred to him. *What if Trelaine were still out there in the black lagoon?* "You fellows, get a useable boat and some gas lamps and go up in the tunnel there and look for anything . . . unusual."

Ransom's latest homicide became a double-homicide as he watched a second body float just beyond the tunnel entrance, facedown if he had one—for as the weak lamplight played over the corpse, searchers could not tell. Using an oar to bring the body, like a lost vessel, into the gunwale of his boat, Alastair found it difficult to get a fix on the man, his size, weight, cut of his jib; impossible with his body floating half under, waterlogged. Ransom and the uniformed policeman on the oars worked to turn the floater in the water, almost flipping the drift boat in which they knelt. The corpse rolled like a log, and the soggy three-piece suit and best shoes tugged heavily back, as if some submerged creature held sway. Then the body hit the boat—hard—and both oarsman and inspector gasped to find it a headless torso.

"Did it fall off—the head, I mean—when we turned him?" asked the oarsman.

"I think not. Likely separated sometime earlier."

"In the depths of the lagoon is it?"

"I suspect so."

Ransom lashed the body to the side with hemp, not wanting to haul it aboard or scuttle the boat. "Fodder for Shanks and Gwinn he is," said the cop turned oarsman.

"Not before we bag all personal effects, do you understand? Your name, Officer?"

"Callahan, sir."

"Callahan, I'm personally holding you responsible for Trelaine's effects, if this be Trelaine—and Mandor's. Understood?"

"Ahhh . . . yes, sir. Yes sir."

After securing Trelaine, they started to shore with the body. Young Callahan, his blond hair lifting with each stroke, perspired until his hair flattened.

"Bastard this one is . . . a true black-hearted monster," commented Ransom.

"Aye, sir, indeed."

Trelaine, like the woman, had tasted of the killer's favorite weapon, but how, here out on the water? Was the monster telling them no place in the city was safe? Nothing sacred? Ransom must know how. How had the killer gotten so near a courting couple out here on the lagoon? The entire crime must be recreated to make sense of it.

Soon, Griffin had rowed out to join them. Ransom put him in charge of the re-enactment, awkward as it was in boats to re-create. He himself played the killer, each of the others playing a part. The one playing Chesley cursed, disgruntled that he'd drawn a woman's role. By now they began in earnest to get it done. And as they walked—or rather boated—through it, Ransom looked for opportunity, imagining himself the killer up to mischief here, and he looked to locate clues, when Griff pointed out a strange mark against the tunnel wall. It turned out to be a black-gray smoky bloody handprint.

"The bastard's teasing us!" said Griff.

"It's sure his hand again, his mark as it were."

"But why would he—"

"Wants us to choke on it."

"Give 'im credit in the papers."

"Wants us to know it's his work?" added Alastair. "Like a bloody artist signing a painting."

"Aye. Still, we must compare it to the one we found at the train station."

"If we can find a sober Philo Keane, get him and his camera on a boat, and to this point."

"With daylight . . . he might do best getting this," replied Griff, sounding optimistic.

"Body set aflame, shoved through the tunnel while the killer grabbed hold of the grating here and climbed the fieldstone overpass. Crowds coming and going, someone had to've seen the bastard come o'er the top."

"People're wrapped up in their own lives, but sure sixty good citizens'll be lining up with perfect descriptions."

Ransom frowned at Griff. "Sarcasm in the young, Griff, is not a pretty thing. Look, we'll get Thom's help, get the papers to claim we have several eyewitnesses who saw the killer exit the water at this point."

"What good would it do?"

"You tell me."

Griff pondered a moment. "Sell papers?"

"It'll serve *our* purposes. To put him on notice, keep him on guard, make him more cautious! All of that, and it may make him take more risks. And hopefully Thom's story will draw some real witnesses as well."

"Actual witnesses. Sounds too good to be true."

"I'm 'sposed to be the old cynic here, Griff."

From all they'd pieced together, the killer had somehow enticed the young couple over to his boat, likely with some pretense of his having trouble with a leak or steerage, anything to lure them close. Perhaps one of the victims or both knew the killer, or at least knew him by sight. He must surely look harmless indeed. *Invisible . . . blends*, Tewes had insisted.

Ransom summed it up for Griff. "As the victim affably attempted to look over the problem, he lost his life, garroted in a matter of seconds, dead and dropped into the water. The killer then leapt into her boat and secured the garrote about her neck. No telling how long he made her suffer. At least this is how I see it unfolding."

Griff swallowed hard. "Then there's a second boat drifting free out here unless . . ."

"Unless all three had disembarked in the same boat."

"And the attendant is of no help on that score?"

"None whatever. Look, if there is a second boat floating in the darkness, it may contain clues, gentlemen," he told the others. "Find that boat and get it to me and touch nothing. Do you understand?"

The young officers concurred, excited over the prospect of contributing to locating and bringing this madman to justice, and having their names associated with the famous Alastair Ransom.

They fanned out, searching for the missing, phantom boat. A pair of the fools singing out, *"Row-row-row your boat, gently down the stream . . ."*

"Trelaine's head could well be lying in that boat, so be prepared, lads!" Ransom's words silenced the chorus of *"Merrily, merrily, merrily."*

Again it was Griffin who'd made the gruesome discovery, alerting the others to the empty boat. When Ransom's boat came alongside, he stared into Griffin's eyes, and he said, "Quite the bloodhound you've become."

"A compliment from you, Rance?"

Ransom lifted his lantern to search the drifting boat, its oars having been secured by Callahan, who now held his head over the side and noisily retched.

Ransom looked into a stranger's eyes, wide and questioning, a man named Trelaine, whose head alone lay at the rear of the boat where he'd been enticed by a killer apparently capable of talking another man into abandoning his boat and a beautiful woman for the privilege of helping out.

How does a soul rest in peace under such circumstances, Ransom silently wondered.

"What next, Rance?" asked Griffin.

Ransom failed to answer, still lost in Trelaine's accusing gaze; a gaze that asked why hadn't the collective "they" stopped this madman before he could do this horror?

Griffin spoke. "Callahan, get into the boat with the head and—"

"Me, sir?"

"—and row it into the dock, Callahan. Inspector Ransom can use the exercise it'll take to get himself ashore."

This reference to Ransom's weight caused only cautious laughter as other search boats had gathered in close for a look at the severed head.

Callahan, tall, angular and fair-skinned blanched whiter, but he shakily made his way into the boat, where the head lay staring up at him. Given its proximity, it lay between his legs where he sat the oars. He could count on its rocking side to side, touching his ankles.

Around him, he heard the nervous twittering and mutterings of others, but Ransom looked him in the eye and said, "Callahan, use your coat."

Callahan nodded and quickly removed his coat and blotted out the staring head. Earlier, Ransom had judged the dead man from his clothes as upper crust. He wore Marshall Field shoes, and his clothes appeared tailored, but the inspector had been surprised on reading the lapel: MONT-

GOMERY WARD. No sign of Carson, Pirie, Scott buttons on the man.

"Griff, did you send for Philo?"

"Sent our biggest lads to fetch him, yes."

"He's likely talked them into a drink."

"Damn, they'll be all night."

"I'm confident they'll have 'im back and waiting for us at the dock."

"We'll have to row him out to the tunnel entrance."

"I can manage that."

"Thanks, Griff, and for earlier . . . for walking my lady friend to a cab."

"Do you know the address she gave the cabbie, Alastair?"

"I do."

"And?"

"She's Dr. Tewes's sister."

"Really?"

"Yes, keeps house for Tewes, perhaps a bit of nursing . . . looks after his daughter."

"*Ahhh* . . . I see, working the relatives, pumping her for information. Smart police work!"

Ransom bristled but also thought of his having measured Tewes. "Old-fashioned foot-to-heel police work. Which reminds me: Did you send those measurements off?"

"Telegraphed. Marvelous invention. Phoned New York, too, just to ask around about Tewes. Didn't he say hc spent some time there? But nothing's come of it, not so far anyway."

Back now through the tunnel, where they bobbed beneath the concrete and fieldstone overpass each eyeing the bloody print marking the killer's escape. Then they were back with Trelaine's parts. His remains were laid out near Chesley Mandor's.

Philo showed up, a brawny cop on each side of him. He'd not brought his usual equipment, carrying instead a hefty handheld camera like a small accordion, no doubt his latest acquisition.

"Hello, my friend," Ransom's weary voice reached Philo. "We've sad work aplenty for you."

"As I heard, but look here, Alastair." He held up his new camera. "Isn't she lovely? It's the latest, a Kombi Night-Hawk detective camera, created for just such work as we engage in, you see?"

"Well and good, so long as you get the cuts, Philo. One's gonna require a boat ride and a bit of balancing, so I'm glad you brought the smaller camera."

"It possesses all the latest improvements known to modern photography, man."

"I'll take your word for it. It's a beauty."

"Morocco leather, my friend, and further, it's fitted with the new rapid rectilinear lens."

The man speaks his own language, Ransom thought. "Let's just get started, Philo."

"It's fitted with a new regulation timer and instantaneous shutter, Alastair, with bulb attachment and—"

Philo, who'd followed Ransom to the corpse, suddenly fell silent, staring, shaking. On seeing the woman's charred remains, he gasped and dropped his camera, and went to his knees.

The victim has a familiar face, Alastair guessed from Philo's contrition, and now apologetic words spewed from the photographer, his hands clasped in the universal gesture of prayer, his body wracked with sobbing. "Chesley! *OhGodno-please-notmysweet Chesley!* Please forgive me! Please forgive . . . ahhhh-haaa."

"My God," said Nathan Kohler now on scene.

Ransom whispered in Philo's ear, a hand on him, trying to get him away and composed, "Tell me she was not one of your models, Philo."

Philo shook off Ransom's touch; he refused help, refused getting up from his kneeling position over the charred body and still lovely face, his hands extended, hovering over the torso and garroted head.

Reporters on scene snapped pictures. Others jotted notes, trying to transcribe Philo Keane's litany of apologies. Ransom knew from experience that a man displaying such vulnerability—beaten and broken in spirit—soon learned how few friends he actually had in this life. Ransom smelled sharks in the water. "Get Philo outta here, Griff," Alastair barked.

"But the photograph of the handprint?"

"Get one of the reporters, anyone. Just get Philo away."

Philo stumbled to his feet, dizzy with death and drink, shouting, "It's Trelaine's doing! That scrawny prick is the garroter! All the while pretending to love her!"

"*Youyouyou* knew both victims?" asked Griffin, but Philo was hearing nothing and understanding less.

"A vile, greedy little man! Joseph Trelaine. I'll swear out a warrant here, now, Ransom! They must've quarreled. He . . . he must've thought after killing her to make it look the work of this Phantom. Dear Ches rejected the prig for me after all, and it . . . I got her killed. No doubt of it!"

Each blathering word another nail in his coffin as Ransom read the feeding frenzy among the press and possibly in both Griffin's and Kohler's heads. Philo had few friends in the press and fewer on the force.

"Here is Trelaine lying dead and headless himself, Philo!" shouted Alastair. "Someone meant to drown 'im after beheading him!"

Kohler added, "He's hardly the cause of her death and his own."

Even young Callahan noticed the triangle here. Philo and Trelaine both vying for Miss Mandor. Philo's reputation for bedding his models, and she sitting for him, rejecting his advances, and Trelaine learning of the sordidness. This is how it played out this moment in curious, disparate interpretations.

Alastair grabbed Philo and marched him off to stand below an enormous tree that'd escaped leveling as the perfect herald of the Agricultural Exhibit. Below the sign of the exhibit, Alastair put it to him. "From where do you know Miss Mandor and this Trelaine chap? Tell me the whole story, and leave nothing out."

"He brought her round after a while."

"After a while?

"He's my accountant for Ward's Department Store, oversees all advertising."

"Ahhh . . . you worked for him."

"Indirectly . . . OK, yes. Insipid man without imagination, turning back all my best ideas. I tell you, Alastair, there were times when I'd've beheaded him, had I an axe."

"Quiet such talk, man!"

"I met privately with Ches, having slipped her a note. I felt . . . thought this was the answer. A way around Trelaine."

"The answer?"

Griffin joined them at the tree.

"You see, he made me test every product before doing a photographic ad. This meant visits to his uncle's farm to test some vet tools. I did all he asked and, God, finally a plumb assignment was offered."

"Which was?"

"Ladies' corsets and bloomers."

"And this is where Miss Mandor came in?" asked Griff.

"Precisely."

"She wanted to do some modeling . . . wanted it badly, I believed at the time."

Ransom gritted his teeth. "I see . . . and you were just the man to initiate her into *ahhh* . . . modeling."

"I posed her in artistic and tasteful displays, showing her incredible beauty and the corsets and stockings and—"

"And made advances," said Griff.

"No, no, no . . . not like that . . . not in that way."

"You mean not like you did with all the others, Polly included?" asked Ransom.

"This is . . . was a lady. I confess love in the air, such beauty and form, and so malleable and willing. I took countless shots, but I ne'er sullied her. She was special . . . laughed at my jokes, and we . . . we talked, Ransom, all night we—"

"Talked?"

"Of hopes, dreams, plans. It felt so . . . so right."

"So what happened?"

"Her body was so expressive. The way she moved."

"Get to the point, Philo!"

"Well, I mean when she put her clothes back on, it was as if . . . well . . . she became a completely different person. Cold and reserved. She made it clear she meant to marry Trelaine for position and wealth—both things she did not dream of, did not pray for, did not speak of when . . . when she lay there before me naked."

"Damn . . . so when did Trelaine discover the nude photos? Did she show them to him?"

"She did not. He never knew."

"But he told you to stay away from her, and you argued."

"I merely told him she was a grown woman, fully capable of making her own decisions, despite her . . . silence on the matter as a whole."

"You mean you *showed* him the photos?"

"Are you kidding? They've made a small fortune."

"You mean you *sold* the photos? to Trelaine?"

"Lock, stock, and barrel . . . save the few I kept in a secret place."

"Do you know how all this looks, Philo? Do you know how this might play in the newspapers should it come out? How it might play in a courtroom?"

"I've never given one goddamn how things appear. Appearances are for fools and are always wrong, right?"

"The appearance of impropriety in the minds of most *is* impropriety, and the appearance of jealousy, anger, murder . . . is in the mind of the beholder truth, *fact,* whether it makes sense or no. And once in the mind, damn hard to disprove."

"What're you saying, Ransom? That I *look* guilty for murder? For garroting Chesley and—and Trelaine? That's . . . why it's preposterous, an outright lie."

"Philo, I want you to go home."

"What? I have cuts yet to make."

"Don't be ridiculous." A reporter had drifted toward them, and his ear alerted like a hunting dog at Philo's last words: *I have cuts yet to make.*

"I'm putting another photographer on the case."

"What? Why that's—"

"Standard practice! You're far too personally involved. You obviously loved her, as much as you *can* love. Now make yourself scarce. You're fired tonight! Go home."

He searched Ransom's eyes and cast a glance at Griff. "I can't believe you . . . that this . . . this is gone so . . . so strangely for us."

"I know you would never do this, Philo. Others who don't know you may perceive otherwise. Now go. Trust me!"

He turned and walked dejectedly off, passing Callahan, who held out his new Wards wonder camera, saying, "You don't wanna forget this, Mr. Keane."

Philo looked at it as if he'd never seen it before. He said to Ransom, "This was what he gave me, free and clear, Alastair, if I'd never see Chesley again . . . and believing she meant what she'd said . . . I took the damn thing."

Ransom didn't know what to say to this. "Take your prize home then, Philo, and either get drunk or get sober, but do it privately."

"Alastair, this is none of my doing, no more than Polly's murder was any of your doing." He threw the camera at Ransom's feet. "Give it to my replacement."

"I can't take your camera, Philo."

"The other man will. Just do it."

Philo rushed away on shaky legs, a dazed stork.

"Poor bastard," muttered Griffin, "but then he always did rush into walls, didn't he? What do you think of his knowing both victims?"

"I knew the last victim. Does that make me a suspect?" Ransom knew the general thinking, that Philo courted problems, but he couldn't be called a murderer on the basis of character defects or bad judgment! He marched off with the camera, Griffin following, saying, "I've a ready replacement for Keane."

"Trust me, Griff, you'll never replace Keane's attention to detail and care in his work."

"Perhaps . . . when he's sober."

"Just get the cuts of the handprint and the bodies. Who's doing the work?"

"Philo's apprentice has volunteered."

"Ahhh . . . Denton."

"He's at the ready . . . came when he heard the news."

"I'm sure he'll do then."

"He's Philo's able *assistant*, as I am your able assistant, Alastair."

"All right, get the *assistant* on it if he can keep from puking."

"He'll do fine."

"Stay with him then, and give him this to work with." He handed over Philo's ill-gotten camera.

"Nathan Kohler seems to be studying your handling of matters, Rance. Go carefully, I daresay. Watch your back."

Ransom noticed something new in Griffin's demeanor and tone; something intangible yet cool wafting ghostlike between them. Had Kohler gotten to Griffin? But he was too worried at Kohler's assessment of Philo's show of emotion to pay close attention. "You get Waldo set up at the tunnel. I'll see to Nathan Kohler."

Griffin became stiff, his eyes filling with a fire. "You're not a man easy to like, Alastair . . ."

"What?"

". . . never giving, never offering a hand, or to buy a cup of coffee, to ask after my day, my family's health, my take on things, life . . ."

"And you think this is the time?"

Griffin marched off with Philo's camera, shouting, "Denton! Come with me!"

Ransom realized that the young detective was right about

his having made little time for him, and that he should treat Griffin with more deference and respect. Worrisome. But he hadn't time at the moment. He had enough on his plate. *Gotta worry about Philo now*, he thought, seeing young Denton salivating over the damned new camera handed him.

"Gawd . . . its morocco leather," Waldo wailed.

CHAPTER 20

Ransom found a park bench where he'd col-
lapsed, fully expecting Nathan Kohler to join him, and he
expected a fight, at least an argument. He expected Kohler to
tell him that an infusion of fresh perspective was sorely
needed as he, Ransom, had gotten not a grain closer.

So when he sensed someone drop onto the bench beside
him, he didn't look up until he heard the irritating voice of
Dr. Tewes. "I called Dr. Fenger . . . pleaded with him to
come to the scene . . . to examine the bodies immediately,
but I fear, he's exhausted and burnt out on murder."

"Dr. Tewes . . . how good of you to come." Ransom's sarcasm sounded harsher than he'd meant.

"Take out all your frustration on me . . . if it gets you onto
what you do best."

"Drinking."

"No, tracking . . . focus on your gift for the hunt, and trust
your instincts."

"Until recently, that is how I managed, but lately . . . the
headaches have become non-stop, the worse since Muldoon's sap."

Tewes ran a hand through Ransom's hair until he found
the knot.

"Ouch! Damn!"

"You're not kidding. No wonder you've a headache."

"Reduce another man to tears." Ransom gave in to Tewes's fingers—both hands now caressing his cranium. Tewes's touch felt light, his hands caring. Alastair gave in further, submitting, too tired to protest. Strangely, he didn't wish it to end.

"I *could* help you." Ransom only half heard as Tewes continued a light massage, careful not to strike the palpitating bulge. "Left you unconscious. Hope they throw the book at Muldoon."

"For striking down a cop?"

"You're the most cynical man I've ever met."

"Cynical or realistic?"

"Do you think everyone is out to get you?"

"Aren't you?"

"I'm not your enemy, Inspector."

"No, you're only spyin' for Nathan Kohler?"

"I . . . I've read your record. You're a fine detective."

"What've you got on Kohler?"

"I'll not say."

"He expects you to muck up my case."

"There is that, yes. But Alastair, I've not sold you out."

"How heartening. You only *spy* for him; you don't *tell* him anything."

"The other day, at the fire scene, I told him I was done with collusion."

"But you're here now."

"I only want to help."

"To help me?" He began laughing. "Like at the train station?"

"Just catch this bastard before his insanity touches us all in ways unimaginable."

"He seems bent on . . . on destroying me . . ."

"Question is," said Nathan Kohler, standing over them now, "who's next?"

"He's going for larger game," said Ransom. "His pattern has been to go up the social scale."

"We should build a record, Alastair," said Tewes. "Should

we ever have this monster in custody . . . well, it could act in our favor."

"Act as a kind of Bertillon measurement of the killer's mind, you think?" he asked Tewes. "And I 'spose you'd like to run hands over this maniac's head?"

"Doing so with enough such madmen, who knows, perhaps over time, if diligent records are kept, similarities in the bone structure, or areas of abnormality in the brain—areas of weak magnetism, for instance—" Jane realized that both men only stared. "But who can say without long-term study?"

"This is why we at top asked Dr. Tewes's assistance, Alastair," Nathan said. "To give our investigation a rigorous scientific, ahhh . . . appearance."

"I see . . . how blind I've been." Ransom grimaced.

"It could have a bearing on the Lombroso controversy, my study," she added.

"Really? And another reputation made!"

"Look, Detective, every brain is as different as the fingerprint."

"It's a proven fact," added Kohler.

She went on. "In cases such as this, with no usable print or a match, today you only have Bertillon and Lombroso, but perhaps one day men like you—*hunters*—will routinely turn to men like me—*scientists*—for answers."

"Glad you're concerned with the future, Dr. Tewes," said Kohler.

"Yeah," added Ransom, "but as for me, I have to deal with the here and now, and while I find the doctor's unusual criminal recording interesting, for now I'd best get back to my duties."

He left Kohler and Tewes to again plot their separate moves in all this. As he turned his back on the odd couple, he felt a definite knife twisting about his spine. Kohler was ever up to no good, and he'd love nothing better than to embarrass Ransom, bring him down, and ultimately put him out to pasture. In fact, he'd been headhunting Ransom for six years now. And to this end, he'd enlisted Tewes's questionable help.

Ransom also feared that Griffin'd been recruited as well.

It's a minefield, he thought when he saw that Dr. Christian Fenger had not only arrived but was looking over the murders. It'd become rare—Fenger out of his labs, on scene. The man had such complete empathy with murdered souls that scenes like this literally hurt him to the quick.

"What of my ring?" Ransom asked him.

"I can assure you, Ransom, my men're innocent. I skewered them, and threatened them."

"And you're convinced?"

"They haven't the ring."

"And their feelings hurt, I'm sure." *If this were true, then the monster has Merielle's ring.* "I'd hoped to bury her with it."

"At heart the romantic, heh?" Fenger sadly returned to the corpses and severed heads. "The man was not torched, only the woman. Should we read any significance into that?"

"Trelaine's body fell straightway into the water, his head into the second boat."

"Heard you did a reenactment. Good a theory as any."

"The killer would've been busy with the woman," Ransom added, "no doubt shrieking, but strangely, no one heard screams."

"She might shriek inside her head, but I have it on reliable authority that Chelsey Mandor is—was a mute."

"A mute? Damn that Philo. Said they'd *talked* all night."

"You've never *spoken* all night without a word?" asked Tewes, joining them. "There're many ways to 'talk.' "

"Damn that Philo. A mute . . . another handicapped woman," complained Ransom.

"Says as much about Philo as it does about the women who're attracted to him," added Fenger.

"Or to his camera," agreed Ransom. "I asked Philo once if he got involved with handicapped and disabled women because he thought it less an investment on his part."

"What'd he say?" asked Tewes, curious.

"Reminded me of his *wheelchair love.* Said she couldn't catch him once it was over. Scoundrel that he is!"

The three of them laughed and Ransom added, "The story does say a lot about our friend Philo."

Fenger's tone went serious. "This Miss Mandor . . . mute from a childhood disease, according to her father—a perfect delicacy for Philo."

"Her father is here? My God."

Ransom feared he'd get no new or useful information out of the distraught father. Another wail escaped the man, who beat the earth with fists from a kneeling position on the grass.

Alastair noticed that Tewes'd returned to Kohler, and they were in a controlled but heated discussion. "Look there, Christian," Ransom said. "I should call on Dr. Tewes tonight, to break the weaker of the two obvious conspirators."

Then of a sudden, Tewes stormed off.

"What's Nathan's game?" asked Fenger.

"The game of Get Ransom."

"Wants an end to talk of an incident that you *alone* want dredged up."

Griffin came back to him. "You were right about the lady victim, Ransom. Nothing on her in the manner of jewelry. Do you think he takes his victim's jewelry?"

"Until now, I thought Shanks and Gwinn were getting rich off these deaths, but Dr. Fenger assures me otherwise."

Griff and Fenger acknowledged one another.

"Ransom, so far as the chief goes, I only let him know what I want him to know when I want him to know. Tell 'im, Dr. Fenger."

Fenger cast his eyes in another direction, but Ransom saw the guilt. "Not you, too, Christian?"

"Kohler runs the man's budget, Rance," said Griff. "Whataya expect?"

Fenger said nothing.

"Let's just work this case, the three of us, and when it's concluded, we can reassess where we stand with one another, gentlemen!"

"Sure, a chance is all I ask . . . a chance to prove myself," said Griff but Fenger remained silent.

"Although I've none left, Griff, I do understand ambition. But mark me, young friend, the prize won can leave a man alone with ambition."

"As may be said of your blind ambition to open the books on Haymarket!" Fenger fired back as if struck.

"Aye . . . touché. You have me there, but who does one trust, Christian, who?"

A deep, painful silence rose among them like an evil child at play. Griffin blasted him. "Alastair, you never put trust in me. Not once've you confided a single dirty secret you've learned about Haymarket. Just a few drunk stories at the bar, yet you expect sympathy and—"

"You're right, Griff. So much I've not confided in *anyone* for fear it'd get back to Kohler. Nathan has a way of getting at people, controlling 'em."

"I want to understand your side of things, Alastair. I do."

"Perhaps one day soon . . . after we apprehend this fiend."

"I'll hold you to it."

Dr. Fenger said, "As to the case at hand . . . I can tell you fellows it's definitely the work of the same garroter. Down to the diamond shape at the neck here"—he paused to point at his own Adam's apple—"about here, on both male and female victims. What utter nerve and swiftness in killing he's perfected . . . practicing his technique over and over to get this efficient."

"What do you suppose he practices on, Doctor?" asked Griffin.

"Melons, fence posts, small animals, who can say, perhaps all and more."

"Or cadavers in a morgue?" asked Nathan Kohler, who joined them. "Gentlemen, whoever this perverted, twisted bastard is, he destroys the peace and happiness of the fair. This kind of thing, four deaths now on fairgrounds, two similar deaths within a cab's ride! It has to stop and stop immediately."

"Not to be contrary," began Ransom, "but it's seven deaths all toll, sir, and I've seen no evidence these killings've made any dent in the number of hotdogs, hamburgers, or trinkets sold, or a decrease in fair attendance."

"In fact, the numbers have increased!" added Fenger.

"Where the deuce're your Resurrection Men, Fenger?" Kohler barked. "Get these unseemly bodies and heads out of here now, now!"

Fenger took great exception to Shanks and Gwinn being called his Resurrection Men, and he stood face-to-face with Kohler on the issue. "Look here, we do not rob cadavers from their sanctified graves!"

"You chest cutters're never satisfied."

"Whatever you're talking about—"

"Potter's Field! A recent disturbance," countered Kohler.

"I was sent to investigate," Griff added. "A woman's body . . . taken without a trace."

"How sick is that?" asked Kohler.

"I recall the incident," said Ransom.

"Who was she, and what end came of it?" Fenger asked.

"No end, open case still, *Drimmer*!" complained Nathan.

"Remains a mystery, even her identity," said Griff. "She was a numbered grave—an elderly Jane Doe."

"And the body in question never turned up?"

"Afraid not."

"Someone likely made a stew of her," suggested Ransom.

Fenger nodded. "Not farfetched, given how swollen our streets are with the homeless, and the city doing nothing to relieve the problem."

"Now they're calling him the Phantom of the Fair over at the *Tribune*," said Kohler in disgust. "Flood gates've opened! Imagine all the ink devoted to this deviant! From what Christian tells me, he doesn't rape his victims—alive or dead! How deviant is that?"

"My God, Nathan, do you think raping his victims might make him a better chap?" asked Fenger. "Somehow more like us and less a monster, somehow less sadistic?"

"Somehow, yes, in my mind."

"Somehow? In your mind." Ransom, his cane beating the pavement here, controlled the urge to reach out and strangle Kohler. *Throw in rape with your murderous act and it somehow made murder more palatable? Normal?* Ransom had to walk off in a circle to not explode.

"At least if he raped them first, we might understand his motive is my point. It'd point to a clear purpose in these *senseless* attacks." Nathan straightened and stood taller. "At the moment, what possible motive have we for his bloodletting?"

"He likes blood . . . likes the smell of it, the consistency of it, likes to wash his hands in it," suggested Fenger.

"Likes the garrote," added Griff, "likes the heft of it, the cunning of it, the handiness of it, the genius behind it. Maybe the history of it."

Ransom shouted, "Come on, he likes the feel of the kill, same as you and I when we hunt deer with a Winchester. He likes the process of the hunt itself . . . the hooking of the bait, the lure, all of it."

"To gain the moment in which his prey is under absolute control," added Fenger.

"Yes, you would understand him, wouldn't you," Kohler coldly replied to Alastair's summing up. "Takes a killer to catch one, or at least to know how one will behave."

"Prove me a murderer, Nathan, and I'll willingly sit for shackles. Until such time, I'd appreciate your not characterizing me as this evil bastard's counterpart."

"But you just did so yourself!"

"Aye . . . I did, but I've not given you carte blanche to do so." Ransom knew Kohler guilty of at least as much evil as himself, but in a time of war, men did evil for a greater good, or at least what they perceive a greater good. During the "war" with labor, Alastair had interrogated an arsonist and anarchist, a known killer of men who set bombs off to make a political point, a refugee of such activities in France. He'd transplanted to America and had drifted to Chicago when news got out about the labor dissidents at Pullman. All this, days before Haymarket and the riot and the bomb that exploded in the square, killing Ransom's fellow officers and doing its best to kill him.

Ransom meant to get information out of the man, and in a warehouse owned by a friend of the police, he'd sweated and beaten the fellow for information. Rumor abounded of a bomb having been planted somewhere in the city. He'd taken extreme measures to get the information he wanted out of Oleander, the man's code name, and the only name he'd disclosed until he screamed his real name from within the flames.

The matchstick slowly burned toward Ransom's fingers as he'd held it to the man's half-opened eyes, blood in his pupils making focusing impossible. No doubt, from the blows to the head. Alastair and the other cops present had pummeled the man's cranium. His bloodied features might've told Ransom that Oleander was, by this time, unable to formulate words much less inform on his comrades.

Then Kohler tossed his lit cigar into the fumes rising off the man. While Alastair's eyebrows and the hair on his hands curled and blackened, Oleander went up like a rag doll tossed into the hearth. As much as Alastair attempted to kill the flames and stop the death, the flames fought harder than he, claiming what was theirs.

Irony of it, *he* and not Kohler had earned a reputation that night. No one had seen Kohler's action. Ransom's reputation had remained intact since then, and word on the street, spread by the grapevine of lowlifes, toughs, snitches like his own Dot'n'Carry, all had him down as a cold-blooded bastard who'd do anything—*anything*—to gain what he wanted. As Dot'n'Carry put it: "If a man finds himself in custody of Alastair, then the only ransom worth talking about was payment in full."

Interrogation meant beatings as a matter of course, routine, expected by those arrested. Certain indigents in particular, when taken into custody and *not* questioned on the latest atrocities in the city, demanded it of their jailers. They demanded a beating regardless, as a beating behind jail walls proved a badge of honor. Further, to leave a Chicago jail without a beating marked a man as a snitch. But in the case of one Inspector Alastair Ransom, the word beating had taken on new meaning in a mix of myth and legend.

"Alastair . . . I think you're so right about this," said Dr. Fenger, bringing him out of his reverie. "The kill . . . the kill being anticlimactic, our boy sets them ablaze for one final rush of excitement. Theoretically, the kill's *not* enough."

Kohler loudly pandered to the press. "So, Inspector, you have no clue as to why a man would set a dead body aflame?"

The pointedness of *aflame* used by the chief made everyone within hearing squirm. It addressed the rumors about Ransom as much as the killer. Alastair's fists clenched, and he took a threatening step toward Kohler.

Griffin, hand raised, stepped between the two larger men, while hazarding a reply, "Fire has always held significance to people . . ."

Fenger agreed as if on cue, "Full of symbolism and mysticism."

"Hmmm . . . Tewes said something similar in his report," began Kohler. "That fire is or may have some weighty import in his head, in a symbolic sense, say of victory or some such . . ." Nathan stepped back from the threat in Ransom's eyes.

"More likely he holds us *all* in contempt," weighed in Dr. Fenger. "It is the act of a contemptuous man, an angry man. I believe Tewes said it best in a brief discussion I had with him."

"Go on," said Kohler.

"Dr. Tewes believes the killer has a fire fetish."

"A fire fetish."

"A fire bug, yes," added Griffin.

"Pyromania is how he put it, a deep-seated insatiable need. Damn, I'm inadequate to the task. Tewes knows the jargon of mental disorder far better than I. I'm, after all, a surgeon."

"Well, if it is some aberration of the brain, a disorder in here," Kohler pointed to his wide forehead, "then he certainly has given into it, carrying about his own portable vial of kerosene."

"He takes their lives and utterly disfigures them. He not only wants them dead, but to control what happens to them afterward—"

"Afterward?" Kohler's features crinkled in confusion.

"After they're dead. A form of necrophilia, Dr. Tewes calls it, but rather than have his way with the dead body, *ahhh,* in a sexual sense, like you earlier spoke of, having some sort of perversion there, you see, he may be getting his sexual excitement from the fire as much as from the garroting and holding another's life in his hands."

"Tewes said all that?" asked Ransom, impressed.

"That way no one, not even the best surgeon—"

"Not even you, Dr. Fenger," added Griffin.

"—can put them peacefully at rest for all eternity. No amount of cosmetics or preservation can help, you see? A burned, dehydrated body cannot e'en be given a proper wake."

"I see," replied Kohler.

Fenger absently added, "Given that every artery, every vein is collapsed by the heat of fire, the body can't receive formaldehydes, and stuffing rags soaked in formaldehyde into body cavities is not really effective."

"It's a sick desire to destroy the remains," suggested Ransom. "By decapitation, then fire. Yet he preserves their features as if they are significant."

"Like photographs," Griff added.

Dr. Fenger lit a slim cigar and smoke encircled them. Kohler coughed, Griff rocked on his heels, and Ransom chewed on his unlit pipe. Fenger said, "You fellows could be on to something. But it's what besets the man . . . the ghosts of his past—according to Tewes—ones gone unfulfilled, ones ne'er put to rest, that have a way of rising from the grave."

Kohler nodded, his mind racing with Fenger's reply. "Then, by God, Ransom, get on to this madman's trail. Find the ghosts that beset him! But first, I need on my desk tomorrow morning a full report for Mayor Harrison!"

CHAPTER 21

The same night at the Tewes residence

"I'm done with it! No more James Phineas Mur-dock Tewes, no more hiding behind this disguise!" Jane Francis announced when she stormed in. She'd just returned from the fair, walking out on Kohler's conspiracy against Alastair and on any hope of helping find a killer. "Who am I kidding? They don't want my help—either of them!"

"Who, Mother?"

"Ransom and Nathan! Alastair at least is honest; he never expected anything of me, Tewes that is. Nathan, on the other hand, lied just to use me. He never believed in the idea of profiling the killer. It was all just part of his ruse."

"Whatever are you talking about, Mother?" Gabby followed her as she stormed about the clinic.

"Only wanted information on Ransom. And to grind Ransom into the ground 'til he can stand no more. Damnable man wants my affections, too!"

"Isn't Chief Kohler married?"

"Yes, but in a Chicago minute, he'd set me up as his mistress."

"Mother! Really!" Gabby tried keeping up as Jane stormed each room, lifted something, banged it or tossed it and continued on. "Slow down, Mother, my God. What has happened?"

She told Gabby of the new horror at the fair. Gabby reacted in sullen silence, a pained look creasing her features. "You were at the fair with Ransom?"

When Jane had left Ransom the first time to come home, Gabby had been away with a study group. It was then that Jane had changed to Dr. Tewes and returned to the scene of the double homicide in Lake Park.

"Never again will I be sucked into doing anything that goes 'gainst my better judgment."

Gabby clapped. "That's wonderful news!"

"I blame these men 'round me! Kohler, Ransom, Fenger, all of 'em."

"I like the sound of this."

"I used to blame your grandfather, for not forcing me to look at reality for what it is! Instead, he taught me to spit in its eye. But too often comes its mocking face, making me the fool!"

"Go ahead, let it all out, dear Mother. You've taken on so much, and you've sacrificed for my—"

"No, I've made my own bed . . . nightmare really. 'Tisn't any of your doing, child."

"Please, you're far too harsh on yourself."

She paced the foyer, wandered the living room to the kitchen again, still fuming. Gabby remained near, recognizing a pivotal moment.

Finally Jane said, "This is it . . . tonight. I make a resolution."

"What resolution, Mother?"

"I resolve to end this damnable charade and any further involvement with Nathan and Alastair's feud." She thought of Kohler's final words to her: "String 'im along, Jane . . . sleep with him if it'll get 'im talking. . . . One confession of overstepping the law, and by God, we 'ave the bastard!"

Kohler acted in the cold certainty of righteousness, weeding out anyone who had anything whatever to do with Haymarket. And what of Alastair? Ransom brought scrutiny on himself like a man who, at least secretively, wanted to confess to someone, anyone, and if she were in the right place at the right time, during a vulnerable moment, then perhaps it would be to *her* that he'd confess his sins. She'd be terrified by it, and she was terrified at the idea of standing in a court docket to testify against Alastair.

Gabby's excited voice snatched Jane from her thoughts. "Good for you, Mother. I agree, and I support your action, whatever you decide, you know that." Gabby hugged Jane, still in Tewes's clothing.

Jane snatched off the mustache and ascot. "Safer to listen to the fairies in my head! The ones that spoke to me as a child."

"Mother, I'll help you if you'll help me."

"Help you how?"

"Define the problem in its particulars, and to your own satisfaction, but I cannot engage in another round of emotional tug-o-war."

Mother and daughter stared into one another's eyes, each seeking answers. Gabrielle nervously laughed.

"Don't laugh. I believe the problem is surmountable, but I'm concerned you hide nothing from me, and that I do likewise, that I should never hide anything, even disturbing, from you if you've a right to know, and I am afraid that . . . I am guilty of this, my sweet."

"Guilty how? What're you talking about, Mother?"

"Tewes."

"My father? But you have told me all about him. How handsome he was, how romantic, how courageously he died for his country in the war."

"I-I've lied."

"Lied?"

"All save that he *was* devilishly handsome."

"But—"

"Let me now tell you the truth about your father, and I do this not to hurt you but to strengthen you. If I'm exposed here in Chicago as a fraud . . . well, within that exposure all manner of things will come to light."

"But how would you be exposed? By whom?"

"Promise to be patient. I will tell you all. In the end, we will regain who we are."

"Then you plan to expose yourself? Before this other party can?"

"Yes."

"Inspector Ransom finally onto you, isn't he?"

"No . . . wish it were so. It's Chief Kohler. Payback, I suppose, for rejecting him."

"You broke Nathan Kohler's heart?"

"If he ever had one." Jane finally sat.

"What you said about my father . . ."

"I started running away from myself a long time ago . . . when your father left me alone with . . . when I was pregnant with you. Felt like damaged goods. So much hurt and misunderstanding. Not toward you, my child, but toward myself."

"So you came back to America to stop the pain?"

"No, to confront it, don't you see? By setting up a practice in New York, but it proved disastrous."

"So now we're here, and talk about hiding from your feelings. You've become a master at it, Mother, right along with having become Dr. Tewes."

"Only an expediency . . . to keep us in—"

"In the money, in the level of comfort to which we've become accustomed? Come on, Mother, out with it. To hide. To hide in plain sight is what you proposed from the beginning."

Gabby grabbed her mother up from her chair and held her. The hug was long and heartfelt. "It's OK, Mother."

"But it's not. In New York, I ran into Nathan, there studying some sort of new identification process he wanted in Chicago, this new fingerprinting thing."

"It is a miracle of discovery this fingerprint business, Mother, and it is all true."

"I've learned from Inspector Drimmer that Ransom is the

one who pushed Kohler to adopt it, he and Dr. Fenger. Christian's known of it for years from his travels to the Orient, but officials ignored his counsel."

Gabby nodded. "Always the way with new ideas. Look at the resistance to the Crapper, the telephone, electricity."

"I so desperately need to calm myself," said Jane.

"Tea. I'll make us some fresh," suggested Gabby.

"Would you? Tea will help."

"Yes, yes, of course." And Gabby was away.

An unpleasant shrill symphony of terror played out in Jane's head, and she feared. She feared what would happen to Gabby should something happen to her. She consciously willed a respite to the panic attack. *Poor Gabby. This is no way to live for either of us.* "Jane Francis," she spoke to herself, "you've got to reclaim your true self." She repeated it until the mantra staved off the attack.

Once the tea had brewed, they went into the parlor where the windows overlooked the boulevard. For some time, they people-watched. They spoke of enjoying the house they'd rented. They spoke of the fair. Gabrielle felt that her mother needed time before broaching a larger, distressing matter.

"When you were just a little girl, I was befriended in New York by another woman very like myself she was . . . her name was Alicia."

"Alicia . . . what a lovely name."

"A lovely soul, and like me, she lived so much inside herself, in her inner world, until . . . well, she was murdered."

"Murdered? No . . ."

"I had hired her in my practice to help keep things in place, to help look after you, to generally take my place when with patients, which, as it happened, was not often, so we spent a lot of time together, and we spoke of ourselves as *problematic* women."

"Problematic?"

"She drowned in the park, but there was more to it. I pointed out the bruises on her neck, her legs, her forearms. Whoever did it knocked her down. I found blood on a stone nearby. I tell you this so you know I understand your pain now."

"Was she . . . garroted?"

"No . . . at the very least all her parts were together when they laid her to rest. But the authorities were not going to be led by some *woman*—even if I did hold a medical degree. They resented my *bullying* them, and they *wanted* it to be an accidental drowning, and so it was labeled. But child, that is not the point of my story."

"What then?"

"Gabby, this poor woman condemned herself for a sense of weakness drilled into her. In fact, we both shared the myth of feminine weakness"—she held up a hand to stop Gabby's protest—"*and,* and shared I daresay with half the female population, even those young women who fall into the abyss of prostitution."

"Now you're speaking of Ransom's Polly Pete?"

"Yes, I suppose her too. Polly, and my dear friend to whom I so often give a prayer, and *myself*. . . . None of us ever saw that *how* we lived—inside our feelings—was power. A positive rather than a negative."

"Women are constantly told this. It's one reason we're uniting. What else are we to do?" Gabby replied, hands flailing like a pair of diving birds.

"We . . . all of us . . . are told feelings are a weakness, something we must struggle to combat . . . to contain if we're to fit into the world—and for how long were we wrong? How horribly wrong in our perceptions?"

"And the other two, dead now, took it into eternity with them."

"So sad . . . only one of three learning the lesson of it."

"I see . . . I think."

"Think how in our day, our generation, child, women were taught to believe every step taken, every dream held was foolish, weak, silly, a woman's ranting, a woman's lot, a woman's hysterics."

"It has not changed so much. I get the same attitude at university!"

"The weaker of the sexes, the highly emotional and volcanic of the sexes, making us out as given more to the animal nature of our evolutionary ancestors. Should we voice an opinion, medical men call it *hysteria femalia*. And only now am I finally *getting it*—"

"Getting what, Mother?"

"That I live with foreign, strange, unfamiliar people around me, like some creature out of one of those mad outer space stories of Jules Verne's, simple as that!"

"You mean as Byron felt . . . not of this world, born into the wrong place and time perhaps?"

"No, this euphoric epiphany is just the opposite."

"But how do you mean, Mother?"

She threw her hands up and shouted, "I am *right* for this world! It is the rest of the population that is strange and odd and foreign."

"Really?"

"Indeed! Look at everyone around you—all the city!"

"I have many times over."

"Look deeper then—it is made up of—of—"

"—of Martian men? Is that what you're saying?" Gabby genuinely wanted to know.

"Men! Men like Chief Kohler, Christian Fenger, Thomas Carmichael, Mayor Carter Harrison, the governor, Philo Keane, Marshall Field, Alastair Ransom! We are simply *not* like them."

"Whataya mean to say?" Gabby asked, confused.

"They will stop at nothing to get what they want, to gain what they perceive are their entitlements!"

"Perhaps it's part of the character of a Chicagoan."

"The character of a man," Jane countered.

"And you believe, Mother, that you're not at all like them? Frankly, going about as Dr. Tewes . . . well how *like them* do you think is Tewes?"

"That's what I'm telling you. There's no way we are like

them under our clothes, under our skin! They are takers, pickpockets, boodlers, and Machiavellians."

"But we're all human, Mother, and—"

"Tewes, for all his faults or due to them, *he is* accepted by Chicagoans—isn't he? Still, you miss my point."

"It all sounds so very cynical, Mother."

Jane became thoughtful, speaking in a near whisper. "No, no child, it's not cynicism I feel. My father alone understood the truth about me, but he could not tell me; he knew I had to learn for myself, and I did today."

"Learned what?"

"Behavior I've thought of as defective—*brainwashed* to think so by men! Behavior that *in fact* keeps me *sane* . . . and Alicia and Polly, and so many trapped women in our society."

"So does this mean you'll support our suffrage march?"

Jane gritted her teeth. "I fear for your safety."

"Oh, come! Who's gonna throw stones and bottles at women standing in their knickers with a brass band playing?"

"I just want you to know how I *feel* now. This is so important."

"Sorry, didn't mean to interrupt, but the vote's important to me!"

"I pray it's not wasted energy, like the senseless self-loathing that is spoon-fed to women. Imagine, a lifetime of apology for being *different*—but no more."

Seeing her mother's tears come freely, Gabrielle again wrapped her arms about Jane, saying nothing, just listening.

"All the lost opportunity. But never again will I hide."

"Hide?"

"Within myself yes . . . Sadly, it's taken all these years to come to an accounting of just how bloody distorted my self-perceptions have been."

"Mother! You never curse!"

"Forget about the cursing and concentrate, child, on what I'm saying. It's so important that you understand early. You mustn't waste your most precious commodity—*time*."

"Per-perhaps this is what we're here for; to find ourselves, and maybe shake things up . . . change things a little!"

"Yes . . . that's exactly what I'm feeling, but look closer, more deeply."

"Sounds like . . . an epiphany."

"A threshold . . . yes, a portal of mind that—"

A rapping noise like a gunshot came at the door. Through the sash, they made out Ransom's silhouette with cane. Gabby said, "Here is your favorite Martian now."

Jane erupted in laughter. "That man! Why doesn't he ring the bell?"

"I rather think he uses that cane for everything."

"So right, including interrogations."

"Are you going to tell him?"

"I'd like to but . . ."

"Surely he suspects by now. After all, he's a detective!"

"It would throw him a good shock!"

Gabby's evil smile shadowed Jane's. "Serve him right after what he did at the train station."

"You've heard?"

"It's all over."

Again Ransom rapped at the door.

"God," Jane wondered aloud, "what do you do with a bear at the door?"

"The truth, now!"

"But it could destroy any chance I might have of—"

"You're attracted to him?"

"Yes!"

"Oh, dear."

Jane secretly feared doing any harm to Alastair's sense of self-worth and professional acumen. She grabbed ascot and mustache. "Gabby, stall him!"

"What? No!" As Jane rushed for mirror and glue, Gabby yelled through her locked door. "But you're finished with masquerades!"

"Not like this . . . it's too sudden. Go, do as I say. Answer the door. I shall pop out the back and come around the front door as though Dr. Tewes is home from an appointment."

"But what of that wonderful speech?"

"Just do it!"

"But your true sentiment?"

"It'll happen when it happens, not before."

By now Jane sat at her secret mirror, applying makeup, planning to exit through a nearby window. She'd stopped short of telling her daughter of her father's ignoble end; perhaps the tale of his dying a brave soldier could stand, at least for now.

So here she was, Tewes again. This time climbing out a back window. She'd given Polly advice to get clear of Ransom, and here she was concerned about the man's sensibilities? *Whatever is wrong with me?*

Despite Gabby's disappointment in Jane's latest decision, she followed her mother's orders, inviting the unsuspecting Inspector into the parlor for tea. As she poured the tea and stalled for time, her mother preened as Dr. Tewes in a back room. Meanwhile, Gabby must field more questions about her "auntie"—Jane Francis Ayers—although Ransom *said* he was here to sec Dr. Tewes.

"Auntie's abed by this hour every night. An early riser, that one."

"And what of you?" he asked between sips, favoring a headache that threatened to blind him. "Shouldn't you be asleep?"

They both glanced at the clock. It was nearing midnight.

"Me? Oh . . . my studies keep me up."

An awkward silence followed until, noticing the pain he was in, she asked, "Are you all right? I heard about the horrible fire in which your . . . the lady you were seeing . . . that is Father told me how difficult it's been for you."

"Your father bailed me out of jail. I mean to make good on

it." He pulled forth a twenty-five-dollar note from the Harris Bank and laid it on the table.

"You must speak to Father about your headaches."

"Aye . . . it's why I came—and to repay the note. But it's rather late for—"

"Nonsense, you must take care of it right away."

"But the lateness of the hour."

"I assure you, for his fee, my father won't turn you away."

"Then the good doctor, he has not—"

"Retired? Wish it were so. I'm afraid, he doesn't take care of himself half so well as his patients."

"He works hard."

Dr. Tewes came through the front door and into the parlor, saying, "So, you've finally come, Inspector, for a complete examination? At such an hour?"

"I do my best work after hours, when others sleep." He stood and filled Tewes's hand with the note to repay the bailout.

"What is this?" Tewes was in the midst of asking when Ransom suddenly became dizzy and wobbly on his legs, almost falling before they got him back onto the settee where he'd been moments before.

Even dazed, Ransom saw that Gabby and Jane showed genuine concern, the caring written in their eyes. Tewes was barking orders and young Gabby, flitting about after cold water and a compress. So unconditional was this response to his near fall. *What would these two be like should I keel over completely?*

"It's his head, Father. He's been favoring it since he arrived."

"Delayed reaction. You must take my cure, now, Alastair," Tewes said. "Can you walk to my clinic? In the chair, under the strap, so your head'll be stabilized as I conduct my examination."

"I am quite all right. No need for a fuss. Don't wanna be a bother or a—"

"Burden? Inspector, trust me. You've long ago surpassed—"

"Why don't you *tell him*?" asked Gabby.

"Tell me what?"

Jane gave her daughter a withering look, warning her not to say another word, but Gabby replied, "To get his blooming arse in that chair! Now!"

The two women each took an arm and helped him from parlor to clinic, guiding him into the doctor's waiting chair. From a haze, he smelled multiple chemicals and concoctions, saw shelves lined with books, and countertops strewn with gleaming instruments and probes.

Alastair felt instantly ill at ease even though the chair he found himself in was as comfortable as sin; in fact, doing as told, he closed his eyes and felt he could easily fall asleep here, finding himself awakened in the morning to the chime of Gabby's voice calling him to consciousness, asking if he wanted one or two eggs with his bacon.

To further relax him, Dr. Tewes's magical fingers began massaging Ransom's neck, moving on to ridges behind each ear. Tewes's thumb at each point, rhythmically rotated. Ransom realized this motion could put a man down fast. He thought what a tool of control is this. He'd never before been induced to such peace, but a sliver of suspicion kept fighting his desire to relax as Tewes repeatedly suggested—as the small, firm hands soothingly continued, careful to apply no pressure to the still throbbing sore point left by Muldoon's blackjack.

Tewes's hands pressed on, precision in each fingertip. Then all thumb action behind the ears ended for the full cranial massage, the talented fingers working to and from each temple, further easing his tension. He wanted to tell the doctor how wonderful this felt, but he felt perturbed, too, ashamed to be feeling so good at the touch of another man. In fact, the idea began to invade his mind—an inky stain fighting Tewes's mantra: "Heal thyself, Alastair . . . heal, heal, heal . . ."

"Tewes, I'm . . . I mean to say . . . I've never . . ."

"Quiet . . . heal, heal . . ."

"I find Jane intriguing. Being a man, I . . ."

She did not tell him to shut up.

". . . that is to say, I like women as you know . . ." Jane realized what he was so clumsily trying to tell Mister Tewes. ". . . and have naught interest in men in that regard . . . if you take my mean—"

"My God, Ransom. Each time I think there's hope for you, a bit of progress."

"I only want it clear that—"

"Please shut the noise out, especially the sound of your own voice! Not another word."

Ransom took the doctor's advice.

"Heal . . . heal thyself . . . heal . . ."

From somewhere nearby, Gabby's sweet laughter erupted. Tewes shushed her.

"Heal . . . heal . . . heal . . ."

Then Tewes's fingers lightly hovered over the huge lump that still throbbed and caused so much pain. He sensed the doctor, using those large magnets he'd seen on the tray near the chair, now performed his patented magnetism treatment.

While Ransom's eyes remained closed, Tewes softly whispered in his ear, "The body is filled with an electromagnetic energy that has the power to heal. I want you to picture this powerful energy inside your body, your head, your will, Alastair. You have it within to will this pain away . . . along with *all* your problems."

But Alastair no longer heard anyone.

"Mother," said Gabby, looking deeply into his features where he'd slid low in the chair.

"Don't interrupt, Gabby."

"But, Mother, he's asleep, otherwise I'd not call you mother."

"Asleep?" She came around and stared. "He must've needed it badly. Tough guy. Doesn't listen to his own body screaming for mercy. Poor man carries a great deal on those big shoulders."

"But why'd he come here to break down?"

"Had to stove in somewhere, so why not my chair?"

"But what's to happen tomorrow when he wakes? Are you going to sleep in that getup?"

"Let tomorrow take care of itself. For now, we leave Ransom to whatever dreams he may find."

"Fine . . . but are you going to stick to your resolution?"

"In time, yes."

"Please, Mother, he's falling for you!"

"Whatever do you mean?"

"He came here to see Jane again, not Tewes."

"You think so?"

"It's time he knows Dr. Jane Francis. Time he knows who he's got eyes for."

CHAPTER 22

Awaking in Dr. Tewes's chair, half on, half off and below a huge metal pyramid of brass, Ransom thought this reality yet another disturbing dream. But this was real. Tewes had put him under, but how? What'd the doctor use? Some sort of gas? An injection? He recalled nothing. Blinking, he realized the distinct absence of a headache, and in the inner coils of his ear, he heard Tewes's voice saying the single word—*heal*—over and over, only the voice coalesced into a woman's soothing voice, a voice that sounded vaguely like Gabrielle's but not quite . . . a voice that came with a visual image of a woman deep in a darkened mental portal—a doorway—and she'd waved him toward her, asking, "Why don't you ask for more?"

He straightened and stood, trying to brush away the wrinkles of the suit he'd worn for Jane. No doubt she knew of his being here, succumbing to her brother's touch. Only the sweet, tangy odor of frying bacon dislodged the terror of being under Tewes's absolute control. *Jane's out there preparing the doctor's breakfast. The perfect opportunity to slip away before anyone should see.*

Carefully, quietly he made his escape from the clinic, the pungent odors of Tewes's various cures filling his nostrils.

Someone'd loosed his shirt and tie and had taken his shoes off. He prayed Jane hadn't seen him so vulnerable. Another thought struck him: *Tewes's hands should be registered as a lethal weapon.*

Whatever else might be said of Tewes's methods, Ransom could not argue with results. His head, even the nasty lump, no longer plagued him, plus he'd gotten through an entire night without interruption or medication—so far as he knew.

He picked up his shoes and tiptoed down the hallway, toward the outer foyer running alongside the parlor. Here he had some vague memory of nearly collapsing as much from fatigue, he realized, as from the steady headache.

He eased the door open. One part of his mind said stay, say hello to Jane, and thank Gabby and her father for not throwing him out the night before, while another part of his mind played tug-o-war with embarrassment at having caved in under this man's touch, even if it were called therapy of a kind, because there was an undeniable attraction to have those hands on him again, and this disturbed Ransom. *An attraction for another man's touch.* He imagined what his friends around the poker barrel, at the tavern, at the station house and the firehouse would say if they should ever hear of it.

Yet he wanted to make successive visits to Tewes's unusual chair, to again take the cure—to be *healed* . . . even if temporarily. But mostly, he wanted to feel the man's hands again against his temples, over the crown, behind the ear.

One foot in, one out the door, hip-deep in indecision, Ransom felt like an unlikely, over-the-hill, misplaced Hamlet unable to decide. Meanwhile, a flood of sunlight raced into the foyer and down the hall, which must announce him. He quickly closed the door and realized some movement in the nearby bushes. "Who is it? Who's there?"

"It's me . . . Bosch!" came the whisper.

"Bosch? Why the deuce're you hiding in Tewes's shrubbery?"

"Your orders—get what I can on the doctor."

Bosch was his best snitch, known on the street as Dot'n'-Carry for the noise resulting from the point-counterpoint between a wooden foot and cane. A decorated veteran of two wars, one of them being the War of the Rebellion, Bosch had previously traveled abroad and had signed up in the British Army and had fought in the Crimean War until he'd had a bellyful of death, and so had deserted, swearing never again. Then came the Civil War, and being destitute, a suit of clothes, hardtack and beans, and a government-issue Sharps rifle ended all horror of war.

"I enlisted for all the reasons that scuttle a man," Bosch told anyone stopping at his tin cup. He sold stories for meager coin. He slavered and spewed forth through missing teeth the entire war and all the reasons for it save the glory of it. Down to how he'd gotten out when his left foot had been amputated in a field hospital while some man with a camera took photos to send off to Washington. He would joke that Old Abe Lincoln, in order never to forget the atrocities of the war, hung Bosch's severed foot in his White House bedroom to contemplate each night, and how this was the chief cause of Mary Lincoln's having gone mad.

Bosch had a lot of stories in his head, many told so often people no longer listened. He had many yet to be told, and many that would never be told, but Ransom knew one thing certain about Bosch, and that was his birthright, his gift, which was the theater and storytelling. His ability with words had never been adequately put to proper use. He ought to've been on the Lyceum circuit, on stage beside the humorists like Twain and Brett Harte and the fellow who told Uncle Remus tales—Joel Chandler Harris. Most certainly, Bosch proved a man in need of a much larger audience, but failing all his life, he now made a scant living at a game requiring a lively imagination along with forked tongue—working for Ransom on the one hand, outlaws on the other. It gave Bosch his only stage, and with his quick wit, he'd managed to survive for a long time on Chicago streets where—should he tell the wrong story to the wrong man at the wrong time—it could be his last.

On the whole, Ransom liked the little ferret-faced mole, and was probably the only one left alive who called him Bosch and not Dot'n'Carry for the sport of it.

Ransom slipped his shoes on and followed the weasel into the bush, and together they found a cow path that took them a safe distance. Below a livery stable sign reading Phillips & Son they talked.

"So what can you tell me of Tewes?"

"He's no kind of man."

"I'm aware he's effeminate. What else?"

"The doctor is a woman."

"Tewes? A woman? What're you saying?"

"I've only me word, but I saw him——errr . . . her dressing down, and I tell you Dr. Tewes has breasts, nice ones in fact."

"Damn you for a fool, Bosch! You saw Miss Ayers! His sister!" Alastair raised his cane for effect. "Get 'way from me now or I'll bash your head."

"I tell you what I see, and this is me reward? Where's me two dollars?"

"I don't pay for nonsense or fiction, Bosch!"

"All right, all right, have it your way, the doctor's a man and keep it that way, but you'll want to know about your friend Kohler and what he's about."

"What is your addled brain spewing forth now?"

"You wanted to know what your Dr. Tewes has on Kohler, so I kicked around, and I tell you, dirt falls away from your chief. If he has secrets, you can't pry it loose on the street, but there is something."

"So what have you, damn it?"

"Confound it, Ransom, you got it backward from the start!" He lifted his own cane, jabbing it at Alastair.

Using his cane sword-fashion, Ransom batted Bosch's off. From Jane Francis's window, they looked like two schoolboys playing pirate, crossing swords.

"So go on, say it, man! Must you be so damnably irritating, Bosch?"

With dramatic flourish, Bosch said, "Kohler ain't the one being blackmailed."

"What?"

"Kohler has something on Tewes, and I done told you what it is!"

"Mark me, if this turns out to be one of your silly fabrications," began Ransom, fuming even as he thrust two silver dollars at the man, the coins falling to the dirt, "I'll find you and skin you alive."

"I'd expect so from a man of your repute, Inspector."

"Now be gone and no more peeking into any bloody windows."

"But 'twas on your say-so! How else to see a lady in Tewes's bedroom?"

"Scat as fast as that stump and cane will allow. Go!"

He made off with his coins, an habitual look back over his gnarled shoulder—a ratlike habit he'd picked up over years on the streets after his medical discharge from the Union Army.

"Damn fool . . . damn old fool," Ransom muttered as he turned and started back toward the busier Belmont Street out front of Tewes's home where he might more readily hail a carriage. He wanted to get home, bathe, shave, get spruced up, look in on Philo, and see Jane again.

He dismissed Bosch's contention that Jane and Dr. Tewes were one and the same as ridiculous. No way he wouldn't've known. He'd spent time with both, hadn't he? He had downed beer with Tewes, drank him under the table, which had been no surprise, and then he'd carried him home. So light he was, yes. And then when measuring the man, he came out even slighter in all lengths than Ransom would have guessed, and the man's ankle had been so thin and fragile, and his waist nonexistent, and on occasion his voice cracked like a youth.

What if Bosch had not seen Jane Francis Ayers disrobing but had watched Tewes disrobe instead? Was he a woman posing as a man, or a man posing as a woman? Jesus! The thought electrified him. Bosch's second contention, that Tewes was being blackmailed by Nathan Kohler seemed unimportant to the first mystery.

It boggled the mind . . . boggled the imagination. If any of it were true, then who had shared a kiss in the gondola on the Ferris wheel with Alastair Ransom? Dr. Tewes or Jane or both?

And then he thought anew of the touch of Tewes's hands, how he'd reacted to that touch, and how his every instinct had recoiled at the thought of a man capable of creating such feelings in him. But suppose . . . it made better sense that . . . *possibly* . . . but then how could he have been so damnably blind if it were so?

He stood on the street down from Tewes's shingle, recently repaired and rehung, as it'd been hit by a clean bolt of lightning during a storm, he'd been told. Someone stood on Tewes's porch, trying to gain his attention. It was Jane, waving him to return. He had so liked her, but now his head had begun to swim with the sharks of doubt and suspicion. If Jane were Tewes, and Tewes were Jane, what possibly could he do with this information? How to react?

He must respond to Jane now. Must return to the home and see the doctor and his sister side-by-side, something he'd not seen in all their association. And as he moved back toward the home, he looked for the third bedroom. He could make out the windows of only one bedroom this side of the house, and Gabrielle's room he'd surmised was on the other side of the house. So where did Jane keep? Which window had Bosch been staring through when he saw a woman disrobing? And could it simply have been Gabby that the little pervert had seen?

"Jane!" he called out.

"I was preparing a breakfast for you, and next I know, you're gone!" she said, all smiles. "Besides, I must talk to you this morning."

"Actually, I really need to speak to your brother. Is he having breakfast with us?"

"I . . . I can arrange it, yes, if . . ."

"If he's not slipped from the house?"

"F-for Cook County."

"Ahhh . . . to view the bodies of the two unfortunates found in the park last night?"

"Unless he's still in."

"Shall we find out if the doctor is in? Does he have any appointments today?"

"I think not in clinic; perhaps a house call or two."

"His work for Chief Kohler has been a help, no doubt. I'm sure the chief can be a generous man."

"Not with Dr. Tewes, I fear."

"I see."

"Shall we go inside?" A horse-drawn trolley went by, a man shouting about rags and bottles to buy and sell—the noise of Chicago awakening. Ransom followed her to the kitchen, where Jane sat him before a sumptuous breakfast.

"Eat," she commanded. "Dr. Tewes says you work too hard, you're not getting enough sleep, and that your eating habits are abominable."

"Once again, your brother's right." He ate while Jane watched, pleased, her smiling eyes not at all like Tewes, yet similar. "You and James, Jane . . . you weren't . . . I mean, were you born twins? Your features, particularly the eyes are so strikingly similar."

"Born a year apart."

"Really, a year apart. Seems it'll be a year before I see the two of you *not* apart."

"You mean together, don't you? He acts my guardian, and it is stifling at times, 'though he has my best interests at heart."

"So now, where is your *older* brother, is it?"

"I think you're being coy with me, Alastair, and I don't appreciate it. Either say what is on your mind regarding myself and the doctor, or get off the subject."

"Where is this coming from?" he asked, dropping his fork.

"I saw you with that ratty little man who's been on our

back stair, not to beg food but to peek through windows. You hired him to spy on us, didn't you?"

"I did not authorize him to come to your home and beat about your windows, no!"

"Oh, wonderful, nice consolation, but he came, and he saw, and he told you what you wanted to learn, that I am Dr. Tewes!"

"I did not . . . that is . . . I failed to believe Bosch."

"But you're here to corroborate—" she began, affecting Tewes's mannerisms now. "Well perhaps it is all for the better that you know."

"I wanted to believe in . . . in you, in some future we might have, but this . . . this . . ."

"Changes things, I know. You should go now, Alastair."

"Go? Go? I have this boulder drop on me, and all you can say is go? Ha!" He near whispered, "What'll the lads make of it? Chicago's greatest detective, Inspector Ransom, could not decipher a woman in drag!"

"The sum total of your concern? What other cops'll think?"

"If the press got wind of—"

"Kohler'd have a good day."

"—and what hooks has Kohler in you, anyway? What goes on between you two? He *knows,* right? God, he must be having a laugh. Is this *all* that he has on you?"

"It is enough . . . along with the story of how Gabby's father died, but last night, I told Gabby everything, so I'm done with lies," she lied, "finished, and I intend, sir, to end all ties with Nathan, this case, and most of all you, sir."

"I see . . . I see . . ."

"I . . . hope you understand."

"It becomes apparent. Right between the eyes, in fact. What a fool I've been. All the things I said to you at the wheel, all the thoughts I had for—"

"For us? You came for Jane only to gather information on James!"

"Will that be your excuse then?" he asked. "To keep us apart? Well, I see you've no need of my . . . of me."

"That's not entirely—"

"But how is it a woman of your caliber can affect such a ruse?"

"How not when a doctor of my caliber is treated as a leper?"

"Act the leper, you become the leper," he shot back, knocking over a chair as he stood. The sound of it, like a gunshot, sent Gabby running headlong to them with her Sharps pointed.

"Out, out! Inspector!" Gabby shouted.

"Fiercely loyal to your *mother*, aren't you, Gabby? A good thing. She'll need all your support—"

"I'll not have you shouting at or harming my . . . my—"

"It's all right. She is your mother now; no need of pretense, Gabby, and please no need pointing a weapon. I am going."

"I understand your anger, Alastair." Jane placed a hand on his, but now her touch didn't feel like the soothing fingers she'd used the night before.

He pulled from her touch. "How ironic that in the most intimate moment I shared with you, you were Dr. Tewes."

"You should come back for more treatments, Alastair, but for now, I think it must be as patient and doctor and nothing more."

"Do you believe I want anything more?"

"Then you will seek help . . . with the headaches?"

He stood silent a moment, considering this. "I can go to any number of phrenologists in this city for my head, and any number of brothels for all else I need, Dr. what is it? Ayers?"

He rushed out to her saying, "Francis . . . Dr. Jane Francis."

Gabby stared across at her, an accusatory look in her eye. "What?"

"You did not do right by Alastair, Mother."

"And I suppose holding him at gunpoint is all right?

Look, I'm doing the best I can! And I'm not about to apologize for my choices. Hell, I tell the truth and what does it earn me?"

"It will earn you scorn and my ridicule. I knew the chickens'd come home to roost."

"Not now, Gabby. I do not need this." Jane rushed to her room and locked the door, where Gabby listened to her sobs. Gabby almost knocked, wanting to go to her mother, but some inner strength told her no, not this time. This time her mother must face her decision alone.

Gabby wondered how she might somehow maintain contact with Alastair. She wanted so to learn from him and from his connections all about police work and police science and police medicine, and to end her own lies with her mother about how her studies at NU were going so well.

Mother can be such a fool, but Gabby saw in Alastair far more than all the stories that orbited around him. She saw so much vulnerability in him, so much hurt and pain and the years of service and misery and professionalism and results. He was so much more than the story of a killing before Haymarket, a killing that may or may not have precipitated the bomb that had killed his mates.

Ransom fumed all the way home. He'd finally been cornered to sit for Tewes's phrenology and magnetic therapy, had placed his misshapen, suffering head unknowingly in Jane Francis's hands, to "take the cure" and not only had Dr. Tewes's touch—*her touch*—cured his recurrent headaches and the localized pain Muldoon had put on him, but the session proved instructive. There might well be something to this magnetism stuff after all. Maybe.

The session had been, he privately confessed, decidedly and strangely appealing and intriguing, and perhaps for Jane as well—for both partners in this unusual coupling of "detectives" searching amid chaos. In her way, she, too, searched for form and structure in a world devoid of shape or sense. Alastair continued to feel a pull toward Jane Francis and their topsy-turvy, fascinating if bizarre relationship.

Now that Ransom had learned the truth, a whole new dynamic between them might naturally arise. So much made sense to him now. From the beginning there'd been a sexual tension, as when he'd become so outrageous in the train station, planting that head against Tewes's—*her* clean white suit, even then there'd been a layer of conflict at work that he'd not fully understood—until now! The wonders of hindsight, and at the back of his head—a head that felt so much better, and a head yearning for her touch again, and filled with a sad truth: *If ever she touches me again, and me knowing it's her touch, how much more wonderful?*

Alastair must work to overcome anger both at the deception and an inability to've discovered it, when all along, it'd been staring him in the face—as all the clues had been there. "Open and shut case," Ransom told himself now, arriving at home. "What in hell was I thinking?"

This made the cabbie and his horse each look back at Ransom. "Begging your pardon, sir?" asked the cabbie. "Something amiss?"

Ransom looked at the man for the first time, a noticeably striking pair of black eyes like olive-sized grapes without seeds. The man's forehead was large as well, his hairy single brow a ledge over the eyes. The man looked like one of Lombroso's supposed villainous types—a real Cro-Magnon. In the old days, and sometimes even now, under conditions of ignorance, police arrested men for their brutish looks, and the stains on their teeth and on their aprons—even if they were butchers—many for brutal rapes, murders, assassinations, and anarchy, like the man Ransom had once killed while hog-tied to a chair. Yes, the cabbie could easily be arrested for a multiple murderer with a garrote and a can of kerosene on his ugly looks alone, and when his picture was splashed across every neighborhood paper in every conceivable language across the city, everyone could sleep better, knowing the Chicago PD had their man under lock and key.

Yes, a man like this fellow would do fine for the Phantom of the Fair; he'd be so easily inked-in by Thom Carmichael's sketch artist. The cabbie even had the attire of a gent, decked in high boots, black cape, and top hat. But then his horse was an ugly creature, too, so maybe the horse would do just as well for the killer. But then, should a horse be arrested for looking suspicious? Should a man?

How anyone could use facial features as an indicator, or the size of a man, or the fact he made a living with an axe or a blade, was beyond Ransom.

"Was it something else you wanted, sir?" again asked the cabbie. "I can hold here for you, if it's your wish, Captain."

"No . . . no, nothing more, my friend. Feed your horse well." He tipped the man an additional two bits.

Ransom opened the door on his flat on Des Plaines Street to the tune of the horse's hooves against cobblestones. He liked his private life, liked the place here, what he had surrounded himself with, his collection of books, paintings, his gramophone on which he played operatic symphonies. He liked being surrounded by his collection of guns and rifles, most hanging on walls or lying under glass. His furnishings had been his father's, mostly heavy oak and leather. His place was warm and brown, and his shelves had dagucrreotypes of his mother and father. The neighborhood was pleasant, tree-lined, green, and well kept. He liked the people in the area, mostly Germans—"Dunkers"—who kept pretty much to themselves, were industrious, opened businesses like food kiosks and beer gardens, and Ransom liked their music and the colorful steins they served their beer in, not to mention the great wienersnitzel prepared at the Frauhouse or Mirabella's. All close to the Des Plaines police station where he worked.

Once inside, Ransom found his soap and indoor shower. Not everyone enjoyed such luxuries, certainly not in Chicago, but Ransom had long ago had the shower installed and more recently the indoor toilet, a Thomas Crapper invention.

A shower and a shave and what was nowadays being called a crap all in the privacy of one's own home.

In the shower, Ransom soaked up and rinsed down, and he thought of nothing but Jane Francis, and he wondered why life is as it is, follows a straight path to disappointment and misadventure. Why'd she feel compelled to lie all this time, passing herself off as Tewes? Why'd she get herself into such a quandary with Nathan—to lie for him. Why he hadn't met Jane far sooner, to've been there when she needed him most? He struggled against a knee-jerk reaction of anger toward her; all anger reserved now for the real fool here—himself! "And that little creep Bosch . . . right all along," he said to the shower stall.

He toweled off and looked at the clock. Eleven-twenty already and he'd not reported in, but who was watching? He often worked the street, checked with snitches, talked to the neighborhood vendors, merchants, tavern owners to learn what was up, and who was doing what to whom, and how often and where and when, and in the end why. So no one would think it strange that he'd not checked in, and if anyone needed him, they could ring the bell or make a call now, as he'd had a phone installed.

He found clean clothes, a nice suit not slept in. A glance at his pocket watch on the end of its fob told him it was half past noon, and his stomach concurred. He wandered out and down the street to Mirabella's, a German restaurant with outside tables and chairs. Along the way, he'd picked up a copy of the latest *Chicago Tribune,* seeing that its headline screamed news of the double murder at the lagoon alongside a photo depicting the flaming boat at the tunnel entrance. Some Johnny-on-the-spot reporter had caught the sight moments before police doused the flames. No doubt whoever the photographer was, he'd collected a fine reward for the startling shot. But nowhere in the frame could a killer be found.

Once seated with a beer in hand, Thom Carmichael stood over him and declared, "*Tribune*'s behind the *Herald*! Take a look at a real scoop!" He dropped his paper onto Ransom's table, the headline screaming: ARREST MADE IN WORLD'S

FAIR PHANTOM CASE. A logline below this read: "Chief Nathan Kohler nabs suspected multiple murderer." This made Ransom sit up and almost spill his beer. "An arrest made? By Kohler?" People at other tables overheard. The more curious waited to hear more.

"Appears Kohler's scored big. For the sake of the city and future victims, I pray it is a good arrest, but I have me doubts, Alastair."

But Alastair only half heard as his rage erupted on reading the name of the accused: *Philo Keane.*

Cursing Kohler, Ransom stood, swilled the last of his beer, tossed down a coin, and rushed for the station house, shouting back, "Where're they holding Philo? Bloody fools! And why didn't you get this news to me sooner?"

"Your own house, of course! Des Plaines lockup—the Bridewell. The story's selling newspapers!"

When he got to the station house, she was there—Dr. Jane Francis, but dressed as Tewes. "Whatever are you doing here like this? I thought once your ruse was up, that you'd've the decency to—"

"I came to plead your case with Kohler, but Kohler is out for your head, you fool, and you go about as if he were manageable. And meanwhile, people around the two of you get hurt."

"Hurt. You speak to me of hurt?"

Police around them began to look askance. *What must the lads be making of this,* he wondered. "Don't dare put yourself between Nathan and me," he said, leading her down a set of steps to a basement area that housed cold case files. "It can only get you trouble beyond your imaginings."

"Alastair, you've not said a word about when we were children together."

"Children . . . you and me?"

"For a brief time, we shared the same teacher, Mrs. *Ornery,* my father called her."

"Mrs. Onar?" he asked.

"Then you do recall the mad Mrs. Onar?"

"She kept a whiskey bottle in her bottom left drawer. Yes, I recall her."

"Good, then you must recall little Jane? Little Jane Francis? Me!"

"I remember the dour old teacher, but you. Francis . . . Jane Francis, I . . . I'm sorry."

"I was pulled from the school, put in St. Albans, as Father could not abide Mrs. Onar and her rules and her lack of imagination and human compassion."

"The milk of kindness she never knew."

"My father was Dr. William Francis. You must remember him?"

"Not a whole lot about those years I've chosen to remember."

"I never forgot you. You were instantly kind to me. You rescued me."

"Rescued?"

"There was a bully named Evan . . . Evan Kingsbury."

"Sorry . . . don't recall him either."

There lingered an awkward moment of silence during which their eyes met. He quickly broke off eye contact and said, "So explain to me now why . . . why all this charade, this living a lie?"

"Economic need mostly. People won't go to a female doctor, unless, I suppose there is no other. I had thought to go westward—"

"California?"

"But there's little hope of good medical schools out west for Gabby, so . . . so . . ."

"So you concocted an even crazier notion?"

"It would've served me well but for Nathan."

"But how did he find you out when—"

"When you found it impossible?"

"Hold on. I was onto you . . . after a while."

"Yes, after I confessed." She began to laugh.

He looked piqued at her laughter, then angry eyed, then he was fighting back his own laugh until he could contain it no more.

People heard their laughter rising up the stairwell, bouncing off stone walls.

When settled, he slapped open the *Herald*'s headline. "Have you seen this? Damn fools've arrested Philo Keane for the murders?"

"Keane? No! Isn't he the fellow with the enormous tripod at the train station?" She scanned the news account. "Says here he knew two of the victims intimately. Chesley Mandor and Polly Pete."

"No, Philo paid them for posing."

"Intimates, he took more than their picture according to—"

"Bloody Carmichael will write anything if he thinks it'd sell a paper. I first met Merielle from one of Philo's photos, and it was Philo who set me on a path of having her."

"She had a very different version of events. Alastair, she felt as indentured to you as she did to Jervis. She had a problem with men."

"But I tell you, Philo would never harm a woman."

"Perhaps."

"Nathan Kohler is trying to bait me and using people I care about to do it, and he's doing a fine job of it. He used you, now Philo. Who's next? Who is safe? Only those who distance themselves from me as Griffin has done."

"Drimmer?"

"According to the paper, Drimmer assisted Kohler in the arrest."

While further scanning the newspaper, she said, "They must've had some provocation, some proof to move on the man . . . I mean police act only if they have something to go on. I mean to raid his home and arrest him."

"I know of many a case where men've been sent off to prison on flimsy evidence, foolish assumptions, prejudices, wrong conclusions, nonsense beaten out of a suspect when all else fails. I also know of cases in which a man was put to death on eyewitness accounts that later proved false."

"If you believe in Mr. Keane's innocence, then you must fight for him."

"Have to see what they have concluded. Why they targeted Philo."

"He'll need a lawyer."

"A good Chicago lawyer, one who knows every loophole."

"I know just the man. Malachi Quintin McCumbler."

"Then hire him on Philo's behalf, and I'll go find where they've got Philo. I fear incarceration alone will kill him. He is an artist, after all."

"I quite understand. Go to him. Tell him others believe in him and are working on his behalf."

She started up the stairwell, but he grabbed her hand and held on. "Why are you doing this? You hardly know Philo."

"But I know *you*." She skipped up the stairs, so obviously feminine now to his eye that everyone in the building must know of her ruse. And by extension all of Chicago.

"How could I've been so confounded blind?" *Maybe I'm losing my edge . . . maybe it's time to find a pasture, Rance.*

As if to answer himself, Alastair added, "You mean like the one in Nathan's dreams? So not right. . . ."

CHAPTER 23

Dr. Tewes's daughter's infatuation with the burgeoning police sciences—from fingerprinting to use of first communications between U.S. cities like New York and Chicago—had not set well with Jane. Not anymore than when Gabrielle confessed a desire to go into a program at Rush Medical under Dr. Christian Fenger to become a pathologist and eventually a coroner rather than a general practitioner or surgeon.

Much to her mother's chagrin, Inspector Ransom had taken it upon himself to instruct Gabby in such matters. Her mother's response only meant a new reason to distance herself from Inspector Ransom. Jane had tried to dissuade her daughter from such prurient interests as she exhibited for pathological medicine, and she'd started out this morning on a major plan to nip it in the bud.

"Why would you trade a medical practice that dealt with health and life for one dealing entirely with cadavers?" she pleaded with Gabby.

"Cadavers don't talk back?" she quipped.

"Give it up, this notion! Along with the insufferable suffragettes."

Finally, Gabby had lost her patience, shouting she'd do

neither. Her mother followed her into her room. "You'll fin-ish your studies at NU, young lady."

"No! I'll either work with Dr. Fenger or I'll quit medicine altogether!"

"And do what?"

"Help the cause of women's suffrage!"

This only heightened the tension. Mother and daughter glared at one another—Jane having just left Alastair, and hav-ing again dressed as Tewes. Gabby, losing all patience, shouted, "I do not intend going through life as a man! And what good've you done, Mother, for women in medicine or—"

"What are you saying?"

"—or for women's suffrage in living a lie like this?"

Her voice shaking, hurt, Jane said, "If you're going to throw away your chance at NU . . . and you believe you would prefer working under Dr. Fenger's tutelage, then I—I'll not stand in your way. But—"

"Naturally, there's a but—"

"But this is the deal: You do not parade about this city in a show of bras, breasts, bloomers, and buttocks in public. Is that understood?"

Gabby frowned. "Really, Mother, you understand so little of public opinion, and you've fallen for the popular view against us."

"Do we have a deal?"

"But, Mother, you make it sound as if we'll be stoned as prostitutes in biblical times."

"Do we have a deal?"

"Iiii-yyyeah, I guess . . ."

"Then I guess I'd best get out and drum up some work for Dr. Tewes."

"But I thought . . . I mean, with a police inspector know-ing, and Chief Kohler knowing . . . that you'd be arrested if you went back to impersonating a male doctor."

"I've checked. There is no law on the books to stop me, as I am not impersonating a doctor, as I am a doctor, and I have a lawyer now who tells me that in fact, a legal suit against

me could bring publicity, and publicity could be made to
work for me. So for now, Dr. Tewes is a fixture, my corporate
figurehead if you will, and that makes it all quite legal."

"But why?"

"Foolish child, how else can I afford the famous Dr.
Fenger and Rush Medical School?"

That is how they'd ended it. Now Gabby crept out while Dr.
Tewes was on errand. Gabby'd made a beeline for the suffrage
meeting. The group intended a march straight through the
fairway at the Columbian Exposition. Their leader had made a
stirring speech a few days before, printed in two papers daring
to support a woman's right to the vote—one in Ukrainian, one
in Polish. The speech spoke of the irony of Chicago's hosting
a world's fair when women in Chicago, and all across America, were denied equality and equal voting rights. "And how
barbaric it all is," Gabby confided to a sympathetic cabbie
who'd gotten her to the meeting on time.

Gabby felt strongly about suffrage. Nothing—not her
word, not her deal, not her chances of working with Dr.
Fenger, and not even her mother—could keep her from her
appointed destiny.

"Philo, what the hell've you done? Get up!" Ransom
slammed his cane into the bars to wake the sleeping man.
"An innocent man doesn't sleep in a holding cell, Philo! Get
up and at least act agitated and appalled and outraged!" But
it wasn't Philo who turned over in the bunk, but a derelict, in
fact the man from the train station who'd been their only
eyewitness. "Orion Saville, right? It's you!"

"They run me down, said I was a material witness. Said I
should cooperate. Had me up all night. Told me I must've
seen this here fella."

"The hell you say? Chicago police planting the seeds of
evidence?"

"Don't know."

"Did they put up men before you? A lineup?"

"Yeah, that's what they called it."

"Not a photo array? Real men?"

"Yes, a lot of different looking fellas I never seen before."

"Did you point one out?"

"I did."

"But man, you just said you had seen none of them before."

"They wanted me to point to one."

"They pressed you to choose one?"

"They did."

"And did you already know which one they wanted you to point out?"

"I knew."

"How did you know which one would please them?"

"How's a man know when a deef and dumb fellow wants to barter?"

"I see. You read their gestures, and all of them pointed to a man named Philo Keane."

"Don't know 'is name, but he shook when I pointed 'im out."

"I gotta go help my friend out of this mudslide he's in."

"Sorry for the part I played, but they had me up all night. Can you get me outta this cell?"

But Ransom was already gone in search of where they held his friend. He stomped up to the second floor, not willing to wait for the lift. The noise of his cane beat a hasty rhythm along the steps as he ascended. Like a rattler on a snake, some observed, the way he used that cane as a warning of an impending showdown.

He burst into one interrogation room and found two fellow inspectors interrogating Philo's landlady, the woman in tears. He slammed the door and moved on to the next bare room, finding Philo half asleep, one hand holding down a piece of paper, the other trying to negotiate his signature.

Ransom rushed round the table, pushing Griffin into a chair when he dared get in the way, while Kohler shouted, "What kind of ass do you intend making of yourself now, Alastair?"

Ransom ignored the others, grabbed up the half-scribbled

signature on the confession and ripped it to shreds. "You bastards are railroading this man! Look at him! He is in no condition to sign anything!"

"The man has confessed, Ransom! Confessed to multiple murder!" protested Griffin.

"And it will stick to the end." Kohler's smug look was that of a preening rooster.

"I'm taking him outta here," Ransom declared.

"Try it and you'll be arrested and stripped of rank!" shouted Kohler.

"Alastair," said Griffin, putting up both his hands in a gesture of pleading.

Kohler pulled out a Smith & Wesson .32 caliber and pointed it at Ransom. "One attempt to take our confessed prisoner from custody, Inspector, and you will be shot."

"He needs no further provocation, Ransom," declared Griffin.

"Why wasn't I consulted? Why did I have to learn of this idiocy from Thom only this morning?"

"We tried to locate you, but afraid—" began Griff.

"You bloody know Kohler didn't want me on hand. Else there'd've been a fight when you attempted an arrest! Right, Nathan?"

"Give you enough rope . . ." Kohler glared across at him, his gun still pointed at Ransom's chest.

"You arrest a man for murder just to bait me?"

"Sheer babbling nonsense from the brook of insanity."

"And you, Griff, you Judas!"

"We have proof, evidence," Griff countered.

"Coincidence only cuts so much ice," said Kohler.

"What proof? What evidence?"

Griff grabbed a closed file lying on the table and spilled forth its contents. "Photos of several of the victims in the nude."

"Jesus! The man makes his living as a blasted photographer! Women go to him for this express purpose. The girls pay for copies, and they in turn sell them for extra cash."

"It's obscene," said Kohler. "Disgusting. Against all decency! He's e'en got the pregnant victim posing in the nude."

"Obscene to you, but they fail as evidence in a court of law."

"You're now a lawyer?" challenged Kohler, still pointing his gun.

"Please, Chief, put the gun down," cautioned Griff, seeing the older man's finger tighten about the trigger.

"What other coincidence have you?" challenged Ransom.

"His words, his *own* words. Several witnesses heard him at the scene the other night." Griffin breathed easier seeing that the chief had lowered his weapon.

"Philo was speaking only of his loss, his grief." Running both hands through his hair, Ransom paced the room like an angry lion. It looked as if he might break down a wall.

Kohler countered with, "He spoke of his involvement with two victims, and now we know of a third."

"I know what he said!"

"You've not sat and read his confession. You ripped it up instead! Pick it up, piece it together and bloody read it, Inspector!" Nathan shouted across the table at him.

Ransom reluctantly found the scattered pieces and puzzled it back together, then scanned the bogus document. "This is crap," he challenged Kohler.

"Crap? What do you mean, crap?"

"What else do you have on Philo?"

"He knew Trelaine and they argued—repeatedly—on each occasion of their meeting, according to the landlord."

Griffin added, "At the top of their lungs."

"What the bloody hell else do you have? Because you take this garbage into a Chicago courtroom, this flimsy bull, and you, Chief, you'll be laughed out of the building. You'd be lucky to land a job selling plumbing fixtures."

Suddenly, Philo shouted out, "I've pleaded with them all night and all day, Alastair. I could not kill my love, never! Trelaine, yes, but never—"

"Shut up, Philo! You'll dig your own grave with these fools!"

The room fell into a deep silence at this.

Still, Ransom saw that Philo had been beaten, and that he'd been deprived of sleep, food, water, facilities. He could well imagine what they'd been telling Philo. Lies, half-truths, and deception in the hands of a skilled interrogator proved powerful tools. What might normally seem absolute nonsense—like elves born of drink and hallucination—became absolute fact over the course of rough interrogation. Ransom knew this too well. He'd employed the same methods to win a much wanted confession and subsequent conviction. These men were trained so well that they could convince an innocent man of any guilt they wished.

Seeing the result of this type of pressure applied to a man he loved, Ransom felt a pang of guilt and shame in himself. Further, he condemned himself on Philo's behalf. Why in the name of all that was holy hadn't he seen this subterfuge reaching toward Philo in its snaking course toward Ransom himself? Foresight appeared to have abandoned him.

Looking across the bare table now at Philo, seeing him stripped of all personal dignity this way—stripped of his cameras, his shield in a sense, and stripped of his gift and his confident manner, left without his calling, without his art— the man looked a child. This image tore at Ransom like a pair of horns coming out of nowhere; terribly disheartening as it was, he could not imagine the depth of Philo's own feelings at what he'd endured here. How much fear Philo must be harboring. Fear not so much over losing his life on the gallows, but losing his art and all future time with his craft.

Ransom stared into Kohler's eyes and spoke to him. "Unless you have some more compelling evidence, I'm taking this man home."

"Home," Philo repeated the single word, his dry throat cracking.

"He blackmailed Trelaine with a series of disgusting nude photos of Miss Mandor. She did not have them made for duplicating, but he kept the negatives, and without her consent or knowledge, he sent a set to Trelaine and attempted to extort money."

Ransom gritted his teeth and recalled Philo's new camera. For a moment he thought of lashing out at Philo, but it would serve no purpose here and now.

"I swear it is a lie," said Philo, sensing Ransom's disappointment. "It is all a lie, all of it, including my bogus confession starved and sweated from me!"

"Don't you see, Ransom," said Griffin. "He knew Polly . . . knew Miss Mandor . . . knew Trelaine."

"And the Polish girl, likely pregnant with his seed!" added Kohler.

"So he is guilty of knowing too many people?"

"Too many dead people, yes."

"Two of whom he admits to having had sex with!" added Kohler.

Ransom's eyes did a saber dance with his one-time trusted partner, Griffin. "Do you have one thing, one document, one fingerprint match, one object, anything to link him to the killings? Does his handprint match the two we found?"

"What of this?" asked Kohler, shaking a small envelope and letting its contents, a ring, roll free. This act surprised everyone in the room.

"Whose is it?" asked Philo.

Nathan dug in. "I trust you can identify the ring, Inspector Ransom."

Ransom had frozen in place, staring at the ring. His mind trying to wrap around the power of this incriminating diamond ring.

Kohler dug in deeper. "After all, it belonged to your Polly Pureheart, your Merielle, did it not?"

"You found this where?" he croaked, lifting the ring.

"In your friend's pocket." Kohler's look of triumph was clean and cold. Ransom hated him for it.

"In his pocket, Rance," began Griff, "as he was brought in, as you always taught me—log all possessions taken."

Ransom grabbed Philo roughly by the lapels, lifting his friend from his seat with the sudden surge of power. "Where did you come by the ring?"

"She owed me . . . money . . . she must've slipped it into my coat pocket without my knowing. She offered it up once, but Ransom, I refused it, reminding her that I was your friend and could not accept it."

"Why did she owe you money?"

"She was constantly borrowing. She played the horses every weekend."

"With whom did she book the races?"

"That scum-bucket Jervis . . . her old keeper, Ransom."

"Damn that ugly man. He's back? Bastard's ten times more likely your killer, Griff!"

"I checked early on, and Jervis is not in the city but back at his old haunts in Alton, Illinois."

Ransom felt his back to the wall. He grabbed up the pieces of the confession and threw them into the air. Then he added, "Send men after that prick Jervis, now you've your explanation for the ring, and if this is all the nonsense you have to book Philo on, you'll be fined for a nuisance, Nathan. Judge Artemis'll dismiss it before it sees a jury, I tell you."

"You are not taking him out of here," Kohler coldly responded. "We have put it out. We have our man. I am not about to send him skipping out the door with you on his arm like a pair of faggots. And as for going to Alton, you do that . . . go right ahead."

"What bloody fools you are, giving it out to the papers, holding a man on evidence of dubious value out of some sense of *embarrassment*?"

"He stays in jail until he is arraigned, bail is set—if any— and then you can have him if you can make his bail, but not before!"

Ransom looked from Kohler to Drimmer, finding both resolute and standing firm and covering the only door out. He looked back at Philo, who appeared about to fall off his chair from fatigue. "At least"—began Ransom—"find the man a cot to lie down on and show him a modicum of decency and—"

"We're not running a juvenile detention center here," interrupted Kohler.

"Fine . . . fine . . . but if I hear this man has been further mistreated, this cane"—he slammed it flat on the table, a gunshot result—"this sir'll find its way into a dark cavity." He lifted the tip toward Kohler, "And you'll look as twirly as a pinwheel. As for you, Philo, not another word to these two! Speak to no one but your lawyer."

"Lawyer? What lawyer?" asked Philo.

"He's on his way!" Ransom stormed past Kohler and Griff and out, slamming the door, in search of a moment's peace. Then he realized he still had Merielle's ring in his hand. He'd just accidentally removed the most damaging piece of evidence against Keane. He pocketed the ring, believing Philo's story, and should the ring disappear, it could only help his friend's cause. He felt no compunction about making the ring disappear since he knew in his heart two truths: Philo was the wrong man for the killings, and Kohler only went after Philo to piss on Alastair. The investigation into Philo Keane was on its face bogus.

But where to put the ring?

No doubt Kohler would be sending a frantic Griffin after him within minutes.

He saw Jane as Tewes with a lawyer in tow coming toward the doors. He rushed to greet them. "*Ahhh,* Dr. Tewes, so good of you to fetch Mr. McCumbler, the best defense in the city."

McCumbler, a hefty red-faced man, had held the jail doors open to many a criminal. Ransom and McCumbler knew one another well. "Usually, you and I are on opposite sides," the barrister commented.

"Not today. Interrogation Room number two, upstairs, *Esquire*, and don't be dissuaded by Nathan Kohler or *his* title, damn him! Our man is innocent and the so-called evidence against him is as weak as the chance of women voting in the next election."

Jane frowned at this.

Ransom then asked her, "Dr. Tewes, any chance you might have a headache powder in that bag of yours?"

"Let me dig about," and as she did so, Ransom dropped the ring into Dr. Tewes's coat pocket.

Griffin showed up just as Ransom was draining a dry headache powder from a folded wrapper, choking it down.

"All right, Alastair, where the deuce is the ring?"

Alastair continued to choke, pointing to his throat.

"My God, man, are you saying you swallowed it?"

"That's right, and to get it from my excrement, you'll need a warrant for search and seizure, and a pair of gloves."

Tewes had seen no ring and attested to the fact the stubborn inspector had indeed swallowed it whole. How he did any of it without a cup of water, Jane could not fathom. But then he had the neck and throat of a bear.

"Dr. Tewes, I want you to stay on Ransom till I get my warrant, and should he pass anything, I want you to still his hand from any flushing away of the evidence."

She stared, her mouth dropping.

"Will you do it?" asked Griffin.

"Do your own dirty work, Inspector Griffin." A smirk on her face, Jane rushed off, unaware of the ring in her pocket.

"Guess, old partner, it'll have to be you sifting through my shit then," Ransom said, pounding Griffin on the back. He then pointed to the streets. "I'm going out there to find the real killer. Keep up if you can."

Ransom rushed out, leaving Griff to his quandary. Ransom imagined what must be going through Griff's mind: *Should I go direct to Grimes to secure a warrant on Ransom's bodily functions, or go back upstairs to ask the boss, or should I keep on Ransom's ass . . . literally?*

Griffin decided to first return to Kohler to tell him the news that Ransom had swallowed the ring. When he entered, the lawyer was taking Kohler through the evidence again, and Philo Keane lay sprawled out over the table, snoring.

"Trelaine employed Keane?" asked Philo's lawyer now.

"And he personally knew three, possibly four of the victims."

"And had nude photos of several victims in a hidden box in his studio?" Defense attorney Malachi Q. McCumbler spoke solemnly, in polite tone. He did so while glancing from the nudes to his snoring client. "Well, on the surface of it, gentlemen, it would appear you have *some* small reason to suspect my client. I will see you at the arraignment."

"That won't be until day after tomorrow."

"Why so long?"

"Ask the court, not me."

"I'll send a man round with fresh clothing. See to it he has uninterrupted sleep and a shower, and any further questioning you do, you do so with me present. I will myself call round this evening to have a word with my client."

"We don't Molly-coddle murderers here, sir," Kohler coldly replied.

"No, I daresay not from the condition of the innocent!" Malachi's voice rose an octave and held in dramatic pause . . . "As, gentlemen, my client is presumed innocent until *proven* guilty."

"Trust me, he is guilty of multiple murder and does not deserve your time!" said Kohler.

"And you chaps, officers of the court that you are, you have some distance to go before that is a reality, sir." Even as McCumbler said this, he knew it true only in some fantasy world. Certainly, the notion of innocent until proven guilty—the reversal of the British Legal system in which a man was guilty till proven innocent—was in itself an ideal to which the American legal system aspired, but the notion could never be wholly attained, not when dealing with human nature. Men condemned first, apologized—if at all—later. Many a man in America and the world over had been lynched by a mob thanks to human nature. It was by no coincidence that every other hamlet dotting the American landscape was named Lynchburg. Malachi had practiced law for almost twenty-five years now in Chicago, and he'd seen a lot of men beaten and broken and convinced of their own guilt by brutal treatment. Torturing a suspect as they had Philo Keane, in Chicago police circles, had a name—routine questioning. Most certainly human nature was well at work here in the Des Plaines Street police house. Well and good and intact, unfortunately.

Griffin waited for McCumbler to leave before he dared tell Chief Kohler of the ring's being lost to the big man's stomach.

From just outside the door, as McCumbler stopped to adjust his glasses before negotiating the stairs, he heard Kohler's gargantuan bellow, a stretched-out *Nooooooo* streaming through the closed door.

He wondered what it might be about when he heard Kohler repeatedly shout the name *Ransom*. McCumbler knowingly smiled.

"I had thought, and happily so, that you were finished with this . . . this disguise of yours," Ransom said on catching up to Dr. Tewes at a cabstand. Several well-fed horses stood harnessed at Union Station.

"Come now, Inspector. Certainly, at times you must use disguises in your line of work—when it suits your purpose?"

Concentrating on her eyes and trying to ignore her mustache, Ransom replied, "Yes, I've used disguises in my work, but Jane . . . what more purpose can this serve you now?"

She backed to within inches of a horse at the cabstand. The horse reacted instinctively, nuzzling her into Ransom's arms. They had a laugh over this when Alastair caught her. To passersby and to anyone standing nearby, they seemed a pair of men quite infatuated with one another. Realizing this, Alastair quickly pulled away.

"Do you know how it's going to look when all comes to light?"

"It might begin to chip away at that brute image you've maintained."

"That image has saved my life on occasion."

"I'm sure I'd faint to hear just how."

"You failed to answer my question."

"The horse did not like the question."

He repeated it. "What more purpose can your disguise serve you? A beautiful woman like you?"

"Thank you for the compliment."

"Don't do that."

"Do what?"

"Deflect the question."

She stepped away from him and sat on a street bench. Busy people passed in and out of the train station. Ransom hovered and, out of one eye, he saw the cab at the front of the line begin its journey. This set off a domino effect, as each horse-drawn cab moved up one space in the line of seven, the exchange creating a soothing cadence of hooves against brick-laid road.

He wanted to hold her hand, but not like this . . . not so long as she looked the part of a man.

"Do you have any idea how long it would've taken me, as a woman, to interest Mr. Malachi McCumbler in taking Philo's case? So, being Dr. Tewes, he hopped right out of his seat and came."

"OK, point taken."

"And walking into a police station, a lone woman? I'd likely have been taken for a prostitute complaining of being robbed by my—"

"All right, point taken. Now I'll be needing my ring back."

"Your ring? What ring?"

"In your pocket."

She reached in, found the ring, and lifted it to the light. "It's beautiful."

"They found it somehow in Philo's possession. Merielle had promised under no circumstance to ever part with it, and the last time I saw her alive, she had it on, and next they find it in Philo's pocket."

"What?"

"Made me, for a moment, believe Keane murdered my Mere, the way Kohler sprung it."

"Nathan's good at that."

"Sure is. Hey, look . . . I wanna thank you for the other night when you eased my pain."

"Easing a headache, *ahhh* . . . that's nothing. To ease a broken heart, now there . . . anyone capable of that will make a fortune and have patients galore. Have I told you how very sorry Gabby and I are for your loss? It was evident you loved Merielle."

"I've arranged for a small wake—Donegan's on Halsted, tomorrow night. If you can be there."

"If you're sure you want me."

"As yourself, yes . . . not the doctor. He will be unwelcome."

He placed the diamond ring onto his pinky finger. "Won it in a card game," he lied, "same as Polly Pete. Thought she and it belonged together."

"How'd Keane come by it?"

"Philo was in no condition to discuss it; he *thinks* she slipped it to him on the sly, something about repaying a debt."

"Keane seems to value your friendship." Jane lifted his hand, again examining the ring's beauty in the sun when a dark cloud came over. "A lovely setting. This could have purchased a lot of photographic plates, film, even a new camera."

"He came the other evening with his newest *baby* in hand, talked nonstop about it, but when he saw the victim was someone he cared for—"

"The Mandor girl?"

"Yes, dropped his new camera, fell to his knees. It proved the start of this trouble for him, that show of weakness."

"Like when the vultures threw you in the Bridewell?"

"Thanks again for getting me out."

She ignored this. "Right now our getting him out of that cell takes priority. I'm sure McCumbler will be successful, and we'll buy Keane's freedom."

"What is all this *we* talk? We've got a problem . . . and we buy his freedom?"

"I want to help you, Alastair."

"And why is that?"

"Because, damn you, I just want to."

"Why?"

"Who knows?"

He looked long into her eyes, until waiting cabbies began staring. "I want to see Dr. Jane Francis open a practice here in Chicago and soon . . . and an end to Dr. James Phineas Tewes for good and all."

She smiled wide, the mustache curling. "I hear a rumor that Tewes has plans to return to New York."

"Yes, I've heard the rumor clackin' about. To catch a frigate to California, start anew there."

"In time . . . in time, Alastair."

A cloud burst released a silver rain that suddenly began pelting them. Together, they stepped into the nearest cab and trundled in through the swinging door not built for Ransom's size. Once inside, laughing, he reached over and informed her that her makeup had begun to run. She leaned into him, preparing to accept a kiss as his large hand touched her cheek, his gentleness causing her pulse to race. But he patted down her mustache instead, telling her, "I'd kiss you if it weren't for the whiskers."

He laughed. After a moment, she laughed. Curious of their laughter, the coachman opened his small window on the cab to study his passengers.

Ransom reacted to the sliding door as it opened, staring back at a pair of eyes that he only half recognized, unable to place. The eyes of the coachman proved most certainly familiar but somehow out of place, out of time.

"Ahhh, begging your pardon, sirs, but where're you off

to?" Water dripped in from the open panel that looked out on the coachman's seat. The sound of an unhappy horse up there came through with the rainwater.

"To the Palmer House, my good fellow," announced Ransom, and to Jane he added, "where we'll drink and dine and—"

"No, no! It's no time for that! Take me straight 'way to my Belmont office. From there, Inspector Ransom can give you his destination."

She hadn't given the young fellow an address, and Ransom asked her about this.

"He knows where Dr. Tewes lives. Most everyone this far north knows where he lives."

"I see. Dr. Tewes tips well."

"True, but this coachman knows you as well."

"Really now, and who might that high-pitched voice and those beady eyes belong to?"

"Waldo, of course."

"Denton?"

"Says he hardly makes a scrapping apprenticed to your friend Keane. Says he makes more money on tips. Afraid he calls your friend a skinflint."

"Skinflint? Philo?" He laughed.

"Waldo says Keane thinks him his indentured servant!"

"OK, he's a skinflint. But at heart, a good man."

"So we haul Denton into the courtroom as a character witness?"

"Perhaps not. The village idiots might draw a straight line between a skinflint and a murderer, as they've drawn a line from Philo's art to murder."

"Art some are calling pornography."

"I've seen it and I tell you it is art."

"Have you . . . ever purchased from him?"

"Yes, photos of Merielle when I only knew her as Polly. Later, I bought up his entire inventory."

"And you still have these, *ahhh* . . . artistic renderings?"

"I do."

"I'm sure of their artistic merit," she teased. "Look, if you want my advice, you will burn them."

"For you, I will do it."

"No for me."

"For myself then."

"Damn it, man, if Nathan can orchestrate Keane's arrest, and if he turns him over to the right interrogators, men like yourself . . . your friend Philo can be persuaded to point you out as having an obsession with one or more of the victims, and then *you* give Nathan the kindling to amass this fire under you in the form of these . . . artistic renderings?"

"Yes, I take your point."

"I'm sure you would've concluded the same, but even had you . . . well, I imagine you'd hold on to one or two of the photos."

"I'll destroy them all."

"Else turn them over to the care of someone you trust."

"That is a rare bird indeed."

"Someone who'd never betray you."

"I am at a loss for a name."

"You thick-headed fool."

"Dr. Fenger perhaps."

"As he works for the police department—which is a travesty, as his office ought to be a separate entity so as to remain completely objective and above criticism and complaint— you'd be placing him in an awkward position, Alastair."

"I can think of no one else."

She gritted her teeth. "What of Dr. Tewes?"

"What of Dr. Tewes?"

"For a detective, you can be demonstratively thick at times."

He reached out and leaned into her, about to kiss her regardless of the mustache, but he was stopped by a whoosh-slap sound.

The flap to the coachman had slapped open again. "Tewes's residence!"

She got out without responding to his last remark, instead

whispering so as Waldo could not hear, "Any prints of the girl you can't bring yourself to burn, get to me."

"I'm not so sure there is any reason to fret over—"

"Remember who you're dealing with. Kohler is your worst enemy. If you've shots of Merielle you simply can't destroy, trust them to me."

"One day . . . Nathan knows that one day . . . I'll find the tie that places his hand on the bomb at Haymarket."

"His greatest fear. You are two men with reason to fear one another."

"I guess I have not looked at it in quite those terms."

"Fear is a great motivator, and when a man sucks fear up his nose, it fills his brain. Nathan Kohler will do anything to frame you, and arresting Philo is just his opening salvo."

"You know a lot about the uncharted territories of the human mind, don't you, Doctor?"

"I have laid hands on a few."

"Like mine? Did I tell you . . ."

"I know you like my touch, Ransom."

"I can ask Waldo to hold if you'll call out Jane . . . two for the Palmer House."

"Perhaps another night. I promised Gabby a special dinner. It's her birthday."

"*Ahhh,* of course . . . of course. Then bring her along and we'll celebrate together."

She realized just how deep-seated was his loneliness. Like an oak in a clearing . . . a lone oak. She couldn't be certain of her feelings for him; she'd not sorted out all of her own fears. He could be so good for her, and she for him, but on the other hand, he could destroy her so easily if he were one of these sorts who preferred the stalking to the catching and the mating. He could leave her as had Tewes in France, again devastating her emotions. "Perhaps if you call round late, you can have coffee and cake on the porch with us." God, she silently cursed herself for being so cowardly and tentative in such matters—neither adjective something anyone anywhere would ever apply to her.

She quickly rushed onto her front porch, turning in time to see him raise his cane in a little wave. He then tapped his cane against the cab and chortled out "Muldoons!"

Jane was soon watching through a window sash from the safety of her home as the cab carrying Ransom trundled off east for Halsted Street.

CHAPTER 24

It was an awkward passing thought Ransom had as he rode alone in the cab. If someone were garroted and set aflame tonight, this would prove Kohler's having arrested Philo as sheer folly. But at what price must folly be proved? Someone would pay dearly—with her life—to see Philo freed, and this vendetta of a chess move that Kohler had made would prove a fool's undertaking indeed. *It must go nowhere.*

Ransom felt certain that Philo wouldn't last a week in a Chicago cell before going stark raving mad, and that Jane was right: This move against Philo was Nathan's direct assault across his bow. *Damn charges'll go the way of the gutter.* But it might take time.

Still, the thought of mopping up after this murdering fiend wandering the Chicago fair, had no appeal. He tried to imagine the next victim, likely another young innocent—the monster's delicacy now. He didn't want to inhale the odor of burnt flesh or take in the sight of yet another decapitated body.

"Lay a trap for the bastard, you should, Inspector Ransom," came a voice reading his mind it seemed.

He looked up through the peep window into the unblinking, glassy eyes of Waldo Denton. "A trap?"

"Yes, a trap, sir, is what we'd use on the farm back home. And who knows, if I was Johnny on the spot with that Night Hawk and was to get pictures, I could make my reputation, I could. Not to mention . . . well, a photo of the killer! Now that'd sell to all the papers in the city at a handsome price, not to mention it'd make us heroes, it would, you and me, coming in with a likeness of the bastard."

The boy had soaked up more from Philo than Ransom had realized. "You'd need a damn wheelbarrowful of luck to be on hand when this monster slips out his garrote and slices someone's throat."

"I read your remarks in the *Herald* and you're going to put 'im in a foul mood with words like that—calling 'im a coward and a weakling, fearful of his own shadow. Words like that, why, you might think he'd come straight for you, and if you were to sort of set yourself up as, say, bait . . ."

"Bait him, heh?" Ransom recalled giving the exclusive to Thom Carmichael.

Waldo kept talking. "Well, sir, I'm no policeman, but I read Mr. Pinkerton's spy book."

"Hasn't everyone?"

"Pinkerton did a lotta what I'm saying, and you've already laid all the groundwork."

"Thanks, Waldo. If it comes to a showdown, and I have time, I'll send for you," Ransom promised, allowing the kid his fantasy. "You bring the Night Hawk. Make your name and fortune on the case."

Denton cleared his throat at this point. "We've arrived at your destination, sir, Muldoon's."

"Thanks." He exited the cab and paid Waldo. "How long've you been driving a hack?"

"Too long and a half. Before apprenticing with Mr. Keane. The day job pays bills."

"I see."

"Good way to get to know our city. Learn it fast having a different fare every ten minutes."

"You keep a close watch on your fares!"

"Personal touch insures they come to me before taking another hack."

"Clever Waldo, quite."

"I try to be. It's not easy."

"Being clever?"

"I mean . . . it don't come easy is what I mean to say, sir."

"Never had an opportunity for college, heh?"

"No, sir . . . not like them born with that silver spoon, what?"

"Ahhh . . . no chance at college myself either."

"Oh, I could've gone to college . . . could've been smart and maybe train for some profession. But . . . circumstances held out against it."

"Know what you mean . . . I do. Guess it was fortunate you took to photography."

"A godsend really. . . . A golden opportunity to work with Mr. Keane, I say. And as for the meagerness what comes from Mr. Keane's hand, it did go a long way to help me in burying Mother."

"I'll give your idea more thought. To lay a trap." Ransom so wanted his hands on the monster who'd turned his city into a daily nightmare. Wanted five minutes alone with the fiend. Wanted to avenge Merielle and all the victims.

"Be sure to get word to me if you do it, sir," Waldo kept on nonstop. "I mean . . . think of it. Even if the Phantom were to give you the slip, which ain't likely to happen to a detective of your stature, sir, but if your trap 'twere foiled, but we still got a shot—e'en of his back as he's running from you, why we'd have him!"

"Dead to rights in the frame."

"Like Mr. Keane says, if it ain't in the frame, it ain't in the frame, and—"

"—and if it ain't in the frame, it doesn't exist."

"Ironic . . . now Mr. Keane is in the frame . . . so to speak . . ."

"Yes, indeed."

"And it's a put-up job, I warrant. When I heard that they'd

put the arm on Mr. Keane, I asked what can the authorities be thinking?" He began a low, curdling laugh rumbling from the diaphragm and escaping nostrils and mouth all at once, a kind of vomiting laugh that Philo had complained about on occasion. Ransom did his best to overlook the torturous sound, but not until Waldo was half a block off, did he feel he could get it out of his head along with the idea of a trap.

"I hope others agree with you about Keane, Waldo," Alastair said to himself where he stood outside Muldoon's. "All you bloody armchair detectives are alike—spoiling for a fight. If young Waldo were not careful, he would indeed attract the attention of the Phantom. An old saying came to mind: *Be careful of what you wish.*

For now a talk with Muldoon was in order.

When he walked into the dark little tavern, Muldoon was waiting for him, a baseball bat extended over his head. "I swear, Ransom, if you've come for trouble—"

"Nothing could be further from my thoughts, Muldoon! What trouble?"

Every rummy and street life in the place mentally braced for a confrontation. Hunched shoulders over the bar stiffened. Men began to move off into shadow, some who owed Ransom in either money or information, scurrying out the back. He had put word on the street that he wanted to know the identity of the infamous Phantom of the Fair, the expert garroter. To date, nothing had come of this effort, and this troubled him immensely, because if the people on the street like Dot'n'Carry could not locate an inchworm's worth of news, then this meant the fellow was not local, not known among the homeless and derelict and deviant street rats.

Such a state made the killer invisible.

But for the moment, Moose Muldoon and the Chicago Bear faced off.

Tension filled the space between Muldoon and Ransom, and everyone could taste the bad blood in the air.

"Muldoon, you stupid cock-sucking motherless swine,

do you know Jim Beckensaw? Your own alderman for this district?"

" 'Course I do!"

"The man got the Sunday dry laws rescinded!"

"Again? already again!"

"He's a political genius, but you yourself know that this is what, the twentieth goddamn time? Ya blockheaded excrement brain! They rescind Sunday laws on a yo-yo pork string, and if you bothered ever to read a paper, you'd've some *passing* knowledge to get by on!"

"Look here, now! Are you here to drink or to fight?"

"German Tavern and Brewery Owners Association laid out a fortune at the doorstep of City Hall, and this ward you are smack in the middle of lies within boundaries of the chosen triangle!"

"Chosen triangle?"

"The bloody city blocks that can serve alcoholic beverages on any given Sunday!"

Muldoon looked stricken. "Nobody told me. I missed the last meet—" He almost finished his sentence before Ransom's cane sent Muldoon flat. From behind the bar, lying on the boards, everyone could hear the moose's moaning.

The bear calmly righted his cane and stepped regally to the door and back out onto the streets where he'd grown up.

He knew that Muldoon could appreciate the balance of it all, blow for blow.

As day turned to night, Alastair decided he must do something—*anything*—to take action against the killer. To this end, he began planting seeds all over the city. Even before leaving Muldoon's entirely, having stepped back into the black interior, he announced, "Take heed, all of you! This blasted Phantom's a fairy is what he is! If he wishes to prove himself anything other than a pussy, then, by God, stand up to a man! No more boys, no girls, no women, but a man!"

After a stunned moment of silence, a cheer went up for Ransom. Men wanted to buy him a drink, others slapped his back. He slammed the cane against the bar to silence the crowd even as Muldoon found his feet. "Buy me drinks and cheer me, lads, *after* I've cut off this bastard's head and handed it to him!"

Cheers went up.

"Let's see 'im take that pussy weapon of his to my neck!"

More cheers followed, and more drinks were pushed at Ransom. Laughter and jokes ensued, most of the jokes leveled at his characterization of the Phantom as a fairy and a coward. But one man in the room watched Ransom's massive neck from a dark corner and thought what a bloody easy ham it'd be to slice through and silence.

"Come on, you baby killer! You little-girl killer. Try your hand with a man!" Ransom shouted over the noise, succumbing to a toast proposed by Carmichael. Ransom had selected Muldoon's as the newsmen's hangout he knew it to be. He imagined the screaming headlines across every late edition. He meant to repeat the performance again—in every tavern he could manage between here and the great fair. "I'll be wandering the darkest, loneliest pathways of the lagoon at Lake Park, where you murdered those two children the other night. So come for me, you little dickless thing! Try to place your murderous guillotine on me!"

So here he was in the lagoon fairgrounds where Trelaine had failed to save Miss Mandor or himself. Ransom strolled one end to the other, *daring* the bastard to leap out from any blackness to slip his bloody wire about Ransom's beefy neck. They had surmised the killer a small man, if a man at all. Ransom was often taken with the fact that many hardened murderers and rapists, once nabbed, turned out to be slight of build and wretched little creatures indeed.

He believed the Phantom would have difficulty just looping the garrote over his head and around his neck, much less slicing through his carotid artery, as he stood six-foot-four, and he had several layers of protective fat that the garroter would likely not figure on. To further complicate any attack on his person, as he paced here, was his cane, his blue steel revolver, and he'd borrowed a pair of specially made horse-hide gloves from a friend working the bovine slaughterhouse at the stockyards. These gloves would slow the cutting power of a garrote if he, like young Purvis, should get his hands between throat and wire. The gloves could slow the expected attack long enough to give him time to wrestle the killer to the ground—if only the bastard would strike!

"Where the devil is the little hellion who obviously has a hard on for me, killing poor Mere in my place?"

Ransom made the return walk from the end of the lagoon, around the water, passing strolling lovers, the occasional homeless who'd be tossed from the park as soon as the first patrolman crossed paths with ragmen, or bums as they were called. How long, he wondered, must he pace in the darkness in this pretense of leisure and calm here in the most poorly lit section of the lagoon, the Ferris wheel high over his shoulder.

In his ears, he heard the faint last death rattle of Miss Mandor out on the water, her boat so near he could leap into it from where he stood. His cop's imagination, his insight, intuition and instinct—*all challenged by this so-called Phantom*—brought the full picture of how the killer had enticed his victims to help out some "poor chap" in a second boat that was listing. Trelaine, in the throes of infatuation with Miss Mandor, perhaps thought he'd impress her with his show of humanity in the form of a dark figure who knew, somehow, enough about the couple to know that she could not scream out. He'd demonstrated on Trelaine what he intended for her. And it had all come to pass so quickly, and seeing Trelaine's head fall forward and into the second boat, his body floating off and away, she most assuredly screamed her silent screams and fulfilled the killer's sick need to see her eyes bulge with fear and her skin prickle, and her extremities fight for life along with her last gasping breath. He'd leapt agilely from the rocking boat he'd himself scuttled, and into the boat transporting her, even as she attempted to leap out over the side to make the shore where Ransom now stood looking out over the black lagoon.

Silent now, the lagoon reflected back a sliver of moonlight and some nearby gaslight lamps, but this small show of light only made the surface look the more like black oil. *Is this Miss Mandor's last pleasant sight? Had she been mesmerized? Hesitated one second too late to make landfall? Had she got into the water, would she've stood a chance of escape? Alerting someone ashore.*

Sometimes his uncanny ability to recreate the scene of the crime frightened Alastair. Just good police work, he told himself, nothing special . . . not like the gift of a wonderful stage voice, an ability at acting, a gift of intelligence for science, or a talent for a musical instrument.

He wished to be home playing badly at that piano he kept as a constant challenge to learn. As a child, he'd dreamed once of being a concert pianist. The memory now made him feel foolish. No, he was born to this . . . to the hunt.

He'd had time to rethink the scene when Philo dropped that camera in utter sorrow over Miss Mandor's unnatural death. He mentally paced to the images of that night, moving on to each murder scene, each impression swelling his mind with a growing hatred of two monsters—one the faceless Phantom, the other himself.

"Where did Griffin get the notion to go after Philo's studio? To uncover evidence there?" he asked himself aloud. "Griffin, you *disappointment.*"

He recalled how Drimmer had so quickly taken up Philo's Night Hawk, handing it to Denton to get the photo of the handprint on the overpass. Dr. Fenger had studied this print from the photo that Denton had taken, and it'd been compared to the onc Philo had taken at the train station, and according to Christian, the prints had indeed come from the same man. But neither matched Philo's hand. *But what of Griffin's hand?*

Again the evidence pointed to a man small in stature . . . a man hardly larger than Dr. Tewes. Griffin was hardly larger than Jane Francis.

"I thought I'd find you here," said Griffin Drimmer who seemed to've stepped from out of Ransom's thought! "Word's all over the city."

"Word?"

"That you've challenged the Phantom to some sort of duel."

"Reckless, I know."

"Foolish . . . to roam about here *alone,* without me at your back?"

"I assumed your back's still up over my ranting and my ring."

Griff held a seething anger just below boiling. "You ought to've come to me first with this plan. We ought to've coordinated on it."

"By the book, is it, Griff?"

"By the book, hell, by the notion we are a team!"

"As when you put Philo behind bars?"

"At the very least, he knows something."

"Were we a team on that solo act?"

Over Alastair's shoulder in the sky, the massive Ferris wheel sent colored lights flitting across Griffin's features, which took on a separate life—as if another man altogether resided within. Possibly a man who felt a deep-seated hatred not only for his mentor, Alastair, and not only for authority and society and rules and regulations, but all the comforts and familiarity of *normalcy*. A kind of Beowulf in sheep's clothing, loose on the world. Even his name, Griffin, spoke of a changeling.

What if Griffin, stymied at every turn, felt that Ransom's

confusion represented some sort of prize? What if the killer felt weak, ineffectual, and in fact *invisible* in the company of other men, especially bulls like Ransom?

While not invisible, suppose Griffin felt invisible? Suppose he had pent-up notions, mad goals, secret anger that'd gone unchecked for so long that it'd all suddenly burst in pure venom in a kill spree? Suppose he'd had a sudden loss of faith, of charity, of humanity, of relations . . . a loss of a loved one, a mainstay . . . someone who'd kept him stable and sane all this time? Hadn't he lost his mother recently?

What did he really know of Griff? He never spoke of his parents, only his wife and children on occasion, and Ransom had never seen them—not in the flesh. So much chicanery went on these days with photographs. Suppose . . . just suppose Griffin Drimmer had created the Phantom in order to make himself visible on two fronts? Visible as the new, young, virile detective who comes on to solve the case, and visible indeed as the Phantom, a killer on page one of the *Tribune*, the *Times*, the *Herald*? And suppose . . . just suppose it was all a way to strike out at Ransom for perceived wrongs?

Ransom wondered how he could live with such a development, that a detective he'd treated as his gopher—snubbed one day, ignored the next, or spoken harshly to—had some larger vendetta to act on? Jekyll and Hyde was now showing at the Lyceum Theater. Could Stevenson's character be alive in the form of Drimmer? Had the killer stood coldly at his side—in each frame—from the beginning? Watching his every move?

The Phantom's first two victims included a prostitute that Ransom had known and had a soft spot for, one too old to ply her trade much longer. He'd not known the Polish girl or Purvis, but the next victim was his Merielle. Suppose it was all working up to Merielle? Suppose it'd been Griffin who had blackened Merielle's eye one day and cut her throat and fired her body the next?

The next two victims—Mandor and Trelaine—implicated

Philo, Alastair's best friend, sending the photographer into a deep depression. *It could all very well be about me,* Ransom determined. *All the killings designed to destroy me.*

And who stood in the best position to know what Ransom held dearest? Who but Griffin? All this rain of suspicion flash-flooded through Ransom's consciousness in a matter of seconds.

"It's not wise, Rance, acting as bait for a madman, one who strikes sudden as a viper, no matter your size or strength or reputation!"

"I appreciate your concern after all the bad blood between us, thanks to your kowtowing, taking Kohler's lead."

"Like it or not, Ransom, I never worked for you. I work for Kohler. Always have, and if you'd bother to check, so do you."

"Yeah . . . right . . ." Ransom purposefully turned his back on *his only suspect. Come ahead, you weasel; make your play . . . attack me from behind and we'll see what happens.* But Griffin made no move. Still, Alastair kept his back to him.

He next laid his bone-handled cane on a park bench, bothered with his pipe, lighting it. Puffing away, his back still to Griffin. Teasing him, disregarding the rawhide gloves. *Do it, you wimp! Do it now! Dare attack!*

Still no supposed attack.

Ransom complained of a shoe button coming unlatched. He cursed the bother and sat down, and he exaggeratedly leaned over his shoes like a Falstaff, complaining of being unable to reach his shoes. *This tease must have Griffin's killing urge, this cure to his invisibility, salivating. The attack will come now!*

Instead, Griffin started talking about his Lucinda while pointing down the lane. "Asked her to marry me under that box elder there."

"What the hell're you talking about?"

"My wife, Lucinda." He launched on a reverie of how feminine and lovely she was. He produced a photo. "An anniversary shot below that same tree. Ran into Denton with that camera."

Alastair saw some elements of the fair in the backdrop. "Denton's taking photos at the fair?"

"Why not so long's he has possession of—"

"Keane's Night Hawk, while Keane is in lockup . . ."

"What's going through your mind now?"

"A payment for services."

"What do you mean?"

"Griffin, tell me, who first led you to believe that Philo could be our killer?"

"No one led me—"

"You needn't answer!" Alastair grabbed his cane, began running and shouting. "We've got to find a phone box and a cab now!"

Griffin gave chase. He'd never seen Alastair move so fast; he hadn't thought him capable of it. He hadn't thought it possible that any man with a cane and a limp could out-distance him, but Ransom was doing just that.

"Where the bloody hell is a phone box? Griffin, we must find a phone box and now!" Alastair was beside himself with agitation, looking the lunatic as the first drops of rain began to fall.

"To call headquarters? Reinforcements? There's a phone a block off the fairway!" Griffin's words stopped Alastair from rushing farther in the wrong direction. "This way, Rance!"

Mayor Carter Harrison in 1880 appointed William McGarigle as superintendent of police, and McGarigle started the patrol telephone and signal system in Chicago—the most important police innovation of its day. The system—375 hexagonal pine boxes—supported lampposts in each police district. Inside one of these locker-sized wood booths, an alarm box dial awaited Alastair, who opened it with his departmental key. He knew that he could not call directly to Jane Francis to warn her, and he did not have direct access to a Bell operator. Nor could he reach Christian Fenger or any individual. The system frustrated such desires, as all he could dial was the local station. This meant, he could not even ring up the station closest to Jane and Gabby, as he believed the two of them in serious danger. However, if he got the right dispatcher, he could conceivably relay the message from station to station.

How long might that take? He could be losing valuable time without result.

He feared risking it, and he feared not risking it.

"What to do," he said aloud.

"How should I know?" replied Griffin. "As usual, I've not the slightest clue what you're doing or thinking!"

Ransom hit a single number on the phone that signaled *murder* to a dispatcher. "I've got to get this message to the home of Dr. James Phineas Tewes, immediately!"

Ransom listened intently to the dispatcher. "Please identify yourself, Officer, by name and badge number, and verify the nature of your emergency."

He lost the connection due to his not having ground the monkey organ mechanism required to keep the connection. He shouted at the dead receiver, pounding it several times into the box. He hated it that he must keep monkey-grinding the damn newly invented thing like he must his gramophone. Why couldn't they make one that worked without all the effort?

And then he erupted when he got the dispatcher back. "What difference does it make who is making the request? Only an officer of the law can call on this bloody phone, so just do what the bloody hell I'm asking!"

Whoever it might be at dispatch, this time switched Alastair off, leaving only a sickening silence on the line.

"Idiot! He didn't even ask what the message was!"

"Try again! But use a bit of civility." Griffin had not as yet seen the interior of a phone box, and so he jammed in at the entryway, examining every corner. He wanted to see the technology in action.

"If it takes civility, then damn it, you make the call! I am off for a cab!"

"But what do I say?"

"Tell them to tell Dr. Tewes to get himself and his daughter out of that house and to a public place, preferably to Dr. Christian Fenger's!"

"But *why?*" he shouted as Ransom and his cane rushed off.

Griffin monkey-grinded the phone and looked at the series of buttons, each coded number standing for a category of offense: accident, drunkards, violation of city ordinance, fire, theft, forgery, riot, rape, and murder in that order. But he did not know which to press. Hesitating for a moment, he reasoned since they were chasing the Phantom that murder was on the bill. He hit the appropriate dial number. This supposedly instantly summoned between five and twenty uniformed officers to his location, depending on the nature of the emergency.

But when the dispatcher came on, the gruff man, still angry with Ransom's swagger, shouted, "Stop muckity-mucking with the call line!"

This did not make sense to Griffin, who'd read statistics on the call boxes. It usually sent out a five-man team of officers in a patrol wagon that carried a stretcher, cuffs, blankets, and their obligatory clubs. Each box cost the city twenty-five dollars! And over the past two years alone some 879,548 distress calls to the various stations had been made. But this fellow at the other end must be reported as derelict or drunk on duty, as again he hung up!

Griffin raced from the box, forgetting to close it, as a storm began to break around him, lightning streaking the black backdrop of sky against the Ferris wheel and the massive buildings of the fair, all the White City bathed in sudden downpour. Griffin knew if he were to make the same coach before Ransom completely disappeared, he'd have to hustle as never before.

Ahead of him, Griff saw the cabstand, some of the horses reacting to the sudden thunder and lightning, raising hooves skyward and in need of gentling. He saw Ransom had stumbled and was now slowed, limping, with the cane working harder for him than ever.

Griffin sprinted now, confident he could catch Ransom. But Alastair was not going to like the news of his failure to get a message to Dr. Tewes.

"Do you think Tewes's life is in danger? Both he and his daughter? Or have you concluded that the phrenologist is the Phantom and may harm the child?"

"You could not be further from the truth, Griff."

"Then who are we chasing amid the storm?"

But Ransom did not answer, instead shouting to the first cab he came to, "To Tewes's—the dispensary and residence of Dr. James Phineas Tewes, now!"

"Address, sir?" asked the cabbie, the same thick-browed Cro-Magnon that Ransom had noticed on an earlier occasion.

"Three-forty Belmont, two doors north of the Episcopal church, and you are paid twice your rate, sir, if you lose a wheel getting me there!"

Something in Ransom feared for Jane Francis and her Gabby. Something deep within whispered a horror, and Alastair imagined a scene of carnage awaiting him at what most in the city knew as the Tewes's residence. He imagined the worst, and at the same time as the carriage pulled away and Griffin slipped through the open door, he recalled how Waldo Denton had seen to it that Alastair would be chasing phantoms of the wrong kind while Waldo, apprentice photographer, sometime cabbie, sometime fair photographer, garroted Gabrielle and Jane Francis in their home!

The cab driver used his whip, and the hansom wheeled

around street corners and clattered insanely over the cobblestones, the sound of the two whinnying horses mimicking the pitiable sounds that Gabby and Jane may be releasing at this same moment. To add to the thunderous assault of hooves beating wildly against stone and the bullwhip cracking, a series of thunderclaps struck as if crashing symbols to this macabre dance they found themselves in.

"What the deuce is going on, Ransom? It's time you treated me as your equal! I demand to know what the—"

The coach lurched, sending Griffin into a corner, pinning him, while Ransom extended his cane at the crucial moment, using it like a wedge against his own tumbling.

"Slow down! You'll get us all killed!" Griffin grabbed Ransom's cane and rammed it against the box overhead and shouted at the driver successively. "Slow up!"

The slot through which the driver communicated shot open and again Ransom saw only the man's eyes, filled with blood rage and ecstatic joy. Loving this, his coachman's fantasy come true: an order to open her full-throttle, and taking two Chicago gents on a ride to terrify and delight. "Beggin' your pardon, sirs, but did ya' not ask that I run the horses?"

"Run them! Run them!" shouted Ransom.

"Whoaaa!" shouted Griffin.

"Hold onto the handrail overhead, Griff!" Ransom said, reclaiming his cane.

"Just tell me what is all the hurry?"

"It's Jane . . . *ahhh*, Dr. Tewes's sister, and the daughter, Gabby! I fear they may be in terrible danger."

"How can you know?"

"Denton."

"Denton? Waldo? What about him?"

"Damn it, man, he is our bloody Phantom!"

"That harmless fellow? He's hardly more than a boy!"

"A warped one, I wager. Look here, he is the one set me thinking of lolling about the damnable lagoon for the Phantom, and that just after dropping Jane . . . *ahhh*, at the Tewes residence."

"Since when do you listen to civilians on matters of investigation, and one so young?"

"He set my mind on it and did it rather subtly. Cunning fellow as it happens."

"I would not have put Denton and the word *cunning* in the same sentence, Alastair."

"Behind those boyish eyes and goofy grin—designed to make him harmless seeming—there lurks a deadly mind, I tell you."

"It just seems so out of the blue, *sooo* farfetched."

"Precisely as he wants you to believe. But more than cunning and deception is at work here, something even more insidious and poisonous. I mean—"

"What do you mean?" Griff's brow creased in consternation. He pulled forth a pipe identical to Ransom's and lit up.

"Suppose he's a bugger who's never once gotten a bloody thing he's ever wanted."

"You mean like not the mother nor father, not the sister nor brother he wanted?"

"Not the circumstances, not the woman of his dreams, for instance."

"Nor the money, nor the education he's chased all his life? Not the profession nor career."

"Not the erection, not the joy, not the release, nor the satisfactions we take for granted as with your life with Lucinda."

"And you think this accumulation of failures leads to deviance and murder?"

Ransom gritted his teeth and held back the immediate word he had for Griffin's thick-headedness. "Put yourself in his shoes. Scrubbing up and about for the likes of Philo, having to push a hack about the city, cleaning up after his horse, seeing every fare he picks up with a woman on the arm. How many times he drove Merielle and me from corner to corner, God only knows!"

"It's still a stretch. Denton's hardly more than a boy."

"We've suspected *small* all along; a weak person, womanish if not a woman."

"But Denton . . . Waldo is . . ." Griffin seemed unable to wrap his mind around this idea. He's so . . . so innocuous, so slight and so . . . so . . ."

For half a moment's flash, Ransom wished for a time when he could be so naïve and trusting as Griffin Drimmer, a time before he'd become so bloody suspicious of everything on two legs. Finally, he placed a hand on Griff's and calmly said, "Invisible . . . is what he is, Griff . . . simply *invisible,* and even more so in that black get-up worn for the hansom cab company, black boot, cape, top hat, down to the Carson, Pirie, Scott buttons."

Drimmer considered this. "A gentleman's attire in any venue."

"And him sneaking looks, eavesdropping, studying each fare in his hack up close, through there." He pointed out the coach hatch.

"Creepy when you think of it."

"And him sitting up on his high seat, looking all about the streets from behind that nag of his?"

The cab thundered down the street, tossing them from side to side. Griffin shouted over the thunderous noise, "No one's going to believe Denton physically capable of killing two people out on that lagoon, unless we catch him in the act, with the tools of death!"

"Press has made of him some sort of Grendel-sized ogre, haven't they?"

"Perhaps the press has overstated the—"

"Overstated? Even Carmichael's taken with the gall and élan of this bastard."

"No one's expecting a Waldo Denton!"

"As for walking water at the lagoon, you and I know how it was done!"

"But people will equate it with the supernatural, that Satan can walk on water as well as Christ."

"Don't attribute satanic powers to him yourself then, Griff."

"But then, they say the Devil doth take a pleasing form."

"This particular devil has chosen an invisible form."

"He is that."

"Don't hold back. Tell me what you think."

"Gut feelings, first impression?" asked Griff. "I thought him harmless, but I soon learned he had no allegiance to Keane."

"Are you saying he's a back-stabbing cock-sucker?"

"OK . . ."

"And why so?"

"At each scene, he laid a seed of doubt about his employer—quietly, mind you."

"Yes, this is his way, and being a small man . . . one you are so much more likely to let your guard down around . . ."

"Yes, many a deadly viper is—"

"Indeed! A small man with a garrote, a man about your own size, Grif—"

"Can do a helluva lotta damage in a matter of seconds."

"Precisely."

"Hey . . . hold on. You thought . . . back there at the lagoon . . . when I came up on you, and you started fooling with your shoe buttons and bending over . . . do you mean to tell me that—"

"I had a loose lace is all."

"You thought me the Phantom, didn't you? Damn you!"

Alastair hesitated, mired in silence, unsure what to say.

"Out with it, big man! The truth!" Griff laughed and muttered, "Wait till O'Malley and some of the lads hear this."

Alastair realized that rather than taking it badly, somehow Griffin found a strange mix of humor and pride in it, somehow still impressed by the notoriety given the Phantom by the newsies. "Imagine . . . thinking me the Phantom of the Fair."

"Will you quit bloody calling him that, please? He deserves no title, no crown, no ink in the damned press; he deserves no 'sir' or 'gentleman' before his name. He deserves none of our respect or misguided ballads written about him, and he certainly merits no admiration."

"Waldo Denton . . . my God, Alastair, how did you figure it out?"

"The ring."

"The one in your bowels?"

"This ring!" he produced his pinky with the ring upon it. "How do you suppose it went from Merielle's hand to Philo's pocket and the killer counting on it's still being there?"

"Philo admitted to taking it in trade."

"How better to implicate his mentor than to lead you and Kohler to Philo's coat pocket or the frock in which you found the ring?"

Griff gave this a moment to sink in as if revisiting the moment. " 'Twas Denton who first identified the disembodied ring as having belonged to—"

"Precisely, yes . . . led you to suspect wrongdoing at the studio. Was he also helpful in uncovering Philo's collection of nudes?" asked Ransom as the cab walls and wheels whined and strained under the whip, the speed, and the angles.

"Yes, and now, tonight," began Griff, "he leads you off on a wild goose chase to stand bait at the park."

"To rid himself of my being on hand tonight at Gabby's birthday celebration. I just know he heard Jane—Tewes and I—speaking of it."

"He's cunning enough to know it'd take an elephant gun or Moose Muldoon to bring you down."

"Well . . . Muldoon's been set straight."

For a moment, they thought the carriage would go over on its side.

"Do you think he'd really dare strike the ladies in their home with Tewes present?"

"He's likely planning to kill them in their beds."

"Why do you think so?"

"Sensationalism, to strike a deeper fear in us."

"To say we're unsafe when snug in our own beds?"

"And he's reaching higher along the scale of respectability, money, and social standing."

"He really is a hatter, isn't he?"

"A mad hatter."

"But why? Just because he can?"

"He alone holds the answer to that."

"Faster!" Griff now shouted even as he tumbled about the cab, banging into every wall and door.

"Get what you can from the whip!" shouted Ransom.

The wheels spun madly beneath them, screaming, and on sharp turns now left the ground.

Stumpf did it . . . he did it all. All the killing, that is.

Waldo didn't even feel he was inside his body when Stumpf, at that moment of taking life—willed the essence of the dying into him. It was why Stumpf liked mirrors, liked killing them before mirrors.

He'd done it both ways of course, but the thrill and satisfaction became so much more heightened if he could stare into both their eyes and those of Stumpf at the moment of knowing. The moment of crossing over. From behind the garrote, before a mirror, he could watch all the eyes!

Stumpf could more readily act at the instant of death to net and catch the soul within his web of wanton lust if he knew the very instant of the soul's leap toward the next dimension. Wanton lust—part and parcel of it—as Stumpf so enjoyed what Waldo Denton's body felt at the death leap. Stumpf got Waldo an erection—that true insignia, emblem of corporeal lust.

"All of life becomes more pronounced and clear and worth the discovery if a man is in his right spirit," Waldo Denton was telling Jane Francis Ayers and Gabby—as he'd come to know their names. He'd first been attracted to them and their home that night he'd killed Purvis at the train station. The same night he'd seen Gabby and Cliffton kissing below the lights near the lagoon. He'd been kicking around the fair, wandering, exploring, one side of him determining good locations for murder as he scouted for Stumpf, while

another side looked and hungered for precisely what that
college boy had—a future, yes, but also a future with a beautiful young thing. A promise at a fulfilling life of happiness,
warmth, camaraderie, mutual respect, admiration . . . mutual
pleasure. All things denied him.

How was it Shakespeare put it in the performance he'd
seen at the theater? *"If I cannot prove a hero, I shall prove a
villain. . . ."* Words to take heart in. Words that indicated to
Waldo that he might be considered important by everyone
he came into contact with, that he could affect their lives.
But even more, the play was the thing that informed Waldo
that deviant thoughts belonged to others as well—even to
the most famous author on the planet, William Shakespeare.
Giving hope that he perhaps was not so absolutely alone and
craven as he'd felt since childhood.

Stumpf and Waldo had wormed past the Tewes threshold
to allow Stumpf his chance. That was what Waldo had
become—a pimp to the base Stumpf inside, who didn't
even want to spare Gabrielle, the most beautiful and innocent and pleasant and most kind person ever to address
Waldo. She, and the idea of a future relationship with
Gabby, remained the only thought in his head that held
Stumpf back now.

So far as the older woman was concerned, Waldo had no
compunction about turning Stumpf loose. When he did let
Sleepeck Stumpf have his way, however, it would destroy
any hairsbreadth of a chance to make Gabby *see* him . . . *really see him* and eventually *see into him* and eventually
somehow *understand* the so-called Phantom of the Fair.
Enough to eventually accept his past ill behavior and forgive
his transgressions as only unconditional love could free the
beast within to slink off elsewhere, back to its den to hiber-
nate and hopefully die of its own loneliness and suffering,
which, in the end, Waldo Denton had no part of and had
never had any part of—and so his mind raced at the moment
of sipping tea and chewing birthday cake.

She had invited Waldo in—dear, sweet angelic Gabrielle,

with the smiling assent of the woman Gabrielle called Aunt Jane.

Earlier . . . it seemed moments earlier, he'd watched Gabby as her aunt called out to her, something about being out alone after dark, that a girl of her social position, being the daughter of Dr. Tewes, she must not give the gossip columnists a scrap to chew on, not even an appearance of impropriety. It had made him, sitting atop the coach, impulsively call back, "Oh, no ma'am, no one could think ill of Miss Gabrielle, never!"

That's when Gabby smiled at him, her attention like a balm. Each time he drove her home from the university, where he intentionally waited, turning away other fares, Gabby gave him all her attentiveness while he spoke of one day owning his own farm and farm animals. No one had ever given him what she offered—attentiveness.

At that moment when she'd smiled up at him, what he saw in her was so amazing. She'd alighted from the cab like a floating princess with hidden wand and invisible wings. She'd forgotten her umbrella in his cab, a memory lapse or an invitation? Of course, she wanted him to return. She *liked* men like him. Cliffton hadn't been so different from him, not really? Save his prospects . . . save his dreams. But even in their dreams, especially their secret desires, to have this angel of earth caress their bodies and touch their trapped souls . . . even in this, he was no different from Purvis. The two of them clinging on Gabrielle, wanting the honor of being possessed by her, and wanting the honor of being able to address her as an enduring love, as her closest intimate on earth, to call Gabby *his*. And if he could not have her, surely . . . surely Stumpf would.

Waldo wanted more for her . . . more for himself . . . more for them. He hated the thought of the empty, lost, acrid feeling in his soul whenever Stumpf finished with him. Whenever Stumpf was sated and fulfilled, the bastard thing just went away with *his* good feelings and left Waldo empty and lonelier than ever, a depression like a dull blunt knife cutting directly into his brain and soul. If the word *lie* had a face, it was Stumpf.

She had *left* the umbrella, rushing off after pushing the few coins through the slot to his fingertips, touching him as she did so. He'd savored the touch and lingered there, noticing the umbrella, but then he'd been distracted by the aunt's calling out from the porch.

He'd momentarily forgotten about Gabby's umbrella, thinking he must get in somewhere, while another part of him gave an evil thought to how he'd manipulated Chicago's so-called premiere detective away from the Tewes home and the Tewes women he'd been watching now for some time, sending Ransom to stand about in the rain at the lagoon on the say-so of Waldo Denton!

He wondered how it'd play in the press to people if it were known that while Stumpf killed someone tonight, the great detective and "last survivor" of Haymarket spent his night in the park!

Stumpf hated Ransom but Waldo Denton had even more reason to hate him. According to all accounts, Ransom had bound and beaten and eventually burned to death Waldo's father. Waldo felt justified in unleashing Stumpf—who had always been in the shadow of his soul, awaiting release. Felt justified in allowing Stumpf to terrorize a city that had allowed Alastair Ransom to operate above the law, and in fact crown him in a sense with promotion and career advancement, and why? Haymarket and his bloody injury? As if being injured carried with it some badge of heroism and honor! Had there been no bomb thrown into a crowd—lobbed from they say twenty or twenty-five feet from some unknown assailant—perhaps authorities would have done a thorough investigation into one Alastair Ransom by now. Would they've concluded him a coward and a murderer instead or a hero? Those men who were hung as anarchist of Haymarket long before Waldo knew their names or their connection with his father—these were the real heroes of Haymarket!

He'd gotten a couple blocks away from the Tewes home

contemplating all this when he recalled the umbrella, his invitation to return to Gabby tonight. What must Waldo do then? He must prove himself to her, prove his case, lay it all out in black and white. The war in which he meant to harm everyone Ransom cared for—Polly, Philo, and now Gabrielle if he could not have her. He'd seen them that night up late, Ransom leaving the house, and Gabby saying goodbye at the door.

"Appearances," the aunt had said on a number of occasions from doorway and window. Hell, it was no *appearance* the way they'd looked at one another, and the aunt in slumber somewhere deep in the house, and the father nowhere to be seen.

And so here he stood in the foyer, Gabby offering him tea, the aunt concerned his wet clothes from the storm might cause him to catch his death.

To catch his death? She oughta concern herself with her own death, he thought from behind the smile as Aunt Jane helped him remove the heavy frock, part of his hansom cabman's uniform.

Jane failed to notice the buttons on the hansom uniform overcoat. Each button read CPS. She merely shook off the rain and hung the heavy coat on the rack beside her telephone.

CHAPTER 25

The hansom coach nearly toppled over as it came around the corner at Broadway and Belmont, and then it came to a screeching halt before the newly chiseled and painted overhanging shingle that announced the residence and infirmary of Dr. J. P. Tewes.

Ransom leapt from the cab, shouting, "Mark me, Griff, that idle carriage over there tied to the lamppost! It'll be Denton's hack!"

Griff stuck his head from the cab into the rain, and he saw the single horse hansom standing idle under the downpour. Could Ransom be more right? He was also surprised at how agile the big man could be when circumstances dictated suppleness. But just as he made this conclusion, Alastair slipped on Tewes's stairs and tumbled into a puddle of mud. With cane in hand, Ransom pushed upward and stood, his suit doused and dripping of mud, his face splotched with it, making him into a creature out of H. G. Wells's books. But the big man allowed nothing to slow him, and like a raging animal, he rushed for the front door, his revolver drawn.

Griffin lifted his collar against the wind-driven rain as he rushed for the rear of the house. "I pray we're in time!" he shouted against the night. "I have the back covered!"

"Good man, Griff!"

Ransom began taking the door down with his boot, chopping directly at the lock. Two kicks, shoulders pulled inward, Ransom crashed through, no warrant sworn out, no caution taken, no thought of anything beyond saving Jane and Gabby from tragedy. The sheer explosion of his entrance sounded like lightning had hit.

Griff found the rear door and hesitating only a moment, he followed Inspector Ransom's example and lifted his foot and kicked out viciously at the lock. The door came way on the second kick, flying open. Just as he kicked open the back door, Griff heard the gunshot—a single huge explosion crackling at the front of the house. Griff had whipped out his own weapon, a Winchester muzzle-loading six-shooter his father had given him the day he'd joined the force. Griff inched toward the gunfire, cautious, prepared for anything, and certain Inspector Ransom needed his help.

He came on the scene in the parlor late. What he found startled him.

Young Gabby held an enormous revolver extended and pointed at a wounded Alastair Ransom whose blood had discolored both the Oriental rug and Waldo Denton, who lay trapped below what appeared a dead Alastair Ransom. "God, Rance's been killed!"

But Ransom's death was not, for the moment, complete. He moaned and shouted, with his face buried in Denton's chest, "Damn you, girl! You've shot me!"

"What do you expect, breaking in here on us!" shouted Jane Francis, tears streaming, on knees over Ransom, doing all in her power to staunch the wound to his side where the bullet had exited, mud from his filthy clothes commingling with blood.

"Get this ape the bloody hell off me!" screamed Denton from below Ransom.

"Do not . . . let him up . . ." Ransom painfully muttered, "till someone shoots *him*!"

"Shut up and save your energy," Jane shouted. "This is a serious wound!"

Griffin's gun now pointed at Gabrielle, a fleeting thought of Gabrielle Tewes's being the monster with the garrote instead of Denton flitting through his mind—and how awful the revelation would be—an attempt at justifiable homicide to stop Ransom's gaining on the truth. "Drop the weapon! Now!" he shouted.

Gabby and Jane both looked at Griffin, both startled. From the look of the room, the items on the parlor table, the overturned, broken dishware and teapot, it appeared that Jane Francis and Gabrielle had simply been entertaining—entertaining a multiple murderer in their parlor, asking young Denton, no doubt questions regarding his plans to become a photographer. No doubt asking what Waldo thought of his employer's arrest. Whether he thought the man guilty or wrongly accused. No doubt, offering Denton tea and cake between inquiries.

The big cabbie who'd gotten them here in record speed without running over a single stray cat or dog, stepped through the torn-open front door and was mumbling something about having been *stiffed* by coppers again. "I'll not put up with it this time!" he called out but froze when Gabby's long-barreled cannon turned in his direction.

"I said put the gun down, Miss Tewes! This fellow and myself mean you no harm, Miss Tewes . . . Miss Tewes . . ." Griffin calmly cautioned in his most authoritarian voice, imagining the horror of it, should she call his bluff. But her eyes met Griffin's and he saw no malice or rancor there so much as a dazed horror that she'd actually shot Ransom. Griff had seen the look before. A look that, in a sense, acquitted her of having had any more sinister plan or thought than simply the reaction that'd resulted in defending her hearth and home and self from a mud-painted man brandishing a huge blue gun.

Still, she held the gun, albeit limply, in her hand.

"Drop the weapon," he repeated coldly, his gun still pointed.

The huge, dark figure of the cabbie stood dripping water below him in puddles, asking, "What the devil is going on here, Inspector?"

Jane Francis shouted, "Get on my phone! Get a medical

wagon here for Inspector Ransom. He could bleed to death if we don't act quickly."

"Where is Dr. Tewes? Surely, he can—"

"He's out of town," she lied. "Besides, Ransom's best chances are with Dr. Fenger. He's got to be carefully transported to Cook County."

"I'm not ready for that bloody coroner yet!" shouted Ransom.

"Just get the ambulance!" Francis shouted. "I've done all I can for him, but it is a nasty wound."

"Yes, to Dr. Fenger," agreed Griffin.

"And quickly, man! Do it, now! Use my phone."

"Who me?" asked the cabbie.

"I'll make the call," said Griffin, "but you—what's your name?" he asked the giant-sized cabbie.

"Lincoln Hardesty."

"Take the gun from Miss Tewes and hold everyone here, and especially the one *under* Ransom. He's under arrest."

"*Under* arrest—I get it." Hardesty laughed at this.

"Just watch him. He's the bloody Phantom."

"Him, that shrimp Denton, the Phantom?" Hardesty laughed. He knew Denton from the various cab stands. He now stood disbelieving, while the two women erupted.

"Impossible!"

"This boy?"

"You must be wrong."

"Alastair, are you mad?"

"You cops have a sense of humor," added the cabbie.

"Just hold him here whatever you do, and do not allow him a moment's chance to ditch anything from his pockets."

"He's no more the Phantom than I am," said Jane.

"You coppers trying to railroad Waldo?" asked Hardesty. "I've seen it happen time and again in Chicago." He then spoke to the ladies. "Cops'll do that. Arrest an innocent man to make him out guilty."

"But they've already arrested Mr. Keane for the killings," said Gabby.

"Makes my point," replied Hardesty.

Griffin had stopped listening to the civilians, but he imagined their conversation would likely be repeated throughout the city once the news of police arresting a hard-working, clean cut, good Christian boy for the Phantom's deeds, only to release a pervert. Everyone in the city would be looking for the next victim still, and Chief Kohler will have gotten what he wanted, a humiliated and broken and demoted Alastair Ransom.

The weapon and jewelry would be crucial. Griffin knew this. After making the phone call, he returned to hold everyone at bay. With Denton, that proved quite easy. From below Ransom's inert body, they heard Denton laboring to breathe.

"Can't you get the inspector off Waldo?" pleaded Gabby.

"No! No, we must not move Ransom until necessary," said Jane Francis, "and even then with great care as to cause no more bleeding. We should leave the moving to those trained in doing the least harm."

"Oh, that's damned great!" shouted a still conscious Ransom. "That'd be those dirty-nailed devils, Shanks and Gwinn. Take me in Hardesty's cab, Griff! I beg you!"

The exertion made Ransom pass out as Shanks and Gwinn started out from Cook County. Soon on hand as they waved an emergency bell overhead when acting as an ambulance, the duo handled Ransom easily, having trained under Dr. Fenger's care, and in the meantime, Dr. Fenger had been located and was said to be prepping for a major operation. When they'd lifted the bloody Inspector, Denton climbed to his knees under the gun of Griffin Drimmer.

They've come for me . . . only matter of time now . . . smells like death . . . blood and decay and death . . . Angel of Death himself will be right at home wherever I am . . .

A huge pothole sent Ransom's body over with the stretcher in back of the meat wagon. The jolt opened his wound and Ransom awoke in the stench-filled darkness. He imagined himself in Hades itself, and rightly so for the mistakes he'd made and the bad judgment that'd gotten him killed.

His thoughts only added to the flame of punishment in this acrid, ambling elephant gut he found himself alone in. After an initial moment of horror and acceptance of both his death and damnation, Ransom realized precisely where he lay. The same wagon that retained the charred flesh odors of Polly and Purvis before her. The back of Shanks and Gwinn's horse-drawn death carrier. The two coroner's men had never heard of soap and water. The interior of the wagon shut out all light and sealed in all rot.

"Get me the bloody hell out of here!" he shouted, raised up and kicked out at the boards of the wagon. He'd chosen the spot where he guessed the buckboard seat holding Shanks and Gwinn must be. He kicked again and again like a bucking angry mustang.

Each kick sent a searing pain through his side where he'd been wrapped mummy fashion by Jane, and he could feel the bandages filling with wetness—his blood.

The wagon bucked back, and Alastair was thrown into the very wall he kicked when the wagon came to a sudden halt. Ransom lay silent, bleeding profusely, passed out on the flatbed below the overturned stretcher just as Gwinn tore open the doors, cursing.

Gwinn sucked in the acrid air without coughing, used to it. Seeing that Ransom had silenced and lay as dead as a stump, he slammed the doors closed again. Taking his squat little body back to the front, he climbed aboard and shouted to Shanks. "Hurry on before that damned maniac wakes again! He's put a hole through the boards!"

"Is he passed out for now?" Shanks needed no second telling as he lit into the horses with a whip.

"Passed out, maybe . . . maybe better than passed out."

"Dead?"

"We can only hope."

In the inky black rear, the patient bounced like a huge sack of potatoes with every pothole and mislaid brick.

"Gawd forgive me," said Shanks. "I hafta hope the bugger dies."

"He's never been no friend of ours," agreed Gwinn.

After locking Waldo Denton behind bars in a cell alongside Philo Keane, Griffin Drimmer looked long and hard at the puny prisoner.

Drimmer still could not believe that this pipsqueak fellow hardly out of his teens might possibly be the infamous Phantom. However, once Ransom was lifted off him by Shanks and Gwinn, Griffin had done precisely what Alastair wanted. He yanked the kid up off the floor, and in quick fashion began to cuff Denton to loud disagreement not only from Denton, but from the ladies.

The only saving grace was that the boy—one hand yet free—put up a fight and tried to go for Griffin's throat when he broke loose. Then he pulled a fancy twirling move to grind about Griffin's body in an attempt to get behind him—a concealed garrote pulled from somewhere. Griffin knew a few Far East combat moves of his own. Realizing the danger if this bony little fellow should get that wire noose around his neck, he upended a parlor table and used it to bash Denton in the temple. As a result of a final blow from Griffin's gun slashing across Denton's face, the supposed Phantom fell hard against a brick fireplace, knocking him senseless.

With no more resistance, over the next hour the suspect, and now assailant, was handcuffed and hauled off to the Des Plaines Street Bridewell. But by the time Griffin turned the key on Denton, his doubts had returned.

The garrote notwithstanding.

When Waldo had come to, he'd told this nonstop tale of how, seeing the success of the Phantom in bringing down his prey, he thought a garrote a good weapon for himself, and so he'd taken to carrying one at all times. "A hackman can't be too careful these days, not with the sort running about this city, I can tell you. I'll tell the judge the same. You've gotta believe me! You've got the wrong man, and that crazy Alastair Ransom—may he die of his wounds, God—he oughta be brought up on charges for breaking and entering. He spoiled me with Gabby, you know. Spoiled the moment, any chance I may've had to please her dear, dear auntie and to impress on Gabrielle my undying love for her! But no—in charges this raging bull, shouting I'm a danger, and making mad accusations. Why, if he does live beyond the bullet that sweet Gabrielle put in him on my behalf, why then he ought to be investigated for being a madman and a maniac, and who's to say that Ransom himself ain't the mad Phantom? Much time as he spends prowling the streets; seeing so much of the gutter trash, living among the rats of this city . . . the man sees shit every day until . . . until all he sees is to kill, kill, kill! What's to say he ain't the Phantom?"

Meanwhile, Philo Keane shouted over his one-time apprentice at Griffin, "It all makes sense now! This creepy little sot here under our noses the whole bloody time! He's the one set me up, isn't it true, Drimmer? Didn't he put the notion of my being the Phantom in your ear? And now he's shifting it to Alastair! Don't you see? Don't you?"

"I know the little rat came at me with this wire in front of witnesses, in front of his little sugar, that daughter of Tewes."

"Then you have him dead to rights! Congratulations! Now release me the bloody hell out of here!"

"Ransom's the one figured it out; he's the mastermind behind the arrest."

"And Rance, is he shot like Denton said?"

"Wounded 'bout here and here." He indicated entry and exit wounds on his own body.

"But he's been spared his life?"

"So far."

"Thank God! Where is he?"

"Cook County Hospital. It'd be the morgue but for his cane—or so said the midwife who patched him up."

"Midwife?"

"Tewes's sister Jane."

"Sister? Look, how so, his cane?"

"I found the cane splintered by the bullet from a Sharps .44, I'm afraid. Could've done a hell of a lot more damage had the bullet not been deflected by the bone handle of Ransom's cane."

"The wolf's-head cane. I give it to him years ago. Carries it everywhere . . ." mused Philo. "That is a wonder indeed."

"Surgeon Fenger is working on Rance as we speak, and from accounts I got over the phone, well . . . only time'll tell if eternity wants the big man or no."

"I gotta get over there. You've got my word, Drimmer. Release me just until I can be sure Rance is all right, and I promise I'll return."

Drimmer's mind raced with what Kohler might do to him in the event he should honor such a deal without either authority or formal paperwork.

"Com'on, man! What's there to think about?" pressed Philo.

"This isn't a Sunday school we're running here. You think for one moment Kohler'd just let you step outta that cell on a *promise* you'll come waltzing back?"

Philo raised both hands to the bars. "Despite all the evil that's passed through these hands, I am a man of my word."

"Bedrock honest, heh?" Griffin half joked. He then stared into Philo's eyes. "One bloody hour, and you're back, do you understand? No one's to detain you."

"*Deal* and thank you, Griff."

Griffin signaled the bored turnkey to let the prisoner out. The Bridewell cage door swung wide and Philo made a dramatic exit, sucking in the air of freedom on the other side of the bars.

"Find a phone and call me here at the station every fifteen minutes. I want to know your whereabouts at all times, Keane."

"Bullshit, you want to know how Alastair is faring under the knife."

"Dr. Fenger's the best in the city."

"The state."

"Perhaps the country."

"Touché!"

"Leave out the basement rear, this way. And call in like I said."

"You've my word, and again, thank you."

"Just don't make a mess of it, Philo. Don't make me come searching for you at Muldoon's or—"

"I've not had a drink in forty-eight hours."

"Then bloody come back here, and I'll see to it you have your drink, but you cannot go running about the city."

"As Oscar Wilde says, 'I can resist everything save temptation.'"

"God, I know I'm going to regret this! Don't be a sot, man! You could be the best photographer in Chicago, the top of your chosen profession—"

"Art, my friend. It is art."

"I know nothing about that, but if you applied yourself a sober man set on a goal, what with your talent, and your contracts with Montgomery Ward and all—"

"What contracts? We never had nothing in writing, Trelaine and I."

"Ohhh . . . mistake."

"Besides, they're not likely to hire a former 'felon' even if innocent, not since the papers carried on how I murdered all those women, and their own account executive!"

"Well look, for the moment, we've . . . we've got Ransom near dead, so think of someone other than your bloody self, heh?"

"Aye . . . you're cut of good cloth after all, Griff. I'll ne'er forget this kindness."

Griffin pushed him out the basement door. "Just go and try to be inconspicuous."

"Yes, yes, of course!" Philo was off, a bounce in his step that Griffin had never seen before, like a man who'd just been satisfied by a woman, but this had to do with freedom.

Given a taste of it, would the man be capable of honoring his bargain? Griff doubted it, and in the back of his mind began to plot where he'd have to hide when Kohler learned of this "early release program" instituted by a second-rank inspector. Then it dawned on him how to handle it no matter what. Claim it by order of Inspector Alastair Ransom, his last order before passing out, and quite possibly a man's dying wish. Pass the bloody buck to a man near death.

The wound sustained by Ransom proved a nasty one. The entry point the size of a silver dollar, and the exit wound a gaping fist-sized explosion of flesh and tissue. If Dr. Christian Fenger couldn't keep Ransom alive, no one could; if Fenger *could* save him, it'd be a testament to genius and skill.

Either way, it remained the will of their unknowable God.

How was one to know, Jane wondered as she watched, fascinated, at Fenger's side in the operating theater, dressed as Dr. James Francis Tewes. What was most excruciating was the interminable waiting—filling Jane with grief and pain. Jane realized how much she'd learned from Alastair, and just how much he meant to her after all.

Perhaps and hopefully, the Almighty had yet to finish with Ransom, Jane thought while watching the surgeon's scalpel flit over his flesh. *But then again, perhaps God was absolutely done molding this man.*

Surgeon Fenger's work was that of an artist. Jane became mesmerized, focusing on the surgery. A voice in her head kept repeating the prayer: *Save him, save him for me, Christian.*

Another voice in her head answered: Ransom's fate lies in the hands of his Maker, not Christian. Still, it seemed a tug-o-war between God and surgeon.

In which case, Jane Francis feared that Ransom's life ended here.